THOMAS JEFFERSON DREAM

Stephen O'Connor has published two coll
Another Lesson and *Rescue*; *Orphan Trains*, a
nineteenth-century child welfare effort; and *Will My Name ~~Be shoulu~~*
memoir about teaching in the New York City public schools. His fiction has
appeared in *The New Yorker*, *The Best American Short Stories*, and many other
places.

* * *

Praise for *Thomas Jefferson Dreams of Sally Hemings*

"What a dazzling experience this book is . . . The most revolutionary reimag-
ining of Jefferson's life ever . . . Have we ever been drawn so close into the
conflicted mind of our slaveholding philosopher-president? . . . O'Connor's
deeply human treatment of Sally, whose actual thoughts will never be known
to us, is the novel's most haunting accomplishment. Ultimately, this is a book
in vigorous debate with itself, as strange and contradictory as the author of the
Declaration of Independence. With its magically engineered collection of fiction, history, and fantasy, and particularly with its own capacious spirit,
Thomas Jefferson Dreams of Sally Hemings doesn't just knock Jefferson off his
pedestal, it blows us over, too, shatters the whole sinner-saint debate and
clears out new room to reconsider these two impossibly different people. . . .
It's heartbreaking. It's cathartic. It's utterly brilliant."
—Ron Charles, *The Washington Post*

"In hundreds of brief, pointillist chapters, Mr. O'Connor reimagines their
decades-long relationship . . . The effect is prismatic and utterly arresting. . . .
Hemings is the novel's outstanding character, eloquent and capable, morally
exacting and self-aware, now overflowing with tenderness, now seething with
hatred. Jefferson cuts a far more ambivalent figure, unmatched in intelligence
but often paralyzed by guilt."   —Sam Sacks, *The Wall Street Journal*

"A brilliant, huge-hearted act of the moral imagination. O'Connor has written a kind of quantum historical novel—simultaneously fiction and nonfic-
tion, wave and particle. With dreamlike fluidity, the story moves from the real
halls of Monticello to Jefferson's musings in the afterlife, from meditations on
the phenomenology of color to what the theft of dignity means. This book
creates new facts to live by; it's stranger and braver than I know how to describe. Open to any page and you will see what I mean."
—Karen Russell, author of *Swamplandia!*

"Everyone knows the story—or thinks they do—of Thomas Jefferson and his en-slaved paramour, Sally Hemings. Stephen O'Connor gives us a vision of how that relationship began (yes, in sexual assault) and, given the obvious inequities in the relationship, grew into something approaching a meeting of minds. His Sally is sharply astute, and sees Jefferson more clearly than he sees himself. Makes you wonder what their relationship would have been like if they'd met today."

—Karen Grigsby Bates, correspondent, *Code Switch*, NPR

"Ambitious doesn't begin to describe the scope of the project O'Connor under-took. And successful doesn't begin to describe the wildly imaginative techniques he used to realize his authorial goal, which is clearly to humanize—equalize, you might say—the two members of this passionate, conflicted couple. . . . What justifies the risk is his insistence on using a full palette and tiny brushes to draw these characters, rejecting broad brush strokes in black and white. Rendered in all their complex, contradictory glory, Jefferson and Hemings seem to stand up on the page and demand of the reader, 'If you found yourself in our situation, what would you have done?'"

—Meredith Maran, *The Chicago Tribune*

"By turns delicate and luminous, then searing and straightforward, Stephen O'Connor's novel sings—it is an epic dream and an epic read. Sally Hemings and Thomas Jefferson come alive in this book, beautifully imagined, and so well-rendered that they become achingly human."

—Jesmyn Ward, National Book Award–winning author of *Salvage the Bones*

"An extraordinary work of imagination . . . A brilliant, unsettling book about power and its abuse." —Mary Ann Gwinn, *The Seattle Times*

"O'Connor compels us to look at both the ugliness in Jefferson's hypocrisies and the hopelessness in Hemings's resistance. . . . [Her] experience is at the heart of this novel. . . . *Thomas Jefferson Dreams of Sally Hemings* gives voice to a woman who was treated as an asterisk for too long. We must not let the next Sally Hemings wait two hundred years to be heard."

—Zakiya Harris, *The Rumpus*

"A brave and wondrous dream of a novel . . . A fascinating, complex, and ul-timately extremely addictive tale . . . [Hemings] is one of history's numberless mystery women, but she comes thoroughly and thrillingly alive in O'Connor's telling." —Jean Zimmerman, NPR.org

"What's striking about Stephen O'Connor's first novel, *Thomas Jefferson Dreams of Sally Hemings*, isn't just that he persuasively invents a relationship almost entirely of whole cloth. It's also a superb argument for why we do this imagining—in the novel's wilder moments where O'Connor weaves Jefferson into the present day, he underscores how hard it is to untangle slavery from the American conversation. . . . O'Connor writes about slavery and intimacy with equal grace. His vision of romance in a society defined by division is wrenching, and proof that dreaming can expose reality better than any hard truth."

—Mark Athitakis, *The Minneapolis Star Tribune*

"Its chapters are short, dense with observation, and precisely aimed at the interior life of the titular characters. Each one reads like a prose poem—elegantly shaped, brimming with indelible images—bearing plentiful revelations about race, colonial life, power, and sexuality. Insights are rendered with abundant craft and arrive—via the author's counterintuitive deployment of the present tense—with bracing immediacy."   —Albert Mobilio, *BOMB Magazine*

"Expansive, riveting, and startlingly original, *Thomas Jefferson Dreams of Sally Hemings* seamlessly interweaves fact and fiction to make one of the most mysterious and politically charged relationships in all of American history heartbreakingly vivid and real. A richly imagined meditation on the human capacity for self-deception and on that troubling zone between exploitation and love."

—Christina Baker Kline, author of *Orphan Train*

"[A] jarring exploration of big themes rooted in the contrary behaviors of ordinary people, presented as a kaleidoscope show juxtaposing straightforward narration with fictionalized memoir, fabulist outpourings, bald listings of historical fact, reflections on the poetry of colors, all moving from past to present and back again. In energetic prose, O'Connor probes how a person's hold over another pollutes them both and examines the inherent conflict in relationships among people involved in an institution as morally repugnant as slavery."

—David Keymer, *Library Journal* (starred review)

"This is an extraordinary book, and I can't remember reading anything like it. It imagines the most intimate aspects of slavery in the way only fiction can—everything is freshly shocking and freshly human. And its wildly original use of dreamscape, fabulism, and philosophy gives us the layers these characters deserve as it reinvents the historical novel."

—Joan Silber, author of *Fools: Stories*

"The book meditates in turn on perception, justice, hatred, and evil, making visible—though never rationalizing—the profound contradictions between Jefferson's philosophical ideals and his private life. This is a challenging, illuminating, and entirely original work that's broad enough to encompass joy, penance, 'complexity, ambiguity,' and 'our muddy human souls.'"

—*Publishers Weekly*

"An extraordinary achievement, six hundred and one pages that fly past—vivid and arresting and expansive and troubling and moving and sad and profound and deeply, deeply complicated, indeed like an unforgettable dream. I admire the novel's wild spirit, the wild spirits it captures, the way it seeks to humanize the demons—and demonize the humans—who populate the terrible era of slavery in America."　　　—Carrie Brown, author of *The Stargazer's Sister*

"Its format is impressively inventive and accessible, and it suits its subject. Using traditional narrative, dream sequences, reimaginings, and excerpts from memoirs and Jefferson's writings, it moves beyond historical fiction to demonstrate the bitter, long-lasting aftereffects of Jefferson's moral hypocrisy. . . . This mind-expanding epic offers much to discuss."

—*Booklist* (starred review)

"This novel is a history of oppression; it's a story of a complex connection; it's an American epic of Homeric proportions. Stephen O'Connor brings to this work a wild imagination, a commitment to social and political concerns, and elegant, at times elegiac, prose. A tour de force."

—Mary Morris, author of *The Jazz Palace*

"Fully acknowledging the tragedy of slavery, O'Connor produces a tale that is overflowing with the range of human emotion; in its depiction of feeling, the novel is often brilliant, dense in poetry and light on unearned sentimentality."

—*Kirkus Reviews*

Stephen O'Connor

Thomas Jefferson
Dreams
of Sally Hemings

A NOVEL

Penguin Books

PENGUIN BOOKS

An imprint of Penguin Random House LLC

375 Hudson Street

New York, New York 10014

penguin.com

First published in the United States of America by Viking Penguin,
an imprint of Penguin Random House LLC, 2016
Published in Penguin Books 2017

ISBN 9780525429968 (hc.)
ISBN 9780143128892 (pbk.)

Printed in the United States of America
1   3   5   7   9   10   8   6   4   2

Set in Adobe Caslon Pro
Designed by Amy Hill

This is a work of fiction based on real events.

To Evan and Brenda Turner,
my other parents

What a stupendous, what an incomprehensible machine is man! who can endure toil, famine, stripes, imprisonment or death itself in vindication of his own liberty, and the next moment be deaf to all those motives whose power supported him thro' his trial, and inflict on his fellow men a bondage, one hour of which is fraught with more misery than ages of that which he rose in rebellion to oppose.

—Thomas Jefferson to Jean Nicolas Démeunier
June 26, 1786

Is he willing to prevent evil, but not able? Then he is impotent. Is he able but not willing? Then he is malevolent. Is he both able and willing? Whence then the evil?

—David Hume (paraphrasing Epicurus)
Dialogues Concerning Natural Religion

So, even though we face the difficulties of today and tomorrow, I still have a dream. It is a dream deeply rooted in the American dream. I have a dream that one day this nation will rise up and live out the true meaning of its creed: "We hold these truths to be self-evident, that all men are created equal."

—Martin Luther King Jr.
August 28, 1963

THOMAS JEFFERSON
DREAMS
OF SALLY HEMINGS

In some ways Thomas Jefferson finds death more appealing than life. Nothing he does matters anymore, and so he is able to lose himself more completely in the moment. Now he is lost in the emerald translucency of locust leaves in dawn light. Now in a cloud of indigo butterflies fluttering over meadow grass. And now his heart is broken by the contest between joy and despair in every note of birdsong. Birds have three springs inside their heads, and seven cogs, and are not actually capable of choice, and yet, all day, every day, they sing of joy's inability to outlast despair. There is something in this that Thomas Jefferson finds unspeakably beautiful.

I

Thomas Jefferson is on his knees in a window seat, looking down a long reddish road shaded by two rows of poplar saplings. He is ten years old and holding a pocket watch to his ear. He hears a dog bark, the whispery commotion of wind in leaves, a crow's caw—but only silence from the watch. As he lowers it to take another look, he can hear and feel the tiny impacts of minute gears and screws tumbling through its complex interior. "This watch used to belong to my father," Thomas Jefferson's own father told him only three days ago. "He gave it to me so that, by marking time, I might learn not to waste it. I hope you will learn the same lesson."

During the first two days after receiving the watch, Thomas Jefferson enjoyed timing things: the length of his sleep—eight hours and sixteen minutes; the time it took to walk from his house to the Rivanna River—thirty-three minutes; the time between the bottom edge of the sun touching the western mountains and the top edge vanishing from sight—three and a half minutes. Yesterday afternoon, however, he noticed along the rim of the watch a small groove, into which he inserted the tip of his penknife. With a quick twist, he popped off the watch's back and discovered an intricate assemblage of twitchily rotating brass wheels partially concealed by a pair of engraved nickel brackets shaped like the scapulae of a mouse. Curious to find the source of the watch's ticking, he used his penknife to unscrew first one of the nickel brackets and then the other, revealing the very heart of the watch: a tiny coiled spring that—at the touch of his gaze—snapped and sent two gear wheels flying into the air. There followed a moment of panicked thrashing, during which he not only failed to capture the flying wheels but scattered the watch parts he had already removed. After much crawling about on the dark rug, and then a good hour of sweaty, groan-punctuated labor, he was forced to admit that he could neither remember nor deduce where all the loose gears and brackets belonged, and he had three pieces (a rod, a sprocketless wheel and a J-shaped wafer of metal) that he had no idea what to do with at all.

Those three pieces lie on the window ledge beside his open penknife.

He was thinking he would make one last attempt at repairing the watch before confessing his transgression to his father, but now, with a voiced sigh, he sweeps the tiny pieces off the ledge into his palm, then slips them into his waistcoat pocket, followed by the watch itself.

As he makes his way downstairs, he can see the look of disappointment on his father's face, and he can hear his father's reprimands: "I didn't *give* you the watch, I *entrusted* it to you"; "You have betrayed your grandfather's memory"; "I would never have believed that you could be so imprudent."

Thomas Jefferson knocks on the door to his father's study. Hearing no answer, he lifts the latch and pushes. The chair at the desk is empty. A window is open about an inch, and the breeze blowing through it flips up one corner of a piece of paper on the desktop again and again. Another piece of paper lies in the middle of the rug in front of the desk. The big chair by the hearth where his father is wont to read historical and scientific books is also empty.

Jillery is sitting motionless at the kitchen table with her forehead resting on the knuckles of her lifted and folded hands. She doesn't turn when Thomas Jefferson walks up behind her. He waits a long moment before he dares to speak, and when he asks where his father might be, she says, "You best not be looking for him right now, Master Tom." She speaks so softly, and with such a weighty expression on her face, that it is a moment before Thomas Jefferson can fully take in what she has said.

"But I need to talk to him," he says. "It is important."

She looks at him for a long time with that same weighty expression, then only shrugs.

He walks out the kitchen door into the garden. That dog he heard when he was kneeling at the window is still barking. It's Captain, he realizes now, from the squeaky yelp in the middle of each bark. No doubt Captain has treed another squirrel. He is seventeen years old and much too slow to actually catch a squirrel, but that doesn't stop him from trying, or from spending an hour barking hopefully at the base of a tree. The barks seem to be coming from the mill, which is where Thomas Jefferson is headed. But there aren't any trees near the mill.

The freshly turned soil in the kitchen garden is black, moist and redolent of what he always thinks of as the smell of earthworms. Someone has been cutting bean stakes on the stool by the toolshed. A small tepee of them leans against the weathered wall, and yellowish whittled slivers make a corona around the base of the stool. All at once Thomas Jefferson hears the low rasp of something sliding along the shed's inner wall, the clank of metal against metal and a soft grunt.

"Jupiter?" Thomas Jefferson stops in his tracks. "Jupiter?"

He opens the door and sees a Negro boy his own age, crouched at the back of the shed, the long handle of a shovel across his knees. "What are you doing in here?" Thomas Jefferson says.

"Nothing." Jupiter pushes the shovel handle up toward the wall, but it swings right back down on top of him.

"What do you mean, 'nothing'?"

Jupiter gives the handle another push, but it falls back down again. Were he only to stand, he could easily rest the shovel against the wall, but he remains crouching in the corner, the handle angled across his knees.

"Just resting," he says softly. He doesn't meet Thomas Jefferson's eyes.

"I saw three big trout by Castle Rock yesterday."

Jupiter looks up at Thomas Jefferson as if he doesn't recognize him.

"I may go down there later," says Thomas Jefferson.

"I don't know." Jupiter's brow is convoluted and dark. "I think maybe I can't."

Thomas Jefferson sighs. "Well, maybe I can't either." He takes the watch out of his pocket. "You know what I did?" He hands the watch to Jupiter. "Listen." Jupiter takes the watch and puts it to his ear, but he doesn't say anything.

"I broke it," says Thomas Jefferson.

"Your grandpappy's watch!"

"I wanted to see what it looked like inside, and I broke it. Now I have to tell my father. So maybe I won't be able to go fishing later."

"Oh." Jupiter hands back the watch.

"If I can, I'll come find you."

Jupiter doesn't reply, only wraps both hands around the handle of the shovel.

"What are you doing in here?" says Thomas Jefferson.

"I don't know."

"You just going to stay in here all day!"

"I'm resting."

Thomas Jefferson shrugs. "All right. I'll see you later."

Jupiter doesn't say anything. But as Thomas Jefferson backs out the door, Jupiter calls, "Don't tell nobody I'm in here."

"All right." Thomas Jefferson lets the door swing shut on its own.

Once he has passed through the garden gate, he walks between the barns and down the creek road. He wonders if he should tell his father that he merely dropped the watch. No. If his father were to have the watch repaired, the watchmaker would certainly notice the missing parts. Maybe he should say that he dropped it, the back popped open and parts spilled everywhere. But how could a mere jolt unfasten all four screws?

Thomas Jefferson's hands are clammy and his throat is constricted. He has to tell the truth. That's all. A lie would only make everything worse.

The sulfur-yellow flank of the mill is now in sight. Captain is still barking, but not the way he does when he's treed a squirrel—more like when he scents a wolf passing in the night. Thomas Jefferson can't see him anywhere.

His father said yesterday that one of the wheel shafts in the mill had split and that he was going to repair it. But the mill's lofty, churchlike interior is empty, and there is no sign that anyone has been working there. It is hard to tell over the hissing rumble of the water in the millrace and Captain's barking, but Thomas Jefferson thinks he hears his father's voice in the yard out back. As he approaches the open rear door, he hears a woman's voice, but then, very definitely, his father says, "One more time." There follows a hoarse whistle and a sharp splat.

At first Thomas Jefferson thinks a side of beef is hanging in midair, but it is a shirtless man, dangling by his wrists from a rope tied to the winch sticking out of the mill loft. The man's slack feet hover two or three inches above the ground, so that he looks as if he leapt into the air and never came down. A lace of red crosses the pale soles of his feet and has made a burgundy mud of the dust below. Captain is running in circles around him, barking.

"Again," says a woman, just out of sight to the left of the door, and it takes Thomas Jefferson half a second to realize that she is his mother. His father speaks. "All right, Jack." Then Mr. Mumphry, who was also out of sight, rushes at the dangling man, swinging his right arm forward. Another hoarse whistle and splat, and the dangling man's whole body arches as if he were a trout leaping out of a pond. Then he goes limp, his body swinging right, then left, at the end of the rope.

Captain ran off when Mr. Mumphry charged. But now he is back, head low. He is barking not at the dangling man but at Mr. Mumphry, who twitches the snakelike coil of his whip in the dust and pays the dog no mind.

The dangling man is Dorsey, Jillery's husband. His back is crossed by bleeding gashes, some bordered with yellowish flecks of fat. "Once more," says Thomas Jefferson's mother. His father grunts, and again there is that hoarse whistle of the whip racing through the air.

Thomas Jefferson does not stop running until he is in the middle of the bridge over Shadwell Creek. He takes the watch out of his pocket and flings it as far as he can downstream. When his father asks what happened to it, he will say he doesn't know; maybe he lost it in the woods.

"... I will make it good. ... Good ..."

. . . But what could I have done? I didn't know what to do. . . .

Sally Hemings' mother Betty was a bright mulatto woman, and Sally mighty near white: she was the youngest child. . . . Sally was very handsome: long straight hair down her back. She was about eleven years old when Mr. Jefferson took her to France to wait on Miss Polly. She and Sally went to France a year after Mr. Jefferson went. Patsy went with him first, but she carried no maid with her. Harriet, one of Sally's daughters, was very handsome. Sally had a son named Madison, who learned to be a great fiddler. He has been in Petersburg twice: was here when the balloon went up—the balloon that Beverly sent off.

—Isaac Jefferson
"Memoirs of a Monticello Slave:
As Dictated to Charles Campbell in the
1840's by Isaac, one of Thomas Jefferson's
Slaves"

Sally Hemings comes to Thomas Jefferson in a dream. She is sitting at his desk, writing with one of his quills. The scratching of the inked tip across the paper makes a sort of thunder in his dream. Periodically, when the tip dries out and a squeaking comes into the thunder, Sally Hemings lifts the quill to her lips and dampens it with a quick dart of her tongue. Only when the thunder is infiltrated by squeaks a second time does she dab the tip of the quill into the ink and tap it twice on the rim of the inkwell. The result of this practice—an effort at economy, Thomas Jefferson can only imagine—is that the right corner of her mouth is surrounded by a corona of saliva-slick black, and a trail of black descends to the edge of her chin, where a droplet trembles without ever falling.

Mr. Jefferson was a tall strait-bodied man as ever you see, right square-shouldered: Nary a man in this town walked so straight as my Old Master: neat a built man as ever was seen in Vaginny, I reckon, or any place—a straight-up man: long face, high nose. . . . Old Master wore Vaginny cloth and a red waistcoat, (all the gentlemen wore red waistcoats in dem days) and small clothes: arter dat he used to wear red breeches too.

—Isaac Jefferson
"Memoirs of a Monticello Slave:
As Dictated to Charles Campbell in the
1840's by Isaac, one of Thomas Jefferson's
Slaves"

The real Sally Hemings comes to Thomas Jefferson in the arms of her mother. It is the first springlike day in March, and he is at his desk trying to work out the etymological connections between "hob," "hobnob," "hobgoblin" and "hobnail." There is a knock that he does not quite hear, and then Martha is standing just inside his door. "I'm sorry, Tom," she says. "I just wanted you to know that Betty is here."

He hears a very small child's irritated "No!" out in the hallway and then a woman speaking in a low, consoling voice. Again the child says "No," but less emphatically. Martha steps aside, and a tall, broad-shouldered woman with skin the tawny gold of August meadow grass enters the room, carrying a tiny girl who takes one look at Thomas Jefferson and buries her face against her mother's neck.

"Ah, yes," he says, though he is not quite sure why he is being introduced to Betty or who exactly she is.

Martha is smiling but seems disconcerted by his lack of response. "Betty," she says, "this is Mr. Jefferson."

Only once he hears the affection in his wife's voice does Thomas Jefferson remember that Betty used to be her nanny and was her confidante after the death of Bathurst Skelton. He has met her several times, in fact, though he has never spoken to her directly.

"Welcome," he says, getting up from his desk. "I hope you had an easy trip."

Betty attempts something like a smile.

"I was thinking she should stay in Ginny's old cabin," Martha says, her words more question than statement. "With her children." Martha glances at the girl in Betty's arms.

"That's a good place," says Thomas Jefferson. "On a clear day, you can look out the window and see a hundred miles."

Betty attempts another smile but looks at the floor as she speaks. "Thank you, Master Jefferson."

"*Mr.* Jefferson," says Thomas Jefferson.

"*Mr.* Jefferson," she repeats.

The little girl turns her head against her mother's neck and looks at Thomas Jefferson with one eye.

"And who have we here?" he says.

The little girl rotates her face back against her mother's neck, but Betty pulls her away and lowers her to the floor. "This here's Sally," Betty says. "She's my youngest."

As soon as the girl is standing on her plump, bare feet, she grabs her mother's skirt and hides her face in it. "Go on, Sally. Say good morning to Mr. Jefferson." Betty tries to tug her skirt from her daughter's hands, but the little girl won't let go.

"We been traveling two days," Betty explains. "And Sally ain't had a wink of sleep the whole time! Ain't that true, Little Apple? You ain't slept in two days."

Touching the girl lightly on the shoulder, Thomas Jefferson says, "Welcome to your new home."

She flings back her head and looks at him with a fierce scowl. "No! Not my home!"

Thomas Jefferson laughs. "Now, that's a girl who knows her mind!"

"Sally!" scolds her mother. "Don't you talk to Mr. Jefferson like that! What's got into you?"

"Not my home!" She pulls her mother's skirt entirely around her head.

Thomas Jefferson laughs.

He is thirty-one. When his wife knocked at his study door, he was supposed to have been writing "A Summary View of the Rights of British North America," a position paper for the Virginia delegation to the first Continental Congress. His hair is the luminous red of a dawn in July; his eyes are the color of roasted peanuts.

The abolition of domestic slavery is the great object of desire in those colonies, where it was, unhappily, introduced in their infant state. But previous to the enfranchisement of the slaves we have, it is necessary to exclude all further importations from Africa. Yet our repeated attempts to effect this by prohibitions, and by imposing duties which might amount to a prohibition, have been hitherto defeated by his majesty's negative: Thus preferring the immediate advantages of a few African corsairs to the lasting interests of the American states, and to the rights of human nature, deeply wounded by this infamous practice.

—Thomas Jefferson
"A Summary View of the Rights of British North America"
July 1774

In Thomas Jefferson's dream, Sally Hemings is wearing only a white linen shift, torn at the front, and revealing an expanse of radiant skin. She does not notice him as she writes. He wants to talk to her, approach her, but is unable to move. And yet, at the same time, he has risen into the air and seems to be drawing nearer to her, although that may only be a result of his altered perspective.

The lamp on his desk has not been lit. The even, sand-yellow glow filling the entire room emanates, Thomas Jefferson realizes, from Sally Hemings's resplendent face, her exposed breast, and even from those parts beneath her shift, beneath the desk and otherwise hidden from view.

And now he can actually see what she is writing—but it is not writing at all; it is a fierce assault of senseless scratches, blots, crossings-out, jabs, loops, squiggles, splashes, gashes, senile quaverings, lightning bolts, comets, eruptions, bullet holes and crevasses, running in all directions, superimposed, without any regard for horizontality, order or even the paper's edge.

After a while Thomas Jefferson realizes that she is compiling notes toward an invention—an iron machine, powered by steam, that moves along an iron road and makes an unending hawk screech, so terrifically loud that anyone hearing it would be instantly struck deaf. "Why would you want to make such a thing?" he is finally able to ask. Sally Hemings fixes him in a gaze of contempt. She cannot speak. She is mute. And her muteness so terrifies him that his legs jerk and arms shoot out, he cries aloud and finds himself awake in the cold, blue night, alone in his bed.

. . . *I cannot bear to be myself. I feel trapped inside my own body, and inside the life I have led. This day I have seen such sorrow, cruelty and injustice that my mind reels at the recollection of it, and my stomach is so sick with loathing that I can hold nothing down. Indeed, I have already vomited three times—twice on that acre of frozen earth where I witnessed the craven depravity of people I have lived with and even loved all my life, and once just now as I held my face over the top of the privy's long, filth-gnarled tunnel. Nothing I believed seems true anymore. As late as this very morning, when I knew precisely what was going to happen, I could not grasp the enormity of it. I allowed myself to believe that I would still be possessed of dignity and decency afterward, and that there were limits to the horror my life—or any life—could contain. How could I have lived in such ignorance? How could I have believed so many lies, and lied so often to myself? Why is it that every time I glimpsed the faintest shadow of the truth, I covered my eyes and ran as far as I could in the opposite direction? I feel as if I never actually lived my life but only sleepwalked through it, dreaming. . . .*

There must doubtless be an unhappy influence on the manners of our people produced by the existence of slavery among us. The whole commerce between master and slave is a perpetual exercise of the most boisterous passions, the most unremitting despotism on the one part, and degrading submissions on the other. Our children see this, and learn to imitate it; for man is an imitative animal. This quality is the germ of all education in him. From his cradle to his grave he is learning to do what he sees others do. If a parent could find no motive either in his philanthropy or his self-love, for restraining the intemperance of passion towards his slave, it should always be a sufficient one that his child is present. But generally it is not sufficient. The parent storms, the child looks on, catches the lineaments of wrath, puts on the same airs in the circle of smaller slaves, gives a loose to his worst of passions, and thus nursed, educated, and daily exercised in tyranny, cannot but be stamped by it with odious peculiarities. The man must be a prodigy who can retain his manners and morals undepraved by such circumstances.

—Thomas Jefferson
Notes on the State of Virginia
Written in 1781–82, published in 1787

E arth has covered the face of Martha Jefferson, and Thomas Jefferson will not come out of his private chambers. Jupiter knocks on the door with the knuckle of his index finger.

"Mr. Tom," he calls. None of the other servants dare call the master anything other than his last name, but Jupiter has served Thomas Jefferson since they were both boys at Shadwell, and is in the habit of saying they are as close as brothers. He knocks a second time. "Mr. Tom, Ursula got some soup here for you. Barley soup! You want her to come in and leave it on the table?"

All four servants—Betty Hemings and Sally Hemings, in addition to Jupiter and Ursula—hold their breath as they wait for a reply. Thomas Jefferson has been locked in his chambers ever since the funeral, two days ago. He hasn't addressed a word to anyone in all that time, not even his three daughters, nor has he had anything to eat or drink. The servants listen but hear only the insistent tweedle of a Carolina wren.

Jupiter knocks a third time. "Mr. Tom?"

Still no response, nor any sound that might indicate a living soul behind the door. The servants craning their ears in the dim hallway cast one another worried glances. "Maybe we should try the library," says Jupiter.

The library is connected to Thomas Jefferson's bedroom and study but has a separate door just a few feet down the hall. Jupiter knocks on that door, waits, then says, "Mr. Tom?" He is about to knock again when a long, doglike moan sounds within the room and ends with an emphatic, "Leave . . . me . . . be!"

All of the servants, except Sally Hemings, exchange relieved glances. Sally Hemings is afraid of Thomas Jefferson. She is nine years old and she can't remember ever having said a word to him.

As they make their way to the kitchen staircase, Ursula says, "Least now we know we not going to have *two* funerals."

"Not yet anyway," says Jupiter.

Ursula doesn't say anything because she is descending the steep staircase and has to concentrate on not spilling the soup.

"Never in my life," says Betty Hemings, "have I seen a man more crazy for a woman than that Mr. Jefferson."

"That's the truth," says Jupiter. "He worshipped the ground she walked on." They are in the kitchen now and can speak more freely.

"She was pretty enough, I guess," says Betty Hemings, "but I never saw the reason in it."

"I'm sorry to speak badly of the dead," says Ursula, putting the tureen down on the table, "but that woman didn't know nothing but how to complain."

"She was always a sickly thing," says Betty Hemings. "I was there the minute she came out between her mammy's legs. Seemed like forever before she figured out she got to breathe if she wants to live. And that's how it always was. That girl was never sure if she wanted to live or die."

"And she made sure everybody knew it," says Ursula.

Jupiter says, "But he loved her."

"He did," says Betty. "No denying that. Of course, he's a sad man, too."

"Oh, yes," says Jupiter. "But Mr. Tom got good reasons to be sad. I know that for a fact."

This is where the conversation ends. Jupiter is always letting on that he knows all kinds of things about Thomas Jefferson, but he'll never say what they are, so there is no point in asking.

Betty Hemings calls out to her daughter, "What you doing?"

Sally Hemings is still standing on the top step of the staircase. She was the last to descend, and so the only one who heard Thomas Jefferson start up again: long, off-key moans that fall in pitch, again and again and again, sounding more like they come from a ghost than a living person. Sally Hemings's fingers are cold and filmed with sweat. Her heart is rattling in her chest.

. . . I am calmer now. I have even had some sleep—on that bed so lately Mr. Jefferson's but now no one's at all. I have arisen feeling that I must solve the mystery of how I came to live this life I have no choice but to acknowledge as my own. Mr. Jefferson often said that he only knew what was true when he was writing. I am sitting at his desk, using his pen and wearing his spectacles. I can only hope they serve me better than they did him. . . .

The story of my own life is like a fairy tale, and you would not believe me if I told to you the scenes enacted during my life of slavery. It passes through my mind like a dream. Born and reared as free, not knowing that I was a slave, then suddenly, at the death of Jefferson . . .

—The Reverend Peter Fossett
"Once the Slave of Thomas Jefferson"
New York Sunday World
January 30, 1898

After an unimaginable length of time, Thomas Jefferson has enrolled in art school. His goal his first year is to do a taxonomy of color, which amounts to an inventory of things—for what is the reality of that red but a sunset in October beyond the steel mills? And of that pale brown—or is it gold—but a muddy road in Thailand? And of that blue but a flash on a raven's back?

He has just taken his seat on the subway, when he spots Sally Hemings standing by the door a bit down and across from him. There is no mistaking that tapering jaw, that long arc between shoulder and pelvis, those narrow eyes, so deeply gray—the summer-storm gray of newborns, which also contains the potential for brown. Her head is bent over a book, but she doesn't seem fully absorbed by what she is reading. Has she, perhaps, noticed him and decided to act as if she hasn't? Should he get up and walk over and pretend that running into her on the subway is only happy coincidence? Would she walk away? Would she join in his pretense? What if he can't speak?

All the while Thomas Jefferson is watching Sally Hemings, their train is rounding a bend, the steel of its wheels grinding against the steel of the tracks and setting off a ragged shriek that mounts and mounts inside the tunnel to such a degree that Sally Hemings tucks her book into her armpit and puts her fingers into her ears. At that moment the lights go out, but the shriek continues, unabated.

Thomas Jefferson cannot speak. He is eleven. His sister Mary is thirteen. Her feet are on a mound of hay. Her back is bent over a hacked beam. Her hair is in the dirt. Blood is filling her eye. His mother is shouting, "Get up! Get up, I say!"

She has been shouting for a long time. Thomas Jefferson heard her from the house. She was shouting, "Do you think I'm so stupid! Do you think I don't know about the sheep!" He was reading a book about India. And in that book it said that trees in India have loaves of bread hanging from their branches. He wanted to keep reading. The loaves are a kind of fruit, the book said. But Mary was shouting, "No, Mammy! No, Mammy! No! No!" But it wasn't really a shout. There is strength in a shout. All Thomas Jefferson heard in his sister's voice was her weakness. All he heard was that she was going to let herself die.

But then the screams started. Like the sound a hinge might make but so loud they cut right into his head. He also heard a sound he could not bear to hear. A very small sound. It was the sound of splitting flesh. He heard it, but he could not bear to hear it, so he didn't hear it. But he saw it. He saw it as he sat over his book. His sister's flesh tearing. The blood flowing out of her body. Later he will remember putting a length of ribbon between the pages and closing his book, but nothing more until the moment he is standing in the doorway of the barn, his back against the jamb. He cannot speak.

"Malingerer!" his mother shouts. She is holding the rake above her head, looking down at his sister, whose blood is overflowing her eye. "For the last time!" The rake jerks high above her head. Thomas Jefferson cannot speak. "Get up! Get up! Get up!" It was a mistake to have come. Nothing good is going to happen now. Now he has been caught in the same weakness as his sister. His mother is looking at him.

"You!" she says. "You!" Her eyes are so wide and fierce they seem to have irises within irises within irises. The eyes say, *You are the one to blame! You!*

Now the rake is falling. Its teeth strike the dust and hay fragments. It balances on edge an instant, then falls flat, teeth up, between his sister and himself.

His mother is gone.

Mary is not moving. Her blood is brilliant on her cheek, flowing into her hair.

Jupiter is standing in the cow stall. "You see it?" he says.

Thomas Jefferson cannot speak.

"You see it? It done happen again. She got the Devil in her good this time."

"She killed Mary," says Thomas Jefferson.

"She'd like to," says Jupiter.

Thomas Jefferson is standing over his sister. He thinks maybe the blood is not coming out of her eye. There is an opening in her eyebrow that is like an eye itself, and he thinks the blood is coming out of that. Jupiter is standing beside him.

"Everything's all right now," says Jupiter.

And Thomas Jefferson says, "She's not moving."

"She'll be all right. We get her cleaned up, she'll be just fine."

"She's dead," says Thomas Jefferson.

Jupiter puts his hand on Thomas Jefferson's shoulder and gives him a squeeze. "Don't you worry, Master Tom. I saw what your mammy done. Miss Mary just got whupped upside her head. She'll be all right."

Mary's lips are moving. Then they stop. Then they move again and her hand lifts to her bloody temple. Her eyes are open. The left eye filled with confusion and fear, the right eye filled with blood.

"You see!" says Jupiter. "What I tell you! Everything'll be all right."

Thomas Jefferson cannot speak.

Thomas Jefferson is watching the movie of his courtship with Martha. He has never seen a movie before, and for a long while he is distracted by the blue beam crossing the darkness overhead. At first he wonders if the beam isn't sunlight channeled through lenses and lighting up a stage where actors are performing. But that doesn't make sense, partly because of the strange, twitchy flatness of the actors and their brilliant colors but mostly because they keep appearing and disappearing in instants and sometimes loom as large as houses. Perhaps the light is shining on some sort of painting in which the colors (through the influence of magnets?) constantly swirl and reassemble. But how can the images speak? Are there actors behind the huge painting? And if so, why are their voices so loud? Finally he decides that what he is looking at are colored shadows of the sort that magicians project onto clouds of smoke, although he still can't figure out how the images move. He gives up all such ruminations when he hears his name spoken by one of the gigantic actors.

He has been brought to this dark room (a theater, it would seem) as a sort of joke by James and Dolley Madison, who are sitting on either side of him. They didn't give him a clue as to where they were taking him but only told him he was being kidnapped so had to be blindfolded. They didn't remove the blindfold until he was seated and loud voices had begun to boom in the darkness.

His name is spoken by a young actor in a copper-colored wig, sitting in a tree and holding an open book, on the spine of which is a single word in huge gold letters: LOCKE. The young man is looking down from his branch at an extraordinarily beautiful young woman wearing knee breeches—a shocking concept for Thomas Jefferson. She is riding a palomino along a forest path and has stopped to converse with the young man in the tree. She looks as if the sun is inside her and it is beaming out through her cheeks, eyes, lips and her brilliantly white teeth. She tells the young man that she had not known there were orangutans in this forest. When he inquires after her name, she laughs, digs her heels into the horse's ribs and gallops down the path, her golden ponytail waving in perfect synchrony with the horse's own golden tail.

In an instant the young woman reappears, but this time in a royal blue gown cut to expose so much of her flawless pink chest that her bodice can only be held up by some sort of adhesive applied to her skin. Chamber music is playing. She is looking with surprise into the eyes of the actor in the copper-colored wig, who asks her debonairly if anyone had informed her that orangutans would be attending this ball. It is not until the young woman at last reveals her name that Thomas Jefferson realizes, with a shock that makes him unable to draw a breath, whom the actors are portraying. It never occurred to him that these two people might be Martha and himself, in part because of their absurd appearance and strange accents and because Martha's hair was a luxuriant chestnut brown rather than blond but mainly because the circumstances of their actual meeting could hardly have been more different.

He was twenty-seven and following the road from Monticello to Williamsburg, where he represented Albemarle County at the Virginia House of Burgesses. It was one of those warm spring days when the sky is glaring white and merely looking across the rolling fields of newly turned earth can put a dull node of pain at the center of each eyeball. Jupiter was driving, and they had been talking for more than an hour about what a sad and lonely man Thomas Jefferson's father had been and about why he had never been able to resist his wife's mad convictions. This conversation had exhausted them both, and they had lapsed into thoughtful silences, listening to the cuffs of the horses' hooves on the rutted clay, the clinking harnesses and the long, buzzy drones of the cicadas.

A large brick house with dormer windows stood about twenty yards off the road. As they approached it, Thomas Jefferson thought he heard the high, clear tones of a woman singing. At first he could see no one near the house, but then a slender young woman, all in black, stepped out of a cluster of boxwoods, took hold of the front of her skirt and climbed the steps onto the portico at the front of the house. She was no longer singing and seemed entirely unaware of being observed as she opened the door and disappeared into the house.

From her slender waist and arms, and the spryness with which she mounted the steps, she seemed hardly more than twenty. But her head hung as she walked, as if she were deep in thought, and her black gown and shawl could only mean that, young as she was, she had been widowed. Her song had been filled with sorrow, yet sung so beautifully that it came to Thomas Jefferson as a perfect joy.

Her voice, her dark silhouette and her light step as she entered her house—these would come back to Thomas Jefferson many times over the remaining day and a half of his journey. And then he simply forgot the young woman—to such an extent that he never even thought to glance at her house on his return trip a month later.

He wouldn't remember her until six months afterward, when he and John Fairfield were traveling from Williamsburg to Monticello and John asked Jupiter to turn their carriage down the muddy drive leading up to the house. When Thomas Jefferson had suggested that John spend a week with him at his mountaintop sanctuary, John had merely said that he knew some "good people" they might spend the night with along the way. He'd said nothing about where the house was or who the people were (except for mentioning that the man of the house had a "nigger wife"), and he certainly hadn't said anything about a widowed daughter with a beautiful singing voice. As their carriage rattled up to the house, Thomas Jefferson's pulse became audible in his eardrums and he wished that he had thought to change his linen before setting out that morning.

He didn't catch a glimpse of the widowed daughter until he was already seated at the dinner table with several members of the Wayles family, adults and children. She arrived late, touching her lips with the middle finger of her perfectly flat hand as she apologized for having been detained. Her father, at the head of the table, looked somberly into his lap as she spoke. When she took the seat immediately to his left, he gave her a knowing, sympathetic glance and covered her hand with his own.

"Mr. Jefferson," he said, looking down the table to where Thomas Jefferson and John Fairfield were seated on either side of the vacant chair, where the woman of the house would have sat (the last of John Wayles's three wives had been dead a good nine years by then), "allow me to introduce my daughter, Mrs. Skelton."

"Pleased to meet you," said Thomas Jefferson.

Mrs. Skelton nodded without quite meeting his eye and said something he couldn't catch.

He was relieved to see that, while perfectly nice-looking, she was nowhere near as beautiful as the woman he had imagined after he heard her singing. She had broad cheekbones and a long jaw, unusually squared for a woman, but she had enormous eyes exactly the pewter gray of her father's, though with a greenish cast by candlelight.

She and Thomas Jefferson were seated diagonally across the table and too far apart to talk. Every now and then, he would glance in her direction just as she would seem to be turning her eyes away. He could never be sure if she had, in fact, been looking at him, and so he glanced toward her with increasing frequency, hoping to catch her before she shifted her gaze—until, at last, worried that she or someone else at the table might think he was paying her undue notice, he forced himself to devote all of his attention to the elderly woman to his left: Mrs. Eppes, who seemed to know a great deal about the art of breeding sheep.

Plates of food came and went. Bottles of cider and wine were opened and emptied. Mr. Wayles's face went redder and redder, and his nose turned a shiny purple.

"Mr. Jefferson!" he called out some two hours into the meal. "Was that your fiddle case I saw my boy bringing into the house a while ago?"

Thomas Jefferson was silent a moment, not sure what he might be getting into. "I suppose it was."

"So you play the fiddle?"

Thomas Jefferson laughed and glanced at John. "I try."

"Well, Martha here"—he took hold of Mrs. Skelton's hand—"is a genius at playing the piano. What do you say you two honor us by playing a duet?"

"Oh, Pappy, no!" cried Mrs. Skelton, putting the middle finger of her flat hand against her lips again.

"Nonsense!" said her father. "I'm sure Mr. Jefferson would love to hear you play!"

Now her eyes truly did meet Thomas Jefferson's, expressing both alarm and a plea for help.

"That's very kind of you, Mr. Wayles," said Thomas Jefferson, "but I doubt that Mrs. Skelton or anyone else would get much enjoyment from my hapless screeching."

Mrs. Skelton gave Thomas Jefferson a grateful glance. "Yes, Pappy," she said. "It's not fair to ask Mr. Jefferson to play for us after he has had such a long ride, even if he is only being modest." She gave Thomas Jefferson another glance, and just as she seemed about to smile, she looked down at her plate.

"Well, then, *you* play for us, Martha!" said her father.

"Oh, no, Pappy. Really, I couldn't." She gave her father a long, imploring gaze, then pulled her hand away from his.

Her father looked at her skeptically for a moment, then slapped the table with his right hand. "All right, then let's have some apple pie! Betty makes the most delicious apple pies!"

Sometime later, when almost all the lamps and candles in the house had been extinguished, except out back in the kitchen, where the slaves were doing the dishes, Thomas Jefferson returned from a visit to the outhouse to find Mrs. Skelton standing at the bottom of the main staircase, one hand on the banister, the other holding a candle. "Forgive me, Mr. Jefferson," she said. "I hope I didn't startle you."

"Not at all," said Thomas Jefferson. "I should be the one apologizing."

She gave him a crumpled smile, then looked away. "I just—" She let go of the banister, transferred the candle from her left to her right hand, then sighed in a way that made it clear she would never finish her sentence.

"It was a pleasure to meet you," said Thomas Jefferson.

"Yes. The same . . . For *me*, I mean." She gave him a worried smile, then transferred the candle back to her left hand and put her right on the banister.

"Good night, Mr. Jefferson."

"Good night."

She took one step but didn't turn away from him. He didn't move at all.

"I'd love to hear you play piano," he said.

"I don't think you'd say that if you'd ever actually heard me." Her face in the candlelight was orange and soft, and her smile was the happiest Thomas Jefferson had yet seen it.

"I'm sure you really are a 'genius' at playing."

She laughed.

"And I also hear you are a very good singer," he said.

"How could you ever have heard such a thing!"

"It gets around," he said. "I've heard that your voice is very beautiful, as clear as a bell."

She took her hand off the banister and wiped it against her skirt. A thickness, like discomfort, came into her smile.

"Good night, Mr. Jefferson."

"Good night, Mrs. Skelton."

I n the movie the blond Martha undresses in the presence of the young
actor in the copper-colored wig before the ball is even over. As Thomas
Jefferson watches the precipitate emergence of her boyishly lean body
with a horrified fascination (how could anyone so besmirch Martha's
reputation by suggesting such heedless passion!), she coughs. It would
seem that she is now entirely undressed, her skin a wavery gold in the
firelight to the young actor's wavery orange—for he, too, would seem to
be undressed, though it is not possible to see the whole of either of their
bodies, since their heads and shoulders alone fill up the entire luminous
wall. That cough is the only thing that seems real in this fevered and
intolerable scene.

Martha did cough—exactly as the actress does—their first night at
Monticello after their wedding, when they were in a state not unlike that
of the gold and orange people on the wall, only they were under a heap of
counterpanes in his two-room cabin, their breath steaming in the lamplight, the falling snow ticking at the windows. Martha coughed, and in
that beautiful moment of their being together, Thomas Jefferson suddenly
feared that she might be sickly and that he would lose her—this woman
who had made him happier than he had ever been in his life.

As he hears that cough in the dark theater, he is bereft once again, and
aghast that fate should have taken her from him a mere ten years later. He
must have made some sort of sound, because he feels a warm hand stroking
his own and looks over to see Dolley Madison watching him with a furrowed brow and sympathetically pursed lips. "Don't worry," she mouths,
then turns her gaze back to the brilliant wall.

. . . When I was a very young child, the fact of slavery—my own enslavement and that of everyone I knew well and loved—was a sort of deadness beyond the world in which I believed myself to live. Before the age of six or seven, I don't think I had any idea we were slaves. In part this was because we were called "servants" and "laborers" by the Jeffersons, and those were the words that we ourselves used. I can't recall ever hearing my mother refer to herself or to any member of our family by the term "slave." Also, I never lacked for food. I lived in a solid cabin that was kept warm in the winter by a stone fireplace, and for much of my childhood I was able to wander about Monticello as freely as a dog. This seemed a good and ordinary life to me—nothing like "slavery," at least insofar as that word had any meaning for me.

I lived with my mother and three of my siblings (I was the youngest) just across the lawn from the great house, and our closest neighbors on the mountaintop, apart from the Jeffersons, were house servants, craftsmen and mechanics—most of them my siblings and cousins. My mother was immensely proud of our family's elevated standing and said that we had achieved it because we were smart, hardworking, and we knew "how to get along." By contrast she had nothing but contempt for what she called "ignorant" or "no-account niggers." I grew up equating these people almost exclusively with the field laborers, who lived down the hill from us and who, those days, mainly picked tobacco on the hilltops a quarter mile and more to the east and south of the great house.

As a child I had little comprehension of how much harder the laborers worked than did my mother or any of the other skilled servants among whom I lived, and so whenever I happened upon them being marched along the roads at sunrise and sunset, I tended to see their filthy clothing, their lowered heads and sullen expressions as manifestations of their fundamental character, rather than of their exhaustion, their bitterness and the injustice of their lot. I was curious about these people and especially about their children, who seemed louder, tougher and more daring than the children who lived near the great house, but I was also afraid of them and kept my distance. At night, when we would hear the laughter and songs, and sometimes the screams and angry bellowing that would come up the hill from the field laborers' cabins, my mother would mutter, "Heathen savages," and offer a prayer of thanks to Jesus for having saved her.

Like most small children, I never doubted that what my mother told me was the truth, and so I shared both her pride and her disdain. If I had imagined that anyone at Monticello might have been slaves, it would have been the field laborers, but certainly not us. I considered myself lucky to have been born into a family of such intelligent and industrious men and women, and to be leading what I could only believe was a good life. When my mother told me to get down on my knees and thank Jesus, the gratitude I offered up was sincere. And yet from a very early age, a small part of me knew—or rather felt, for I could not allow myself to truly know—that my good and fortunate life was not what it seemed.

When I was five or six, a circus came to Charlottesville and my mother decided to take me to it on a Sunday—her day off from her duties as Mrs. Jefferson's body servant. Everyone was talking about the circus's dancing bear and trick riders, but I was most eager to see the acrobats, who, from my mother's description, I thought could actually fly and so must have had wings like angels. I was also very excited because my mother dressed me in my favorite gown, which was dark blue with red trim on the hems of the sleeves and skirt. It had been passed down to me from my sisters Thenia and Critta, but it had originally belonged to Mrs. Jefferson when she was a girl.

We were in the kitchen of the great house getting some water and bread to take with us on the ride into town when Mrs. Jefferson suddenly appeared. I all but ran up to her, hoping that she would notice that I was wearing her gown.

"Ah, Betty!" she said, not giving me a glance. "I've been looking for you all over. I need your help."

My mother put her hand on my shoulder. "But I'm taking Sally to the circus."

Mrs. Jefferson seemed to notice me for the first time and gave me a curt smile before speaking to my mother in a firm voice. "I'm sorry, I'm afraid this is an emergency, and there won't be time for that."

My mother darted her eyes at me, and for an instant she looked shocked, as if she had just been slapped—but in the next instant she shook my shoulder, her face knotted with irritation, and said firmly, "You be good, baby girl!" She followed Mrs. Jefferson out of the room, as if the whole idea that she and I might have gone to the circus had been my own foolish fancy.

This was the moment when I had my first intimation that my proud and strong mother was afraid of Mrs. Jefferson—a woman whom I had always thought of as elegant and kindly. And as that stunning realization dilated within my consciousness, my mother's fear instantly became connected to dozens of other odd events, many of them ordinary (a grimace turning into a smile, a heavy sigh followed by a cheerful "I'm coming!") and a few so troubling that they seemed inscribed with fire upon my brain (the time my sister Mary, who was already a grown woman when I was born, cried out and clutched my mother's arm when she saw Mr. Corbet, one of the overseers, walking toward her and then calmly let him lead her away; or the night my mother's friend Johnny sat in the corner of our cabin, speechless, his face like stone, his eyes fixed on something invisible). All of these events seemed to be instances of adults not allowing themselves to admit to plain, if very troubling, facts. Even as I stood in that kitchen after my mother had gone, I experienced another such evasion, though a far more modest one: Ursula crouched beside me and said, "Don't worry, honey pie—that circus isn't any fun anyway!"

All of these recognitions came together in a mind too young to make sense of them, but I do believe that they were the origin of an unsettling feeling or vision with which I became afflicted not long afterward. Night after night throughout my childhood, as I lay upon the verge of sleep, the events of my day—conversations, squabbles, games and chores—would come back to me but seem to be surrounded by something that I came to think of as "the deadness." I didn't have a clear conception of the deadness, except that it was bleak, dark and profoundly frightening. And in its shadow all the events of my day, which had seemed so vital and real as they were happening, would become thin and pale—a pathetic charade. There were nights when the deadness was so all-encompassing that I would writhe in panic, feeling I could not take enough air into my lungs and wanting desperately to escape. . . .

Facts

The average life expectancy at birth in late-eighteenth-century Virginia was thirty-eight years for males and forty-one years for females. The equivalent figures for nonwhite men and women were thirty-three and thirty-five years, respectively. If a white male were to survive adolescence, his life expectancy rose to about fifty years, whereas the female life expectancy did not increase appreciably, in part because four percent of women died in childbirth. The average woman, white or black, had six or seven children, a third of whom would die in infancy. One factor contributing to these high mortality rates is that doctors and midwives did not habitually wash their hands before procedures until the late nineteenth century.

Women's finances were controlled by their fathers before marriage and, afterward, by their husbands. If a widow or unmarried woman was not independently wealthy or being supported by relatives, she could become a governess, shop clerk, seamstress, domestic servant, field-worker or prostitute. The wages for most legitimate jobs were so low, however, that many single women, especially if they had children, had no choice but to make money on the side by prostitution. It is also true that female domestic servants were commonly expected to grant their masters sexual favors—discreetly, of course. Those who were not discreet enough generally lost their jobs and, their reputations ruined, often could find no other work than prostitution. On average a woman lived four years after becoming a prostitute, with the most common causes of death being venereal disease, murder, suicide and alcoholism.

The male head of a household was called "master," as were male shopkeepers and teachers. One attribute all of these men had in common was that they were allowed to beat their subordinates. Although violence within the home was generally looked down upon, husbands were understood to have the right to physically punish their wives for such transgressions as adultery and persistent insubordination, and most people considered the occasional beating a necessary incentive in children's moral and even academic education, so much so that teachers often had a rack of canes behind their desk or a paddle leaning against the wall in the corner.

Shopkeepers—craftsmen especially—were allowed to beat their employees for moral failings such as laziness or stealing—although the term "employee" does not adequately represent the relationship between the master and the one or more boys or girls who worked for him as apprentices or indentured servants and who were bound to him, generally until the age of twenty-one, receiving no compensation for their work other than food, clothing and a place to sleep—often just the floor of the shop. Industrial workers of the time got a mere pittance for their labors and worked in brutal and dangerous conditions that could make today's sweatshops seem luxurious.

This was the context in which slavery existed during Sally Hemings's lifetime and which conditioned her attitude toward her own servitude and her relationship to Thomas Jefferson. Although freedom was always preferable to the brutality, indignity and injustice of slavery, the actual difference in the quality of life between the free and the enslaved was not as dramatic as we are prone to imagine today—especially when we consider that as hard as life could be for the white working class and poor, it was massively harder for African Americans, even those who had gained their freedom.

And while according to our own standards, marriage during the eighteenth and nineteenth centuries might also seem close to slavery, people of Sally Hemings's time still cried for joy at weddings, and Jane Austen, who was Sally Hemings's almost exact contemporary, could write as if marriage were the greatest happiness that could befall a woman. People adjust to their circumstances. People subject to the most barbaric cruelty can still delight in a baby's laugh or feel moments of perfect contentment lying on a grassy hillside in the sun. There is something beautiful in our capacity to accommodate atrocity, even if it can also be our undoing.

"I will make it good. . . . I will be gentle. You will see. . . ."

... *It was impossible, of course, that I could remain in ignorance of my true situation for very long. The first person to tell me that I was a slave was a girl named Elsie, who was a year older than me. I must have been close to seven at the time. I knew instantly that what she said was true, but I denied it anyway. She laughed and said, "Are you stupid! Don't you know all colored folks are slaves?"*

Not long afterward I began hearing tales from other children about masters putting their slaves in iron collars or whipping them until the skin was torn off their backs. Most of these stories were told by boys, who wanted nothing more than to see me shriek, gag or burst into tears. I resolutely deprived them of that satisfaction by gritting my teeth behind an expression of world-weary indifference, but of course I could not help being affected. The most horrifying tale I heard was of a master who hung his slaves from hooks on the rafters as if they were meat. The image of those poor people impaled and writhing seized control of my thoughts and kept me awake for nights on end.

I did not, at first, give these tales much credit—in part because of the salacious delight with which the other children told them. It seemed clear to me that if these boys believed the tales they were telling, they would have been aghast and afraid for their own skins. I also didn't believe the tales because I had never heard of anything comparable at Monticello. There were no iron collars here, no meat hooks; there wasn't even a whipping post. Yes, there were thrashings from time to time, but nothing like the senseless and extreme cruelty of the masters in the stories the boys told me.

People were thrashed for stealing, for being drunk and belligerent, for not doing their work. While there were some overseers who were excessively assiduous in the detection of such crimes, or in the execution of punishment, a semblance of order prevailed at Monticello that, although it might only have resembled actual justice, nevertheless did make the punishments predictable and therefore substantially avoidable ("Keep out of the woods and the bear won't bite," was how my brother Peter put it). But more to the point, whatever excesses did occur never seemed extreme enough to transgress common notions of ordinary human cantankerousness.

Yet, as today's events have shown only too clearly, while Mr. Jefferson was not without principle, he was nevertheless criminally self-indulgent and self-deceived, and as repulsive as it is for me to consider—indeed, I am again overcome by nausea as I commit these words to paper—such horrors could never have come to pass were there not some cold and dank precinct of his heart impervious to even the faintest sympathy for those who labored and suffered so that he might live in comfort. . . .

In an 1806 letter to his grandson, Thomas Jefferson writes that when he was fourteen and his father died, "the whole care and direction of myself was thrown on my self entirely, without a relative or friend qualified to advise or guide me." What is notable about this statement is that at his father's death Thomas Jefferson's mother was still very much alive, and he was living with her, although he would very shortly board at the Reverend Maury's school in Williamsburg. The fact that she is not listed as a relative "qualified to advise or guide him" is not, however, surprising, because among his nearly twenty thousand surviving letters there is only one reference to his mother, in a note to her brother informing him of her death: "This happened on the last day of March," Thomas Jefferson writes, "after an illness of not more than an hour. We suppose it to have been apoplectic." There is also a single sentence in his account book, dated March 31, 1776: "My mother died at eight o'clock this morning, in the 57th year of age."

The *m* in "morning" in this entry is malformed as a result of a violent drilling sensation in his temple. By the time Thomas Jefferson has finished the sentence, he is so overcome by pain that he thinks he might vomit. As he pushes away from his desk and staggers to his bed, radiant white, purple and pink globes begin to hover on the right side of the room, bobbing slightly, like shy, silent ghosts. And, indeed, as he feels his right hand and leg going numb, his first thought is that the ghost of his mother has come to take her revenge by afflicting him with the very illness that killed her.

This is the first of what he will come to call his "periodical head-aches," which will strike him every few years during the spring (almost always in March) until the end of his presidency—with the most notable perhaps being the one that confined him to his chambers for thirteen days after Martha's death.

This particular bout, however, is the most intensely painful. Every day for a week, from the moment the sun glimmers orange amid the trees over the eastern mountains until it settles beneath layers of gold, rose and lavender in the west, he has to lie in his bed with a moist towel across his face and a porcelain spittoon on his bedside table, waiting to catch his watery vomit. Only when the fields outside his window are lit by stars can he draw his curtains and breathe fresh air. Sometimes he steps barefoot onto the dew-chilled grass, so that he might feel the breezes on his body and hear them whispering in the budding tree branches. He wants to know again what it is like to be a living man in a living world. But mostly, even out on the lawn or as he walks after midnight through his own pitch-dark house to the table where Ursula has left him a glass of water, a cut of meat and a slice of bread, he feels that his mother has succeeded after all, that his illness has left him a mere ghost, haunting the places where he used to live.

It is April 16, 1757. The Reverend Maury is about to climb the stairs to fetch a nightshirt with a missing button when he spots fourteen-year-old Thomas Jefferson slouched in the parlor window seat, knees up, a heavy book spread across his thighs. Maury lingers a moment just outside the parlor door, watching his young student absently coiling locks of his red hair about his finger as he reads, apparently oblivious of the fact that he is being observed. Maury has to acknowledge that Thomas Jefferson is very clever, possibly brilliant, but he finds the boy sullen and odd.

Just the previous evening, Maury happened to be pacing in the front yard, enjoying a pipe, when a carriage pulled up, returning Thomas Jefferson from an Easter visit with his family. As Maury helped the boy drag his heavy satchel off the seat, he said, "I hope you had a fine stay with your dear mother." But Thomas Jefferson gave him no other response than to turn his back and walk toward the house, clutching his satchel with both arms.

"Young man!" Maury called after him. "Is that how you behave when you have been addressed by your master?"

The boy stopped but didn't turn around.

Maury walked up beside him. "What have you to say for yourself?"

Still not meeting the older man's eye, Thomas Jefferson said, "I'm sorry."

"What made you think you had the right to behave so rudely?"

"I didn't have the right. It was only . . ." The boy lowered his head and pinched his lips together before finishing his sentence. ". . . that I did *not* have a good visit." As he pronounced the word "not," the boy finally lifted his head and looked his master in the eye. And then, with a disconcerting coldness, he announced, "And what is more, I have resolved never to return home again. Henceforth I would prefer to lodge here with you and Mrs. Maury during all school vacations."

"What happened?"

"That is my own affair," the boy said firmly. "If it would not be possible for me to stay with you, I shall look for temporary lodging in the village."

With that, Thomas Jefferson walked into the house, climbed the stairs to the dormitory and refused to come down for supper.

Needless to say, the Reverend Maury dispatched a letter to Mrs. Jefferson that very night.

In the morning he received word from his wife that the boy wouldn't take so much as a cup of tea, and during church services (it was a Sunday), Maury noticed him staring vaguely into space, a distraught expression on his face, not even moving his lips when it was time to sing. And now here the boy is, slumped by himself in the window, staring into a book with a crumpled brow.

Last night Maury had been irritated by the boy's rudeness, but now he is beginning to worry.

Only once his master steps into the parlor does Thomas Jefferson look up with a start and realize he is not alone. He snaps his book shut and swings his feet to the floor. "Sorry," he says.

"Don't worry, Jefferson," says Maury. "Window seats are made for reading."

Just past the boy's head, Maury can see Carr, Molyneux and some of the other boys kicking an inflated cow's bladder around on the muddy green across the road.

"But it's a beautiful spring day," Maury says. "You should be out there playing football with your classmates."

"I don't like football."

"Don't be silly. Every boy likes football. Best thing in the world for the lungs."

"I don't like sports. I think they encourage the worst tendencies in human character. They're all about who can dominate whom."

It is a long moment before Maury knows how to respond to this objection. Finally, deciding that the boy is showing signs of melancholia, he says, "But you must take care to amuse yourself."

"I have *Don Quixote* to amuse me." Thomas Jefferson pats the book balanced on his knees. "I think it is much more amusing to read about a mad old man doing battle with wineskins in his sleep."

"Very well," says Maury, thinking that the Lord will only help those who help themselves. He nods, backs out the door and continues on his mission to fetch his buttonless nightshirt for his housemaid.

. . . *I was a melancholy child. I did not have many friends, and I grew unhappy in groups, largely because I lacked a quick wit. Whenever other children mocked me, I would merely stand there, wagging my tongue in my open mouth, unable to utter a single word and feeling more ashamed every instant. But I could be happy on my own. As a little girl, I had great fun playing with a doll that Bobby carved for me. It had wool for hair, a painted face and hinged arms and legs, so I could make it walk, run, turn somersaults. The doll's name was Parthenia, and her closest friend was a sea captain, who happened to be invisible to everyone but her and with whom she would travel around the world, riding lions and enormous fishes, climbing mountains and having dinners with kings and queens.*

As I grew older, I found most of my joy by having my own adventures. From the age of four or five, I would steal away from whichever sister was supposed to be watching me to wander alone through the woods for hours, listening to robin song, crow cries and the ghostly piping of owls. I made houses for myself under bushes and in the branches of trees and would sing myself songs and tell myself stories. My mother scolded me for spending so much time in the woods. She said it was dangerous for a girl, that I might lose my soul.

Apparently, there was one time when I returned from my wandering and told my mother that I had met a talking groundhog who had taken me to an underground world lit by flowers that had flames for petals. This world was ruled by two golden snakes—a king and queen—who sat on thrones shaped like wagon wheels and hissed their commands to all their subjects: groundhogs, moles, voles, mice and foxes. I have no memory whatsoever of telling this story, but when I refused to admit for several days that I had not actually visited this world, my mother decided I had been possessed and took me to see an old man who lived on another plantation—and him I remember vividly.

His name was Popo, and his fingers were so misshapen they looked as if they were made entirely out of chestnuts. He had my mother take off my clothes and lay me faceup upon the ground in a copse behind his cabin. With a foul-smelling greenish paste, he drew a cross on my breast, and then, as he chanted in an African language, he grabbed my shoulders so fiercely that I thought my arms were going to snap off. After some minutes he let me go, and then, still chanting, he slaughtered a chicken and poured its blood into a small bottle that he told my mother to bury in front of our cabin door. Years later, when my mother brought up my story about the underground world and I told her I had no memory of it, she said, "That's because it went right out of you with the Devil."

When I first thought to tell this story, I intended to conclude by saying that although I never believed for a second that I had been possessed, there was a way in which I did lose my soul on my walks, because all on my own in the sun-shot green dimness under the trees it was a simple matter to surrender to the illusion that my life was easy and full and that I was entirely free. But just now I remembered that during those nights when the ordinary events of my life would seem shrouded by the deadness, my solitary walks were never among them, which is to say that my walks never seemed pale and unreal. And so, as I prepared to condemn them as a soul-stealing delusion, a voice cried out in my heart, saying, "You cannot deprive a poor slave girl of her only joy!" . . .

Not hours before Martha dies, her voice hardly above a whisper, she draws Thomas Jefferson's attention to a strange beetle with a tiger-striped cowl that is crawling across her bedclothes. "Look, Tom. I've lived all this time, and yet every day I see an insect unlike any I've ever seen before." He tells her that as soon as he has a moment, he will find its name in a cyclopedia of insects that he has recently acquired. That moment never comes. Not long after Thomas Jefferson has taken the beetle between his thumb and forefinger and deposits it on the window ledge, Martha closes her eyes and her soap-white skin goes ash gray. Soon her breathing becomes irregular, with the gaps between breaths growing longer and longer, until finally, just before noon, she takes three enormous breaths, each followed by an impossibly long silence, the last of which never ends.

The flame stretches, and its tip flaps into a rippling wisp of smoke as an elderly white servant lowers a lamp chimney into place. The atmosphere inside the yellow room, already dense with the sausage-and-tobacco odor of ceaselessly yammering men, is cut by the thin acridity of whale oil. It is nearly eight on an evening in June 1775, and Thomas Jefferson is thirty-two. Although he washed his face on arrival in Philadelphia, his fingertips detect finely granulated road dust along his jaw in front of his ear. He has been standing against the back wall for nearly half an hour, clutching his right elbow with his left hand, and keeping his right hand aristocratically poised against his cheek in an attempt to look contemplative and at ease, but thus far he has spoken to no one. He is perhaps the youngest of the thirty or so men present and feels something of an interloper, given that he is at this meeting—the Second Continental Congress—only as a replacement for his cousin Peyton Randolph.

When Thomas Jefferson first arrived, a small man in spectacles with an almost feminine voice was saying that he would not be able to take a position on the resolution—a funding matter as far as Thomas Jefferson could tell—until he had consulted with the people back in Carlisle who had elected him.

"Good God, man!" shouted another delegate (from New York, Thomas Jefferson thought). "Don't you have your own mind? Do you think the good people of Carlisle sent you here to be a stuffed pillow?"

The original speaker replied mildly, seeming nauseated with disdain, "I thought this body was meant to be a democratic assembly of representatives, not a parliament of petty monarchs." With that, he left the lectern and took a seat at one of the tables, where a neighbor gave him a pat on the back. The New York delegate flung both hands in the air and said something that Thomas Jefferson couldn't hear but that inspired a round of hoots and guffaws at his table.

After that, a bemused-looking man of about forty walked to within an arm's length of the lectern and spoke in a voice that reminded Thomas Jefferson of the jingling of sleigh bells. "The committee will be making its report momentarily. Please don't leave!" This announcement was met with groans, but the words were heeded. No one left. Servants were summoned. Bottles of cider and wine were brought to the tables. Pipes were lit. And very soon the urgent matters this meeting had been convened to discuss were entirely abandoned in favor of tales about the catastrophes and feats of athleticism known to have occurred in and around bordellos.

At present, the only people who truly seem to be considering matters of war and independence are seated at the table in the corner to which the bemused-looking man retired. Thomas Jefferson would like to eavesdrop on their conversation, but, having suffered his whole life from a morbid shyness in large groups, he doesn't dare go anywhere near. At the mere thought, a trembling comes into his fingertips and he is taken by an irresistible restlessness.

He lowers his hand from his cheek, sticks his thumbs into the waist of his breeches and begins to pace along the wall, keeping his head lowered and his brow furrowed, in the hope that anyone observing him might think he is deep in cogitation. Each time he stops and reverses direction, he cannot help but glance toward the corner table, and on one such occasion notices the bemused man scrutinizing him. Feeling that he has been unmasked as a charlatan, a twist of dizziness comes into his skull and his whole body breaks into a hot sweat. He has to leave the room.

A door at the end of the hallway leads into the dark garden behind the State House. No sooner is he standing in the moist coolness of the deepening evening than his head begins to clear. Already he hates Philadelphia. He wonders if he shouldn't just have Jupiter and Bob Hemings pack his carriage in the morning and take him back to Virginia.

The sky is a metallic navy blue directly overhead and lightening toward a deep teal in the west. Thomas Jefferson can make out the silhouette of the roofs of the buildings across the street and of the trees and bushes in this very yard—which is surrounded by a high brick wall, faintly visible in the gloaming. He hears the mumble-grunt of two men talking to his right and a splattering of urine on bare earth. He cannot make out a word either is saying, but he also feels the need to urinate, so he walks toward the opposite wall, where he waits, legs spread, his penis in the evening air, until the two men have gone back inside. Once his own urine begins to flow, the relief is so great that he groans aloud.

As he rebuttons his breeches, he contemplates walking right through the building and back out onto the street, where he might perhaps find a hospitable tavern. He is now distinctly hungry. But instead he returns to the yellow room.

He is not even through the door when the bemused man—no longer seeming remotely bemused—is eyeing him again. As Thomas Jefferson makes his way back to the spot against the wall that he occupied for most of his time in the room, he wishes he knew someone well enough to ask for a glass of wine.

He reinserts his thumbs beneath the waist of his breeches and prepares to resume his contemplative pacing. But now the man who has been watching him has gotten to his feet. As the man starts across the room, the bemused expression comes back onto his face. Thomas Jefferson looks away, his entire body simultaneously heating and chilling with sweat. The man is smiling as he walks, though perhaps there is a faint perturbation on his brow. Attempting a smile of his own, Thomas Jefferson wipes his palms against his waistcoat and takes a step in the direction of the advancing man.

"Pardon me," says the man. "You wouldn't by any chance be Peyton Randolph's nephew?"

"Cousin," says Thomas Jefferson, having to force himself to speak above a whisper.

The man wrinkles his brow and leans his head closer. "Pardon?"

"Randolph's *cousin*," Thomas Jefferson says more loudly. "I'm his cousin."

"Ah!" says the man. "But you're Jefferson, are you not?"

Thomas Jefferson nods. "Yes."

The man's eyes squeeze into arcs of delight, and his small mouth forms a distinctly U-shaped smile between his heavy cheeks. "Welcome! Welcome! I am so happy to meet you!" He shakes Thomas Jefferson's hand vigorously with both of his. "I'm Adams. John Adams."

Thomas Jefferson cannot speak. There is no person he has been more eager to meet than this very man still clutching his hand so forcefully.

"I must confess to being a great admirer of your 'Summary' for the Virginia delegation," says Adams. "I don't think that anyone has argued our cause half so memorably and succinctly as you have. It is masterful work—absolutely masterful!"

Thomas Jefferson can hardly believe that he has even met John Adams, let alone that he is hearing such praise. It is a long moment before he can bring himself to utter a quiet "Thank you."

"I think we would all be much enlightened if you were to honor us with an address concerning your ideas." At last Adams lets go of Thomas Jefferson's hand. "Tomorrow afternoon perhaps?"

A small noise comes out of Thomas Jefferson's throat.

"Excuse me?" says Adams.

The younger man's lips move, but still no words emerge. His face has gone paper white. Droplets tremble on his upper lip.

"I'm sorry," says Adams, a sharp concern in his large brown eyes. "Are you ill?"

"No . . . I just . . ."

Adams leans yet closer and turns his right ear toward Thomas Jefferson. "Yes?"

"The address . . . I . . . Thank you, but . . ." Thomas Jefferson has to lick his lips before he can continue. "But . . . I . . . I . . . can't."

Thomas Jefferson is not able to stop his dream. He lies, flushed and sweating in the frigid darkness, willing his mind to be clear, his thoughts to be practical and significant—*Should a democracy grant citizens the right to resist subpoenas?* But the dream moves within his thoughts as if it were their true nature.

And in his dream Sally Hemings's invention has become a countryside of steel wheels, leather bellows and chains. And she herself is so resplendent it is almost impossible to look at her as she leads him across shuddering metal bridges, between house-high pistons that plunge and surge and jet shrieking towers of steam, between massive brass cauldrons, the polished flanks of which reveal his face as a gnarled dab of pink that smears and shrinks with his every step and his arms and legs as the ungainly stilts of a mantis or a giraffe.

Up diamond staircases that ring underfoot, past rows of copper clocks whose numbered faces tell something other than time. Smell of oil and dust and steam. Ceaseless throbbing. A kettledrum rumble. Bangs and clanks and rattles. And through it all, Sally Hemings, her white shift little more than a mist about her dazzling body, drifts up ladders, down corridors, across humming fields as if she herself were only a shred of steam, while Thomas Jefferson must wrench his feet off the ground with every step and feel his throat go raw from lack of breath and his heart kick in his chest.

At last she leads him out onto a steel balcony with a riveted floor, from the center of which rises something like a wagon wheel, but made entirely out of brass. He knows that if he can only turn this wheel, the machine will stop; he will be able to leave. But the wheel is jammed. He cannot budge it. Neither left nor right.

"Let me try," says Sally Hemings, and with a single finger she sets the wheel spinning. Her machine lurches, then rises into the air.

"What are you doing?" Thomas Jefferson asks.

"I don't know," she replies, the ever-quickening wind whipping her hair straight back behind her head. "I don't know why any of this is happening."

She is smiling. Her storm gray eyes are radiant with delight.

. . . I have had to pace the room for some minutes in order that I might summon the resolution to finally write about Mr. Jefferson. My head is throbbing, I feel bile rising in my throat and my fingers are cold with sweat. This man is the author of the evil that has ruined the lives of so many good people. It is not possible to forgive him. Nor can I forgive myself. He is my shame, and yet—

I don't know what to say.

My mother's words come to me: "Well, he is a man, but the Lord didn't make many men as fine as Mr. Jefferson."

The problem is that I cannot conceive of Mr. Jefferson as only one man. So many of the memories I have of him are entirely incompatible with the man I know him to be. And perhaps this is only the mirror image of the way I see myself. Never once did I imagine myself to be evil, and yet I have lived a life in which I can no longer discover the girl who once looked back at me from every mirror with such artless contentment. . . .

The movie seems to go on forever. Thomas Jefferson wants to leave, but he is in the middle of a row in the middle of a crowded theater, and James and Dolley Madison are seated on either side of him, their expressions somewhere between stupefaction and worship, as they each stare at the wall where brilliant colors swirl and pool and are replaced every instant by other colors or by utter blackness, which, in an instant, explodes into light again—and into noise!

The noise is staggering. Voices thunder and wail. Tiny sounds—chains jingling on a wagon's undercarriage, dry leaves scraping across a slate roof—are like cannonades and banshee shrieks piercing the skull from ear to ear. And the music! This must be what music would sound like to a mouse trapped inside the reverberation chamber of his violin.

Thomas Jefferson slumps in his seat and wants to slide all the way to the floor. He wonders if, in fact, it would be possible to escape the room by crawling between the seats.

After a long period of looming, booming and frenzied flashing, as well as yet more shockingly intimate behavior on the part of the actors (do they know they are being watched? can they see him in the audience?—Thomas Jefferson finds everything related to these scenes profoundly disconcerting), all at once he is watching a far more static scene, set in a huge room—illuminated, it would seem, only by a full moon—in which the man in the copper-colored wig (now purple) is writing the Declaration to the accompaniment of a stately movement from a concerto grosso by Corelli. This is not so bad, except that Thomas Jefferson's many days and nights of solitary labor all seem to take place within a single moment and in a room that gradually fills with people, who look over his shoulder as he writes, then cheer when he is done. Also the hand sliding so glibly across the page never hesitates, never crosses out a word and writes in the perfect script of Timothy Matlack.

Jefferson proposed to me to make the draft. I said, "I will not," "You should do it." "Oh! no." "Why will you not? You ought to do it." "I will not." "Why?" "Reasons enough." "What can be your reasons?" "Reason first, you are a Virginian, and a Virginian ought to appear at the head of this business. Reason second, I am obnoxious, suspected, and unpopular. You are very much otherwise. Reason third, you can write ten times better than I can." "Well," said Jefferson, "if you are decided, I will do as well as I can." "Very well. When you have drawn it up, we will have a meeting."

A meeting we accordingly had, and conned the paper over. I was delighted with its high tone and the flights of oratory with which it abounded, especially that concerning Negro slavery, which, though I knew his Southern brethren would never suffer to pass in Congress, I certainly never would oppose. . .

We reported it to the committee of five. It was read, and I do not remember that Franklin or Sherman criticized anything. We were all in haste. Congress was impatient, and the instrument was reported, as I believe, in Jefferson's handwriting, as he first drew it. Congress cut off about a quarter of it, as I expected they would; but they obliterated some of the best of it, and left all that was exceptionable, if anything in it was. I have long wondered that the original draft had not been published. I suppose the reason is the vehement philippic against Negro slavery.

—John Adams to Timothy Pickering
1822

. . . *In my mother's opinion, all white people—the males especially—were lazy, irritable, corrupt and foolish children whom we, like so many Brother Rabbits, were constantly outsmarting—but Mr. Jefferson was the exception. "He's the smartest man who ever lived," she used to tell me. "He's read every book ever written and knows how everything works—and if he doesn't know, he can figure it out." And then, of course, he was famous—so much so that, as she put it, "When he walks down the street in Philadelphia, everybody clears out of his way"—an image that when I was a little girl did a good deal more to confirm my fear of Mr. Jefferson than to help me share her veneration.*

My mother, however, had only the most indefinite idea of what Mr. Jefferson had done to become so famous—and she wasn't alone. I remember her telling my sister Mary that he was the king of Virginia and Mary saying, "No, he's the burgess. General Washington is the king." My brother Bobby was Mr. Jefferson's body servant in those days, and he once told us that Mr. Jefferson was a "delegate" and a "governor," but I had no idea what either of these words meant, and Bobby was unable to explain them in a way that made sense to me or, I think, to anyone else in our family.

One thing that everyone at Monticello knew very well, however, was that Mr. Jefferson was important. We knew that he was written about in the newspapers almost every day and that he was visited by other important men, like General Washington and Mr. Madison. Elegant carriages were always pulling up in front of the great house, and they were filled with men and women dressed in silks and lace and wearing shoes so highly polished they gleamed like the sun on water. Some of these people came from as far away as Boston and New York, and they were clearly thrilled to be in the presence of our master, some so thrilled they were reduced to blushing and stuttering. I remember once helping my mother serve water to guests at a particularly large dinner party and seeing a woman so entranced by what Mr. Jefferson was saying that she kept her full fork hovering over her plate the entire time it took me to make a circuit of the table.

And even we servants shared a small portion of our master's fame. On Sundays when we were allowed to go into town for prayer meetings or to sell our livestock and the products of our gardens, men, women and children would point at us and stare. They'd ask in low, hushed voices, "You're Mr. Jefferson's people, aren't you?" They'd want to know what he was like or how it felt to work for such a man.

There were those among us who hated Mr. Jefferson—the wisest, I now know. But many more were prone to say things like, "Mr. Jefferson is a good master" and "We're lucky." My mother told me many times, "Don't you forget how lucky you are to have Mr. Jefferson for a master!"

This all seems so pathetic to me now. And cowardly. Yes, we were lucky to be able to go into town on Sundays, and to sell what we grew and raised, and to keep the profits. Yes, Mr. Jefferson had a genuine abhorrence for the cowskin and a desire to be just, even kind. But there was still that dank precinct in his heart and that part of his brain that saw Negroes as more animal than man. Yes, we were lucky, but such luck is a mere drop in an ocean of misfortune. That we counted it as more than that only shows how impossible it was to keep off the deadness. . . .

P rudence, indeed, will dictate that Governments long established should not be changed for light and transient causes; and accordingly all experience hath shewn, that mankind are more disposed to suffer, while evils are sufferable, than to right themselves by abolishing the forms to which they are accustomed. But when a long train of abuses and usurpations, pursuing invariably the same Object evinces a design to reduce them under absolute Despotism, it is their right, it is their duty, to throw off such Government, and to provide new Guards for their future security.

—Thomas Jefferson
Declaration of Independence

"What is the matter? Why do you look so sorrowful?" *I don't know. I was just staring at my hand and thinking that it is not my hand. I have been having such odd thoughts.* "You have been too much indoors. I will ask Jupiter to saddle Castor and Diomede. It is a fine, clear day. The new leaves are like a green mist on the mountains." *No. I would rather not. I just want to stay here. For the moment, at least. I can't even imagine getting out of this chair.* "You must be catching something. Go to your cabin. I will bring you hot chocolate and biscuits, and I will read to you from Henry Fielding." *I keep having the feeling that I am not myself. That I am not even here. I wonder if I am going mad.* "I have often felt a spectator at my own life, that the person I am is only what the world expects of me and that the real me is standing to one side." *Yes. It is something like that. I feel as if I can't do anything.* "It is fancy. It will pass." *I am not sure.* "Go lie down and I will read to you from Henry Fielding."

. . . I was not myself. Is that possible? For almost my whole life I was not the person I imagined myself to be. . . .

I am Thomas Jefferson. I have Thomas Jefferson's flowing, frizzed, red hair. I have his ocher eyes. And I look down on the world from a height that is greater than my own. I am on trial. And John Marshall is standing in front of me, in his black robe, his thick black eyebrows arrowed in contempt. "Prove yourself," says Marshall.

"What is there to prove?" I say, my voice spreading wavelike to the four corners of the room, where it crashes and returns to my ears as a complex echo. "Do you doubt that I stand before you?"

"I doubt everything about you," says Marshall. "You are incoherent. I don't believe in you at all." He has several loose sheets of paper on the desk in front of him. He shuffles them, scowling at each in turn as it passes before his eyes. Then he stands them on end, lifts, drops and pats them until their edges are aligned. "You hear only the sounds of words," he says, "and care nothing about their sense. A word without sense is only so much gas passing through the vocal cords. It is nothing."

It is true that I am listening to the sounds of my words—or Thomas Jefferson's. They have a capacity to boom and reverberate in a way that I am not accustomed to. They are a sort of weapon, but I am not sure how to use them. "I stand for liberty," I say experimentally, "and for equality." As these words pass my lips, they have the effect of increasing my stature. Marshall has to crane his head back in order to reply.

"Whose liberty?" he says. "Whose equality?" His own words cause him to shrink. He is shouting, but his voice grows tinny and small.

"I stand for the liberty and equality of all men."

"All men are as nothing to you!" Marshall shouts in his tinny voice. "They are a concept entirely devoid of meaning. You care about no one's liberty but your own. And no man can be equal to you by definition. 'Equality' in your parlance is a rock, a cudgel, a battering ram! A cannibal in the raiment of a patriarch!"

"You are a monarchist!" I tell him, my voice rattling the windows, causing plaster dust to sprinkle from the ceiling cracks. "You are a corrupt artifact of an obsolete era! A monocrat! A tyrant! A consolidationist!"

Marshall, gray-haired, storm-browed, is nevertheless a child sitting at a child's desk. He folds his papers impatiently, stuffs them into a leather satchel and stands. "We are judged," he says as he moves toward the door, "not by how we understand our words but by how our words are understood by others." He opens the door, then slams it behind him, but its sound is obliterated by my booming laughter.

. . . Far worse than the scars of lash or club is the theft of one's dignity. When one's human value is seen only in regard to how thoroughly one surrenders one's own desires to those of the master and how effectively one's labors contribute to the comfort, dignity and freedom of the master, and especially when one has no freedom whatsoever but to submit to this state of affairs, it is almost impossible to believe that one might be admired, loved and treated with respect in one's own right, and that one might deserve to be treated so, and that one is equally deserving of the rights to life, liberty and the pursuit of happiness.

The narrow compass one is allowed for the exercise of freedom—within one's own home and mind and, under the more beneficent of masters, on one's scant acre of land—can only confirm one's sense of worthlessness. As every farmer knows, a man can work to the point of exhaustion every day and still end up penniless and starving, and such a fate is only more likely for the slave who can only tend his garden or his stock after he has finished his master's work, which often lasts until after dark. Likewise, when the secrets of domestic harmony can elude even the wealthiest of men, how likely is it that they should be accessible to the poorest? And when one has been denied the basic comforts and freedoms of life, even one's own mind offers no sanctuary. One's very desire to live a decent and ordinary life can be an unending source of humiliation, and one's outrage at injustice can be exhausting and all too easily transformed into self-loathing. And so the desire to lie to oneself or to make much of small blessings becomes irresistible, and thus a further humiliation. The very songs we sing to escape our chains themselves become our chains. . . .

Thomas Jefferson is holding a candle in the corridor outside Sally Hemings's room. "I'm sorry," he says. "Might I come in?" He goes into the room, and the corridor is dark. Nothing can be seen. But his words are audible through the door: "My sweet girl! . . . So lovely . . . I will make it good. . . . I will be gentle. You will see. . . . Gentle . . . I will make it good. . . . Good . . ."

James and Dolley Madison's faces pulsate orange and red. A sound like a river of peanuts pouring over a cliff fills the dark room. Although Benedict Arnold actually set fire to Richmond in the morning, at which point Thomas Jefferson had long since resigned as governor of Virginia and fled on horseback, in the dark theater Richmond's pulsating orange and red flames rise from the city's crumbling rooftops to encompass the entire night sky, and the actor in the copper-colored wig—in silhouette against the towering flames, except for one handsome cheek and the flank of his noble nose—shouts "Hah!," whips his horse with his cocked hat and rides off bareback into the impenetrable night.

Not long afterward the actor in the copper-colored wig is again on horseback (saddled this time) and again using his hat as a whip as he careens down one slope of Monticello while a detachment of British dragoons marches up the other.

Then comes the famous moment, the one that Thomas Jefferson has recounted with gratitude and pride scores of times and that his children will recount in their turn, as will their descendants for generations to come: Martin Hemings is standing in the dining room of the great house. One of the dragoons is holding a pistol to Martin's chest. The British commander, who would seem to be General Cornwallis, although, in fact, Cornwallis was a hundred miles away at the time, has just told Martin he will be shot unless he confesses where his master has gone, and Martin replies, "Fire away, then."

After these words the British commander's plump, pink face looms gigantically in the dark theater. It is possible, by observing the alteration of the actor's features, to actually track the progress of Martin's statement as it slowly makes its way to the center of the commander's plump, pink brain. There is a moment of stillness, followed by a nod that is mainly a lowering of eyelids, and then there is a gun blast and the appearance of a single dot of blood on the rim of the commander's right nostril.

"What!" cries Thomas Jefferson, leaping from his seat. "No! No!"

James and Dolley Madison have also leapt to their feet, but only to drag their friend back down into his seat. People in the back of the theater are shouting for them all to sit down.

"That never happened!" says Thomas Jefferson. "That simply never happened!"

A man sitting behind them taps Thomas Jefferson on the elbow. "For chrissakes! It's only a movie! Would you just sit down?"

Dolley Madison speaks softly into his ear. "It's all right, Tom. Just wait, you'll see, the ending is quite uplifting."

"Why did you do that?" says Max, dropping the script onto his desk. "Do what?" says Jeremy, who has been lying on the couch under the window, texting his girlfriend.

"I liked that scene."

"What scene?" Jeremy rests his phone on his solar plexus.

"The one where Sally's brother says, 'Fire away!'"

"Oh." Jeremy swings his bare feet to the floor and sits up. He puts his phone facedown on the couch beside him. "I like it better that way."

"So what?"

"I think it's better."

"But they didn't shoot him."

Jeremy shrugs just as his phone sounds the electric *clink-clonk* of an incoming text. At first he seems to be ignoring the text, but then he picks the phone up, looks at it and puts it down.

"I want to change it back to the way I wrote it," says Max.

"Why?"

"Because that's what actually happened, and I think it's a cool scene."

"How do you know it happened?"

"It's in every single one of the books. And anyway Martin was alive until—"

"I don't believe it."

"What?"

"That he said that. It's so fucking corny! So morally fucking uplifting! 'Fire away!' That's like something out of a fucking Victorian children's story. Like Sunday school." His unanswered text *clink-clonk*s a second time. "Hold on a second." He thumbs a one-word message into the phone and hits SEND.

"But you have him say it," says Max.

Jeremy looks at him blankly.

"'Fire away,'" says Max. "That's the part you left in."

"Yeah, but shooting him makes it all ironic."

"I don't know what you're talking about."

"He gets all moralistic and full of himself, then—whammo!—he's dead. I think that's funny."

"I think you're a fucking sick individual."

"It's ironic." There's another *clink-clonk*. Jeremy picks up his phone, smiles and sets it down. "But the main thing is that it puts Jefferson in more danger. Now the audience knows that the British are these actual evil bastards, so . . . you know, everybody will be on the edge of their seats. Maybe we can even have a chase scene."

"Oh, come on!"

"But it also makes Jefferson look better. The way it really happened, he seems like a total coward. Quitting being governor and everything. And Martin seems way braver than him."

"Maybe he was."

"But Jefferson's our protagonist. Who's going to want to see a movie about a slave-owning, slave-fucking hypocrite who's also a total coward? We've got to give the audience something to hang on to here. We've got to give them someone they can love."

"But he wrote the Declaration of Independence."

"So the fuck what!"

"He invented the swivel chair!" Max laughs as he swivels his own chair, first left, then right.

"Is that true?"

"Absolutely! You can look it up on Wikipedia."

Jeremy laughs.

"Let me finish this fucking thing." Max picks up the script.

Jeremy picks up his phone. "Clare's mother's hassling her again. Maybe I better just go call her." He's hitting keys on his phone as he walks out of the room.

. . . *When Thenia was seven, she took care of Critta, Peter and me. And when Critta turned seven, it was her turn to take care of her younger siblings, while Thenia went on to learn sewing and how to clean house. But by the time I was seven—the age at which all children begin to work at Monticello—there were no younger children for me to care for, so I was given a job in the nursery, which was where Negro children who did not have sisters old enough to care for them were watched while their mothers worked, mostly in the field.*

The nursery was a large cabin divided into two rooms, the smaller of which contained two or three cots and was for the babies. The larger room, furnished with a table and a pair of benches, was where the older children could play or sleep on the floor. The nursery was run by a pair of old women, whose infirmity had made them unsuited for labor, and there was always at least one wet nurse there to feed the babies. I was one of three girls whose primary duties were to wash the babies' clouts and to entertain the older children.

I was happy with this work. While I had no great fondness for washing the clouts, it did mean that I got to spend an hour by myself at the stream running behind the nursery. I very much liked being with children, however, and they liked me, I think. I would tell them stories, sing them songs, and sometimes I even took them on expeditions into the woods—the very things I would have done had I been on my own. But, in fact, it was the children themselves whom I most enjoyed. They had their moods, of course, and the boys in particular had a fondness for teasing me, but I always fell in love with at least one of the children in my care, and I disliked almost none of them. I took my work seriously, thought of myself as a little mother and looked forward to the day when I might actually be a mother. I was meant to continue at the nursery until I was ten, at which point I, too, would be taught to sew, or to cook, or any of the other female labors. But my life took a different course one hot August day when I was nine.

I was leading three small boys past the great house on my way to a cow pond, where I hoped we could all cool off, when I thought I heard a woman calling out.

I looked around, and under the shade of an enormous copper beech, lying on a couch that had been carried out of the parlor, I saw Mrs. Jefferson waving. "Sally!" she called. "Could you come here please? I'd like to have a word with you."

Mrs. Jefferson had been ill ever since her baby died, more than a year previously. That baby had been named Lucy, and three months ago she had had another baby, also named Lucy, and had grown even sicker. She hardly walked anymore, and a couch had been brought out under the tree for her because Mr. Jefferson believed that the fresh air would do her good.

I had been with Mrs. Jefferson many times, but never on my own, and so the notion that she wanted a private conversation with me filled me with apprehension—especially as my mother had told me that as Mrs. Jefferson's illness had grown worse, she had become increasingly irritable and vindictive. As I crossed the lawn, the boys trailing along behind me, I tried to think of what I could possibly have done wrong and what I might say to my mother if Mrs. Jefferson were angry with me.

But, in fact, she only smiled as I approached—though it was one of those smiles that seem to have been born out of pain. She was in her mid-thirties but she looked almost twice her age. Her skin was the color of trout flesh, and there were purple hollows under her eyes. Despite the heat she had a woolen shawl drawn up around her neck.

I told the boys to sit down on one of the tree's enormous, serpentine roots and that if they were very good, I would teach them how to catch pollywogs at the pond. When at last I stood in front of Mrs. Jefferson, she reached up and caressed my cheek with her cool hand. "You're such a pretty girl!" she said. "You have such lovely, kind eyes."

The intensity of her gaze disconcerted me. I lowered my head and couldn't bring myself to speak.

She had been lying diagonally on the couch, her slipper-shod feet not quite touching the ground, but now she sat up properly and patted the empty space beside her. "Sit down. I have something to say to you."

When I didn't move, she smiled and said, "You don't have to worry. I promise not to bite!"

When I still didn't move, she asked if anything was the matter, and I nodded at the boys, who had found an anthill and were looking for a twig to stick into it.

"Oh, don't worry about them." She laughed. "They'll be fine. And this won't take a minute."

She stroked the silk upholstery with her pale hand, then patted it.

I turned and sat down, but only at the very edge of the cushion. I folded my hands in my lap.

"I've been watching you," Mrs. Jefferson said. "And I see that you are very good with children. You never threaten to thrash them, you never even raise your voice, and yet the children do exactly what you say. It is because they want to please you."

"Thank you." I swallowed to suppress a smile of pride.

Mrs. Jefferson smiled and took my hand. She had grown so thin that I could feel every one of her bones, even in her palm. She looked at me for a long moment, with her soft, faintly pained smile. I wanted to pull my hand away.

"You know that I have a very small baby," she said.

I nodded.

"Ever since she was born, it has been difficult for me to devote as much attention as I should to her sister, my dear little Polly." Mrs. Jefferson let go of my hand and pulled up her shawl, which had begun to slip from her shoulders. Then she took my hand again and gave it a squeeze. "And so I have an offer to make to you. I am wondering if you would like to be little Polly's companion. She is not even five years old, and I am afraid she spends too much time alone."

When I didn't respond, she continued, "Do you know what a companion is?"

"No, ma'am."

"I want you to spend the day with her and do whatever it is that she would like to do. If she would like to play a game with you, play a game. If she would like to go for a ride, you should accompany her in the carriage. And, of course, I would like you to tidy up her room and look after her clothing, as your mother does for me." She gave my hand another squeeze. "So is that something you think you could do?"

I knew that what I was being asked to do was only what I was already doing at the nursery, but for some reason it filled me with dread. I hardly knew Polly and didn't understand why she should be lonely when she had another sister—Patsy—who was almost exactly my age.

There was, however, only one answer I could give, and so I gave it.

"I'm very happy," Mrs. Jefferson said, although she looked anything but happy. "I think that you will be the perfect companion for little Poll. I am sure that one day you will be as dear to her as your mother is to me."

I thanked Mrs. Jefferson again, collected my boys and continued my journey to the cow pond, wondering if there was some way my mother could talk Mrs. Jefferson out of using me in this fashion.

Poor Mrs. Jefferson. She was never anything but kind to me. Even when she could no longer speak, she would still cast me lingering glances and smiles.

In less than a month, she was dead. . . .

It is 1784. In the months after Martha died, Thomas Jefferson lost three stone, and now, more than a year later, he is still so thin that the contours of his teeth are visible through his cheeks, and multiple deep creases fan vertically on either side of his mouth. He arrives late for every session of Congress and leaves early whenever he can manage it. For several weeks he throws himself into preparing a bill that will determine how the Northwest Territory is to be managed, but when his provision banning slavery within the territory after 1800 is deleted under pressure from southern delegates, his exhaustion is total, and more spiritual than physical. He is through with politics. He will return to farming. If he never sets foot in a congressional meeting again, he will count himself a lucky man.

He is sitting at the table of the Virginia delegation, dull-eyed, staring into space, tearing strips from a newspaper, crumpling them into balls, then unfolding them. James Madison is seated beside him. They are alone. Night has fallen so recently that they are unaware of it. The panes on the windows all around them wobble and swirl, like a full stream in April frozen midflow. The light from their solitary oil lamp and their illuminated faces is broken into yellow twists on the glass, like the topmost flames in a fireplace, just before they vanish into black.

"I don't want to," says Thomas Jefferson.

"You will be working with Adams," says Madison. "And Dr. Franklin loves Paris."

"Then why is he leaving?"

"He's not," says Madison. "Not yet. At least not officially. He's old, though. Eighty if he's a day. And if he waits much longer, he won't be strong enough for the return voyage."

"I get seasick in a canoe."

Thomas Jefferson places a ball of paper on the table, then flicks it away with his middle finger.

Madison speaks in the low voice of reproach. "Tom." And then his eyes widen and he slaps his hand on the table. "It's *Paris*, Tom! *Paris!*

There's no more beautiful city in the world! And when Adams goes to London and Dr. Franklin returns home, you are certain to be minister."

Thomas Jefferson gives Madison a leaden glance. "And spend my days negotiating tobacco duties with fat aristocrats and singing the praises of our blubber oil to quartermaster generals across the Continent?"

Madison leans close, his voice thrumming in Thomas Jefferson's ear. "The French women, you know, are very fond of Americans and very free with their affections. Dr. Franklin is an old man, but by all reports, he has no shortage of female company."

Thomas Jefferson places another crumpled ball of paper on the tabletop.

"And the wine!" says Madison. "The French wine!"

Flick. The crumpled ball arcs off the edge of the table and hits the shadowy floor just in front of the vacant speaker's desk.

"Please stop," says Thomas Jefferson.

"But our minister to France must be a cultivated man. A philosopher. Dr. Franklin has set a precedent. No one can better take his place than you."

"I said *stop*."

Madison flings himself back in his chair and sinks into brooding.

"I'm tired of political life," says Thomas Jefferson. "And in any event, I don't have the mettle for it. I disgraced myself as governor—"

"Tom!"

"Don't!" Thomas Jefferson smacks the flat of his hand down onto the table. "You of all people should allow me to speak plainly."

"You're too hard on yourself."

"I'm not hard enough." Thomas Jefferson screws shut the top of his inkwell and wipes the tips of his quills. "But the main point is that I despise myself when I engage in politics. I entirely lack the stomach for bullying and bribery. Compromise so enrages me that I have not had a moment these last weeks free of headache." He places into his satchel the remainder of the newspaper from which he has been tearing strips. "I serve my country best with my pen. And I am happiest at home, among my books. There is no point pretending otherwise." He wraps the inkwell and the quills in a chamois bag that he also places into his satchel.

All at once Madison leans forward and touches his friend on the shoulder. "You're too much alone," he says. "I fear for you this winter, alone on your mountaintop."

"Then you must come visit me." Thomas Jefferson's half smile fades into something like irritation.

"Stop it, Tom!"

"Stop what?"

"You're being a fool."

"I hate politics! I loathe politicians! I just want to return to the life I was born for. How can you forbid me that?"

Madison sinks back into his chair. Thomas Jefferson inserts a strap into the buckle of his satchel.

"Lafayette specifically asked that you be sent to Paris," says Madison.

Thomas Jefferson stops, his fingers resting on the buckle. He does not look around. He is staring but not seeing anything. He has grown perfectly still.

The subway lights flicker and come back on, but the ragged metallic screeching continues. Thomas Jefferson knows that if he doesn't stand up now, if he doesn't cross the car and find a way of speaking to Sally Hemings, he will never have another chance. He knows this, but he cannot move.

II

In Sally Hemings's dream, she is walking down a street of very tall buildings with jagged, glinting roofs, and she is lost. She is walking with Thomas Jefferson, but he is a shadow, and he disappears when they pass through the shadows of buildings. He is holding her hand—or she thinks he is holding her hand. "Hurry!" he says. They are going someplace very important, and only he knows the way. At first she doesn't know where they are going, and then she realizes that she is a baby and that he is taking her to the place where she will be born. "Hurry!" he says. "You have to hurry!"

She wants to be born. If she isn't born, she will have to be a shadow in a world of shadows. She is not a shadow now. She is a baby. Except most of the time she doesn't look like a baby; she looks like herself: long-legged and long-armed, and with a face that is almost a woman's face. And sometimes Thomas Jefferson is not a shadow. She can see him, or parts of him. And she can feel his hand, which is very, very strong—so strong that she worries her hand will be crushed.

"Hurry!" he tells her. "They will leave without us!"

Thomas Jefferson is angry. He is running, but she can't run with him, because she is barefoot and the streets are covered with jagged, glinting shards and her feet are getting cut. "Run!" he tells her. "You have to run! They are almost gone!" But she can't run. The shards slice and tear. Her feet are bloody.

She wants to call out to him, but she can't make a noise. All she can do is clutch his hand, his arm, and claw at the lapel of his coat. Her feet are bleeding, and she knows that she is about to fall onto the shards.

But then he is holding her in his arms. She has her arms around his neck, and his arms around her are so very strong, and he is running so fast that everything is turning white, and there is this horrible noise that is also like a form of whiteness, and she wonders if this means she is being born or if she is dying.

. . . I am trying to tell the truth to its "teeth and forehead," as Shakespeare says. Yet I am afraid that I am building a big lie out of tiny facts, that everything I say about who I was and how I lived will imply that I could have lived no other life, that I was entirely dispossessed of freedom of will. The simple fact that tortures me to this very instant is that I was never without freedom of will, that at any of countless junctures I could have said, "No," and I would have lived a different life. Nothing was truly inevitable, and even when I didn't know I was making a choice, I was—and I must bear the burden of those choices. Most troubling of all, however, are the times when I did know I was making a choice and a voice inside me told me that the choice was wrong but I didn't listen—because I didn't believe the voice, or I didn't want to believe it, or because I couldn't really hear it among a thousand other voices. But never- theless, it spoke, and I didn't listen, and now I am damned. . . .

In history every fact is an element in a mathematical equation: Thomas Jefferson + John Adams + Philadelphia + skinny red ponytail over broad blue collar + pen = Declaration of Independence = the world as we know it. In history almost the entire human race exists in dusklight, murmuring inaudibly, ankle-high to Thomas Jefferson, who is perpetually effulgent with sunrise, who strides the cobbled spaces between monuments with chin raised, eyes fixed on distant prospects, and who knows cumulus clouds mounting aesthetically in ethereal blue but has never known rain.

There are other people in history. George Washington, for example, who is also dawn-effulgent, also massive, a monument in and of himself, maybe a little larger than Thomas Jefferson or a tad smaller. And that bald head, draped around the edges by long, gray hair, those wire-rimmed spectacles, that expression indicating something between peptic distress and discombobulation—that's Ben Franklin, of course. In history the three men come together, and their speech is of such august profundity that it can never be adequately imagined.

But in life almost everything that Thomas Jefferson eats makes him sick, and so the indoor privies of his Paris mansion, the Hôtel de Langeac, are an endlessly renewed blessing, night and day.

In life Thomas Jefferson is lost. One moment he is imagining that if he were to mount a four-sided book stand on casters like those he devised for his swivel chair, he could switch from book to book with the flick of a finger, and in the next moment he is lost. The streets of Paris are so narrow, disheveled and labyrinthine that a minute's distraction is enough to erase the connections between where he is, where he was and where he wishes to be. Thomas Jefferson spots a liveried footman, asks directions, but his French fails him so miserably that he can only pretend he has understood. And so he walks off and arbitrarily turns left, then right, and abandons himself to fate.

S emen, of course, is the most vital source of masculine energy, but it is also true that if too much semen accumulates within a man's body, he can go insane. Dr. Richard Gem, the preeminent American physician in Paris, is concerned that, as a grieving widower, Thomas Jefferson is not adequately venting his semen and so is putting his reason at risk. Onanism is not, Gem insists, a safe method for keeping bodily fluids in balance, as it can also lead to madness, in part because of its tendency to inspire excessive indulgence (it is a well-known fact that the insane are universally addicted to this practice). According to the doctor, the only healthy way to discharge excess semen is in the embrace of a young woman. Gem prescribes weekly visits to the house of Madame Benezet. Thomas Jefferson attempts to comply with this prescription but finds the women chez Madame Benezet wholly insincere in their friendliness, and he is disturbed by the presumptions they make about his character. Lafayette and Danqueville suggest that there is no reason for him to pay for the favors of women, since, as a dashing and cultured American, he can have his pick of the belles of Parisian society. But his friends' forthrightness and ease in female company are all but unimaginable to Thomas Jefferson, and so he takes to maintaining the proper balance of his vital fluids on his own, by expelling semen once a week, or sometimes twice, but never more often.

It is September 6, 1786. Thomas Jefferson has drunk two bottles of wine over dinner and believes that he is in love with Maria Cosway, who is a portrait painter, seventeen years his junior and married, and who has drunk nearly as much wine as he has. He wants to prove to her that his love is a mad joy and that he is as vigorous and adept as a man half his age, so he leaps a cistern in the place Louis XV, but his toe catches on the far rim and he descends to the flagstones in an inverted position, breaking his right wrist so badly that he will have to write with his left hand for much of a year and suffer, for the rest of his life, unpredictable squawks whenever he plays even the simplest tunes on his violin.

Maria Cosway laughs and laughs, thinking, *What a silly man!*, thinking he is only playacting as he rolls back and forth on the flagstones, howling. And as he howls, Thomas Jefferson thinks that Martha would never have laughed at the sight of him in such pain, and he thinks that he doesn't, in fact, love Maria Cosway. And as she comes to realize that he is not playacting, she, too, thinks that she does not love him—this clumsy American, with his farmer's accent—that he is pompous, and a bore, and that she was a fool to have betrayed her husband for him, though, in fact, she will continue to write to Thomas Jefferson long after he has left France and returned to Virginia and long after she has left her prodigiously unfaithful husband and moved into a convent in Italy, and Thomas Jefferson will write to her—two letters a year, three, sometimes more—and their correspondence will continue until she is an old woman and he is a much older man, and there will, in fact, be an unfinished letter to him on her desk the day she receives word from John Trumbull that Thomas Jefferson has died.

But that drunken night in Paris, Thomas Jefferson cannot see Maria Cosway as she bends over him making sympathetic noises that he knows to be insincere. There are no streetlights, and he and she only dared take a walk after their dinner because the sky was cloudless and there was a gibbous moon—although now that moon is pumpkin orange and steeple-pierced, and in a minute it will have been absorbed by its own flickery fire on the Seine. Thomas Jefferson can see stars around the amorphous obscurity that is Maria Cosway, bent over him, uttering low coos and singsong consolations such as are normally addressed to children, and he is not so drunk that he doesn't know that the darkness on the streets soon will be of such profundity that he will be all but blind after he has seen her to her hotel and then as he makes his way home, in agony, by starlight, and that the journey will take hours.

But those hours, unrecorded, will never exist in history, nor will the starlight and the pumpkin moon, nor those bottles of wine, nor Thomas Jefferson's laughter, nor Maria Cosway's, nor their kisses across the dinner table, nor those deeper kisses just before he tells her, "Watch this!" and begins to run toward the cistern.

It is June 26, 1787. Sally Hemings is fourteen and has arrived in a country where the air smells of rancid meat and of flowers too long in the vase, and all the people speak in grunts, coughs and fluting whinnies. In one hand she holds the canvas bag that contains her every possession in the world. Her other hand is on the shoulder of Polly Jefferson, whom she clutches against her side. Beside them on the stone quay is a waist-high sea chest stuffed with Polly's belongings. Her little sister, Lucy, is dead of the whooping cough, and Polly has come from Virginia to live with her father and her big sister, Patsy, in France. But this mud- and gravel-colored city is not France. Sally Hemings does not know what this city is. She thinks it might be London.

"What's happened to Captain Ramsey?" says Polly, who is nearly nine years old but so small and frail she looks six. Her hair is exactly the rich earth-brown of Sally Hemings's, and the two girls have done their hair in an identical fashion, with hanks drawn back loosely from the temples and framed by the ruffle of their cotton bonnets. Sally's bonnet, however, is topped by a straw hat, partially eaten by mice during their passage (at the crown and the back), and pinned, through the bonnet, to her hair.

"He'll be right back," she says.

"But where did he go?"

"Didn't you listen?" Sally Hemings is irritated, but she knows she shouldn't be, so she gives Polly's shoulder an encouraging squeeze and speaks softly. "He's just looking for the porter. He'll be right back."

"But why didn't he send Mr. George?" says Polly. "Or one of the mateys?"

"They're busy, I reckon." Sally Hemings gives Polly's shoulder another squeeze, but more for her own encouragement this time.

She doesn't like Captain Ramsey. Throughout their five weeks at sea, he was always coming up behind her, slapping her on the bottom and shouting, "Get along there, girl!" One night when she was on her way back from emptying Polly's chamber pot over the gunwale, he stopped her at the top of the companionway and put his hand on her bodice, just over her left breast. When she pushed his hand away, he said, "What's the matter! I just want to see how healthy you are." That is the worst he ever did, and he has never been anything but grandfatherly to Polly—who loves him as if he actually were her grandfather—but Sally Hemings suspects he's one of those white men her mammy has told her about, the ones you have to keep your eye on.

She looks down the long marble quay toward the building with the huge windows into which Captain Ramsey disappeared. He ought to have been back ages ago; it can't take that much time to find a porter.

When their ship docked, brilliant silver and white clouds with gray undersides were scattered across a powder blue sky, but since then the clouds have grown steadily denser and darker, and she can see a heron-blue smear of rain falling diagonally beyond the big building.

A sudden chilly gust blows down the quay, and she has to hold on to her hat. This is a cold country, she thinks. It is nearly July, and yet she and Polly have to wear their shawls tight across their shoulders if they want to keep from shivering. France will be nicer, she hopes.

Polly makes a small noise and flings her arms around Sally Hemings's shoulders.

A bearded man in a black coat is standing just behind Polly, holding the grips of a wooden wheelbarrow and shouting, in a low, angry voice, words that sound like English chopped into pieces and rearranged in a nonsensical order. The front edge of his wheelbarrow is actually touching Polly's skirts, and the girl seems to want to climb into Sally Hemings's arms.

"Did Captain Ramsey send you?" asks Sally Hemings, thinking the man may be the porter. But her question only makes the chopped-up English tumble ever more rapidly and loudly out of his three-toothed mouth.

He keeps jerking his wheelbarrow back and forth on the cobbles. It is stacked high with oil casks and has no room at all for Polly's chest.

"He just wants us out the way," Sally Hemings says, and pulls Polly back until they are both standing with their heels half over the quay's edge. The bearded man grunts and pushes his wheelbarrow through the gap between their toes and Polly's sea chest.

"Where's my papa!" cries Polly. "I hate this country! I wish we stayed with Aunt and Uncle Eppes."

"There, there." Sally Hemings pulls the weeping girl into her arms, feeling that it will be only a matter of seconds before she, herself, will be crying.

Polly was furious at being left behind when her father and Patsy went to France, and she only became more so when little Lucy died of whooping cough, a disease she might never have gotten had she and Polly gone to Paris, too. And when her father finally wrote to Aunt Eppes saying that he wanted Polly to join him, she said that she wouldn't go. "Don't you want to see Patsy?" her Aunt Eppes asked her. "Don't you want to live in a real castle and see real princesses walking the streets?" No! Polly was determined. If her father didn't love her enough to come and take her to Paris himself, then she wouldn't go, and no one could force her.

Finally Aunt and Uncle Eppes told her that they would go to France with her. They packed valises for themselves and carried them onto the ship at Jamestown. When she was settled in her cabin, they gave her a medicine they said would keep her from getting seasick, but that actually just put her to sleep. And when she woke up, she and Sally Hemings were all by themselves on a boat full of men, miles and miles at sea. Sally Hemings had never felt so lonely and afraid as she did during the hours she sat beside the sleeping Polly, and she feels a little of that loneliness and fear now.

She squeezes Polly against her chest and kisses the top of her head. "Your papa loves you," she says. "That's how come he sent for you. He'll be here soon, and you'll see how much he loves you. Everything'll be just fine." She kisses Polly's head a second time, and the little girl returns her squeeze. "Who knows?" says Sally Hemings. "Maybe Captain Ramsey found your papa already and they're just talking down there in that big house."

Polly is no longer weeping, but she keeps her head tight against Sally Hemings's breast.

It's been more than half an hour since Captain Ramsey left them. All of the other passengers on their boat are gone, and Sally Hemings feels more alone every instant. Maybe this isn't London. Maybe all these gruff men in their leather aprons and grease-stained clothing aren't speaking English at all but some other language she's never heard of. Maybe Captain Ramsey has just abandoned them here.

She gently extracts herself from Polly's grip and says, "You wait here, Polly-Pie. Let me go see what's taking that Captain so long."

"No!" cries Polly, grief-stricken all over again. "Don't leave me!"

"I'm not leaving you. You can see me the whole time. I'm just going down this dock here, so I can see in the windows of that big house. You got to wait here, because someone's got to look after our stuff."

Polly's eyes are jittery with tears, and there is a groove of worry between her eyebrows, but she doesn't complain. Sally Hemings steps backward and, after a few yards, begins to hurry sideways, alternately looking where she is going and back at her charge. She knows there is no reason Polly shouldn't come with her. All of the men on the dock are busy with their own labors, and they could never make off with that big chest without her noticing. But somehow she can't stand the idea of Polly coming with her. The two girls have been together every single minute of the last thirty-seven days. Sally Hemings would just love a few moments alone. Nothing bad could happen in so short a time.

She has gone only a dozen yards, however, when she spots a heavy-shouldered woman in a blue gown hurrying down the quay, clamping her feathered hat onto her head with one hand, her knees thrusting, one after the other, against her shimmery skirt.

"Polly!" the woman is calling. "Polly!"

She is close enough to see Sally Hemings's smile of relief, and she, too, starts to smile, even as she continues to run.

"I am so sorry!" the woman says between wheezing gasps when at last she is at Sally Hemings's side. "We were told . . . you wouldn't be . . . getting in . . . until tomorrow . . . or the next day. . . . When I heard . . . your boat . . . was here, . . . I ran all the way. . . ." She stops talking, grips Sally Hemings's wrist and places her other hand against the base of her own throat, gasping so fiercely that she makes a ghost moan with every breath.

"Forgive me!" she says at last, letting go of Sally Hemings's wrist. "I haven't introduced . . . myself. . . . I'm Mrs. Adams. . . . A friend of your father."

"I'm Sally," says Sally Hemings. "That's Miss Polly over there." She points toward the little girl who has already taken several tentative steps in their direction.

"Yes. Of course," Mrs. Adams says briskly. "So sorry." And with that she runs toward Polly with both arms extended. "Polly! Oh, Polly! It is so good to see you at last!"

My dear Sir

I have to congratulate you upon the safe arrival of your Little Daughter, whom I have only a few moments ago received. She is in fine Health and a Lovely little Girl I am sure from her countanance, but at present every thing is strange to her, and she was very loth to try New Friends for old. She was so much attachd to the Captain and he to her, that it was with no small regret that I seperated her from him, but I dare say I shall reconcile her in a day or two. I tell her that I did not see her sister cry once. She replies that her sister was older and ought to do better, besides she had her pappa with her. I shew her your picture. She says she cannot know it, how should she when she should not know you. A few hours acquaintance and we shall be quite Friends I dare say. I hope we may expect the pleasure of an other visit from you now I have so strong an inducement to tempt you. If you could bring Miss Jefferson with you, it would reconcile her little Sister to the thoughts of taking a journey. It would be proper that some person should be accustomed to her. The old Nurse whom you expected to have attended her, was sick and unable to come. She has a Girl about 15 or 16 with her, the Sister of the Servant you have with you. As I presume you have but just returnd from your late excursion, you will not put yourself to any inconvenience or Hurry in comeing or sending for her. You may rely upon every attention towards her and every care in my power. I have just endeavourd to amuse her by telling her that I would carry her to Sadlers Wells. After describing the amusement to her with an honest simplicity, I had rather says she see captain Ramsey one moment, than all the fun in the World.

I have only time before the post goes, to present my compliments to Mr. Short. Mr. Adams and Mrs. Smith desire to be rememberd to you. Captain Ramsey has brought a Number of Letters. As they may be of importance to you to receive them we have forwarded them by the post.

Miss Polly sends her duty to you and Love to her Sister and says she will try to be good and not cry. So she has wiped her eyes and layd down to sleep.

> Believe me dear Sir affectionately
> yours &c &c,
> A Adams

Dear Sir

I had the Honour of addressing you yesterday and informing you of the safe arrival of your daughter. She was but just come when I sent of my letter by the post, and the poor little Girl was very unhappy being wholy left to strangers. This however lasted only a few Hours, and Miss is as contented to day as she was misirable yesterday. She is indeed a fine child. I have taken her out to day and purchased her a few articles which she could not well do without and I hope they will meet your approbation. The Girl who is with her is quite a child, and Captain Ramsey is of opinion will be of so little Service that he had better carry her back with him. But of this you will be a judge. She seems fond of the child and appears good naturd.

I sent by yesterdays post a Number of Letters which Captain Ramsey brought with him not knowing of any private hand, but Mr. Trumble has just calld to let me know that a Gentleman sets off for paris tomorrow morning. I have deliverd him two Letters this afternoon received, and requested him to wait that I might inform you how successfull a rival I have been to Captain Ramsey, and you will find it I imagine as difficult to seperate Miss Polly from me as I did to get her from the Captain. She stands by me while I write and asks if I write every day to her pappa? But as I have never had so interesting a subject to him to write upon [corner torn off] I hope he will excuse the hasty scrips for the [corner torn]y intelligence they contain, and be assured Dear Sir

> that I am with sentiments
> of sincere esteem your
> Humble Servant,
> A Adams

Thomas Jefferson gets two letters from Abigail Adams at once, six days after they were sent. In the same post is a letter from Maria Cosway, telling him for the second time that her visit to Paris will be delayed and all but begging, since she remains in London, to be allowed to visit Polly at the Adamses'. Thomas Jefferson feels a sinking ache as he reads her letter. He would love for her to meet his darling Polly and for the little girl, perhaps, to come to love her. But Mrs. Adams is a veritable savant of what she calls "secret life." Were Maria to utter one item of intimate knowledge—say, about Mistress Jelly, Polly's favorite doll, whose name Thomas Jefferson has more than once applied to Maria herself—then all would be revealed. The mere fact that this woman, whom Mrs. Adams knows only as an acquaintance of John Trumbull, should be so interested in visiting a mere child would be suspicious enough all on its own. No. Impossible. Out of the question.

But Thomas Jefferson suffers another sort of ache as he reads Maria's letter, because this new delay means there was simply no reason for him to have pretended to be off in Tuscany negotiating a trade agreement when Polly's ship arrived. He could easily have met her at the dock in London as he had promised and returned to Paris in time for Maria's visit—if, in fact, she will be visiting at all. He might also have been able to see Maria in London, though that could have been decidedly unpleasant, given that he would most likely have had to see her in the company of her husband.

As he thinks about it now, he knows for certain that Maria will not be visiting—and this is the most potent source of his ache. She already loathes herself for having betrayed Richard; how is it possible, then, morally and emotionally (to say nothing of practically), that she will manage so complex a deception as getting to Paris on her own? And how could Thomas Jefferson have let himself imagine she would! No doubt, in her heart, she doesn't want to see him ever again. Hasn't she told him repeatedly that Richard is a good and tender man? And that she couldn't bear to live if he were ever to find out? This is how it has always been for

Thomas Jefferson. The only woman who ever returned his love with all her heart was Martha. As soon as he revealed the strength of his passion to Becca and to Betsy, they vanished like quail into the forest. And now it is the same with Maria.

And the worst of it is that he has already sent Petit to London in his place. Were he to go there now, he would probably find that Petit, Polly and the Hemings girl had already set out for Paris. So he has nothing to do but wait. And nothing to distract him from thinking about Maria. And nothing whatsoever to stop him from pitting the ever-more-hopeless possibility that she might, in fact, visit against the ever-more-monumental-and-oppressive certainty that she won't.

He is standing in his study off the garden, in front of the cabinet where he keeps his wine, and he is pouring himself a second glass. How could he have strayed so far outside his better nature? Isn't this relentless agony his punishment for having betrayed the memory of his tender and beautiful wife and for having neglected his dear daughters? He is nothing but a monster and a fool, who will be unloved and lonely in his old age, a pathetic, neglected, ridiculed, gout-ridden inebriate and an incurable onanist—and that will be the only fate he deserves! It is an unfortunate fact of his nature that his moral instinct is strong enough only to punish him for his transgressions but not to preserve him from transgressing in the first place. He pours himself another glass.

"Are we here!" Polly says. "Are we here!"

The coach passes along a grand boulevard lined with row on row of geometrically shaped trees through a massive wrought-iron gate and then turns right, with a lurch like a ship surmounting a swell, into a small courtyard before a magnificent marble-and-limestone house with columns on either side of its portico and marble steps cascading down to the sandy paving.

"Are we here!" says Polly.

"I don't know," says Sally Hemings, although, in fact, she does know; she just can't bring herself to say it.

"Are we here!"

"Yes, you silly girl!" says Monsieur Petit. "This is your new house, the Hôtel de Langeac. Your father is waiting."

"We're here, Sally! We're here!"

Polly has grabbed hold of Sally Hemings's forearm and is shaking it up and down in her excitement. For some reason Sally Hemings is not excited. She is the opposite of excited. There is an ache in her heart and stomach, as if something bad is about to happen.

"Yes, my little Polly-Pie," she says softly. "We're here."

A female voice is calling, "Polly! Polly!"

At the top of the steps is a huge black door, half open, with a young woman standing in it. "Polly!" she shouts, waving her plump, pale hand. "Polly! Dear Polly!" And now the young woman has lifted the skirts of her embroidered green gown and is drifting down the stairs, her little feet appearing and disappearing beneath a white cloud of lace.

Can this possibly be Patsy? The last time Sally Hemings saw her was almost exactly three years ago. They'd both been eleven years old then, and it was the day before Patsy left Monticello for Paris. She had just been to say good-bye to her horse and was sitting on a box in front of the stable, scraping manure off her boots with a stick, tears making pale trails through the dust coating her cheeks. When Sally Hemings had asked her what was wrong, she had wailed, "I don't want to go! I'm going to hate

Paris! Why can't I stay here with Polly and Lucy?" How is it possible that this young woman, in her flowing gown, with her hair pinned high atop her head and a cameo pendant at the base of her neck, should ever have been so filthy and abject with grief? It is not just that Patsy's clothes are so elegant and her manner so refined, but that she seems even at fourteen (though she is almost fifteen) to have shot right out of girlhood and be ready for marriage.

"Patsy! Patsy! Patsy!"

Polly is so excited that she can't get the coach door unlatched, and Monsieur Petit has to walk around from the other side to do it for her. The little girl leaps straight to the ground and races up the steps. By the time Sally Hemings has lowered herself to the gritty, yellowish driveway, the two sisters already have their arms around each other and are rocking from side to side.

A number of other people have emerged from the big black door, servants mostly, though none Sally Hemings recognizes—

But then she sees a tall, dark-skinned young man in a burgundy frock coat, a yellow waistcoat and yellow stockings. It is Jimmy, of course, but somehow she can't allow herself to believe it. He smiles and waves but doesn't come down. He seems to be waiting for her to mount the steps and greet him. Jimmy is twenty-two, and except for his fine clothing, he looks almost exactly as he did at nineteen, when he left Monticello. The big difference is in his manner. There is a somber hesitancy in the way he holds himself at the top of the stairs. Or a seriousness. Maybe he, too, has shot into adulthood.

Just as Sally Hemings is about to rush up to her brother, someone else steps through the door—a tall, rangy man with white-laced red hair and alert hazel eyes. He holds his shoulders square and his head high and seems possessed of immense strength. He descends the steps with the fluid rapidity of an athlete.

Sally Hemings knows that this is Thomas Jefferson, and, indeed, he has changed less than any of the other people with whom she has been reunited. But he scares her. There is something in the length of his legs and arms, in the confident elevation of his chin and even in the happy squint of his eyes as he sees his daughters that makes it impossible for her to look away from him but that also makes her dread the moment when his eyes will turn in her direction, and he will speak, and she will be compelled to answer.

. . . My mother didn't like to talk about my father. That was another topic that would make her face go still and drab. When I asked about him, she would say, "He was just a man. But he's gone now." Maybe it was the flat hush in her voice, but from the very beginning I understood "he's gone now" to mean he had died. I remember thinking that knowing my father was dead was my secret, as if it were something I had stolen from my mother without her noticing. But then, when I finally worked up the courage to ask her about it, she said, "That's right. Your pappy's dead and gone. You were just an apple pip when he died. He hardly got to hold you in his arms."

I never actually grieved for my father, but I did miss him. I'd watch other children riding on their fathers' shoulders, and I would wish I had somebody who would do that for me. Or I'd see some big, strong man get down on his knee and tickle his little girl, then hug and kiss her while she laughed and laughed, and I would feel pierced through by loneliness. Of course, Bobby and Jimmy were eleven and eight years older than me and most of the way to being men—in my eyes, at least—by the time I started paying attention to these things. But they didn't love me the way a father would. Every now and then, they'd give me a little squeeze, but the main way they showed their love was by teasing. Jimmy's nickname for me when I was little was "Cider Jug." He was always saying things like, "How come your belly's so big and round, Cider Jug?" or, "You best stay away from the men after sunset, or they'll pop your head like a cork and drink you down."

Often when I was wandering in the woods, I'd imagine my father walking beside me, maybe holding my hand. Sometimes he'd be the one telling me the stories I told myself. I would even talk to him. I would ask him questions, then answer them aloud for him. Other times he would come to me in the middle of the night, especially when I had had a bad dream. He would sit beside my bed, stroke my hair and tell me in a low, kindly voice, "Don't you worry. Your pappy's here. Everything's going to be just fine." And that really would help me feel better—most of the time, at least.

My father was never just some vague masculine presence; I saw him clearly in my mind's eye. He was very tall and very smart and had the mahogany skin and baritone voice of Reverend Hodder, a free man who came to Monticello to hold prayer meetings. And partly because I had such a clear and vivid image of my father, when a girl named Buttercup told me, "Your pappy is a white man," I just couldn't believe her. "Yes he is," she insisted. "My mammy told me. That's how come you're so high-toned and have white-girl hair."

At first the main thing that troubled me about what Buttercup said was that she used the word "is," which meant that my father was still alive. I went straight to my mother, who told me, "Of course he's dead! Why would I lie about a thing like that? He died when you were five months old." And when I asked if he was white, she said, "Don't you listen to that fool talk! Your pappy was just a man. Just a plain old man." I tried to take my mother at her word, but even at age six, it was clear to me that if my father had been a Negro, she would have said so straight out.

Once the idea that my father was white became lodged in my brain, I began to conceive of myself differently. Up until that point, I had hardly given a thought to my skin and hair—maybe because I knew many Negroes with pale skin and many "white" people whose skin had a decidedly dusky cast, especially in summer. For me, "white" primarily signified people other than "us," those difficult, sometimes cruel, never reliable people with whom our life was inextricably and mysteriously intertwined. I didn't even know what the term "race" meant at the time and never imagined that I could be anything other than Negro. But almost as soon as I identified "white" with the color of my own skin, I began to tell myself a story that I actually was white, that my mother wasn't my real mother and that I was only being raised as a Negro by mistake. At the end of this story, the mistake would always be uncovered and I would be radiant with the sort of glory that surrounded Mr. Jefferson. I imagined everyone at Monticello, colored and white, being extravagantly happy on my behalf and staging a sort of celebration for me, after which Mr. Jefferson would adopt me, and I would live in the great house with him and his family, and I would bring my mother and siblings along as my servants, and we would all dress in silks and lace and wear the shiniest of shoes.

This story felt like another secret I had stolen from my mother, but one so complexly shameful that I could never mention it to her and, indeed, have kept it to myself my entire life. One August night, however, when it was too hot to sleep, Critta and I took our ticks outside and spread them on the grass behind our cabin, where the faintest breeze blowing across the field cooled our sweaty limbs and faces. I had in mind a question that I had wanted to ask Critta for days but had never actually dared to speak. Now that the two of us were lying side by side, all alone under the night sky, and our privacy further ensured by the din of crickets and peepers, I drew my lips to her ear and whispered, "Buttercup said my pappy was white."

"So?"

Critta's complacent response surprised me, and it was a long moment before I could ask, "Was he?"

"Of course!" she said. "Everybody knows that!"

"Who told you?"

"Jimmy. He was Jimmy's pappy, too, and mine. He was all of our pappy."

This news was such a shock that I couldn't speak. Finally I asked, "Does Peter know?"

"Of course. Everybody knows except you, because you're the baby!"

"Why didn't you tell me?"

"You know that Mammy doesn't like us talking about things like that."

And that was where our conversation ended.

Years later, when I was fourteen and packing to bring Miss Maria to live with her sister and father in France, my mother was seated at the table behind me. She didn't talk while I packed, only sighed heavily and kept rubbing the palm of her left hand with the thumb of her right. I thought she was angry at me, so I did my best to fold my belongings quietly and not disturb her with questions. When I finished, I turned around and saw that she was looking straight at me, her brow all wrinkled and her eyes two sharp points, as if I'd done something horrifying.

"Come here," she said firmly, nodding at the chair beside her. When I hesitated, she said, "I've got something important to tell you."

I sat beside her at the table, and she cupped both of my hands in hers and squeezed them. "I never told you this," she said, "because I didn't want you getting into trouble. Bobby, Jimmy and Thenia know, because they were old enough to remember him. But I thought it'd be easier—"

"Remember who?"

"Your pappy."

"I already know he was white."

She smiled, almost as if she were proud of me. "Well, that's not all he was." Her smile got thin and crooked. She looked away. When she looked back, she wasn't smiling. "Your pappy..." She took a deep breath and licked her lips. "Your pappy... was Mrs. Jefferson's pappy. You and Mrs. Jefferson were sisters. Miss Patsy and Miss Polly are your nieces."

My mother told me that she'd kept the identity of my father secret because she thought that if I knew I was a servant to my own family, I might say or do something wrong or I would get ideas that would only make me sad. There wasn't anything she could do about Bobby, Jimmy and Thenia, but she had told them that if they ever breathed a word to Critta, Peter and me about Mrs. Jefferson being our sister, she would "whip their backsides till they caught fire!"

"Only reason I'm telling you now," she said, "is you're going to France. I don't think Miss Patsy or Miss Polly knows, but Mr. Jefferson surely does. And you're most ways to being a young woman now, so you've got to understand that Mr. Jefferson most surely knows you're his wife's sister, and that's a fact."

As she said this, I started to sob and couldn't stop. The news was more than I could bear, especially as I had already been terrified about getting on a boat and traveling to a country where nobody would speak a word I could understand. My mother took me into her arms, pressed my head against her bosom and kissed my cheek over and over. "Don't you worry," she said. "Everything's going to be fine. You're such a smart girl. Everything'll be just fine."

Sally Hemings is fourteen years old, and she has been in Paris for two days. Thomas Jefferson almost doesn't see her as he enters the upstairs parlor, partly because it is five-thirty in the morning, an hour at which no one else is normally awake, but mainly because she is so silent and still, a streak of darker gray before the gray of the window. She is leaning her forehead against the wobbly, bubbled glass, looking out onto the rainy courtyard, clutching the fingers of one hand in the near fist of the other. At the sound of his shoe scuffing to a stop just inside the door, she becomes a burst of flutter and flight, like a ruffed grouse startled from a hedge. "I'm sorry!" she cries. "I'm sorry! I just—" She shoots past him and out the door so rapidly that if she ever finishes her sentence, he hears not a syllable.

Q: When did you first find out that you were free?

JAMES: The marquis told me.

Q: The Marquis de Lafayette?

JAMES: [Nods.]

Q: When?

JAMES: Oh, I don't know. It must have been . . . Uh . . . I'm pretty sure it was the first time he came to dinner. I remember hearing him in the foyer. He had such a loud voice, and he was laughing. He and Mr. Jefferson were both laughing. And then, no more than a minute later, he came into the kitchen. *"Zheemmee! Zheemmee! Zheemmee!"* He was so happy to see me again, he said, and why hadn't I come out to greet him at the door? I didn't know what to say to that, because I'd only met him once before, when I was a kid. But then he stopped shouting, and he leaned close to my ear. "I want you to know that slavery is not tolerated in this country," he said. "It is contrary to the laws. As long as you are here, you are as free as Mr. Jefferson."

Q: What did you think of him telling you that?

JAMES: I don't know.

Q: Did you think it was strange?

JAMES: Well, the marquis was a strange man. I liked him, though. He was always good to me.

Q: Maybe not to Thomas Jefferson?

JAMES: Oh, he and Mr. Jefferson were best friends. In fact, I bet he told Mr. Jefferson what he was going to say before he even came back in the kitchen. He was just like that. The really strange thing, though, is that he had a slave himself when he was in Virginia.

Q: Really?

JAMES: His name was Jimmy, too, now that I think of it. There's even a famous picture of them together, isn't there, Sally?

SARAH: A painting.

JAMES: Who's it by?

SARAH: I don't remember. A French painter. I think he even came to the Hôtel once, but I don't remember his name.

Q: What about you, Sarah? When did you find out you were free?

SARAH: The marquis told me, too. But Jimmy told me first. Didn't you, Jimmy? It was that first day, when you showed me my bedroom.

Q: What did you think?

SARAH: It was beautiful! It had red silk wallpaper, padded and soft, like a pillow. But it was freezing in the winter.

Q: No, I mean about being free.

SARAH: Oh! [Laughs.] I didn't know what to think about that. It was strange, mainly.

JAMES: You were tired.

SARAH: Exhausted! And I was in a new country. Everything was strange. Everything was just hard to think about then. For a long time, really.

Q: But what about after?

SARAH: It was still strange.

Q: Why? How? Did you really not understand?

JAMES: *I* understood. I understood right away. It was easy. [Stops talking. Squeezes SARAH's hand.] Sorry.

SARAH: That's okay. Go ahead.

JAMES: No. You first. You're the one everyone wants to hear about anyway! [Laughs.]

SARAH: That's not true!

JAMES: Tell her to stop being so humble!

Q: [Laughs.]

SARAH: Okay. . . . [Glances at JAMES, who takes a sip from the flask he keeps in the breast pocket of his jacket.] Uh . . . What was I saying?

Q: You didn't understand.

SARAH: Okay . . . well . . . The thing is, everything is so different now. Things that seem simple now just weren't then. Even after all these years, it's still very hard for me to put it into words. I guess the main problem is that I can't think like that anymore. Nobody thinks like that anymore. But anyhow. For me, at the time, it was like I had two minds. In one of those minds, I knew, of course, that slavery was wrong. It's like what Mr. Jefferson wrote: Certain truths are self-evident. Everybody just wants to be free. We're born thinking we're the center of the universe and that we can and *should*—I think it's a moral issue for babies!—that we *should* get everything we want. Which we do for a while, because babies don't actually want very much. And that's where the second mind comes in. Because I was born a slave. Jimmy and I were both born slaves. That's just how the world was—

JAMES: That's not how it was for me. [Covers his mouth.] Sorry.

SARAH: No. Speak. You've got something to say.

JAMES: [Looks at Q.]

Q: Go ahead. If it's all right with Sarah.

SARAH: Speak, Jimmy.

JAMES: I only ever had one mind about slavery, and in that mind I knew that the world had made me a slave and that slavery was wrong—a crime against humanity! Unforgivable! And I knew in my heart I wasn't actually a slave, that I had never been a slave and that I was never going to act like a slave. I would only do what I chose to do, just like every other free man.

Q: And were you actually able to manage that?

JAMES: Yes. Absolutely! . . . But, of course, I was lucky. Sally and I were both lucky. Because of—you know: Mr. Jefferson. . . . But anyhow, that's how I felt for as long as I can remember. From way before I went to France. And, of course, from way before Mr. Jefferson gave me my manumission and I really was free. In the eyes of the law, I mean.

Q: And how was it then? After your manumission.

JAMES: It was the same.

Q: No. I mean . . . Well, I hadn't actually intended to bring this up until later. But . . . I mean . . . Given what happened?

JAMES: I don't actually want to talk about that. [Long silence.] Okay?

Q: I'm sorry.

JAMES: [Takes a sip from his flask. Puts it back in his pocket.] I refuse to talk about that. . . . It was . . . Well, it was all very complicated, and there's no way I can explain it. And I don't want to. [Silence.] Of course, slavery entered into it, but it wasn't really how you think—

Q: I—

JAMES: Anyhow, Mr. Jefferson only gave me my manumission because he wanted to get rid of me.

SARAH: That's not true!

JAMES: Sure it is. He was just sick of dealing with me. I could see it in his face when I asked him. I could see how relieved he was.

SARAH: No, Jimmy.

JAMES: But I didn't care. Fuck that. I thought—you know: I'd just go to Philadelphia and make a new life for myself. Friends and . . . maybe travel. I wanted to go to Spain. Back to France. But the other thing is—I mean . . . Maybe if I'd been white as Sally. And . . . Well . . . you know— [Silence.] But fuck that shit!

SARAH: Jimmy!

JAMES: What? Fuck it!

Q: I—

JAMES: I told you I didn't want to talk about it. So it's over. Okay? Finished! Let's just forget about it. None of that really matters anyway. That's not how it was.

Q: I'm sorry.

JAMES: Go on, Sally. I interrupted you. Say what you were going to say. [Long silence.]

JAMES: Go on. *Really*. I'm sorry. I shouldn't have interrupted.

SARAH: Don't be ridiculous. [Silence.] I said it all anyway. There's nothing to say. . . . Mainly I was like you. I knew I was a slave, and I knew it was wrong. But . . . There were just these people I'd grown up with. My family. Mammy, of course. And you, Jimmy. Peter. And Critta and . . . Well, the Jeffersons were family, too. I mean, Martha and Maria were my nieces! And, of course, there was Mr. Jefferson—

Q: Do you mind if I ask you something?

SARAH: Uh.

Q: I'm surprised that you call him "*Mr.*" Jefferson.

SARAH: He wanted us to. He hated the term "master." He didn't want anybody to call him "master."

JAMES: Maybe. But that didn't change anything, did it?

SARAH: [Silence.]

JAMES: I mean the words we used—"mister," "servant," "laborer"—those were just his way of getting us to go along with the lie he was telling himself.

SARAH: Not really.

JAMES: Well, you can believe what you want to believe.

SARAH: [Silence.]

JAMES: [Lifts his flask. It is empty. He balances it on his knee. SARAH is looking at him, but he does not meet her eye.]

Q: But still. To get back to— You know: names . . . I'm just wondering. Didn't you ever . . . ? I mean, considering—

SARAH: You mean Thomas? Tom? . . . Sometimes . . . Of course there were times when I—when we were— [Silence.] Oh! . . . Oh! . . . [Weeps.]

Q: I'm sorry!

SARAH: No. Really. It's nothing. Ridiculous! I guess I just got a little . . . you know: emotional. I mean, this conversation—

Q: I'm turning off the recorder.

SARAH: No. Really.

Q: I'm turning it off. Maybe tomorrow—

[End of recording.]

. . . During our weeks at sea, I was like a mother to Miss Maria. I scolded her for not changing her linens or for failing to wash behind her ears, and she could not sleep unless she was enfolded in my arms. But we were also like sisters: each other's only friend on the ship, the only one who knew anything about the people and places we loved most. We were also the only children and the only females not accompanied by a man (in fact, there were only two other women on board). Our intimacy was the shield by which we warded off fear—and in truth, I, too, might not have been able to sleep were I not enfolded with my dear little Polly—as I called her then. We vomited over the gunwales together; we gossiped about the people we had left behind; we traded memories about the beauty and comfort of Monticello, which now seemed a paradise to us both; we speculated anxiously about the lives we would have in Paris and told each other jokes about this sailor's red ears, that passenger's dewlap and another's fondness for the phrase "in a manner of speaking." Amazingly, we never once fought or even got annoyed with each other during our passage, perhaps because neither of us could imagine how we might survive without the other.

Everything changed once we arrived at the Hôtel de Langeac. We would never share a bed again. I would never be her mother, sister or friend. I couldn't even call her "Polly-Pie" or "Pollarina Bumble," as I had during our passage, but only "Miss Polly" or, on very formal occasions, "Miss Mary," for that was her real name.

At the end of August, she and Miss Martha went to live at l'Abbaye de Penthemont—a convent school, about an hour's walk and on the far side of the Seine from the Hôtel. They would come home Wednesday and Saturday afternoons and return to the school early the next mornings. During their absences I would help my brother Jimmy, who was the cook, with shopping and kitchen duties, and Clotilde, the housekeeper, with dusting, mopping and making the beds. But when Miss Martha and Miss Maria were home, they were my sole concern.

At nights I helped them undress and would put away their gowns, shawls and undergarments. In the mornings I brought them cups of hot chocolate in bed, put out whatever clothes they requested and would help them fasten their stays and do up the buttons at the backs of their gowns. I would also brush and pin up their hair, a chore I particularly liked, because we would talk about their friendships at school and the young men who interested them. Mr. Jefferson had hired a tutor for Jimmy and me, and as my French improved, I was able to give Miss Martha and Miss Maria gossip I had heard from other servants about the foibles and secret loves of their friends. The girls would laugh, hoot and exclaim at my reports and ask for more when I had done.

My other main duty was to mend the sisters' clothing and do other sorts of sewing—tasks I would usually perform in a window of whatever room the girls happened to occupy and that were no obstacle to conversation. Often we talked all morning and afternoon—about anything from types of hair powder to whether Paris or Virginia was the better place to live or how it was possible, if God controlled all things, that we were the ones thinking our own thoughts. And from time to time, I would put down my sewing and we would play at cards, charades or the Devil and the Woodman.

Such days passed swiftly and happily, and I allowed myself to believe that there prevailed between us something like the familial affection that would have existed as a matter of course had our true relationship been known—and this, I have no doubt, was one of the "ideas" my mother hadn't wanted me to get, because, of course, there was a big difference between what I thought of as our true relationship and the one we actually lived.

The girls had the right to tell me what to do, and I had no right to refuse, or even question a command—in which fact, of course, our actual relationship was at its most naked. We might be in the midst of friendly chatter—I could even be telling a story—when one of them would feel a pang of hunger and send me off to fetch some fruit or cheese. The command might come peremptorily, yet whichever sister issued it need not have felt the slightest ill will toward me nor have any sense that she had been impolite. This was just the way one spoke to servants. And as I had long been used to doing what I was told, I would simply walk off to the kitchen—though often feeling a lonely throb deep in my breast. Those were the times when I most missed my own family, Critta and Peter especially.

There were, of course, days when the girls were consciously impolite or even cruel, days when my job seemed mainly to suffer remarks like, "How can you be so stupid?" "Faster, you layabout!" or, "Of course, you are never troubled by the admiring gazes of young men." Most of these remarks came from Miss Martha and were particularly painful because I admired her and wished that I could be as intelligent and poised as she. Miss Maria was rarely cruel, though she was prone to sulks, during which she would claim to hate school and to detest Paris and would continually pull single hairs from the side of her head, to the point that she developed a small bald spot about an inch above her left ear that I would have to be sure to cover when I did her hair in the morning.

Worst of all was when the sisters fought, which they did frequently and, often, for no apparent reason. One of their most impassioned disputes commenced when Miss Maria referred to a bird giving itself a dust bath at the Tuileries as a "popkin" and Miss Martha laughed derisively. "How can anyone be so stupid!" she said. "That's a sparrow!" The truth is that Miss Maria was more often the first sister to attack, but given that Miss Martha was six years the elder, her counterattacks were so sophisticated and aimed so precisely at her sister's most tender points that it was hard not to pity the poor girl, even when she was in the wrong. Often, at Miss Maria's lowest moments in such fights, she would throw her arms around my waist and bury her face in my lap as a means of escaping her sister's insults and gibes.

As servant to both sisters it was in my interest never to appear to take sides, although I had to be especially careful not to offend Miss Martha, since as the elder and her father's clear favorite she was the one who could do me more damage. Even if my heart were breaking for poor Miss Maria, I would do my best to seem mystified by the girl's embraces. That strategy had only limited effectiveness, however, since Miss Martha found the fact that Miss Maria should want to embrace me exceedingly irritating all on its own—particularly as it was not uncommon for Miss Maria, even in her most contented moods, to throw her arms around my neck and declare, "I love you!" Not since both sisters were in Virginia had Miss Maria made such a declaration to her sister, nor had Miss Martha to her.

I know that in many ways I was fantastically lucky. Miss Maria truly did love me, and I loved her. My relations with Miss Martha were always more complex and have remained so until this very day. But in Paris she and I were *in a position not unlike Miss Maria's and mine during our Atlantic passage. As fluent as Miss Martha was in French, she would never be truly accepted by the French girls at school. As gracious and erudite as she might have been, and as expensive and fine as the gowns her father bought her most certainly were, in her own heart she would never cease to see herself as a rustic from a crude settlement in a savage wilderness, whereas with me she never had to feel the least self-conscious. We had known each other practically since birth; our toes had squelched in the same mud; we missed the same balmy summer nights, the heady fragrances of magnolia and jasmine and the dry sweetness of sun-warmed pine needles. . . .*

It is the voice that stops Thomas Jefferson in the dark hallway outside the kitchen. "Juh voo dray sal-ly see."

"*Non, non, non*," says Clotilde. "*Encore: Je voudrais celui-ci.*"

"Juh voo dray sil-ly see," says Sally Hemings.

When Thomas Jefferson hears that voice, he remembers Martha on the veranda at the Forest. She was still wearing black, Bathurst Skelton only nine months dead, but already she was nothing like a widow. "In three weeks exactly," Thomas Jefferson told her, "you must send me a letter consisting of one word, 'yes' or 'no,' and on that very day, I will send you a letter consisting of only one of those same words."

It was then that Martha laughed, and fifteen years later, in this dark hallway, Thomas Jefferson hears that laugh again.

"But what if we each write a different word?" Martha said.

"That's the beauty of it!" he replied. "When 'no' and 'yes' are read together, they spell 'noyes,' and noise is not an adequate answer, so we will have to try again until we get it right."

They were talking about whether, when he returned from Monticello, they would perform a duet—he on violin, she on piano, a prospect that terrified them both—but as she laughed, Thomas Jefferson understood that she had, in fact, agreed to marry him, although she would never have admitted this, not even to herself.

"Mr. Jefferson," she said, "I had not realized you could be so silly!" And she laughed again.

"Juh voo dray sil-ly see," says Sally Hemings.

"*Non*," says Clotilde. "*Je . . . je . . . Répète: je . . . je . . . Et: ce . . . ce . . . celui-ci.*"

"Zhuh . . . zhuh," says Sally Hemings. "Zhuh voo dray suh-ly see."

That voice on the soft air of an evening in June so many years ago. Martha was so happy when she laughed, and so was he. It was as if happiness were something they had discovered together, something no one else in all the history of humankind had ever experienced, their secret, their gift to each other.

And now that voice again. In the dark hallway. From the throat of a fourteen-year-old servant girl. That voice of silk and sand. Thomas Jefferson stops in midstep, and for a moment he cannot move, he cannot even breathe.

"Mieux," says Clotilde. *"Mieux, mais pas tout à fait correct, ma jolie petite sotte!"*

Sally Hemings laughs and laughs.

What is the truth of blue but midocean under a storm cloud? But that flash on a bird's back as it skims a field of sunlit grass? Blue is not a word, not 631 THz, nor 668 THz, not a chip or a pie slice. It is a funeral suit. It is sobriety. It is one's share of divinity as one stands on a shard of granite underneath an empty sky, a hundred mountains at one's feet. Swimming-pool blue. Policeman blue. The actual blue on the wall of one's childhood bedroom and the blue that one remembers. Ice blue. Moon blue. The truth of blue is inexhaustible, and Thomas Jefferson knows that his taxonomy will never be finished, not even if he devotes his every remaining minute of life to it. His taxonomy is a form of obeisance, a way of humbling himself before truth. Eye blue. M&M's blue. Blue under black light . . .

The Marquis de Lafayette has a face like a naughty fox and cannot keep still. Even when seated, he constantly flings his hands into the air, as if to give shape to his words, and his feet move so restlessly on the floor that he seems perpetually on the verge of leaping into a jig.

Sally Hemings has been in Paris only a month the first time he visits the Hôtel de Langeac. She stands against the wall while Thomas Jefferson introduces the marquis to Polly. After kissing Polly's hand and then Patsy's, the marquis announces that seeing the two girls side by side the image of their dear and beautiful mother has arisen so vividly within his imagination that it is as if she herself were in the room. Then he walks over to Sally Hemings and kisses her hand as well.

"What is your name?" he asks. When she tells him, he says, "I can see that you, too, have a beautiful mother, *but*"—he raises his index finger with a flourish—"I also think you have a beautiful gown!" He leans toward her, his brows lifted in impish delight, and looks her directly in the eye.

Merely fourteen, and unused to being spoken to so familiarly by a dinner guest, let alone by an aristocrat, Sally Hemings can only blush and giggle, and then, embarrassed by her embarrassment, she blushes even more deeply. But the marquis continues to smile and look into her eyes.

"Do you know why I think your gown is so beautiful?" he says.

When she shakes her head and blushes yet again, he tells her, "Because I wore one exactly like it, with a wig *et un grand chapeau*, when I first set sail to your country! I was forbidden to go, you see, and the soldiers of the king were looking for me everywhere. So as I walked down the hill to the quay"—he walks in a small circle, with one hand on his exaggeratedly swaying hips and the other near his face, wrist bent, fingers dangling—"every time I saw a soldier, I would say, *'Bonjour, Monsieur! Vous êtes très beau!'* I do not think I was a very beautiful woman, *pas comme vous, les trois jolies filles.* But soldiers are so vain, and they can never receive enough compliments—even from ladies who look like pigs in fancy dress! So every single soldier smiled and let me pass. And that is the story of how I had to become a woman so that I might be a general in your Continental Army!"

Everybody laughs at the marquis's pantomime—Thomas Jefferson included, although he ends by shaking his head and saying, "I don't think we should take our good friend entirely at his word."

After that evening, every time the Marquis de Lafayette sees Sally Hemings, he goes straight to her and says, "And how is my beautiful little *Sah-rah*?" And she always laughs and feels a trembly warmth inside her chest that robs her of the power of speech.

One afternoon Thomas Jefferson overhears Patsy tell Sally Hemings, "If you are to make a good impression in society, the first requirement is that your speech be flawless, in both English and French," and it is soon clear that the girl has taken this advice completely to heart. On more than one occasion, he has seen her at the kitchen table gazing with fierce intensity at her French tutor as he clarifies some nuance of the language, and she even asked if she might have three rather than two lessons a week. By October—barely two months after her arrival—she is able to hold rudimentary conversations with Clotilde and other French servants—and in this regard is far more advanced than Polly, even though all of Polly's classes at school are in French. And while Sally Hemings is never able to completely banish the kitchen from her consonants and vowels in English, she listens carefully to Patsy and Polly, with the result that her vocabulary expands rapidly, and she gains complete mastery of her verbs.

Another afternoon Thomas Jefferson hears Sally Hemings exclaiming out in the garden, "Oh, look! It's like an emerald! Even the bugs are beautiful in Paris! They're all made out of jewels!"

And then he hears her laughter amid the rolling pigeon coos and the wind seething in the plane trees.

A nd now the actor in the copper-colored wig is on horseback amid a crowd of Negroes in spotless rags, who are speaking all at once in a dialect that Thomas Jefferson finds almost impossible to comprehend—all of the language assaulting his ears in this dark room has sounded jagged and warped, but none has been as impenetrable as this. The one word he can understand is "Massa!"—and these people shout it incessantly, many of them smiling, their eyes avid, wide.

This would seem some sort of joyous celebration, but the voices of the people are so loud, their cries come so thick and fast and they press so close upon the actor in the copper-colored wig that his horse whinnies, snorts and lurches away. And then, in an instant, the illuminated wall is entirely filled by the face of a young Negro man, whose expression morphs from jovial good-spiritedness to stone-eyed fury.

In the next scene, this same young man—who can't be more than sixteen—is high in an apple tree with half a dozen other boys and one extremely pretty girl, whose skin is almost the same honey gold as her glinting, tightly curled hair. A cocked hat is visible, bobbing up and down as it drifts just over the top of a nearby hedge. The young man snatches an apple off a branch, and, his face now filled with devilry, he flings the apple and knocks the bobbing hat right off its owner's head—which immediately rises (along with the head of a rearing, whinnying horse) a good yard above the top of the hedge and inspires new cries of "Massa! Massa!"—for the man rising above the hedge is, of course, none other than the actor in the copper-colored wig.

There are images of boys leaping and bare feet striking the ground, then a cluster of backs disappearing over a grassy hillside. But the solitary girl has had the misfortune of catching the hem of her dress on a sharp branch of the apple tree. Her shocked face dropping between leafy branches yields to the bemused expression of the man in the copper-colored wig, who has rounded the hedge on his horse and is in the process of dismounting.

The girl is now hanging upside down, only her head, arms and shoulders visible beneath the lowest branches of the tree. "I'm sorry!" she shouts as her arms flail in the empty air. "I'm sorry! I didn't do it! I'm sorry!" The actor in the copper-colored wig's bemusement is clearly inflected by an appreciation of the girl's beauty, absurd as her position may be.

"Let me help you," he says, reaching over his head and seeming to fly into the tree. With one hand he supports the girl beneath her shoulders, while the other lifts her impaled hem off the sharp branch. The struggle to get her safely to the ground, with her feet down and her head up, involves something very like an embrace. The embarrassed girl continues to apologize, making liberal use of that word, "massa." But finally the actor in the copper-colored wig silences her with a handsome smile and asks her name.

"Sally," she says. "Sally Hemings!"

"Oh, no!" cries Thomas Jefferson.

Dolley is patting his arm. "It's all right, Tom," she says. "Everything turns out all right. You'll see."

The man seated behind them leans his head between theirs and says to Dolley, "Could you please keep this guy under control!"

Dolley gives Thomas Jefferson a wry smile and a final pat on the forearm, then resumes her expression of idiot's wonder.

During her first weeks at Hôtel de Langeac, Sally Hemings is afraid of Thomas Jefferson. He is always so quiet, and his quietness seems like anger to her—or, at the very least, like the claustrophobia-inducing stillness before a summer storm. But soon she comes to understand that he is quiet only because he is shy. She watches him in society and sees that he is always doing an imitation of himself. He wears a wide, fixed smile, but he never displays much of a sense of humor and is never relaxed, even though he often drinks prodigious quantities of wine. He is far happier when he is with just one other person. Often, when he is sitting with Mr. Short or with the Marquis de Lafayette in the upstairs parlor, she will hear their laughter spilling out into the corridor, sometimes until late at night. But he seems happiest of all when he is entirely alone in his study with his books and his writing and drawing (his desk is always covered with sketches of buildings and machines). When she brings him tea in his study, he often greets her with a light in his eye, as if he is keeping a secret he cannot wait to reveal. On these occasions his gestures are easy and unstudied. He seems entirely at home and to have no wish to ever be anyplace else.

But most of the time, Sally Hemings thinks Thomas Jefferson is sad.

During those days that Patsy and Polly are at their school, there are many occasions when she can observe him without his knowing she is present. Often when she is sitting in the parlor window, restitching Patsy's and Polly's fallen hems and split seams, she watches him passing from room to room like a ghost. Other times she will catch sight of him looking up from a book by the fire, and he seems so lost, as if he has entirely forgotten where he is. This is a man who owns so much, who can do almost anything and who knows more than anyone she has ever met, but there is something wrong in his life. Something is missing.

A year passes. Sally Hemings is fifteen, and now she never sees anything to be afraid of in Thomas Jefferson, only tenderness. His lips are almost womanly. His hands are huge, but his fingers are slender and their movements are so delicate that she can't imagine him ever doing harm. He is a wounded giant, she thinks. He is a paradox of tenderness and power.

1. Kitty Church, an American classmate of Polly's, always makes a point of including Sally Hemings in card games when she visits the Hôtel de Langeac and seems especially interested in her opinion of the boys who are a part of their social circle. Sally Hemings is almost absurdly grateful for such attention, even though she is often humiliated when she tries to keep up with the conversation. There are many things that she doesn't understand even in English: ironic remarks, certain jokes and especially references to literature, art and politics. There are times when she feels so profoundly stupid that she can't help wondering if she has only been invited to join the girls' games and conversations so that everyone might have someone to laugh at.

2. Marie de Botidoux, one of Patsy's best French friends, draws Sally Hemings into the corridor outside the upstairs parlor. "You must be honest with me, dear Sally," she says in French. "Is it true that there are slaves in Virginia?"

Sally Hemings, seeing no reason to deny the obvious, answers in the affirmative.

"I knew it!" Marie replies. "I have inquired of your mistress a thousand times on this point, and she would never tell me the truth."

Sally Hemings is suddenly possessed by cold dread.

"And now I need you to be completely honest with me on one other point," Marie says. "Is Monsieur Jimmy your brother?"

Sally Hemings hesitates, but again she answers in the affirmative.

"If that is true, then you must be a Negress."

Sally Hemings flushes. Her mouth falls open, but she doesn't speak.

"Of course you are! One can see it in your lips! You are a white Negress! Who has ever heard of such a thing! A white Negress! But if you are a Negress, then you must also be a slave, is that not true?"

Sally Hemings answers that she is as free as anyone else in France.

3. Renaud is sixteen, one year older than Sally Hemings. He has a dimple in the middle of his chin, a fog of rust-colored freckles

across his nose and cheeks, and he always seems to be thinking of something funny. She asks him why he wears his blue knitted cap tilted to the left, and he tells her it is to hide his donkey ear. Another time she spots a dead rat in the gutter, and he says, "Shhh! That's my brother Fernand. He's sleeping." Every Monday, Wednesday and Friday, shortly after nine in the morning, she hears the jingly clink of his milk barrow coming down rue Neuve-de-Berri and is always ready in the doorway with a pewter flagon when he reaches the Hôtel de Langeac, and he always greets her with a merry, "Good morning, Mademoiselle Salée!" ("Miss Salty")

Renaud's lips are raspberry red and are often chapped. One Wednesday, Sally Hemings finds herself wondering what it would be like to kiss those cracked and flaky lips, and she is unable to stop looking at them the entire time he is ladling milk out of the ceramic pot in his barrow. It is the same when he comes again on Friday, but this time as she watches his lips pucker and stretch to form words or press together crookedly while he tilts the ladle over her flagon, a warm urgency radiates from deep within her belly all the way into her throat, and she wishes he would pull her toward him and press his lips against hers. She has never felt like this about a boy before, and she cannot tell if it is a very good or a very bad thing.

When he comes again on Monday, the warm urgency is so powerful that she can hardly put one word coherently after the other. When she inadvertently speaks in English, she breaks off in the middle of her sentence and, after a moment of silence, says in French, "I'm looking for my French, but I've lost it."

He laughs as if she's made a joke. "I saw it a few minutes ago running down the rue de Faubourg Saint-Honoré. If it's still there when I am done with your neighbors, I'll grab it by the ear and bring it back to you."

Renaud smiles at her merrily, picks up the handles to his barrow and sets off down the muddy street, his ladle jingling against the side of the crock.

The next time he comes, she notices a limp white tulip lying in the barrow, just in front of the crock. He picks it up and holds it out to her. When it flops over the edge of his hand, he grips the the base of the stem in one hand and then makes a whistley zip as he slides the thumb and index finger of his other hand from the base all the way to the flower. Then he holds the flower erect as he hands it to her. "I couldn't find your French," he says, "so I thought I'd bring you this."

Sally Hemings is smiling so hard as she accepts the flower that she worries she might burst into tears. A long moment passes before she can thank him. "It's so beautiful!" she says.

"It used to be more beautiful. But I think it's a little thirsty."

Then they are both silent. Renaud is smiling, but for the first time ever he seems to be uneasy. Sally Hemings wonders if she shouldn't thank him with a kiss. Perhaps that is what he expects. In her mind's eye, she sees herself getting up on the tips of her toes and pressing her lips against his. That hot urgency has become so powerful it is like a magnetic force drawing her toward him. But she doesn't budge. She is too afraid.

"I almost forgot!" he says. "I have cheese!" He pulls a board draped with cloth from behind the crock. "My grandfather made it." He pulls off the cloth with the finesse of a magician. "A Camembert!" The white wheel is about a foot wide. A third of it has already been cut away, and the yellow cheese is oozing onto the greasy wood. "You have never tasted a better cheese."

"It looks delicious," she says, though she doesn't actually like French cheese.

"How much do you want?"

"Let me go ask my brother."

"Your brother?" Renaud looks perplexed.

"He is the chef."

"No!" Renaud laughs derisively. "The chef is not your brother!"

"He is," she insists—but then she realizes what is happening. "Monsieur Hemings?"

"Yes," she says weakly.

"How can that be? He is black!"

She gives her shoulders a helpless shrug. "He is my brother."

"Then you are black, too."

She doesn't answer.

He laughs incredulously. "Are you a cannibal?"

"No!" She does not understand how Renaud could say such a thing. "Of course not!"

"I thought all blacks were cannibals! I thought there was nothing you liked more than a plump little baby for breakfast!" He seems to think his joke is very funny. "From now on I will have to call you Miss Pepper!"

She asks for the milk.

The next time he comes, she puts her flagon on the doorstep with a single sol even before she hears the jingling clink from the end of the street. And when the sound has receded in the opposite direction, she opens the door and picks up the full flagon. The money is gone.

Time passes. Sally Hemings is fifteen. She is sixteen. The food prepared by Jimmy agrees with her. She grows three and a half inches and becomes almost as tall as Patsy, at whose height everyone exclaims. Her once node-knuckled fingers grow pleasantly plump, the hollows around her eyes fill in and there is a pinkish light in her cheeks that Thomas Jefferson associates with mornings in early spring, just after the leaves have come in.

He often thinks of his wife when he looks at her. Her eyes are exactly the zinc gray of Martha's, and her hair is the same coffee brown. She is much taller than Martha, however; her cheekbones are higher, and her jaw is more delicate and tapered. But it is less the way she appears that reminds him of his wife than how she sounds and moves. Most striking is the way, when she is between activities or when she thinks no one is looking, her expression will go inert, as if she has just received terrible news. When he was first courting Martha, this expression would make him worry that he had somehow offended her, but in the next instant she would smile or even laugh. And it is exactly the same with Sally Hemings. She has what people call "laughing eyes." When she smiles, they narrow with delight and seem themselves to be smiling. And her laugh, like Martha's, starts with a hoot, then tumbles into a low, merry gurgle. Every time Thomas Jefferson hears it, he cannot help but smile himself. Sometimes he, too, laughs.

Thomas Jefferson is returning to his study from the kitchen, his cheek bulging with a ripped-off piece of bread that he is rather awkwardly trying to make swallowable without having to remove it from his mouth. On Saturdays, Jimmy always has a lavish dinner waiting for Patsy and Polly when they get home from school—but it is two o'clock; they are almost an hour late, and Thomas Jefferson simply has to put something into his stomach.

Just as his hand touches the latch on his study door, he hears the screech of the huge front door opening and Patsy speaking loudly. He can't make out her first words, but then he hears, "Perhaps the mothers were being punished for some evil they had done."

"But the babies!" says another voice. It is Sally Hemings. "The babies were punished, too. Why couldn't he punish the mothers in some other way?"

"Perhaps they were evil."

"But they were babies! Babies can't be evil."

"No, I mean that they were fated to do evil and God let them die with their mothers so that that evil would not come into the world."

"If he knew that the babies would do evil, then why did he allow their mothers to give birth to them? What is the point of bringing them into the world only to kill them?"

"Oh, Sally!" Patsy cries. "Stop being so thick! If you'd given it two seconds of thought, you'd know that the world is far too complicated for us to comprehend. Only God understands the millions of things that must happen so that this world can be just and the virtuous get their due reward."

By this point the three girls have passed through the foyer into the dining room, where Thomas Jefferson is also standing. Patsy and Sally Hemings seem so engrossed in their discussion that they haven't noticed him, but Polly cries out, "Papa! We're home!"

"So you are!" he says. "And you're late! I've been wasting away with hunger!"

He walks around the big table at the center of the circular room and receives kisses from both of his daughters. Sally Hemings stands by the door with the pinched brow and turned-down lips of someone who wants to speak but has decided to remain silent. She is carrying both of the girls' satchels.

"But you were in the midst of quite a debate," says Thomas Jefferson. "Don't let me interrupt!"

"Oh, it's over!" says Patsy.

"Is it really?"

"Sally was just committing the Manichean heresy, but now there's nothing more to talk about."

Sally Hemings has backed toward the door and will clearly be bringing the girls' satchels up to their bedchambers in two seconds.

"Is that true, Sally?"

She looks down at the floor and doesn't speak.

"Have you committed the Manichean heresy?" says Thomas Jefferson.

She looks up, blushes and looks down again. In an almost inaudible voice she says, "I don't know, sir."

"She was just telling us this awful story she heard in the *marché*," says Patsy.

Thomas Jefferson turns toward Sally Hemings. "What is it?"

Patsy speaks. "Two mothers and their babies were found dead—"

"Let her tell it," says Thomas Jefferson.

"Oh . . ." Sally Hemings seems about to excuse herself, but then she says, "That's it, mostly. Except they were in a *canot*. Madame Aubier, who sells onions—she has a brother who is a sailor. And he was making the voyage back from Montreal when he spotted a *canot* floating in the empty sea. It was filled with people—the survivors of a ship that had gone down, he thought. Except when his ship drew up alongside the *canot*, he saw that all the people in it were dead. Frozen to death. It was winter. And there were two mothers in the boat who had frozen solid with their arms around their babies and small children. That's what we were talking about." She glances at Patsy.

"And what did you make of that?" Thomas Jefferson asks Sally Hemings.

She glances again at Patsy, who just shrugs. "Well, the main thing is that I didn't see how a good God could allow all those people to die—especially those babies, who couldn't have done a thing wrong in their lives.

So I was just saying that either God isn't all good or he isn't all-powerful. I didn't see how he could be both and let something like that happen."

"And I was saying that the mind of God is vast," says Patsy, "and that it is foolish to pretend that our own weak minds can ever fathom his rationale, his motives or even the true consequences of his acts."

"And what do you think, Polly?" says Thomas Jefferson.

"I wasn't listening." Polly casts the other two girls a worried glance.

"But what do you think?"

"I don't know. . . . God moves in a mysterious way, I suppose."

Thomas Jefferson smiles ruefully and shakes his head. "This is what I get for letting you two be educated by nuns." He points at Sally Hemings. "This girl has not been to school one day in her life, and yet she can see the essence of the problem more clearly than either of you. What you have both said is exactly what popes and monarchs would have us think about them and their actions. There will be no justice on this earth unless we can look plainly at the facts before our eyes and draw the most rational conclusions. Our abilities to observe and evaluate are the surest manifestation of God's grace. Everything else is occult superstition and plays into the hands of tyrants."

The two sisters look down at the floor in shame, but Sally Hemings can feel their irritation—Patsy's especially—radiating in her direction.

"You have a good head on your shoulders, Sally," says Thomas Jefferson.

"Thank you, sir." She glances at Patsy, who pays her no mind. Then she lifts the two satchels she has been holding. "But if I may be excused . . ."

Thomas Jefferson nods, and Sally Hemings, allowing herself a small smile, backs out of the room.

Thomas Jefferson believes that he should love the world—an ambition continuously obstructed by the fact that one cannot have the good without also having the evil. Thomas Jefferson wants purity, but there is no purity, not in this world and least of all in his own heart. There is beauty, however, and mathematics—which are one and the same sometimes, as in the golden rectangle, which when manifested in architecture can make walls and whole rooms seem weightless and floating. But this impression is only a production of the mind, which is to say: an illusion. In fact, all physical manifestations of the golden rectangle are as solidly earthbound as any other existing thing. Thomas Jefferson knows that all purity is illusory, and yet he still wants his love of the world to be pure, which is to say: illusion-free.

. . . *I have tried to sleep, but it is useless. My mind whirled with infernal thoughts, and my limbs were possessed by such writhes and twitches that I could not keep them still for half a second. I have no idea what the hour is. Sometime after eleven, I imagine. The clouds have parted to reveal a low, ice-white moon that has infused the snowy lawn with pallid brilliance. A mouse is gnawing at something inside the wall.*

I finally surrendered all hope of sleep when a voice spoke inside my head, telling me that I had committed nothing but self-exculpatory lies on these pages and that the whole truth of my last forty years could be conveyed in four words: I BETRAYED GOOD PEOPLE.

Just this instant a moonbeam so brilliant it cancels out the wavery orange of the candle has crossed the paper-littered corner of the desk and struck the foot of a chair beside the door.

Would I be justified in taking this as a sign?

But of what?

In any event, what finally got me out of bed was the thought that what I must do here is disentangle the strands of ignorance, inattention, self-deception, fear and desire out of which my life is woven so that I might see clearly and finally how truly damnable I am—and once I have laid that truth bare, these pages will be meaningless and I had best throw them onto the fire and go on to whatever life remains to me. . . .

I tremble for my country when I reflect that God is just, that his justice cannot sleep forever. Commerce between master and slave is despotism. Nothing is more certainly written in the book of fate than that these people are to be free.

—Thomas Jefferson
(as quoted on the wall of the Jefferson
Memorial in Washington, D.C.)

Thomas Jefferson spends his days arguing with men over pieces of paper or flattering them over plates of meat and glasses of wine. He argues interest rates with Dutch bankers, proposes trade agreements to the Spanish. He tries to convince the French not to pay ransom to the Barbary pirates. Some days are consumed entirely in journeys from *palais* to embassy to *hôtel*. On others he sits in his study dashing off letters as fast as he can think, then summons Petit and commands him to deliver the letters within the hour, only to have another packet of urgent missives waiting when Petit returns.

But all of this stops in the evening, when it is Thomas Jefferson's habit to sit in front of the fire in the upstairs parlor, sipping from a bottle of wine and reading Latin or Greek. One such evening he has Vergil's *Eclogues* open in his lap when Sally Hemings enters the room.

"Excuse me, Mr. Jefferson," she says, and when he neither looks her way nor answers, she speaks again. "I'm sorry to disturb you, Mr. Jefferson."

It is a long moment before he turns toward her, spectacles halfway down his nose. He seems not to have any idea who she is.

"I'm sorry," she says.

"Not at all!" Thomas Jefferson is smiling now. "I'm the one who should be sorry. I was so—" He holds up his book, shrugs. "I didn't even know you were there."

She explains that she has come to fetch a miniature porcelain shepherdess that Polly left on an end table and will surely want in her room tomorrow when she comes home from the Abbaye de Penthemont. As Sally Hemings walks past Thomas Jefferson to the table where the shepherdess is standing, she asks, "What is it that you are reading?"

He lifts his book and reads, *"Pastorem, Tityre, pinguis pascere oportet ovis, deductum dicere carmen.'"*

When he looks at her again, she is smiling uneasily.

That's Latin," he tells her. "Vergil."

She laughs. *"Je soupçonnais que ce n'était pas du français!"*

He also laughs and lowers the book into his lap. "Actually, what I read happens to be about a shepherd. A god tells him that his sheep should be fat but his poems should be lean."

Sally Hemings picks up the shepherdess figurine and rolls it thoughtfully between her thumb and fingers. Her lips are pursed, and one eyebrow is lifted in exactly the expression Patsy wears when she is troubled.

"Is something the matter?" asks Thomas Jefferson.

"Oh . . ." She looks as if she is going to make her excuses and leave, but then she says, "I was just thinking how wonderful it must be to read."

"Well, it is," he says. Then he is silent, because he can see that she is sad. "You should get Jimmy to teach you. He's an excellent reader. I taught him myself."

She crumples up one corner of her mouth. "I asked him to, but he says I have no head for learning."

"Nonsense! You're a bright girl! It's easy."

He splays his open book over the arm of his chair and turns to the table where there is a heap of correspondence that he browsed through earlier in the evening. Taking a sip from his wine, he points to the figurine. "Put that down and come over here." He examines the letter on top of the pile, then flips it over and opens the brass lid of a star-shaped inkwell. As Sally Hemings comes up beside him, he dips his quill and writes her first name in big letters.

She laughs. "That's the one word I can read!"

"Good," he says. "That's a good start."

He dips his quill again, and to the left of her name he writes, "I am."

"Do you know what those words are?"

She doesn't, so he asks if she knows what the first letter is. When she shakes her head, he tells her what the letter is called and explains the sounds it could signify, with the one in this case being the letter's own name. Then he tells her what the names and sounds of the next two letters are and asks her to figure out what word they spell.

She drawls the sounds out as she says them over and over: "Aaaahhhh-emmmm, aaaa-emmmm."

"You sound like a sheep!" he tells her. "Also, you're trying too hard. Look at the other two words and see if that helps you."

No sooner has he made this suggestion than she laughs out loud and reads the sentence.

"Brava!" cries Thomas Jefferson. "You're already reading!"

She claps her hands beneath her chin and laughs again.

"Now let's teach you to write!" Thomas Jefferson dips his quill once again and hands it to her, telling her to copy each letter.

She squeezes the quill between her thumb and the tips of her four fingers and holds it over the page as if she is trying to balance it on its point. She knows that what she is doing is wrong, but she doesn't know how to correct it. While she is holding the quill in midair, a droplet of ink falls to the page and lies there like a black bead.

"No, no, no!" Thomas Jefferson laughs and takes the quill out of her hands. "Here." He dips the quill again and puts it between her thumb and forefinger, then positions her other fingers with his own.

Her fingers are rough, but warm and very moist. Her face is just beside his, her gray eyes glinting avidly. She is smiling. Her breath is meaty and lush, and he can feel the warmth of her shoulder and arm, which are touching his own.

He lets go of her hand, and as she makes a rough approximation of the sentence he has written, he realizes—fully realizes for the first time—that she has become a beautiful young woman.

When she is finished, he gives her the piece of paper and says, "Show that to Jimmy. Tell him I command him to teach you to read and write!"

Sally Hemings clutches the page on both sides and reads it aloud over and over as she walks out of the room, leaving the porcelain shepherdess lying horizontally on the table where it was previously standing.

Later that night Thomas Jefferson decides that his vital fluids have gotten out of balance again. But the following day he discovers that his attempt at self-regulation has had no effect. It is the same the next day and the one after. After a week he discontinues the practice, lest he endanger his sanity.

Sally Hemings is a slave girl, he tells himself, three months younger than Patsy and partly African. How could he possibly have any sort of feeling for her? Absurd! Preposterous! He need only wait, and all will be well.

A landscape of wooded hills, green and yellow fields and scattered brick houses accelerates from the horizon, seeming to stretch as it approaches, and then shoots in a blur beneath the steel balcony of Sally Hemings's invention. The sky is roaring. The studded balcony bucks on irregularities in the wind. It shudders and heaves, and Thomas Jefferson has to clutch the brass railing to keep from whirling into oblivion.

"Isn't this wonderful!" says Sally Hemings, who is leaning out over the railing—so far out that she seems to be lying on empty air. "Come," she says, her white shift snap-flapping ceaselessly along the length of her body. "It's easy!" She reaches back toward him with her open hand. "Really! You'll love it! It's exactly like flying!"

"No," Thomas Jefferson wants to shout. "It's dangerous!" he wants to tell her. "Come back! Come back! You'll fall." But every time he opens his mouth, the wind crams his words back down his throat. Again and again he tries to speak, and every time his lips mouth silence.

First Sally Hemings is puzzled. Then she is hurt. Now disappointment is slowly suffusing her face. In a moment she will look away. Thomas Jefferson knows this. She will turn her face into the wind. She will forget him. It will be as if he'd never lived.

In the days that follow their writing lesson, Thomas Jefferson notices that Sally Hemings is watching him. He walks into a room, and she instantly looks up from her sewing or dusting—sometimes it would seem expectantly, though almost always she immediately looks away, as if embarrassed or ashamed. It is perfectly ordinary, he tells himself, for one person to look up when another enters the room and mere vanity to imagine anything else afoot, especially as he is a man on the verge of old age and she but a girl of sixteen. Why would she even give him a second glance? The problem is that she does give him second glances. And third glances. If, by any chance, he and she should be in the same room for any length of time, it is perfectly common for him to look up from whatever he might be doing four, five or six times—and, on each occasion, notice her eyes darting away.

Perhaps it is my fault, he thinks. *Perhaps she has noticed that I am always staring at her, and she only looks up involuntarily to see if my gaze—no doubt unwanted—is once again turned in her direction.* On most occasions this explanation seems entirely sensible—but then there are times when their glances meet and she will hesitate a half second before looking away, or when he will think he sees a faltering smile on her lips. And on such occasions the effect upon him can be so powerful that he will have to leave the room.

Thomas Jefferson tells Patsy that he has decided she and Polly should have a maid with them at Penthemont. Other girls have servants lodging with them, but heretofore Patsy said she didn't want to have one herself, because she is an American, and a democrat, and so it is better that she learn to manage on her own. While Thomas Jefferson finds this sentiment wholly commendable (indeed, Patsy is only repeating what he has said to her himself), he tells her that he is worried she is not spending enough time on her Greek and Latin and believes that she would do better work if Sally Hemings were there to attend to her domestic needs.

"What do you think, then?" he asks.

"*C'est comme vous voudrez, cher Papa,*" she answers. "My duty is to accede."

"Excellent! I will inform the abbess of our decision this week, and Sally will return to the school with you next Sunday."

But Sally Hemings does not return to the school with Patsy and Polly the following Sunday, nor the one after. And on both occasions, when Patsy asks her father why, he tells her that he has been too busy to write to the abbess but that he will do so immediately. He never does do so, however, and Patsy finally concludes that either he has changed his mind or he has simply forgotten.

Thomas Jefferson contemplates the rock that is his self. There are days when it seems massive: not a planet but possibly a lesser moon or a comet. What most troubles him about his self is a quality that might be referred to as its weight, or its rigidity, or its implacable constancy. There are times when Thomas Jefferson feels there is no greater limit on his freedom than his self.

Here is a definition of life, or of the world, or of this medium in which being elaborates: *an infinity of possibilities*—and it is Thomas Jefferson's self that prevents him from fully inhabiting this medium.

Oh, the noble sentiments he wishes he were capable of feeling! Oh, the moments of golden contentment that he has turned into debaucheries of self-loathing! Oh, the cherubic unities of actuality and belief that his self has suffocated in the crib with a pillow!

The Princess Lubomirsky will be throwing a ball on New Year's Eve, and Patsy and Polly insist that they must have new gowns. Thomas Jefferson agrees—especially as Patsy has reached that age when, as he puts it, "impressions are of the highest consideration." He also says that if Sally Hemings is going to attend them at so lavish an event, she, too, needs to make a suitable impression.

The dressmaker, Madame Palatin, has a nose like a hawk's beak, a figure like a pigeon and she hoots like an owl as she measures Patsy and Polly, telling Thomas Jefferson she has never seen two such pretty girls. *"Comme des princesses!"* she adds. *"Vraiment!"* Her voice descends to one of the lower mammalian registers, however, when it is time to measure Sally Hemings. *"Dépêche-toi!"* she grunts, and although Sally Hemings leaps from her chair by the door, the old woman grunts again, *"Dépêche-toi!"*

As she jabs her thumb into Sally Hemings's armpit and runs her measuring strip down the girl's ribs to her waist, she complains to Thomas Jefferson about the character of modern serving girls. *"Elles sont toutes si paresseuses,"* she says with a sigh.

Then she is grunting again. *"Tourne-toi! Vite!"* She grabs Sally Hemings by the elbow and yanks her around. *"Tourne-toi donc! Tu as les oreilles bouchées, ou quoi?"*

When Thomas Jefferson suggests that it is not necessary to be so rough, Madame Palatin tells him that he is spoiling the girl and that there is only one thing servant girls understand. Then she flicks her cupped hand in the air, just missing the back of Sally Hemings's head.

A month later Thomas Jefferson, his daughters and Sally Hemings are back in Madame Palatin's studio. Polly, who is now eleven, is the first to try on her gown, and when she comes out of the dressing room and takes a turn in front of the mirrors, Madame Palatin exclaims that she has never seen a more beautiful child. Polly's gown is very plain—blue silk, with a high, square neck and a lace vest—but her father and sister applaud as she grins and rocks from foot to foot. From her seat by the door, Sally Hemings also applauds.

Patsy's gown is truly spectacular: rose pink silk with rose red trim, an embroidered band around the base of the petticoat and a lace bodice cut to reveal the uppermost swellings of her bosom. She swirls in front of the mirror, the skirt of her gown swaying in a waltzlike rhythm, even after she has stopped and is stepping toward her grinning, applauding family. She curtsies with a shy smile that reminds Thomas Jefferson of her mother on the night that, for the one and only time, she and he performed a duet in front of an audience. But Martha's shyness that night was partly due to the fact that she knew she had not played her best. She hated public events of any kind, in fact. Patsy has no such anxiety. A good thing, Thomas Jefferson thinks. He cannot help but connect Martha's almost constant fearfulness with her early death.

Madame Palatin seems to feel that there is no need for Sally Hemings to try on her gown, but Thomas Jefferson insists she have her turn.

"Oh, no!" the girl cries from her chair by the door. Her face is bright red, and she can't lift her eyes from her lap. "Really! There's no need."

"On the contrary," says Thomas Jefferson. "If we find at home that something is wrong with it, then we will have to come all the way back, and that would be a waste of valuable time."

Madame Palatin holds the gown out by its shoulder so that its dangling skirt just clears the floor. It will fit like a second skin, she declares, but if the gentleman insists, *"C'est comme vous voudrez."*

The gown is less intricately ornamented than Polly's and in yellow silk with a slightly higher neckline and a full, lace-frilled underskirt. Sally Hemings emerges in small steps from the dressing room, her gaze lowered to the floor, her forehead and cheeks crimson and, Thomas Jefferson can just make out, her lips crumpled and white in an attempt to suppress a grin.

"Come, Sally, take a turn," he says. "Let us see what it looks like from all sides."

"No," she says. But then she does do a quick and graceful swirl. She is so embarrassed afterward that she bends over double and nearly backs into the mirror.

"Beautiful!" he says. "You've grown into a very fine young woman, Sally."

The words aren't even out of his mouth before he can feel Madame Palatin's disapproval chilling one corner of the room. He doesn't care about her. In fact, he is glad if he has offended her. But then he glances at the chair beside him and sees Patsy looking up, her expression an amalgam of disbelief, mockery and alarm.

They are more ardent after their female: but love seems with them to be more an eager desire, than a tender delicate mixture of sentiment and sensation. Their griefs are transient. Those numberless afflictions, which render it doubtful whether heaven has given life to us in mercy or in wrath, are less felt, and sooner forgotten with them. . . . Comparing them by their faculties of memory, reason, and imagination, it appears to me, that in memory they are equal to the whites; in reason much inferior, as I think one could scarcely be found capable of tracing and comprehending the investigations of Euclid; and that in imagination they are dull, tasteless, and anomalous. . . . Among the Romans emancipation required but one effort. The slave, when made free, might mix with, without staining the blood of his master. But with us a second is necessary, unknown to history. When freed, he is to be removed beyond the reach of mixture.

—Thomas Jefferson
Notes on the State of Virginia
Written in 1781–82, published in 1787

It is April of 1789, Thomas Jefferson is forty-six, and his mind is as busy with discontinuous thoughts as the sky is busy with birds. He knows that his constant distraction is wrong, and many times a day he wills his mind to be more disciplined. And yet it is also true that cerebration has never felt so fruitful as it has during this one year in particular. And he has, perhaps, never felt so intensely alive as at this very moment, when, strolling the shore of the lake at the Bois de Boulogne, he is in conversation with his great friend, Marie-Joseph Paul Yves Roch Gilbert du Motier, Marquis de Lafayette. They are preparing for the first meeting of the Estates-General, Louis XVI's response to Lafayette's call for a national assembly, and are in a delirium composed in equal parts of rhetoric, philosophy, egotism and hope.

"Government," Thomas Jefferson is saying, "should exist only as a mechanical apparatus with no power of its own, inert except when it is executing the public will. Its highest purpose should be to preserve the absolute freedom of its citizens."

"Absolute?" says Lafayette, one jet eyebrow uptilted, lips in that nearly straight smile signifying his delight at having detected an error in reasoning. "*Absolute* freedom? For *all* citizens?"

"*Absolute*," Thomas Jefferson affirms, "except insofar as the exercise of that freedom would injure other people or deprive them of their own freedom."

"Aha!" Lafayette points his index finger toward the clouds. "Deprive other people of their freedom!" The delight in Lafayette's smile has multiplied considerably. "That brings to mind an old bone I have to pick with you."

Thomas Jefferson hopes that his own smile also expresses delight, for as much as he enjoys debate, there are many times when he feels ashamed before Lafayette, who, as a mere lad of twenty, was a general in the Continental Army and took a musket ball in the thigh in defense of Thomas Jefferson's dearest beliefs, and who, once Thomas Jefferson had fled Richmond ahead of the British, retook the city, and then, after Cornwallis attempted to capture Jefferson at Monticello, did battle with the British on the banks of Jefferson's own Rivanna River, and then continued to battle the British at Green Spring and Jamestown and Richmond—during which time Thomas Jefferson, hiding out in a cottage on his most remote plantation, Poplar Forest, was drafting his one and only book, *Notes on the State of Virginia.*

"... I will make it good. ... Good ..."

The fire shimmers copper and orange along the planes of Thomas Jefferson's forehead and cheeks and gleams gold on the tiny droplets adhering to the stubble on his upper lip. A freestanding candelabra behind his chair lights the pages of his book, and there is an empty wine bottle on the table beside him. His elbows rest on the arms of his chair, while he cups a full glass with both hands in front of his belly. A solitary creak sounds in the hallway just outside the parlor door.

"Sally?" calls Thomas Jefferson. After a short wait, he calls again. "Sally."

Sally Hemings appears in the dark doorway, her face a wavering orange in the firelight—except for her right cheek, which is lit a steady sand yellow by the candle she is holding.

"I was wondering if that was you," says Thomas Jefferson.

Sally Hemings doesn't speak. Her lips purse in something that might be a smile.

"Is everything all right?" he asks.

"I've just finished for the day." She lifts her candle as if it is evidence.

"Good," says Thomas Jefferson. "Good." He sips from his glass. "It's cold tonight, don't you think?"

The expression that might be a smile becomes something more like a grimace.

"For April, I mean," says Thomas Jefferson.

"There's a draft downstairs," says Sally Hemings.

"It's very warm here by the fire, if you'd like . . ." He gestures to the empty chair opposite his own.

Now the expression is very definitely a smile, but an uneasy one. "Thank you, Mr. Jefferson . . . but . . ." She shrugs and lifts her candle a second time.

"Certainly," says Thomas Jefferson.

"Good night." The uneasiness has vanished, and her smile is only happy—and radiant with her generous spirit. Sally Hemings doesn't always look beautiful, but right now she seems a vision to Thomas Jefferson.

"Good night, Sally."

"Good night," she says.

And then he is alone.

In Thomas Jefferson's mind, there is only one thought, and when Sally Hemings is kneeling before the fireplace, stirring the embers; when she stops by the window in the hallway and sweeps a strand of hair off her forehead as she looks out into the morning light; when he sees her down on the street talking to the knife sharpener, *"Pardonnez-moi, monsieur"*—at such moments his one thought grows until it is like a mob storming the capital of a failed nation. Thomas Jefferson knows that he has rights, but he also knows that not all rights are equal. *Yes*, he thinks as paving stones fragment the window glass of the capital. *You can do as you please. There is no reason not to.*

. . . When I first arrived in France, I was indeed everything that is meant by "innocent." I was lonely and afraid. I understood nothing of what was around me and had no taste for any of it. I kept to myself and longed for the day when I might return to Virginia and my family, whom I missed terribly. Even as I began to enjoy the world in which I was now living, my delights were entirely childlike. It seemed a simple wonder to me that Paris should contain so many beautiful and beautifully dressed people and that I could not only move among them but actually talk to them, that their language should turn out to be not the assemblage of grunts, groans, belches and throat-clearings that it had seemed to me at first but a wonderfully textured mechanism for expressing oneself, understanding others and making sense of and savoring the world. Even before I could put more than ten words of French in a comprehensible row, I had already adopted the Gallic sense of humor and would puff out my lip and blow in that classic expression of French mocking surprise, or I would utter that singsong "Oo-la!" which has almost the same meaning, and I became particularly attracted to the phrase "C'est la vie," perhaps because I took the same comfort as the Parisians in the notion that the most extraordinary actions and events were, in fact, entirely commonplace and therefore incapable of disrupting one's daily existence. During those months and years when every new increment of my burgeoning Frenchness was a sheer delight to me, I was, in so many ways, exactly like a child who has wandered into a primeval wilderness and who can do nothing but exclaim at the brilliant flowers, the massive trees, the strange and beautiful birdsongs, having no inkling of the crocodiles lurking under the lily pads, the snakes coiling in the branches, the panthers stalking at her heels, the vultures circling above the treetops.

And yet I have come to fear that I may never have been entirely as innocent as I would like to believe. While I was certainly deeply flattered and even touched by what I viewed as Mr. Jefferson's kindly and paternal interest in me, I was also always keenly aware of his physical presence—as evidenced by my otherwise unaccountable blushes and quickenings of the pulse when he might walk into the room or when I felt his attention upon me. My mother had, of course, warned me about the possible consequences of the attention any white man might pay to me, but I simply could not imagine that Mr. Jefferson could harbor such crude desires. No doubt my naïveté was partly the natural result of my ever-growing awareness (from the things I overheard, from the deference with which he was treated by visitors to the Hôtel) that he was a famous and very important man, but the fact remains that I was not merely thrilled by his glances and smiles, I actually longed for them.

At the very least, I fear that these involuntary responses were misinterpreted by Mr. Jefferson and encouraged inclinations that perhaps he might not otherwise have indulged. But I also fear that they made me susceptible within my own being to those particular attentions that ultimately brought me to what I can now only think of as my damnation. And it is this possibility, perhaps above all others, that makes me writhe with shame. . . .

Thomas Jefferson is forty-six and Sally Hemings is sixteen. They are in Paris, and it is late April 1789. Patsy and Polly are at school, and Jimmy is in Le Havre, picking up a shipment of books, surveying equipment and seeds that have been sent from Virginia. Thomas Jefferson finds Sally Hemings in the scullery cleaning the breakfast dishes.

"*Mademoiselle Sally,*" he says, "*j'ai une petite surprise pour toi.*"

"*Oui?*" She puts the dish has just finished into a rack and picks up another. "*Est-ce que Patsy et Polly—*"

Thomas Jefferson cuts her off. "*Non, non, ce n'est pas ça!*"

"*Qu'est-ce que c'est, alors?*"

"*Un miracle!*"

"*Ah, non!*" Sally Hemings crinkles the bridge of her nose. The last "miracle" Thomas Jefferson presented to her was a lump of cheese that looked and smelled exactly like clotted matter scraped out from under a toenail.

Thomas Jefferson laughs. "*Non, non!* Nothing like that!" He laughs again, remembering how, during the instant she held that morsel of cheese in her mouth, he could see the white all the way around her gray-blue irises and how, in the next instant, she spat the cheese onto Madame d'Arnault's Persian rug and ran straight out onto the street. "*Je te le promets,*" he says. "This will be like nothing you have ever experienced. A real miracle— you'll see!" Thomas Jefferson observes suspicion doing battle with curiosity on Sally Hemings's forehead and lips. "Come along," he says. "*Allons-y!*" And then he tells her, "Perhaps you should put on that yellow gown. And your embroidered cape. You will want to look your best."

After an interval of muddy streets and a brisk trot along a country road, during which Sally Hemings sits beside the driver, she finds herself in a mown field, at the center of which a crowd surrounds a bonfire. Something like a gigantic purse—blue, yellow and red silk, frilled on the seams—is stretched out on the grass.

At first she cannot imagine why Thomas Jefferson asked her to wear her finest clothes to this rural ceremony (or whatever it might be), but then she notices that the crowd contains a substantial representation of Parisian high society. Although Thomas Jefferson steers her well away from them, she sees the Princess Lubomirsky, and Monsieur and Madame de Corny, and Baron Clemenceau, with his crooked mustache. What on earth could draw such men and women to some peasant's hacked pasture? And why is it that they are all chattering with such excitement and staring at the activities of the men around the bonfire?

The mouth of the purse stretched out on the grass is propped open by a six-foot-high wicker ring that two men hold on edge, while four others blow smoke into it by waving sailcloth fans. There seem to be other men inside the purse, because a sort of dome—mounted on poles, perhaps—keeps rising and falling within its far end. As the men blowing the smoke grow tired, they are replaced by others, while still more men keep heaping wood on the fire. The dome, rising and falling inside the purse, grows larger and looms higher with every new waft of smoke.

"Now look!" says Thomas Jefferson, leaning so close that his lips practically touch her ear. "It is about to happen. You will see. A true miracle!"

But Sally Hemings cannot pay attention. She is trying to figure out if Thomas Jefferson's lips might, in fact, have touched her ear. And she is still feeling the low burr of his voice inside her head. She looks around to see if anyone is staring at her, but all eyes are on the enormous purse.

"It is happening!" Thomas Jefferson says, standing tall again, entirely removed from the vicinity of her ear. "Watch! A man is going to fly!"

Sally Hemings does not believe him, of course. A man flying? Impossible!

But then, with a sound like the earth itself heaving a sigh, the giant purse lifts off the flattened grass, and guided by shouting men pulling ropes and pushing with poles, it swings, bottom up, directly over the fire, some ten yards above the flame tips, where it is held in place by four strong ropes tied to four stout stakes. Sally Hemings waits for the men inside the purse to tumble into the fire, and when they never appear, she imagines them hovering within the purse's shadowy interior, just as the purse is hovering in the air.

There is a platform beside the fire and, on top of the platform, a wicker canoe connected by slender lines to the inverted purse. A young man, also wearing blue, yellow and red silk, climbs a ladder and steps gingerly into the canoe. His curly chestnut brown hair falls well past his shoulders.

Thomas Jefferson touches his forehead to Sally Hemings's temple. His breaths puff against her ear, and his voice is low. "That is le Comte de Toytot."

The man sitting in the canoe is making a speech, but Sally Hemings's French has vanished. She understands nothing—except that he is about to fly.

And then, in a single instant, four men with swords cut the four ropes and the inverted purse lifts from the earth with the fluid grace of a wave at sea. As the wicker canoe swings off the platform and also begins to rise, the foolish young count with the long brown hair laughs—as if he has not committed an abomination, and is not about to die, as if he has never, in fact, been happier in his life.

"What is he doing!" Sally Hemings cries, grabbing Thomas Jefferson's sleeve.

"Nothing." Thomas Jefferson smiles. "Just this: He is going to fly like a bird. And then, when the air inside the *ballon* cools, he will sink slowly to the earth. It is all safe. All under control."

This time she believes Thomas Jefferson, not only because he knows more than any man on earth but because she can see that what he is saying is true. The man and the *ballon* continue to rise with a breathtaking grandeur, sideways, drifting with the breeze.

But then something changes: A hollowness comes into her throat, and the whole of her body goes cold, and all at once she becomes aware that Thomas Jefferson has taken hold of her hand, the one with which she had grabbed his sleeve.

The hollowness in her throat expands and becomes a sort of dizziness. What is happening makes no sense. Why would he do such a thing? Again and again she wonders if the pressure she feels on her fingers could possibly be the pressure of his hand, and again and again she tells herself, *No, it can't be.*

But then her hand is empty, and Thomas Jefferson is running. The entire crowd is running. She can still feel the pressure of his hand and the sweat their hands made together, but now he is far enough away that she would have to shout for him to hear. She lifts the skirt of her yellow gown and runs across the field after him, along with the rest of the crowd, until finally, at the edge of a wood, they must all stop, while the *ballon*—now higher than several houses piled one atop the other—glides silently over the trees.

Over the trees! A man flying *over* the trees!

Now Thomas Jefferson is next to her again. "Should I ask *le comte* to take us with him next time?" he says, his lips once again beside her ear. "Would you like to fly with le Comte de Toytot?"

"Oh, no!" says Sally Hemings. "I'd be too afraid!" Then, almost immediately, she thinks, *Yes! I do want to fly with* le comte! *I do! I do! Oh, please ask him! Please take me with you!*

But these words never pass her lips.

S ally Hemings is dead. The yard behind her house in Charlottesville is loud with the braying of mockingbirds. The rag-and-bone man's cart clatters on the cobblestone street out front. Her children are gathered around her bed: her three slump-shouldered sons and her daughter, who has not been back to Virginia in thirteen years and who arrived only minutes after her mother breathed her last.

Sally Hemings's dead children are there also: the daughter taken by fever after she had learned to walk but before she could ever run; the daughter who, small enough to cradle between elbow and palm, never recovered from the trial of being born; and the one Sally Hemings always called "La Petite," who had been conceived in Paris and who, no bigger than her mother's fist, came into this world on a river of blood and was buried at Monticello in a ceramic pot.

The dead children grieve, but their grief is gentle, like a winter fog over a yellow field. The grief of her living children has turned them to stone. They do not talk. They are waiting for something to change, and nothing will ever change. The youngest son is holding a violin, but he has left the bow in the front room.

Outside the window the trees heave in a sudden wind. The sky grows dark, and the mockingbirds fall silent. For long moments rain is about to fall, but after a rumble of thunder the wind recedes and the sun returns.

Now Thomas Jefferson, who has been dead himself for more than eight years, is also in the room. Sally Hemings looks at him but doesn't say a word.

Minutes pass before he finds the strength to tell her, "I wanted you to be happy, but you were never happy."

"I was happy," she says.

"With me?"

"Yes," she says. "I was happy."

But Thomas Jefferson does not believe her. He does not believe her because he himself was never happy. There were many, many times when he pretended otherwise: the time when she acted out the story of Cinderella with a teacup, a soup spoon and two forks, and the two of them laughed and laughed and laughed; or the time they spent the whole day riding, then cooled off with a swim in Johnson's Creek and then made love on a horse blanket spread over a bed of mint; or that afternoon when he was sitting beside her on her bed, bouncing three-month-old Beverly on his knee, and suddenly the tiny boy's delighted squeaks and coos came together in a chuckle and then a full belly laugh—his first ever. Thomas Jefferson knew many such moments with Sally Hemings and managed to believe, each time, that he was happy, that Sally Hemings was happy, that no two people could be happier. But now he knows that on every one of those occasions his own happiness had been infected by fear, by his sense that what he believed was happiness could not, in fact, ever exist in this world and that in a moment he would have to live in the world as it actually was: a place of unending loss and shame.

He takes the empty chair between two of their living sons and across the bed from the third son and their daughter. "No," he says. "You were never happy. There is no need to lie anymore."

"I am not lying," she says, but after that she can think of nothing else to say.

For a long time the silence in the room only deepens. Then a mockingbird launches into a fleet and fragmentary improvisation.

"You cannot pretend to be ignorant of the effect you have upon me," says Thomas Jefferson.

It is the evening following le Comte de Toytot's flight. Thomas Jefferson and Sally Hemings are seated across a corner of the dining-room table, before the fire. There are two wine bottles between them, one empty, the other not quite. There are also two glasses. Thomas Jefferson has just finished his. Sally Hemings's is almost full. This is her third glass. He has been counting. Or maybe her fourth.

"And what is more," he says, smiling tenderly, "you cannot pretend that you do not share my feelings. I can see it in your eyes."

Sally Hemings is not, in fact, looking at Thomas Jefferson. She is looking at her hands, her right thumb massaging repeatedly the center of her left palm.

"I could see it," he says, "when you took my hand out on the field. Do you remember? Just as le Comte de Toytot was borne into the air?"

Thomas Jefferson wants her to look at him again. He reaches across the table, places the edge of his bent index finger beneath her chin and lifts.

Now she is looking into his eyes, her own eyes tremulous in the flickering firelight.

There is a plunging in his breast that is equally pain and joy. "My God!" he says. "You are so beautiful."

Sally Hemings pulls her chin away from his still-extended finger. "No." She is looking again into her lap.

"Yes!" he insists, allowing his finger to lightly stroke her cheek as he withdraws his hand. "You are a vision!" He refills his glass, then swirls the dark fluid once.

"No," she says, still not looking at him. "I *didn't* take your hand." At the word "didn't," her head lifts and she looks him straight in the eye. Her gaze is firm, but he can see that she is trembling, that she is afraid, that in a moment she will begin to cry.

"I'm sorry." He takes a deep sip from his glass. "I am sorry. I have been presumptuous."

"No," she says. "You have—"

He cuts her off: "I am *sorry*." There is anger in his final word, and he is ashamed of his anger. Now he is the one looking down. "I have allowed myself to be blinded by feeling."

"No."

"Please," he insists. "I am sorry." This time he speaks the word with a suitable tenderness. "You are a beautiful young woman, Sally, but that does not give me the right—"

He stops speaking when he sees that her gaze has fallen to her lap.

"What?" he asks softly. When she doesn't answer, he slumps in his chair. "And now I am making everything worse."

"No," she says. And she looks up at him with a small, shy smile. Again that plunge of joy and pain. He wants to pull her into his arms but only takes another deep sip from his glass. She is still smiling, and he begins to wonder if he might hope.

"What?" he says again, even more softly. He leans toward her.

"Nothing," she says. "I had a lovely day. I will never forget it. *C'était un vrai miracle de voir un homme voler dans le ciel.*"

"Yes," says Thomas Jefferson. "Wonderful. *Vraiment.*" She has stopped smiling. He sees the trouble in his own face reflected in hers. "Perhaps you had better leave me alone, Sally. I have work to do."

The smile returns weakly, then vanishes as she pushes her chair back from the table and stands.

"Certainly," she says and, as she backs away from the table, "Sorry."

Then she is gone.

Alone in the warm, illuminated room, Thomas Jefferson finishes his glass and pours another.

. . . It was a true miracle to see a man flying in the sky. . . .

First Sally Hemings sees a golden shimmer along the top of her door, and then she hears the whisper of a leather sole on wood. A knock. So light that she is able to pretend to herself she hasn't heard it. Then another knock. She has been lying flat on her back for more than an hour, unable to sleep. For much of that time, she felt herself listing sideways in the darkness, as if her bed were a boat swept along by the current of a mirror-smooth river. It was the wine. She has never drunk so much wine. She feels it still, as a wisp of nausea at the base of her throat. And the listing. That is still there, too.

But it isn't only the wine.

No sooner did she stretch out under her covers than the moments of her day began to repeat inside her head: le Comte de Toytot waving happily as he drifted over the trees, the low vibration of Thomas Jefferson's voice filling her ear, the feather touches of his lips, his sweating hand—but also what he said while she was drinking her wine: "You are so beautiful. You know that, Sally, don't you?" His nose was red, his eyes and mouth drooping, as if his face were melting in the heat of the fire. "Beautiful," he said. Over and over. At first, as she heard these words, the hot thickness in her throat felt like embarrassment, but then it hardened into a sense of something wrong—maybe something very wrong. "Beautiful," he said. "You cannot pretend to be ignorant—"

Another knock. "Sally?"

Him.

He knocks again. "I'm sorry to disturb you."

It is raining. She hears the echoey clatter of water in the gutter pipes and the gust-driven rain like sand flung against the windows.

"Sally?"

"One second," she says.

She is already standing, her bare feet on the cold floor. She doesn't know what to do. The cold is creeping up her body inside her shift. She wants to find her yellow gown, but she doesn't know where she left it. There is no light in her room. She can't see anything at all except the wavering glow around the door.

"I'm sorry," says Thomas Jefferson.

Maybe she threw the gown across the chair beside her chest of drawers. As she takes a step in that direction, her middle toes slam against the corner of her night table. A flare of pain illuminates the blackness. The enamel chamber pot clanks but doesn't spill.

"Sally?"

"One second," she groans, balancing on one foot, clutching her throbbing toes with both hands.

"Are you all right?"

"I'm fine."

She has found the chair—nothing on it but a single stocking. Now her knee collides with the chest of drawers, but only enough to rattle the glass knobs. No pain, but somehow the fact that she keeps knocking into things leaves her feeling helpless and faint. She is trembling.

She knows what is happening, or what seems to be happening, but she doesn't know it at the same time. White men do such things. Her own father did. But she cannot make herself believe—even now—that so gentle, sad and wise a man as Thomas Jefferson could be like that. And the disparity between what she is able to believe and what seems manifestly to be happening makes her feel disconnected from the world.

"I'd just like a word with you," he says. "One word."

She steps toward the wavering golden outline of the door. There is something soft under her foot. Her gown. And now she remembers that in her haste to bury herself under her covers she simply threw the gown onto a chest, from which it must have slipped to the floor. She picks it up, puts it over her head and slides her hands down the sleeves. Now she is standing just inside the door, the back of her gown unbuttoned to her shoulder blades.

"It's late," she says.

"I know. It won't take a minute."

The door is not locked. He could have opened it and come in at any time. Maybe everything she's been thinking is foolish. Maybe there's nothing at all to fear.

She lifts the latch and pulls the door inward, peering around the edge, keeping her body out of sight, pressed flat against the paneled wood.

"Oh, Sally!" Thomas Jefferson gasps softly, and then gives her a happy smile. His hair is a mess, as if he has been gripping it in his closed fists. His eyes look gelatinous in the glow of his candle. Even as he stands without moving, he is clearly having difficulty staying on his feet.

"Might I come in?"

For reasons that Sally Hemings will never be able to comprehend, she backs away from the door as soon as he asks this question, and then she runs to her bed—which she realizes instantly is exactly the wrong thing to do.

Thomas Jefferson is in the room, and he has closed the door behind him. He hurries toward where she stands, puts the candle on the night table and takes her hand as he sits on the edge of the bed.

"My sweet girl!" he says.

He is holding her hand in both of his. She does not resist. She is paralyzed and feels as if she is hovering a few feet above her own head, watching what is happening and not particularly caring—feeling nothing but a hurtling sort of numbness.

Thomas Jefferson squeezes her hand gently. "I just had to see you," he says. "Do you understand? I couldn't stop thinking about you." He smiles crookedly. "I think you do understand. You are, of course, the most innocent and modest of girls, but"—he looks straight into her eyes—"I think you do."

He stands, looming so large in the darkness that he seems twice her size. Now his mouth is on hers. She feels the prickliness of his lip and chin, his tongue attempting to push between her lips. "Oh, Sally!" he gasps. "Oh, Sally! You are so lovely! So utterly lovely!"

Now he is kissing her neck, her throat. His hands are running up and down her body, touching her in places, front and back, where no one has ever touched her before. The feeling of his fingers on her body fills her with loathing. She wants to slap his hands away. She wants to shout, "Leave me alone!" She wants to bite his tongue. But she does none of these things. Looking down from above, she sees herself as a limp rag doll. If he weren't holding her up, she would fall to the floor.

"I will make it good," he says between kisses. "I will be gentle. You will see. Gentle. I will make it good."

And now he has lifted both her gown and her shift over her head. And now he lays her naked body on the bed. He is kissing her breasts, her belly, that part of her down below. He is making the husky groans and ripping sighs of animals.

All at once he pulls away. He is standing beside the bed, tearing at the buttons on his breeches. She knows what is going to happen. It cannot be possible. But that makes no difference. It is happening. It is inevitable. And there it is. Like a club sticking up out of him. Like a skinned fish.

Like an enormous mushroom that is practically all stem. She never imagined that it could be so repulsive.

But now something else has happened. Her entire body has gone rigid. He tries to move her legs apart, and he can't. He cannot move her hands from her sides.

He laughs softly. "Sweet girl! Don't worry. I will be gentle. You will see. I promise. I understand. I will make it good." He is talking between kisses. And he is kissing his way up her body. She feels his blunt, hot thing bump just above her knee, then press into her thigh—lightly at first, then harder.

When his mouth reaches hers, she keeps her lips clamped shut. She is shivering. Her whole body is icy in the icy air, and she can't stop the shivering.

He pulls back his head. "Sally?" He starts to smile, but then his smile fades.

She makes a small shriek, like a rabbit in the jaws of a dog, and shakes her head once, hard. She cannot speak.

"Are you all right?" he says.

Again she shakes her head.

For a long moment, he only looks at her, his disconcertion resolving slowly into something like profound exhaustion.

"Oh, God!" he says. "Oh, God! How could I be such a fool?" He turns away from her. Sitting on the edge of the bed, he puts his elbows on his knees and his forehead into his hands, clawing at his hair. "I'm sorry! I am so sorry! Oh, God." He stands and pulls his breeches up from around his ankles. "I can't believe I . . . I can't believe . . . What a fool . . . Unforgivable . . ."

Then he is gone. The door has closed behind him.

His candle is still on her night table. The flame drops and flutters as a gust seeps around the window casing.

Outside her door she hears an abrupt, hollow thundering. He has stumbled on the stairs. Quiet. An exhalation. He cannot see. Unsteady foot thumps quieten as they recede. He must make his way in total blackness. By touch alone.

Colors are illusions. Better yet: They don't entirely exist. A particular blue will look radically different in a field of orange than in a field of green. Show ten people a blue wall. Then take them into another room, present them with a hundred cards in assorted varieties of blue and ask them to pick out the color of the wall they were just looking at. It is highly likely that each person will pick out a different blue and likelier still that none of the blues they choose will match the wall in the other room. What is blue in sunshine might be green by candlelight and purple under fluorescent light. A blue on a smooth surface will appear a different blue when the surface is rough. There is a color that, especially in its paler tints, most men see as blue and most women see as green. It is a fact that the colors we see are never actually present, and yet, at the same time, they are absolutely present, as present as our emotions, memories, hopes, desires, beliefs—our very selves. And, of course—individually, but more commonly together—colors can constitute that most vivid and immediate form of truth, that truth also known as beauty.

The huge clamor of steel shrieking on steel recedes into the rumble and roar of the train hurtling through the soot-blackened tunnel. As Thomas Jefferson watches, Sally Hemings lowers her fingers from her ears, pulls her book out from under her arm and reopens it. She sighs, and her face settles into peaceful concentration—so maybe she hasn't noticed him after all. Gradually a faint tribulation darkens the center of her brow, but maybe only in response to some sorrow or worry experienced by the imaginary people about whom she is reading. He remembers, years ago, watching her through a window as she sat in a wicker chair out on the porch, gazing idly into space, her feet up on the railing. He felt, as he studied her then, that he was seeing her as she actually was—which is to say, as she was in his absence. It was a moment of terrific intimacy.

III

III

S ally Hemings stands in the dim hallway thinking about different kinds of knowledge. Some things that you know leave you alone, like the way bread tastes, or your name, or the stink of butcher shops on a summer afternoon. But there are other things that once you know them won't let you be yourself anymore. You can remember who you used to be, but you are no longer that person. And you never will be again.

The fear came first and the disgust afterward. As she lay alone in her bed once Thomas Jefferson had gone, she was haunted by the images of his sweating, red face, distorted by drink and by the brutal, animalistic urges that had taken him over. He had, in fact, become an animal as he threw himself on top of her, grunting, groaning, clawing at her, rubbing himself against her. How is it possible that a man as dignified, gentle and wise as Thomas Jefferson could have yielded to such crude impulses?

If she could find a way to go back to when he'd asked if she would like to see a true miracle, she would say no. And when he told her to put on her yellow gown: No. And when he asked her to get into the carriage with him, she would say it was not proper for a gentleman to ride with his serving girl. And when he offered her wine, she would say, "No. I won't drink it. No."

But now, in the cold morning—gray sky in the window at the end of the hall—she thinks that as horrified as she may have been last night, it is probably for the better that she now knows that Thomas Jefferson is no different from any of the brutal men her mother warned her of, that his civility is merely a subterfuge, as it is perhaps for all men. She is wiser for this knowledge, and maybe also stronger.

Last night she had thought that she was weak, that she was nothing, not even a leaf blowing down the street. But now she knows that Thomas Jefferson is the one who is weak—because he showed her that he needed something from her; he needed something so badly that it turned him into a wordless animal. And he also showed her his shame—which per-haps is what matters most.

He sat there on the end of her bed, his head in his hands, talking to himself, moaning, cursing, and then he left, staggering as he pulled up his breeches in midstep. And as Sally Hemings watched his shame, all of her own went away. *I am blameless*, she told herself. And now, in the hallway, she says aloud, "I am better than him." Never before did she imagine that she could be better than Thomas Jefferson. The world as she knew it simply didn't allow for that possibility. And now it does.

There is so much room inside Thomas Jefferson. I shout, and there is no echo. I have been walking for days and am not sure I will ever traverse the distance between his head and his feet. Nights I unroll my sleeping bag and make a fire from the dried sticks and punky logs that are scattered everywhere in here. Last night a man walked out of the darkness and asked if he could sit down and warm his hands at my fire. A fresh-killed rabbit dangled from his belt, and he said he'd be happy to share it with me. He, too, has been walking for days and days, and he has come to the conclusion that Thomas Jefferson does not exist, that this is only a sort of purgatory or perhaps one of the upper rings of hell—the one reserved for those who can't distinguish fact from hope.

Tonight a different man is warming himself by my fire. He has no food to offer, but he is happy to help me cut potatoes and beets for a soup. I tell him what the man said last night, and he tells me he knows for certain that Thomas Jefferson is real and that we are inside him. It's just that these fires of ours make him lighter than air, and so he is constantly drifting among the clouds. "That's why you can never get to the end of him," the man says. "He is everywhere."

I tell him I don't understand why that should be true, and he tells me he has conclusive evidence. "A couple of weeks ago," he says, "I happened to be near one of his eyes, and I could look down at the moonlight shining off the tops of the clouds. And below them I could see the orange lights of a huge city—London or Los Angeles. Or maybe Tokyo."

I don't see what this proves but decide not to argue.

After we have finished our soup, we put a couple of big logs on the fire and get into our sleeping bags. Sometime later I am awakened by the clicking of clawed feet and by soft but emphatic woofs, exhalations and semivoiced yelps, which all together sound remarkably like speech. I sit up and place a couple more logs on the fire. At first they only smoke, but after I have blown on them awhile, flags of yellow flame ripple up into the darkness.

As I pull the top of my sleeping bag back over my shoulders, I notice two perfectly round coals glowing in the gloom about a dozen yards from the fire. I hear a low noise, something between a grunt and a howl, and find another pair of coals hovering about the same distance away in the opposite direction. I grab a stout branch and drag it into my sleeping bag with me, just in case. There is no horizon here and no real dawn or daylight—just a cataract-colored luminescence that lasts about as long as a regular day.

T homas Jefferson walks hurriedly along the sandy path through the Champs-Élysées, head down, hands in the pockets of his breeches, coattails kicked again and again by his striding calves, a grid of plane trees spreading out for acres on either side of him. He hardly slept last night and was too bleary and restless this morning to work. It is April 21, a month past the vernal equinox, but the air is dank, cold. Heaps of cloud, white and gray, drift over the rooftops, intermittently releasing showers of musket-ball-size drops, but so far never intensely enough to merit his turning around and heading home.

He is trying to convince himself that what he had wanted last night would not have been a theft but a gift, that the girl, with all the modesty that is natural to her sex, had been looking on him exactly as he had been looking on her and that, unable to acknowledge the depth of her own feeling—

But this line of reasoning is quashed by his memory of her rigid body, her averted face and the noises she had made—noises of childish fear and grief.

He veers off the path and into the geometric forest, where identical tree trunks angle through his peripheral vision in perfect diagonal and perpendicular rows. He stops, his forehead against smooth, mottled bark, and gasps in panicked despair at the impossibility of escaping his own being. But then, hearing that the sounds he is making now are the sounds he made last night, he falls silent.

This is self-pity, he tells himself. *You have no right to self-pity.*

Pushing away from the tree, he continues walking, his head down, hands in his pockets. He feels tears rising to his eyes, but they never come. He hasn't cried in years, not since Martha died.

How could he have allowed himself to get so drunk? How could he have allowed such low urges and repulsive ideas to take possession of his judgment? It is true. He cannot deny it: *le droit du seigneur.* That foul aristocratic presumption had come to mind last night every time his resolve wavered, every time he was overcome with anticipatory shame. *Who would blame you?* he had thought. *They all do it.* Lafayette has told him that he has had *un goûter* of every single one of his serving girls. Even James Monroe has confessed to a dalliance with his chambermaid. *No one will blame you,* he had told himself time and again.

And yet once he was actually in the girl's room, he never gave a thought to his "right," nor did he think of himself as "taking" anything from her. All that was in his mind were his nights with Martha—especially those first nights of their marriage, by the fireplace, when the snow was falling outside the windows. Stupidly, blindly, selfishly, he had imagined that all that was needed was a little patience, some loving words, a gentle touch here and there with hand, lips and tongue, and all at once Sally Hemings's desire would overwhelm her modesty and, as with Martha, her thighs would loosen, her arms would fly up and she would cover his neck and lips with her kisses. But instead he'd inspired nothing but her loathing, and now he feels nothing but loathing for himself.

He hears a pattery drumming in the leaves overhead. A cold drop strikes his cheek. In a matter of seconds, the rain is falling so thick and fast that it hits the sandy earth all around him with a sound like millions of tiny feet stamping.

Thomas Jefferson has never called her "Miss Hemings" before. She came upon him under the portico, squeezing water out of his sodden coat by twisting it into a thick rope. The sleeves of his white shirt were sodden, too, and perfectly transparent where the wet linen clung to the skin of his arms. As soon as he realized he was being observed, he shook out the coat and attempted to put it on. After prodding several times at the interior of a still-drenched and twisted sleeve, he gave up, flung the coat over his shoulders and pulled the lapels across his chest.

His lips were blue, his hair a mass of tarnished copper coils, his face dripping. As he looked at her, a shiver passed through his whole body. This was when he said it: "Miss Hemings, I know that I don't deserve your forgiveness, but I want you to know that I profoundly regret my actions. They were utterly inexcusable, and they will fill me with shame until the end of my days."

Now he is silent. His clearly rehearsed speech over, there is nothing he can do save wait for her reply.

But Sally Hemings is too filled with rage to talk. Her ears roar with it, and everything turns white. By the time she comes back to herself, she is already at the bottom of the steps and making her way rapidly but unsteadily toward the gate to the street.

She has no idea what she said or did while the world was roaring and white. She has no idea what she looked like, but she feels as if she were shaken into a vibrating cloud of light and noise.

And now she is out of the gate and on the street, which smells of feces and wet stone. The tremulous weakness fades from her legs; her stride grows purposeful, strong.

It is Saturday. She is going to pick up Patsy and Polly at their school across the river, on rue de Grenelle. It will take her an hour to walk there and longer to walk back. Maybe when she returns, she will know what to do.

The guard tightens her belt. She speaks.

—Wake up.

—Uh . . .

—Wake up. It's morning.

—Wha . . . ?

—Get the fuck out of bed.

—Who are you?

—Get the fuck up, I told you!

—Why?

—Because I told you so.

—It's the middle of the night.

—No it's not.

—I've only been asleep for ten minutes.

—It's been three hours.

—What?

—Three hours. I've been on duty three hours, and the whole time I've been sitting here watching you. So now it's morning.

—It's *not* morning.

—How do you know?

—Leave me alone.

—How do you know?

—Because I'm fucking exhausted, and I want to sleep.

—Answer my question.

— . . .

—Answer my question.

—I just did.

—Just because you're tired doesn't mean it's morning. You think the sun rises and falls according to when you feel like sleeping?

— . . .

—When was the last time you saw daylight?

—How the fuck do I know?

—I rest my case.

—Why are you doing this?

—Well, there are two reasons. First of all, I'm the guard and you're shit, so whatever I say is the law. That's the most important reason. The second reason is that I've been reading your file, and I'm interested in you.

—Great.

—Don't you want to know why?

—Why?

—Because I know you think you don't belong here.

—Does anybody think they belong here?

—Nobody likes being here, but that's not the same thing as thinking they don't belong.

— . . .

—Some people know they don't deserve freedom. Murderers, mostly. Even the really heinous ones. On the whole I prefer working with murderers.

—Why?

—Because they know the difference between right and wrong. They know that some people are good and some people are evil and there is no in-between.

—How can you say that?

—You see! That's exactly what I'm talking about.

—No in-between. How can you say that?

—Because that's the way it is.

The prisoner makes a vocalization that commonly precedes speech. The guard speaks.

—Shut up! I'm still talking. I know what you are going to say. You're going to tell me about complexity, ambiguity, our muddy human souls. But none of that matters. So what if you wanted to do the right thing? So what if you thought you *were* doing the right thing? Or if you had a terrible childhood? Or even if you were insane? If the thing you did was evil, that's all that matters: You're evil. You belong here. End of story.

—How can you say that?

—Hah!

—What?

—Didn't I just tell you? You're shit in here. And I'm *God.* Right? I'm the big, fucking, all-powerful mystery. Where wast thou when I laid the foundations of the earth? Didst thou create Behemoth? Leviathan? Have the gates of death been open unto thee? Get down on thy knees! Repent in dust and ashes!

The prisoner is laughing. The guard speaks.

—What's so funny?

—Nothing.

—Then shut up!

— . . .

— . . .

The prisoner speaks.

—But still, there's a flaw in your reasoning.

—I knew you'd say that.

—So you know what I'm talking about?

—Why don't you tell me?

—You said *if* the thing you did was evil. That implies that you have to have a way of distinguishing evil from ordinary wrongdoing, or even from virtue—because, after all, sometimes evil is just a matter of perspective. The theft of a loaf of bread might seem evil to the baker, but to the starving man—

—Just like I said: Complexity. Ambiguity. Our muddy human souls. You're like a robot.

—Don't evade the point.

—What is the point?

—The point is that conclusions about whether a person is good or evil have to be based on evidence, and evidence can be misleading, or just hard to interpret. And then there's the matter of terminology. How exactly do you define evil? And where do you draw the line—

—Are you actually paying attention to what you are saying?

— . . .

—I mean, do you actually think it takes a rocket scientist to figure out that a man who buys and sells human beings is evil?

— . . .

—Well? What have you got to say for yourself?

—That's not what I . . .

—You think there's any way that trading in human beings isn't evil?

—I'm just talking about what you said, about there being no in-between.

—Well, you know what? I don't give a fuck about what you were talking about. If you're evil, you're evil. That's all there is to it. We're not talking garden variety screwup here, or even mean fucking bastard. We're talking evil. There's no such thing as being a little bit evil. Evil is an all or nothing proposition. That's it. And all your talk about ambiguity, definitions and all that other bullshit is just a way of avoiding the simple truth.

—And I'm saying that there is no such thing as simple truth. For better or for worse, reality is always complex and ambiguous, and a failure to recognize that fact leads straight to tyranny.

The guard shakes her head and smiles. The prisoner speaks.

—What?

—If that's what you think, then it looks like you've got a lot to learn about tyranny.

She bangs her billy club against the bars of the cell. The prisoner leaps backward. He speaks.

—What the fuck!

—Get down on your knees!

— . . .

—You heard me! Get down on your knees!

The guard pulls a ring of keys out of her pocket and unlocks the cell door. The prisoner speaks.

—What are you doing?

The guard bangs her billy club against the cell bars once again, but far more forcefully. The bars ring. The ringing reverberates down the corridor. The prisoner speaks.

—What are you doing?

—I'm going to teach you a lesson about tyranny.

The door swings open as if of its own accord. The guard and the prisoner look into each other's eyes. She speaks.

—And about your fucking pursuit of happiness and your fucking created equal.

The guard enters the cell. The prisoner backs away. The guard speaks.

—That is so fucking over.

A day has passed, and a night during which Sally Hemings did not sleep. Now it is morning, but so early that there is only a blue vagueness in the garden outside the kitchen door. An armful of wood has already burned down to a mound of glowing, irregularly popping and snapping coals, and a ten-gallon iron stewpot is already filling the air with onion-scented steam. Jimmy, who got back from Le Havre last night, is standing at the chopping block transforming peeled carrots into a heap of thumbnail-long cylinders. He doesn't know that Sally Hemings is standing in the doorway behind him, watching.

Her first thought is that her brother seems so gentle as he gives himself to his work, and so unhurried, even though the extraction of each new set of three or four carrots from the heap, their alignment against his knife and then the rocking chops that transform them into orange cylinders are accomplished in scant seconds. It's his grace that makes him seem unhurried, or even in a sort of trance. He hardly looks at what he's doing, his eyes turned toward the empty space above a shelf of soot-blackened copper pots, and yet his knife blade strikes with the regularity and precision of a ticking clock.

But in the next instant, all Sally Hemings sees is her brother's humiliation. His movements are not so much graceful as supremely controlled. His back is rigid, his expression blank and his head held high in the manner of a man struggling to endure the unbearable. There is a great deal of rage inside Jimmy, but it is humiliated rage—rage lacking not intensity but the power to be expressed in action.

At these last thoughts, Sally Hemings becomes so weak with sorrow that a groan escapes her throat.

Jimmy's head jerks around. "Oh, Sally!" He smiles. "Don't do that! I thought you were a ghost."

"Sorry."

"Don't you know better than to creep up on a man with a knife in his hand!?"

Sally Hemings can't bring herself to laugh. Jimmy's smile is replaced by the slightly parted lips and crumpled brow of concern.

"What's the matter, Cider Jug?"

"Nothing." She looks away, then back.

Jimmy is still looking at her but doesn't say anything.

"I just heard someone in here," she says, "so I thought I'd look in."

"Hunh."

"What are you making?"

"Boeuf bourguignon."

"Oh." Sally Hemings wasn't quite listening to his response. So after an instant she asks, "What's that?"

"Beef and wine and vegetables—potatoes mostly." He looks back at the chopping block, lines up some carrots and places his knife across them. "Mr. Jefferson's having a whole bunch of people over tonight." Chop.

Sally Hemings doesn't say anything for a moment. Then she says, "I better be going."

Jimmy rests the hand holding the knife on the table. When she doesn't budge from the doorway, he says, "Come over here."

"No. I've got to go."

"Come over here." He points his knife blade at the floor beside him.

She wipes her hands on her apron, then crosses the room to stand beside her brother, though not as close as he indicated.

When she still doesn't say anything, Jimmy says slowly, with a knowing smile, "You look like the dog sneaking out of the hen yard."

"What are you talking about?"

He smiles again. "I don't know. I'm waiting for *you* to tell me. All I'm saying is that you look like you've been up to no good."

"I haven't done anything," she says angrily. She wants to leave, but she can't.

"Well, something happened."

"No." She picks up her apron absently and wraps both hands in it. "I have to go." She takes a step away, then turns around. "Something happened, but I didn't do anything."

His smile is gone. "Oh, Sal."

Her eyes grow hot with tears. She squeezes her lips together and shakes her head.

"You don't have to say anything," he tells her.

She wipes her fingers across her eyes, then says, "I can't talk here."

She walks toward the door and out into the yard, where the powdery light is going pinkish. She hurries between beds of the rotted leaves and stems of last year's peas and squash, pressed flat by a winter of snow, and she doesn't turn around until she is behind the toolshed. Once Jimmy joins her, she leans forward and speaks in a voiced whisper beside his ear.

"Mr. Jefferson came to my room the other night."

Jimmy pulls his head away from hers and covers his mouth with both hands. "Oh, no!" After a moment he lowers his hands and says, "You mean that he . . . that . . . that he . . ." He cannot complete his sentence.

"He came to my door," says Sally Hemings. "He was drunk, and he wouldn't go away."

"Did he force himself in?"

"No. Not really. He just kept saying all these things. . . . I didn't know what to do, but . . . And when I realized he was already in the room, I didn't know how I was going to get him out."

"Did he—" Jimmy cuts off his own question. He gives Sally a firm, interrogatory glance but then cannot bear to look at her.

When he looks back, she is staring him straight in the eye. Then she nods slowly.

He makes a small gasp but says nothing.

She realizes that he has probably misunderstood what actually happened, but she can't bear to speak any of the words she would have to use to make that clear—and maybe it doesn't matter. It was bad, that's all. Just bad.

After a long moment of silence, Jimmy moves his open hands back and forth horizontally, as if sweeping something off a table. "You can't talk about this to *anyone*," he says. "Anybody finds out about Mr. Jefferson or if Mr. Jefferson finds out you been talking—" He doesn't complete his sentence.

"But what am I going to do?"

"I don't know." He makes the sweeping gesture again. "You best hope Mr. Jefferson doesn't come around again. The best thing you could have done was never open up your door in the first place."

"Jimmy!" She puts both hands on top of her head, as if she has just been struck.

"I'm sorry." He comes back to her, throws his arms around her and crushes her against his chest. Then he lets her go. "I've got to think about this. The main thing is, we've got to see what's going to happen. Maybe nothing's going to happen . . . and then everything will be all right . . . and we can just forget about it."

"I'll never forget about it."

"Well . . ." Jimmy backs away. "Just wait, and we'll see."

For almost a week, Sally Hemings keeps to her room as much as she can stand to and as much as she can manage without neglecting her duties to such a degree that everyone in the house will guess what has happened.

She cannot bear the idea of anyone's knowing, partly because if no one finds out, then it is almost as if nothing actually did happen, but mainly because she knows the conclusions that everyone will draw: Some will blame her for having led on the good Mr. Jefferson, or for having lacked the fortitude to make clear to him the inviolability of her virtue, and the rest (the majority, she believes) will simply be indifferent to what she has suffered. She is a slave, after all, and a young woman; it is her duty to serve her master in any way he requires. All of these conclusions fill her with such fury and dread that she sometimes feels insane.

So by day she is careful to respond to every greeting, question and command exactly as she would have responded had nothing happened and to devote exactly her ordinary level of attention to her every task and action—even to actions as simple as walking down the hall (in fact, she devotes much *more* attention than normal to how she places each foot as she walks, and how she holds her hands, and where she allows her eyes to stray).

By night she jams a wooden peg into the slot above the latch of her bedroom door so that it can't be opened.

By night she looks up into the swirling plasma of darkness between her bed and the ceiling and hears the tick of every contracting or expanding floorboard and the whisper of every breeze, and she thinks only of the danger gathering force in every corner too dark to see.

By night she does battle with her memory and her imagination and with her rigid, sweating, sleepless body, which wants to do nothing but run from her room and out into the streets and never see the Hôtel de Langeac again, or Paris.

"Come with me, child," says Madame Gautier, the laundress, a potato-shaped woman of about sixty, with very small eyes and an imperious pout. She visits the Hôtel twice weekly, to drop off cleaned linens, towels, undergarments and shirts and to pick up dirty ones. She is speaking in French. When Sally Hemings greets her command with only an uncomprehending stare, Madame Gautier asks, "Are you not Mademoiselle Sally?" Sally Hemings answers in the affirmative, and Madame Gautier takes her by the hand, saying, "Good. You must come with me. Monsieur Jefferson desires that you should live in my house."

Sally Hemings yanks her hand free. "One moment! I know nothing about this."

"I am afraid that is none of my affair."

"Did he tell you this himself?"

"Yes. Just now, when Madame Dubois was paying me. Monsieur Jefferson came into the kitchen and asked if he might rent a room for you."

Many thoughts are shooting through Sally Hemings's mind, most of them concerning the significance of Thomas Jefferson's decision. Is she being banished from the Hôtel de Langeac? Will this impatient and stupid woman be her new mistress? Will she never be able to see her brother again? Or Patsy and Polly?

"I'm sorry," she tells Madame Gautier. "I must speak to my brother."

The old woman seems on the verge of scolding her, but then her scowl softens. "Very well," she says. "But hurry. I have many things to do."

She knows, Sally Hemings thinks as she hurries to find Jimmy. *Everybody knows.*

She has to pass through the dining room on her way to the kitchen, and this is where she spots her brother, who rushes right up to her.

"Jimmy!"

"Oh, Sally!" He holds out a small envelope. "He gave me this."

She takes it, removes the single page inside, on which she recognizes her own name and Thomas Jefferson's handwriting. She stares at it a long moment, her trembling hand making a blur of the page's edges.

"Do you want me to?" asks Jimmy.

She hands him the letter, and he reads:

"'Miss Hemings, I am writing to inform you that I have procured a room for you with Madame Gautier, which shall be your refuge whenever your services are not needed here by Patsy and Polly. During the days that my daughters are in residence at the Hôtel, I think it best that you reside in your present chamber, though if that should not be agreeable to you, alternate arrangements can certainly be made. Whether you wish to continue your duties at the Hôtel in the absence of my daughters is also a matter I leave to your better judgment. I hope you will understand that I have made this arrangement only in the interest of your greater comfort. If I have erred in my judgment, or if you have any questions or requirements, please do not hesitate to express them to me through the good offices of your brother. Respectfully yours, Th. Jefferson.'"

S ally Hemings's new room is just off the yard where Madame Gautier does her washing. The walls are fieldstone, the floor is dirt, the bed is a straw-stuffed tick on a wooden frame.

Sally Hemings thinks the room might be pretty if she can whitewash the walls, put dried flowers on the sill in front of the folio-size window and find a small dresser or trunk for her clothes. "You can do whatever you want," says Madame Gautier, "but Monsieur Jefferson must pay for it."

Sally Hemings does not want to ask any favors of Thomas Jefferson.

Madame Gautier's twenty-year-old daughter, Thérèse, is as big as a man. Her fingers are as thick as her thumb, her mouth is chapped purple all around from constant licking. "Who are you?" she asks Sally Hemings five times in a row, and seems satisfied with nothing Sally Hemings and her mother tell her.

Sally Hemings goes to sleep every night to the sound of the mice stirring inside her tick and wakes every morning to steam clouds scented with lye soap.

Her eyes water and her nostrils burn.

She is determined to only return to the Hôtel de Langeac when she escorts Patsy and Polly home from school and to stay away when they are not there, but she has nothing to do during her days except wander the streets.

"Monsieur Jefferson is paying for your room but not your food. If you want to eat, you must buy your own food or you must ask Monsieur Jefferson to buy it for you."

Sally Hemings cannot read, but she is able to add and subtract in her head, and so she figures that her wages are enough to allow her to buy bread and a piece of cheese every day.

Jimmy gives her meat and soup during her days at the Hôtel.

She cannot store her food. The mice eat it when she keeps it in her room, and Thérèse eats it when she keeps it in the kitchen larder.

She is walking through Les Halles on her way to Penthemont and spots a young man lying in the street, the top quarter of his head missing. A young woman standing in a doorway tells her that he was brained by a rock thrown by a *"sans-culotte."* Sally Hemings does not know what a *sans-culotte* is.

"You really must take better care of yourself," says Patsy. "How can we bring you anywhere if your linens are so gray and you smell like fish?"

When Monsieur Gautier gets drunk, Madame Gautier makes him sleep in the yard. On those nights Sally Hemings gets no sleep, because her door does not lock and she is afraid that he will come in and because his snores are as loud and enduring as a two-man saw cutting through an endless piece of wood.

Polly says, "Clotilde told us you no longer live here because Papa is angry at you. That's absurd! If you would like, Patsy and I will tell Papa he is being ridiculous this very minute." Sally Hemings glances at Patsy, who looks away. "Don't," Sally Hemings tells Polly. "Thank you, but don't."

Every morning Thérèse comes out into the yard and gathers her skirts into a bundle between her knees. She holds her bare buttocks over an enamel chamber pot until she has entirely voided both her urine and feces. Then she flings the contents of the pot over the rear wall into a vacant lot—or she tries to. About a third of the time, she misses and the mess remains on the wall until her mother can sluice it away with a bucket of used wash water.

Sally Hemings feels the heat on her cheek first, then looks down a street to see a house towering with flame. A pawnshop, she discovers when she has joined the curious crowd. Black timbers enveloped in roaring orange. Bricks bursting with a sound like gunshot. Once again: the *sans-culottes*.

"I insist!" says Polly. "I think Papa is just being stubborn. I am going to talk to him this instant." "Really," says Sally Hemings. "There is no need.

I'm perfectly happy as I am." Patsy takes no part in the conversation, but when she looks at Sally Hemings, she seems to have an extremely painful stomachache.

Only once it has sunk its teeth into the flesh just to the left of her chin does Sally Hemings realize that the animal she woke to find sitting on her chest is a rat.

Sally Hemings has always loved the main staircase, which descends in a crazy, angular spiral along the walls of the cockeyed space between the ballroom and the front hall, but once she resumes living at the Hôtel de Langeac after her five-week absence, she takes only the rear stairs, which let out in the narrow corridor just outside the kitchen, and she uses the Hôtel's side entrance onto rue Neuve-de-Berri when she goes shopping for Jimmy or Clotilde or when she has to fetch the Misses Jefferson from their school.

As a result of these practices, she only rarely catches sight of Thomas Jefferson during the days when his daughters are not present at the Hôtel. And on those occasions when she does spot him at the end of a hall or in a room she is passing, she always averts her head, pretending she doesn't see him, but not without noticing that he, too, shifts his gaze away from her.

One morning she descends the rear staircase and comes face-to-face with Thomas Jefferson as he is leaving the kitchen. He blushes so deeply that his hair looks yellow, and after a moment of flustered fidgeting he presses himself against the wall and gestures for her to pass. Neither of them says a word.

True hate is effortless. It is called into being spontaneously, inevitably, by the hateful object. When the object is not purely hateful, however, hate requires effort, and if such hate regards the complexly hateful object as if it were purely hateful, then the hate itself is not pure. The world abhors purity. The world abhors most things proclaimed true. The world abhors perfection.

And because we ourselves cannot be perfect, there are moments when the effort of hating the hateful thing is more than we can manage—moments of indifference, or of forgiveness, or even of admiration. And if the hateful thing is sufficiently deserving of our hate, those moments in which we are not sufficiently hate-filled can inspire us to hate ourselves, just a little or sometimes a great deal. This is because hate is so intertwined with morality as to make the two seem almost indistinguishable.

Love, too, is intertwined with morality, but far less intimately. We are more than capable of loving someone without thinking him or her morally perfect. But when we hate someone, it is almost impossible for us not to think of that person as evil.

It is a well-known fact that hate not unambiguously anchored on moral condemnation tends to degenerate over time into gentler emotions, or into no emotion at all. And it is also true that hate anchored only on fury can spontaneously flip over into love, that most capacious of emotions, that emotion which can not only thrive in the presence of hate but be intensified by it. And for this reason our tendency to think of love as life's greatest blessing is, alas, little more than sentimentality.

Sally Hemings is standing at the window at the top of the kitchen stairs, looking down into the garden where Thomas Jefferson is kneeling on the flagstone path between the beds of black earth that will soon be lush with cabbage, squash, beans, cucumbers and corn—all grown from seeds sent from Monticello. He licks the tip of his index finger and sticks it into an open envelope he is holding in his left hand. Carefully pulling his finger straight up out of the envelope, he peers at something on its tip and pushes his finger deep into the soft, moist earth in front of him. Then he smooths earth over the hole he has just made, licks his finger again, puts it back into the envelope and plunges it once more into the earth. He repeats this exercise twenty or thirty times before, with a childlike concentration on detail, he folds down the flap of the envelope, folds the envelope itself in half and slips it into the pocket of his frock coat.

Batting the earth flecks from his hands, he stands up and takes a step back to survey his work, not noticing the rake lying teeth-down directly behind him. His left foot steps on the rake handle, and he staggers, catching his right heel on the uneven pavement and toppling backward into the next vegetable bed, where he attempts to halt his fall with his right hand—which is to say with the arm he broke so badly not long before Sally Hemings's arrival in Paris.

He remains seated in the vegetable bed, rocking back and forth, clutching his right wrist in his left hand. After a couple of moments, he rocks onto his knees and, still clutching his wrist, gets to his feet. When he is vertical, he gingerly lets go of his wrist, opens and closes his fingers several times, then rotates his hand. From where she is standing, Sally Hemings can see no sign of pain, but he does clutch his wrist again as he walks toward the kitchen and disappears from sight.

. . . *The erosion of my virtue began, paradoxically, with my diminished regard for Mr. Jefferson. From my very first days at the Hôtel de Langeac, I had never quite seen the awkward and morose Mr. Jefferson as a real human being. He was more like a creature out of a nursery story, a prince put under a curse or pining away for a lost love—and, indeed, I attributed most of his sorrow to the death of his dear wife. It was only after he had committed the unthinkable that he became a mere man in my eyes and thereby became both pitiful and, eventually, capable of being pitied.*

The transformation of my feelings from contempt to something much closer to sympathy occurred during the month or so I lodged with Mr. Jefferson's laundress, an arrangement he made on my behalf. I would return to the Hôtel de Langeac only when Miss Martha and Miss Maria were home from school, and inevitably, from time to time, I would be forced to stand in the same room with Mr. Jefferson, while he and his daughters discussed arrangements or merely chatted. He would never look in my direction on these occasions and seemed reluctant to even meet the girls' gazes, afraid perhaps that I might have said something to them or that they might have heard rumors from some other quarter. I never breathed a word to either daughter of what had happened between their father and myself, though they clearly had intuited that something was wrong, Miss Martha in particular. Whenever Mr. Jefferson caught sight of me, his face would blanch and his voice would go low and soft, devoid of those modulations of pitch that signify joy, enthusiasm or even anger.

I must confess that I relished these manifestations of his discomfort, in part because they seemed just retribution for what he had done but more because they increased my own stature—in my eyes at least. After a period during which I would tremble in his presence (though more out of humiliation and suppressed rage than fear; I am not sure I ever truly feared Mr. Jefferson, and I never felt physically endangered), I began to take delight in intensifying his discomfort. I would stare at him whenever I was in his presence, and anytime he would glance my way and then wince or avert his gaze, I would have to struggle to keep myself from smiling.

Perhaps it was my growing sense of my power to unsettle Mr. Jefferson that transformed my contempt to pity—though I don't know; emotions are like a stew, the taste of which is determined by no one ingredient but by all together. What I do know is that one night when I was lying in my bed at the laundress's house, it occurred to me that Mr. Jefferson had shown true consideration for my feelings by arranging this refuge for me and that had he been the debauched brute I'd been imagining, he never would have allowed me out of his sight, let alone made it possible for me to regain my sense of decency and composure. And as soon as these ideas came into my head, all of Mr. Jefferson's winces, shrinkings, averted gazes, blanches and troubled expressions—the very things that had filled me with a self-satisfied contempt for him—began to seem manifestations of his tender nature and of his remorse, and thus of his desire to be good. And with this recognition, I began to feel his sufferings and humiliation as if they were my own and to remember how, on the night he had come into my room, no sooner had he realized that I truly did not share his desires than he cried out, clutched his head in shame and ran from the room. And now I, too, felt ashamed. My body was possessed by a paroxysm of tearful remorse, and for some hour or so during the darkest time of the night I imagined that I, myself, was heartless and evil.

In the morning, of course, all of this seemed nonsense, and I resumed my determination to cut Mr. Jefferson no quarter and to preserve my dignity and modesty above all else. . . .

Thomas Jefferson is walking amid the lush stench of the open sewers and the rankness of butcher shops and slaughterhouses, the smoke of coal and tobacco, the smell of wet wool and of houses hollowed by fire, then drenched by rain. But mostly he is walking among faces. So many faces.

Although he is reluctant to cede any advantage to Europe, he feels that the variety of faces he sees on the streets of Paris is vastly beyond that of any city in America, even Philadelphia. The variety is almost entirely due to disease, however, and to the fundamental cruelty of life under a monarch. The pitted, leathery faces of the pox sufferers, for example, or the dwarf-eyed faces of the blind-since-birth, or the toothless and the potato-nosed, or the mad and the aghast.

But there are also noble faces. He cannot deny this. The hawk-sharp gaze of the broad-shouldered ironmonger. The creamy cheeks and blue-eyed concern of the barefoot mother, hurrying her two small children out of the path of the clattering phaeton. And even the face of the duchess riding in that phaeton, who, lost in her own musings, her head and shoulders shaken in the shuddering of wheels over cobbles, lets her eyes fall on Thomas Jefferson's and gives him a glance that cuts like a cool arrow straight into his heart. And then she is gone.

Just that morning Thomas Jefferson looked at his own face in the mirror above his washstand, and he believed he was looking at himself. But now he thinks that he was mistaken. Our faces are not ourselves. They are only the façades behind which our selves perpetrate their histories, shrouded in obscurity and human wishes.

Thomas Jefferson's heart pounds, and he is sweating.

That plump woman smiling blandly as she stands behind her board table in the market square: What secret sufferings lurk behind those brown button eyes? What does she long for and fear as she stokes the fires under her pots of fruit? As she seals her preserves in porcelain jars under layers of wax, paper and twine?

Strawberry. Red currant. Apple. Apricot.

Thomas Jefferson's fingertips have gone slick with sweat.

He has conceived the desire to buy a jar of the apricot preserves from the woman, and now, mysteriously, he cannot breathe. A nugget of pain throbs in each of his temples. What is happening? he wonders. Then he remembers one sunny morning some two or three months past, when Sally Hemings licked her fingers, laughed and proclaimed, "Nothing on earth was so delicious as French apricot preserves!" He turns his back on the woman and her preserves and strides empty-handed out of the market square.

And then, minutes later, his fingertips having gone ice cold, he is hurrying home with a jar of apricot preserves in the pocket of his greatcoat.

He has to wipe his hands on his breeches before taking up his pen to write on a scrap of paper torn off the bottom of a cobbler's bill: "For Sally."

After he has left the jar of preserves atop his note on the table in the empty kitchen and has walked halfway down the hall, he decides he must return and retrieve his pathetic and shameful offering. He ventures back as far as the kitchen door, but then the notion that he should be ashamed of so innocent a gesture only seems more pathetic and incriminating, so once again he hurries down the hall.

And then: the bemused surprise of Clotilde when, an hour later, she comes across the jar and the note.

And then: Jimmy's somber gaze when, some hours after that, his sister walks into the kitchen.

"What's the matter?" asks Sally Hemings, stopping in the doorway.

He nods in the direction of the jar.

She recognizes not just the one word she can read but the handwriting. What she cannot make sense of is the blue scrawl on the label glued to the jar.

"What flavor?" she asks her brother, and he tells her. She picks up the jar, and then she puts it down and leaves the room.

But Jimmy has not had time to skin an onion before she is standing again beside the table. "It won't hurt to taste," she says.

Fingertips glossed with sweat, she tugs at the twine and paper, then picks up a knife and breaks the wax seal.

It is nine at night, and Sally Hemings has just finished washing and putting away the pots used by her brother and Clotilde when she hears the Marquis de Lafayette's laughter coming down the corridor from the direction of Thomas Jefferson's study. It would have been faster for her to go up to her room via the staircase just outside the kitchen, but she decides to take the main staircase instead, in the hope of catching a glimpse of the funny and kind marquis.

As she passes, candle in hand, in front of Thomas Jefferson's door, she sees a paper-strewn desk, a lit oil lamp and, just to the right of the lamp, somebody's knee, but she doesn't dare hesitate long enough to determine whose knee it is.

No sooner has she passed the door than she hears the marquis's voice: "Is that my beautiful little Sarah?"

"Sally!" Thomas Jefferson calls. "Sally! Would you mind coming here for a moment?"

Straightening her hair and her apron with her one free hand, she returns to the door. "Yes, Mr. Jefferson."

The two men are leaning forward to get a better view of the door, Thomas Jefferson behind the desk, the Marquis de Lafayette in front of it. (His was the knee she had glimpsed.) Both have shiny red faces and glittering eyes. A half-empty bottle of wine and two full glasses are on the desk. Two empty bottles stand beside the marquis's chair. He is looking at Sally Hemings with his usual merry smile. Thomas Jefferson is also smiling, but less easily. Sally Hemings feels a piercing sorrow as she looks at him, but she is not sure why.

"Thank you, Sally," says Thomas Jefferson. "You remember the marquis?"

"Mais oui," says Sally Hemings. *"Bien sûr."*

"And how is my beautiful Sarah?" says the marquis.

"I'm fine, thank you." Sally Hemings knows that she should say, "And how are you, my lord?" but she can't bring herself to ask him a question.

"We need your advice!" the marquis announces, his smile growing just a touch mischievous. "Your good friend, *le philosophe*"—he gestures at Thomas Jefferson, who has ceased smiling altogether—"and I are trying to come up with a document that will help this benighted monarchy acquire some of the virtues of your wise and civilized country."

"Gilbert," Thomas Jefferson says reprovingly.

"Nonsense," says the marquis. *Je veux vraiment savoir ce qu'elle pense.*"

Thomas Jefferson takes a deep sip from his glass and leans back in his chair. His face grows darker as it recedes from the lamp glow, but the flame still gleams in his eyes.

"Come in, *chère* Sarah," says the marquis. "Would you like a chair?" He looks around the room. Every other chair is stacked with books, papers, surveying equipment or other mechanical devices.

"That's all right," says Sally Hemings.

"*Mais non!*" He turns to Thomas Jefferson. "We can clear off one of these chairs for the young lady, can't we, Tom?"

"No, *really,*" insists Sally Hemings.

The marquis is leaning forward to rise from his chair but now hesitates.

"Are you sure, Sally?" says Thomas Jefferson. His voice is kindly, and there is a tenderness in his gaze that brings back her sorrow. Her sorrow and something else. This is the first time he has looked into her eyes for more than an instant in the six weeks since the night he came into her room. Her knees are trembling beneath her petticoats and gown.

"Yes," she says. "I was just on my way upstairs."

The marquis leans back in his chair. "Well, we won't keep you." He takes a sip from his own glass. "But we would both like to know what you think about something." He glances at Thomas Jefferson, who presses his hands flat together as if he were praying and holds the tips of his fingers against his mouth. "We'd like to know," the marquis continues, "what you think of an idea that we have been discussing. It concerns the definition of liberty or, more exactly, the liberty of people living together under one government. We would like to define liberty as the freedom to do whatever one wants, as long as that does not cause injury to anyone else or deprive people of their basic rights, including the right to liberty. What do you think of that idea?"

Sally Hemings is silent. She feels Thomas Jefferson looking at her, but she doesn't look in his direction. Her knees are trembling so violently now that the skirt of her dress has begun to shake.

"It's all right," says Thomas Jefferson.

"Let the girl answer," says the marquis. He is not smiling now. He no longer seems the least bit funny or kind.

"Sally," says Thomas Jefferson, "you don't have to say anything if you would rather not."

"It's a simple question," says the marquis. "Should people be free to do *whatever they want* as long as they don't hurt anyone else?"

After a long moment, Sally says, "I suppose that would be all right. If they don't hurt anybody, I mean. But I don't know. I'd have to think about it for a bit. It seems to me that there are a lot of things that don't hurt anybody else, but I'm not sure if people should really do all of them. Like hurt animals. I don't know if people should be able to do that if there isn't a good reason."

"Well said," says Thomas Jefferson, who is leaning forward now, his hands still pressed together in front of his mouth.

"What about depriving people of their liberty?" says the marquis. "Do you think that one man should be free to deprive another man of his freedom?"

Thomas Jefferson falls back into his chair again, his forehead gnarled with uneasiness, his eyes still gleaming.

"What do you think?" says the marquis. "Do we have the right to deprive other people of their liberty if they have not committed a crime?"

"Gilbert," says Thomas Jefferson. "I think you are being inconsiderate."

"Let her speak," says the marquis.

"I think . . ." says Sally Hemings. "I think that's another question I have to think about some more."

"But you *must* have an opinion!" the marquis says impatiently. "Do you think that someone should have the right to deprive you of your liberty if you haven't broken the law?"

Sally Hemings's eyes are hot with tears. Her vision blurs.

"Gilbert!" Thomas Jefferson slaps his hand down on the desk. "This is pointless and cruel."

"Let her speak," the marquis says firmly. "What do you think, Sarah?"

"I think," she says, her voice trembling, "that there is a difference between the way things are and the way they should be."

"Is that all?" says the marquis.

"Yes, my lord."

S ome days later I make my camp in a shallow declivity that gives me partial shelter from a cold wind that has been blowing steadily from the northwest since first light, though never with very much force. The wind is strong enough to keep blowing out my matches, however. And I am only able to get my fire going by first crouching to shelter the match and kindling with my body and then by standing upwind of the fire with my sleeping bag open and stretched out behind my back as a windbreak.

I sit back down once the larger logs have begun to burn steadily but soon realize that far from blowing out the fire, the steady wind is causing it to burn much faster than normal and that I am going to have to gather considerably more wood if I want to stay warm until it is light again.

I am casting a long-legged shadow at that dim fringe where the fire's flickering light fades into the surrounding gloom when I notice two white coals hovering in the darkness some twenty or thirty yards in front of me. Acting as if I haven't seen anything unusual, I carry the wood I have already gathered back to my camp at an unhurried pace, drop it beside the fire and sit down next to the backpack, where I have left the open buck knife I used to shave sticks into kindling.

I watch the hovering coals only out of the corner of my eye and can tell that they have come considerably closer since I first spotted them. They waver as they approach, and sometimes they disappear. Then they begin to fade into a vertical smear of lesser darkness that gradually, as it brightens, coalesces into the shape of a man. His long, wispy hair is blown across his face by the wind and looks golden in the firelight. He is barefoot. His jeans are worn through at the knees. His T-shirt is filthy and webbed with holes in the vicinity of his belt buckle. His vaguely military jacket is also filthy and missing every one of its buttons. Even before he has stepped into the full light, that lush and acrid odor of a body unwashed for weeks has begun to affect my sinuses and eyes.

"I'm sorry," he says. "Do you mind if I sit down?"

I shrug. He sits.

Then I move my sleeping bag and belongings about a yard away from him, so that more wind can pass between us. If he notices, he doesn't show it. For a long time, he just stares wordlessly into the fire.

Only when he sweeps his long hair—more gray than gold—out of his face do I realize that he is Thomas Jefferson.

"Oh, my God!" I say.

"What?" He looks at me with a sick-dog squint.

"What are *you* doing here?"

"I don't know." He shakes his head and lifts his hand in a way that indicates weary befuddlement. "I don't know how I got here. I don't even know where I am. Do you know where this is?"

I don't know how to answer this question.

"I've just been . . ." he says, ". . . well . . . just walking. And . . . I don't know. This place gives me the creeps. You know? It's like . . . I mean I don't know how I got here. I don't know how I'm going to get out. I walk and walk and walk, and nothing ever changes. You know? I don't ever get anywhere. I'm just here." He shakes his head again, but this time expressing only weariness. "This is no way to live." He looks me straight in the eye. "No. Way. To. Live."

Thomas Jefferson hears the front door slam and light, hurried footsteps, then feminine exhalations in the corridor outside his study and the whispered words, *"C'est pas possible!"* Leaving his desk, he finds Sally Hemings, gasping with her back to the wall, bonnetless, her hair undone on one side, her eyes wide, looking right at him but showing no trace of recognition. Her hands are flat against the wall, as if in the next instant she is going to push off and flee back down the hall. "Sally?" says Thomas Jefferson, unsure if she has even heard him. "Sally, what's happened?"

"I'm sorry," Sally Hemings says between gasps. "I've just been running." She takes a step away from the wall and lifts one hand to tuck the hair splayed across her shoulder behind her ear.

"Did something happen?" says Thomas Jefferson.

"A madman." She puts her hand to her throat.

"Were you attacked?"

"I was at the *marché*. I only wanted onions and flour. Then a man. He started shouting. He pulled off my bonnet and threw it into the gutter." Sally Hemings cries, "Oh!" as if the man has attacked her again. The hand at her throat twitches, flutters. Just below her jaw, the skin is red, chafed, blood-specked.

"Come here," says Thomas Jefferson, backing away from his study door. "You must sit down."

"I'm sorry." She looks at him with pleading eyes.

"I insist. Sit down. Let me give you something to drink."

He walks into his study and pulls a chair away from the front of his desk. It is the very chair in which the Marquis de Lafayette was sitting a week or so earlier. As Thomas Jefferson goes behind his desk to open a cabinet low to the floor, Sally Hemings enters his study and sits on the front edge of the delicate, silk-upholstered chair. She hears a clinking of glass on glass. Thomas Jefferson places an etched flask of whiskey-colored liquid on his desk and a tiny tumbler, not much bigger than a thimble.

"Cognac," he says. "Drink it all in a gulp. It will settle your nerves."

Sally Hemings picks up the little glass and does as she is instructed. She has never tasted cognac before. It is like liquid fire against her palate and tongue and like bitter acid in her throat. But as it goes down, she can feel the muscles in her chest relax. She breathes more easily.

"Do you know why the man took your bonnet?" says Thomas Jefferson as he walks back around his desk.

"He was shouting. I could hardly understand anything he said. I think he was drunk. He kept calling me 'une traîtresse.' And I think he said he was going to kill me. 'À mort!' he kept shouting. And 'Tiers état!'"

"Ah!" says Thomas Jefferson, now sitting at his desk. He has taken another tumbler from the cabinet and fills it with cognac.

"Other people were saying that. The man was shouting, and a whole crowd gathered. He pushed me to the ground and he spat on me. I thought—"

Sally Hemings's mouth is open, but she makes no sound. Her eyes have grown wide again. She sits erect on the edge of the chair, then gives her head a violent shake. "I'm sorry," she says at last. "Forgive me."

"No, no, no," Thomas Jefferson says kindly. "Please." He takes the flask in his right hand and holds out his left. "Here. Give me your glass."

Sally Hemings does as she is told. And when Thomas Jefferson returns the glass, she swallows its contents in a gulp. He pours himself a second glass. "You must have been so frightened," he says.

Her eyes grow wide for an instant. "I thought—" Again she cannot speak.

"You don't have to say it."

"I thought— What they were saying. I was sure—" Her eyes brim with tears—although they do not fall. Her lips remain motionless in the shape of a word she never speaks.

Thomas Jefferson leans forward, as if he is going to get up, but then he sits upright again, holds out his hand, and she gives him the tiny tumbler. The cognac has made her feel better. Less afraid. More herself. When he returns the tumbler to her, she sips it more slowly this time and decides that she likes the taste.

"How did you get away?" Thomas Jefferson asks.

"La dame helped me. La dame with the onion cart and the jerky. She called the man fou and cochon. And when she picked me up off the ground, the crowd called her traîtresse, too. And the man. 'À mort! À mort!' he kept saying. I thought he would—" Sally Hemings looks down at her glass." But la dame said she wasn't afraid of stupid children. 'Crétin!' she said.

Everyone was shouting at her. They all seemed to have gone mad. But then she picked me up and helped me walk out of the market. And no one did anything or followed us. They just let us go. None of it made any sense. They just let us go, and they were still shouting when *la dame* bade me good-bye on the next street. I didn't understand any of it. She didn't either."

"These are remarkable times, Sally," says Thomas Jefferson. "Do you know what the *tiers état* is?"

"No."

"It is the French term for common people. The French common people are rising up against their monarch. Our spirit of republicanism is a great wave rolling around the world, and right now it is cresting here in France."

Sally Hemings is quiet. She does not meet Thomas Jefferson's eye, and he realizes he has been insensitive.

"I'm sorry, Sally. I don't mean to imply that what you experienced was not . . . *terrible*. I only hoped that you might . . . I don't know—" Thomas Jefferson falls silent.

There is a long moment during which he wonders if it is time for her to leave.

"But why did the man attack me?" she says at last. "I am not the king. I am not a princess or an aristocrat. *Moi aussi, j'appartiens au tiers état.*"

"Perhaps he was only angry. Perhaps he saw your clothes and decided you were the servant of an aristocrat. Though that is still madness. Revolutions become necessary when one people is oppressed by another. But that does not mean they are an unalloyed good. There is no such thing as moral purity in history. Even the most beneficent of revolutions necessarily entails injustice and the shedding of innocent blood. Our one consolation during moments like this is that they shall be followed by the dawning of a better world—" He cuts himself off, once again feeling he has been insensitive. "I am terribly, terribly sorry, however, that you should have suffered as you did today. I feel as if it is my fault."

Sally Hemings looks Thomas Jefferson straight in the eye. "Why?"

He is blushing. He shrugs. "Mrs. Adams and Captain Ramsey both thought that you should have returned to Virginia straight from London, and . . . Well, I, too, have often thought that would have been better—"

"I am glad I stayed here," says Sally Hemings. She is still looking Thomas Jefferson straight in the eye. "I have become a different person in Paris, and I am glad of it."

Thomas Jefferson is standing up. A restlessness has come into his legs and eyes. "I am very happy to hear that, Sally. Still, I think it might be best if you did not go to the market alone for the next week or so. I doubt that these difficulties will last very long. But caution is advisable for the time being. Venture outside only in the company of another servant. I'll speak to Petit about it immediately."

Sally Hemings is standing up. She puts her tumbler down on Thomas Jefferson's desk. "Thank you. That *did* help me feel better." She smiles but avoids Thomas Jefferson's gaze. "Well, I better let Jimmy know about the onions."

Thomas Jefferson continues to stand behind his desk for a long moment after she leaves, his smile gradually fading. He takes his frock coat off the hook behind the door. His work is done for the day. It is time to see what is happening in the streets.

A day has passed. Sally Hemings is standing in the doorway to Thomas Jefferson's study, but so silently that he doesn't notice until she draws her breath to speak. "Mr. Jefferson," she says, softly but emphatically. She looks stunned. Her eyes are wide but focused on nothing. The rest of her face seems frozen.

"Are you all right, Sally?" he says. "Is something wrong?"

"I need to talk to you."

"Certainly." Thomas Jefferson has been writing a letter. He wipes the tip of his quill with a rag and flips shut the top of his inkwell. "Sit down." He gestures at the chair in front of his desk.

"No, thank you."

He places a piece of blotting paper atop the letter he has been writing and smooths it down with the side of his fist.

Sally Hemings has taken a couple of steps into the room, and when he looks at her, she takes a couple more, but not toward him, only away from the door.

"What is the matter?" he says.

She swallows. And when she speaks, her voice is trembling. "I have something to say."

"All right." He folds his hands on top of his desk, in part to conceal his own slight trembling. When she doesn't speak, he asks, "What is it?"

"I have been struggling with my conscience." She is silent a long moment, then takes a deep breath. "And I have realized that I must . . . that unless I tell you—"

Her words cut off as if she has been grabbed by the throat. Her wide eyes and still face express something closer to fear.

"Go ahead, Sally," Thomas Jefferson says softly, his own throat going dry. "What is it you have to say?"

"I have to tell you that you shouldn't—"

Again she stops, looking so frightened and lost.

Her face hardens. "I have to tell you," she says, "that—" Another pause, but this time she is only gathering strength. Her words come all in a burst. "I will never forgive you for what you did."

A tremor runs through her whole body, and then she is looking at him with a fierce alertness.

For reasons that Thomas Jefferson does not comprehend, he is glad at what she has said. He has stopped trembling.

"You are perfectly justified," he says at last. "I neither deserve nor expect your forgiveness. But I am sorry. Very sorry."

Sally Hemings continues to stare into his eyes, breathing heavily—and looking utterly beautiful. She says nothing.

"I don't expect you to accept my apology," he says. "I only want you to know what I feel."

Once again her words come in a burst. "Why did you do it?"

Thomas Jefferson gasps. "Hah!"

"Why are you laughing?"

"I'm sorry. I was just surprised."

Sally Hemings has taken another step toward the center of the room.

"I had no good reason," he says. "I was a fool. And I had had too much wine. Also . . ." He looks away from her, picks up his quill and gives it a turn. Then he puts it back on its tray, looks at her and shrugs. "The most foolish thing of all, I suppose, is that I hoped that you might"—he looks away again—"welcome my . . . attentions."

When he looks back at her, her expression has softened, though she is still looking him straight in the eyes. Her voice is so quiet he can hardly hear it.

"I didn't."

"I know."

They look into each other's eyes for a long moment. Then Sally Hemings turns her gaze toward a framed map of France on the wall.

"Perhaps you had better go, Sally," he says.

"Yes, Mr. Jefferson."

She is gone from the room in three steps.

The air in the ballroom is dense with the odors of meat, burning whale oil and male sweat. More than twenty men are gathered at the round table at the center of the round room, the majority of them standing and all of them shouting. They are also consuming prodigious quantities of duck, salmon and potatoes—new plates of which Sally Hemings and the other servants are constantly ferrying into the room (the entire staff of the Hôtel has been impressed into service for this meeting, including Monsieur Petit), and, of course, the men are also emptying dozens of bottles of Bordeaux.

This morning Monsieur Petit told the staff that a very important meeting would be occurring at the Hôtel that night, that the most courageous and brilliant men in all of France would be coming to discuss matters of utmost importance "to the future of humanity." He did not say what those matters might be, but as Sally Hemings has moved among the men carrying bottles and trays, she gathers that they are intending some sort of confrontation with the king, and she wonders—though she hardly dares to hope that this might be true—if this meeting isn't like the ones that Thomas Jefferson attended in Philadelphia when she was a baby and that led to the Revolution. The thought that she might be a witness to a great moment of history fills her with an intense excitement that expresses itself as a buoyant sense of well-being—as if she has gotten mildly intoxicated on the fumes of the wine she's been pouring.

Most of the men are crowded at one end of the table, where an old man whose wig rests crookedly on his bald head sits, flanked by candelabras, plume in hand, and occasionally transcribes phrases shouted to him by one or more of the men. The Marquis de Lafayette, standing just behind the old man, sometimes claps his hand on the man's shoulder and gives him commands to write additional phrases or to cross out ones he has already set down. Most of the time, these commands are met by incredulous roars and upraised hands and then a new round of shouting, in which the marquis actively participates, his expression alternating between mischievous delight and the conviction that he is surrounded by imbeciles.

Apart from the elderly scrivener, Thomas Jefferson is the quietest man in the room. He stands beside the marquis, his arms folded tightly across his chest, although his right hand does clutch a wineglass. Every now and then, the marquis will move his mouth close to Thomas Jefferson's ear and they will confer behind a cupped hand. Some of the other men standing around him also address remarks to him or ask questions, but none of his responses are audible above the cacophony. Sally Hemings can't help but feel disappointed that he is not taking a more active role in this important discussion. She feels that he is letting himself down and worries that his moment in history may have passed.

At one point late in the evening, as she is walking down the dark corridor from the kitchen, a bottle of wine in each hand, she hears that the room has gone silent and that Thomas Jefferson is speaking. She stops just inside the door, in the wavery brown dimness, far from the lamps and candles on the table.

He is one of the tallest men in the room, and seems even taller standing next to the much smaller marquis, yet his stature seems diminished by a vagueness in his eyes, as if he can't actually see the people he is addressing, and his voice is pitched higher than normal and sounds thin.

All at once Sally Hemings realizes that he is afraid.

"*Le premier principe doit être que tous les hommes sont créés égaux,*" he says. "*Tous les droits découlent de cela.*"

He is quoting his own writing: "All men are created equal." Is he doing that because he is nervous? Do the other people notice? Do they think he is a fool for repeating a phrase they must all have heard a thousand times?

She looks around the room. A couple of men just in front of her are murmuring to each other, but she can't hear well enough to tell if there is anything derisive in their tone. The faces of the other people in the room are unreadable masks. There is a snakelike fixity in the shining eyes of the marquis. Is that his way of trying to hide his embarrassment? Or could it be an expression of his anger that Thomas Jefferson is making a fool of them both?

Sally Hemings cannot move from her spot by the door until Thomas Jefferson, after a pause that reminds her of nothing so much as that of an old man who has forgotten what he meant to say, closes his mouth, looks down and shrugs, and then the men around the table begin to cheer and applaud. The applause isn't so loud that it might not just be polite, but then she sees that a shy, happy smile has come onto Thomas Jefferson's face. He suppresses the smile, looks up at the crowd and says, *"Nous avons encore beaucoup de travail à faire!"*—sparking a new surge of applause.

To Sally Hemings's utter surprise, her eyes fill with tears.

A short time later, when she is pouring more wine for Lafayette, he grabs hold of her hand and says, *"Merci, ma jolie Sarah!* This is a very good night! You must get your friend Mr. Jefferson to tell you what we are doing." As he lets go of her hand, he gives it a light squeeze and he smiles at her, his eyes flaring with excitement. "I think the world is changing tonight!"

She glances toward Thomas Jefferson, and, finding that he is already looking right at her, she has to turn her head away. But when she looks back, she manages to hold his gaze just long enough not to appear self-conscious—or so she hopes. "Would you like some more wine, Mr. Jefferson?"

He smiles warmly and holds out his glass. "Thank you, Sally."

Hours later, as Sally Hemings and Anne are clearing the abandoned table, Thomas Jefferson walks back into the room after having said good-bye to the last of his guests. He seems thoughtful and contented, if very tired.

Anne fills her tray with clinking glasses and walks toward the corridor to the kitchen. Sally Hemings deliberately slows down her collection of glasses but doesn't look in Thomas Jefferson's direction until Anne has left the room.

He gives her a weary smile. "I'm sorry to have made so much work for you, especially so late at night."

She shrugs and makes a smilelike crinkle of her mouth. She doesn't know what to say.

His smile fades. He takes a step backward, as if he is ready to leave the room.

"Has the world changed?" she asks.

"I don't know." He pauses thoughtfully, and then his smile returns. "What do you think?"

"It doesn't look much different to me," she says. "Maybe a bit messier."

Thomas Jefferson laughs, and Sally Hemings can't stop herself from laughing, too. After a moment he says, "Do you know what we were doing here tonight?"

"Well . . . apart from eating, drinking and shouting, not really."

"We've been putting together a French document that is a lot like our own Bill of Rights, about which Mr. Madison and I have been corresponding so much lately."

Sally Hemings has heard Thomas Jefferson talk about the Bill of Rights, but she isn't entirely clear what it is.

"So what does the document say?"

"Well, it starts out by saying, more or less, that all men are created equal. It also says that liberty is the freedom to do everything that will injure no one else."

"Oh." She looks away, unsure why Thomas Jefferson has chosen to refer to that very awkward night.

"So you see, Sally, that you, too, played a role in what happened here tonight."

She is blushing. Her ears go hot. "I didn't."

"I don't know about that," says Thomas Jefferson. "I think that the marquis has had you in mind often as he has contemplated the issue of individual liberty."

"I don't think that's true." She is still blushing. "Anyhow, I didn't do anything."

"You're too modest."

"No I'm not."

"Yes you are," he says firmly.

She has been looking down at her tray, but when she raises her eyes, she sees that Thomas Jefferson is looking at her with a smile that is both weary and tender.

"You make a very good impression on people," he says. "I think you should know that."

1. Men are born and remain free and equal in rights. Social distinctions may be founded only upon the general good.

2. The aim of all political association is the preservation of the natural and imprescriptible rights of man. These rights are liberty, property, security, and resistance to oppression.

3. The principle of all sovereignty resides essentially in the nation. No body nor individual may exercise any authority which does not proceed directly from the nation.

4. Liberty consists in the freedom to do everything which injures no one else; hence the exercise of the natural rights of each man has no limits except those which assure to the other members of the society the enjoyment of the same rights. . . .

> —From the Declaration of the Rights of
> Man and of the Citizen, introduced at
> the National Assembly by the Marquis
> de Lafayette on July 11, 1789

. . . What I am trying to do here is simply pin down the process by which I became complicit in the crime that has brought so much misery to the people I have known and loved—many of them for all of my life. And it becomes ever clearer to me that it happened by a process of twilit thinking—by thoughts behind the thoughts I was aware of, thoughts—and feelings, too—that I could ignore or even pretend I had never had, thoughts whose immorality and gross impracticality might have been blatantly obvious had I ever had the courage or wisdom to drag them into the full light of my awareness. . . .

Near noon on a Sunday morning, Sally Hemings is walking home after having escorted Patsy and Polly back to school. It has rained, and although she is carrying an umbrella, the skirt of her gown is wet and hangs heavily against her knees and shins. The clouds have parted. The sun is brilliant white. Leaves on the treetops hiss and turn up their pale undersides in fierce gusts. Bits of blown grit sting her cheek and make her squint.

She is walking along the road between the Tuileries and the Seine when she notices a gentleman about twenty yards ahead running toward the bank of the river. The wind flips his hat off as he runs, and, turning an ungainly pirouette, he grabs it off the ground and resumes running to the edge of the quay. Only once he has stopped does she realize that the man is Thomas Jefferson. Slump-shouldered, he stares down at the water, and then his right arm twitches, as if he were uttering a curse—though Sally Hemings can hear nothing. She comes up beside him just as he is turning away from the river.

"Oh, Sally!" he exclaims. She has startled him.

"What happened?"

His mouth puckers unhappily. He points behind her, at a wooden box—his writing desk—atop a low wall on the far side of the road. "I was doing a drawing, and I'd nearly finished when I stopped to sharpen my pencil, and then a gust of wind picked the drawing up and flipped it end over end into the river." He turns and points. "There—you see?"

A piece of foolscap rises and falls on the waves, not far from a man rowing a small boat.

"You could ask the man to get it," she says.

"It's not worth it. The drawing is ruined." He turns away from the river and shrugs resignedly.

"I'm sorry," she says.

His eyes meet hers long enough for her to feel an uncomfortable warmth pass through her breast and into her throat. She looks back at the rapidly flowing water. The foolscap is now one hundred feet downstream.

"It's all right," he says. "I can do another. It wasn't good anyway." He puts his hat on his head and crosses the road toward his writing desk. Sally Hemings follows.

"I hate to lose things," she says.

"I do, too."

"No, I'm ridiculous about it. Sometimes, when I'm coming back from the *marché* or from the school, I kick a stone along the street, and if I manage to kick it all the way home with me, I can't bear to leave it outside. I feel as if I am abandoning an old friend!"

Thomas Jefferson makes a small laugh. "What do you do?"

"I take it inside with me. I have a box up in my chamber full of stones."

He laughs again, heartily. "You have such a tender heart, Sally."

She smiles, blushing. "It's stupid."

"Not at all."

They are standing beside his writing desk. He picks up a pencil lying against the bottom edge of the desk's sloped top and puts it into a chamois sack. His penknife is lying in the dust at her feet. Sally Hemings picks it up and hands it to him. He puts that into the sack.

"Thank you," he says.

"It's stupid to care so much about a stone," she says.

"On the contrary, I think that shows how engaged with life you are and how generous you are with your affections. In my experience most people are so lazy, hurried or frightened that they close themselves off to life. That's such a waste of our brief time on this earth."

Thomas Jefferson is smiling with an almost paternal tenderness that embarrasses Sally Hemings. She is momentarily flustered.

"Well, I don't know," she says at last. "It seems to me that we should only care about little things a little bit and save our real feelings for the most important things."

"Perhaps . . ." Thomas Jefferson is still smiling. "But theologians say that God cares as much for the death of a sparrow as he does for the destruction of a city."

Now Sally Hemings is the one to laugh.

"Why are you laughing?" asks Thomas Jefferson.

"I shouldn't say."

He flips open the top of his portable desk and puts the chamois sack inside, then tucks the desk under his arm. "Why not?"

"I just shouldn't."

They are walking now, back toward place Louis XV and home. The brilliant sun heats the paving and the tops of their heads, but a mountainscape of white and slate gray clouds is advancing over the trees of the Champs-Élysées.

"But I want to know what you think," says Thomas Jefferson.

"Well . . . I don't know. . . . That just doesn't make any sense to me."

Thomas Jefferson grunts. "I'd forgotten what a skeptic you are!"

"To me it just seems insane that God would feel exactly the same about the death of thousands of people as he does about one dirty little bird."

"Well, perhaps I've phrased it badly. I think what theologians say is that God's heart breaks for the death of a sparrow as well as for the destruction of a city."

"That's just as insane."

"Not really. What we are talking about is *feeling*, not rational evaluation. The theologians want to draw our attention to the beauty—the *moral* beauty—of the all-powerful creator of the universe being heartbroken at the death of a dirty little bird. Don't you find that beautiful?"

"What I want to know," says Sally Hemings, "is if God feels so bad about the death of a little bird, why does he kill it? And it's the same with destroying cities."

"That's the big mystery, of course. But still there's the beauty. It seems to me that the idea of a God caring for a creature as insignificant and humble as a sparrow has a beauty all by itself—maybe in part because it teaches the lesson that all things of this world are important—political revolutions, great works of art, falling in love, dirty little birds and even stones one kicks home on the street."

"But what I was saying is that I *don't* care about everything. I care much more about some little gray stone than I do about half the beggars I see on the street. In fact, I *hate* some of those beggars and can't bear to look at them. That's what I meant by stupid."

"I'm sure that's not true."

"Oh, yes it is."

"But even the fact that you feel bad about hating beggars proves the point I am making. Think about Christ's injunction to love our enemies. I find that a supremely beautiful moral challenge. It may not be possible for us to truly love our enemies, but the suggestion that we *ought* to love them can help guide us in life, especially if we think that what it really means is that we should try to understand our enemies, to see the world from their point of view and, most of all, to understand that they are human beings, struggling in a hard and confusing world, just as we are, and that their fundamental rights are exactly equal to ours. They may not do the right things or think the right things, but that does not mean they are inhuman or should be treated so. I think Christ's injunction is, in fact, the foundation of all morality."

"Well, I don't know about all that. But I do know that it's not possible to love your enemy. And so saying that impossible things are beautiful makes about as much sense to me as crying over a stone."

"But you *do* cry over a stone."

"And that's stupid."

"You don't think there is anything good about tenderheartedness?"

"It's good to be tenderhearted to your children. And to your mother."

"Not to your father?" Thomas Jefferson smiles wryly.

"Your father, too." Sally Hemings laughs. "But only if he is a *good* father!"

Thomas Jefferson also laughs. But after only a few seconds, their smiles fade.

They have crossed place Louis XV and are walking amid the colonnades of trees bordering the Champs-Élysées. The sky straight overhead is crystalline blue, but the sun has been obscured by the clouds. The air has grown distinctly cooler, and the wind is continuous. There is a sound in the tops of the trees like air being sucked through teeth.

After a couple of minutes, during which they only stroll, never even exchanging a glance, Sally Hemings speaks. "Mr. Jefferson, might I ask you a question?"

"Certainly."

"You knew my father well, didn't you?"

The center of Thomas Jefferson's brow furrows. It is a while before he says, "I am not sure."

Understanding that he is only trying to be discreet, Sally Hemings's throat tightens. She feels a prickling of sweat at her temples and in her armpits. She, too, should be discreet—all the more so because she is a servant. And yet she is so curious to hear what Thomas Jefferson might have thought of this man of whom she has no memory.

"I know who he was," she says at last. "My mother told me."

"Oh." Seeming both surprised and embarrassed, Thomas Jefferson falls silent, and Sally Hemings decides to let the topic drop. But after a couple of moments, he says, "Yes, I knew him, but not as well—or as *long*, I should say—as I would have liked."

"Can you tell me about him?"

Thomas Jefferson is silent another extended moment. "He was a good man, and very capable. You would have had every reason to be proud of him." Thomas Jefferson falls silent again, an indecisive expression on his face.

After a moment Sally Hemings asks, "Is there something else?"

"He was a spirited man, and possessed of many powerful enthusiasms. But like all men, he had his weaknesses. . . . And beyond that I do not feel qualified to speak."

They traverse the length of the Champs-Élysées in silence, except one time when Thomas Jefferson points to a magpie and says, "That is the only animal, apart from the human race, that can recognize itself in a mirror"—a remark that Sally Hemings responds to with only a grunt.

At the Chaillot Gate, immediately beyond which they can see a southern wall of the Hôtel de Langeac, Thomas Jefferson stops and turns to face Sally Hemings.

"Miss Hemings, there is something on my mind that I suspect I should keep to myself, but . . . Well, I can only hope that it might actually be better for you and . . . for both of us . . . if I speak. . . ."

Sally Hemings looks down at the toes of his black boots on the yellow sand and waits for him to continue.

". . . I simply want you to know that despite my unforgivable behavior several weeks ago, I have the utmost respect for you. You are a charming and very intelligent young woman, and I regret deeply that my utter foolishness might have led you to believe I had any other opinion."

Sally Hemings allows her gaze to meet his for half an instant before she says, "Thank you."

. . . I could have said no to Mr. Jefferson. Even at sixteen, when I knew so little of him, I still understood this essential fact. If I had said no, emphatically, and on every occasion when he first began to broach his intentions, he would have respected my virtue, both because he himself was ashamed of his desires, particularly when he considered the feelings of his daughters and dearest friends, and because, as ardently carnal as his nature might have been, he was ultimately less interested in sensual pleasure than in love. This was one of his greatest weaknesses. He craved adoration, not just of the people he knew but, in a very real sense, of the entire world—which was why he couldn't stay away from politics, even though he detested political life.

But I didn't say no—"no," of course, being a word Negroes simply never speak to white people. That said, I could easily have conveyed my feelings without having to actually speak the word. I could have pretended, for example, to be indifferent to his small kindnesses and continual readiness to engage in conversation. Had I done so, then none of the events that now seem a poison in my soul would have come to pass. The difficult relations that followed his having come into my bedchamber would certainly have continued a while longer, but I still would have been his daughters' maid throughout the remainder of our time in Paris and, most likely, at Monticello as well.

And what is more, even had I rejected him when his expressions of desire became more emphatic and overt, I knew that the worst I would have had to suffer would have been life as a scullery maid or a washerwoman. Mr. Jefferson would never have sold me away from my family or subjected me to any form of severe punishment. Had he done so, he would have had to face the fact that his supposed love for me was a sentimental sham and that he was as capable as the most brutal slaveholder of acting out of revenge, cruelty and spite. It was essential to Mr. Jefferson's self-esteem that he believe himself to be nothing like the majority of his neighbors. . . .

One morning, as Sally Hemings is walking past Thomas Jefferson's study on her way to the kitchen, he calls out, "Mademoiselle Sally!" And when she looks in his door, he says, "I've been thinking. . . ." He makes a circular gesture with his hand. "Come in! Come in!" She takes a step inside the door but goes no farther, and he does not insist. "I've been thinking," he says, "that you have too good a mind to be so entirely unlettered. What's happened with Jimmy? Has he been teaching you to read and write?"

"Not really."

"Did you ask him?"

"I did, but he didn't seem very interested." She sighs. "I think he doesn't see the point of a girl learning to read."

Thomas Jefferson slaps his hand down on the table. "That's absurd! Go ask him again. And if he continues to be so contrary, you must tell him that I order him to teach you reading and writing."

Four or five times over the next several days, Thomas Jefferson asks Sally Hemings if she has commenced her reading lessons, and on each occasion her answer is the same, that her brother has agreed to teach her but that he never seems to have the time. "Nonsense!" Thomas Jefferson invariably replies. "All you need is fifteen minutes a day. He must have fifteen minutes!"

But then one day, when Sally Hemings gives him the same report, he says, "Well, I suppose *I've* got fifteen minutes. Come by the parlor after you have finished your duties, and let's see what we can do."

S ally Hemings finishes her labors at 9:00 P.M. and arrives at the parlor to find that Thomas Jefferson actually went out that day to buy her a primer, which he has placed open on the same table where he showed her how to write her name. There are two chairs beside the table, so close to each other that she could barely fit her fingers between them. The table is lit with a candelabra and an oil lamp.

Thomas Jefferson commences by going through the alphabet letter by letter, explaining the possible sounds that each might make. When it becomes clear that she is confused by all the variations, he assures her that it will be much clearer when she actually tries to read.

The primer consists of twenty-six rhymed couplets, each featuring a different letter of the alphabet. He begins by reading aloud several of the easier ones—those without biblical or classical names in them. First he reads the couplet and then goes through it a second time, making the sound of each letter as he passes a pen point underneath it. The sounds he makes, especially as he exaggerates them for clarity, are nothing like English, and Sally Hemings cannot help laughing. "You sound like you're talking in your sleep!" she says.

Thomas Jefferson also laughs. "I'll get my revenge when it's your turn!"

And, indeed, when he asks her to read "Whales in the sea / God's voice obey," the only words she manages to read on her own are "in" and "God's" and even those require a lot of help. By the time they have decoded the couplet together, she is exhausted and embarrassed.

"It takes time," says Thomas Jefferson, smiling. "You'll catch on after a while."

"Maybe it would be easier if the words weren't so silly," she says.

His brows buckle. "My dear Miss Hemings, I am beginning to suspect you are something of an atheist."

"A what?"

"An atheist. Someone who doesn't believe in God."

"Oh." She is not entirely sure he is joking. "Why do you say that?"

"Because you have laughed at every one of the religious couplets!"

He is smiling. She smiles, too.

"That's because they are so funny. What language does God speak to fish? Bubble language? And what does he say, 'Thou shalt love the man with the harpoon'?"

Thomas Jefferson leans back in his chair and tugs on the bottom of his waistcoat as if he has just finished a good meal. He looks her straight in the eyes—his own coppery bright in candlelight. "So you *do* believe in God?" he asks.

"Yes," she says. "I think so." She is worried that she shouldn't have spoken so freely, that she might come off as impious, but Thomas Jefferson seems pleased by her remarks.

"Do you believe that God is good?" he asks.

"Perhaps. In his heart."

"What do you mean?"

"I mean God wants to be good. And he tries to be good. And he is good a lot of the time. He made this beautiful world, after all. He made babies. He made sunsets and roses. But he also makes mistakes. He created diseases. Earthquakes. He made it possible for people to be cruel. People are cruel all the time."

"But is that God's fault? Or are people alone to blame?"

Thomas Jefferson continues to look at her intently, a slight smile on only one half of his face. Sally Hemings blushes.

"You must think what I am saying is stupid," she says.

"Not at all. In fact, I have just been reading a dialogue by an eminent philosopher who seems to share your opinions, though he is not nearly so forthright."

Her blush intensifies, and her right ear goes hot.

Thomas Jefferson smiles, leans forward and lifts his hand in her direction, but then he draws it back and folds his arms across his chest. "So what do you think: Is God the cause of cruelty?"

"Well . . ." For a moment Sally Hemings doesn't know what to say, but then her original point comes back to her: "The preachers are always saying that God controls everything. And that he knows all, sees all. So if that's true, then God is making people do cruel things, and so their cruelty is God's fault. But that's the thing I'm not sure I believe. I can't believe that God would intentionally make people do cruel things. So maybe God *doesn't* control everything. And people do cruel things on their own. But even if that is true, I still think that God is partly to blame, since he put the ability to be cruel into human beings."

"Why would he do that?"

"I don't know. It doesn't really make sense. That's what I mean about mistakes. Maybe God wasn't paying attention when he made people. Or he didn't think it all the way through." She glances at Thomas Jefferson, then looks away. "Or maybe he was just in a bad mood."

"That makes him sound a lot like a human being."

"I suppose. Except that he can do so much more than a human being can. He's just not perfect."

"But if he's not perfect, then why worship him?"

"Because he made so many beautiful things, too. How could I not be thankful for those things? But maybe 'worship' is the wrong word. Maybe all I really feel is thankful. Though sometimes I'm also angry and disappointed." She looks down into her lap, where she is massaging the center of her left palm with the thumb of her right hand. She glances up and shrugs. "But I probably shouldn't say that."

Thomas looks at her a long moment, then speaks in a measured voice. "I think everything you are saying is extremely courageous and rational."

Sally Hemings does not know how to respond.

"Do you believe in the Devil?" Thomas Jefferson asks.

"I don't know. I mean, of course, that could explain why bad things happen. God and the Devil are fighting over everything. But I don't know, I find it harder to believe that someone would want only terrible things. That just seems too pointless to me. If I think about the Devil, if I really try to imagine him existing, he ends up seeming a lot like God—or a human being. Someone with good and bad sides. Good and bad moods. Maybe wanting to do right but also wanting other things. So . . . The main thing is that I don't see the point in there being a Devil . . . or in there being two mixed-up magical people controlling the universe. So it makes more sense that there be only one. God."

"Why not only the Devil?"

"I do think that sometimes, but it scares me, so I hope that I'm wrong. But on the other hand, if the Devil is running the world, he's still made all the beautiful things, so maybe he's just like God, and not that scary after all."

"Do you ever think that there may be no God?"

"Sometimes. But how could this world just be here? Someone had to create it."

"You could ask the same question about God. How could God just be here? And if it is possible for God to just be here—this being who is infinitely more complex than the earth, since he created it, just as the watchmaker is infinitely more complex than the watch—if it is possible for God to *just be here*, why not the earth?"

An openmouthed half smile comes onto Sally Hemings's face. She shakes her head. "That's an interesting idea. I never thought about that before." Her smile broadens, and she is silent a moment. "I guess the real reason I believe in God is that it makes me feel happier to believe that someone is there, behind everything. And sometimes I feel his presence. Every now and then, when I am in a particularly beautiful place or I am feeling especially sad or afraid, I feel that God is there somehow."

"Does he ever talk to you?"

"No. Not really. I just *feel* that he is there. But I don't know if he really is. Maybe I only feel him because I want to."

Now Thomas Jefferson is the one who seems not to know what to say. He shifts uneasily in his seat.

"What do *you* think about God?" Sally Hemings asks.

"I'm exactly the same as you. Except sometimes I think there is no God, but that God's existence doesn't matter, because we have the idea of God. Or rather, we still have the idea that God is good and that we should also be good. And the idea that we should worship the beauty of the world. And as long as we have such ideas, it almost doesn't matter whether God actually exists."

Sally Hemings makes a small grunt and then thinks for a moment. "The only thing is that I don't see God as good—or good enough. That's my problem."

Thomas Jefferson smiles weakly, but then disconcertion crosses his face. He looks down. He pushes the primer an inch or two away with the tips of his fingers. "I'm sorry, Sally, but I think we had better stop this."

Her forehead darkens, and her mouth falls open. He sees that he has hurt her.

"You must think I'm an idiot," she says.

"No! Not in the least. You have nothing to apologize for—on the contrary."

She closes the primer. "I'm sorry I have been such a bad learner. It's just that there are so many letters and sounds."

"That's not it," he says, still looking away. "I have enjoyed our time tonight."

He casts her a furtive glance, and all at once she becomes aware that their calves are not more than an inch apart. She thinks that she should move her leg away from his, but she doesn't. Instead, in a soft voice, she asks, "Then why?"

"I just think it would be better if Jimmy taught you after all. I will speak to him myself. It's his duty as your older brother."

"He won't do it. Jimmy's not like that. He just won't."

Thomas Jefferson throws himself back in his chair. Half in despair, half in entreaty, he says, "Oh, Sally."

"What?"

"I shouldn't say this."

She remains silent.

"You are so beautiful," he says. "You are utterly beautiful, you have an excellent mind, you are so kind and full of life—but this is impossible. I had thought that I would be able to keep my feelings within the bounds of decency, but I was—" He cuts himself off, looks at her with sad and yearning eyes. "Oh, you dear girl!"

After a moment he sits up and tugs once again at the bottom of his waistcoat.

"So I think you had better leave, Sally. For your own good. I'm terribly, terribly sorry. I will talk to Jimmy. Or maybe Patsy. Perhaps *she* could be your teacher. But if neither is willing, I will hire you a tutor. I am determined that you shall read."

Sally Hemings feels as if something is spinning inside her head. She stands and speaks breathlessly, almost whispering. "Thank you, Mr. Jefferson."

Thomas Jefferson squeezes his lips together. His face is red, but the skin about his lips is yellow. His eyes look enormous. As Sally Hemings puts her hand on the latch of the door, he calls out her name. Then he says, "Please understand that this has nothing to do with you. You are a darling, darling girl and entirely innocent of blame. I am the one who is enslaved by feelings he ought never to have conceived."

Sally Hemings lifts the latch and leaves.

. . . I knew I could say no—and yet I didn't. My reasons were shameful and obvious. I was vain. I was weak. I had been the baby of my family and, of course, nothing more than a poor colored serving girl—a slave. No one had ever listened to what I had to say. As a child, whenever I had ventured to speak some idea I might have had while wandering in the woods, my mother would laugh and tell me my head was "stuffed with foolishness." My brothers and sisters just told me I was stupid—and I really was stupid around children my own age. My jokes always seemed obvious; my insults seemed to have been translated from another language. I would rehearse them inside my mind, but the words never came out in the right order.

But there was something about the quality of Mr. Jefferson's attention that made me eloquent. Even when I was swooning in disbelief that such an important man was listening to me, I was still able to speak what I actually thought. And, of course, the fact that he didn't laugh, that he took seriously what I had to say, that he constantly drew out more of my thoughts, proffered his own and wanted to know what I made of them—all of this filled me with such exhilaration that I would have to work to calm myself, sometimes for hours afterward. And this was true, even in those instants when I suspected that he was condescending to me. (At sixteen I hardly dared expect more than condescension from a man of Mr. Jefferson's stature.) I was always a little afraid in conversation with him, but it was the best sort of fear, the kind that inspired me to make the most of my abilities. The truth is that I don't think I had ever felt so completely myself—the self I most wished to be—as when he and I were talking.

I was much less easy regarding that other aspect of Mr. Jefferson's attention, but I cannot say that it, too, did not also work a sort of glamour upon me. I had always seen myself as gawky and ratlike and thought I could never compare with the beauty of my two older sisters—Thenia especially, who was tall, graceful and possessed of all the female attributes most attractive to the male *eye and who had always seemed entirely delighted by the attentions of boys and young men. Not only had I never received such attention, but in Paris, where the fact that I was a slave made me an* objet de scandale, *I had been the target of disparaging remarks about my supposedly African features, and once an extremely handsome young man had subjected me to a torrent of barbarous and filthy adjectives, most of them appended to the nouns* "négresse" *and* "noir." *And so it was hard for me not to feel flattered by Mr. Jefferson's adoration, even as I was also frightened and disgusted.*

Thus I didn't say no. I would smile and nod at Mr. Jefferson's greetings; I would blushingly accept his offers of chocolate or apricot preserves; I would talk to him for as long as he would seem interested in talking to me and feel grateful for every instant; and when he told me that he wanted to teach me to read, I came at the appointed time, even though I knew in advance that I would be sitting so close to him that I would have to concentrate to avoid brushing his arm with my own or letting my knee fall against his. . . .

Sally Hemings is sleeping. She has been turning over and over in her bed. Her shift is twisted around her waist, and her ankles are twisted in her sheets. A minute ago—maybe two—she tugged one of the top corners of her sheet up to her throat, but now her hand lies limply on her breast and the corner of the sheet curls like a stilled wave beneath her fingertips. Odd noises are coming out of her throat, toneless bird squeaks. She is dreaming of Thomas Jefferson. She is dreaming that he has taken hold of her hand and is licking her palm, again and again. She can feel the slick wetness of his tongue and its warmth. His tongue is exceedingly large, so large she cannot imagine how he will ever be able to get it back into his mouth. When his tongue has finished licking her palm and every one of her fingers, it moves to her wrist and then forearm. When it touches that soft, blue-veined hollow on the inside of her elbow, she awakes with a start. She is gasping in the night. Her eyes are wide open, but she sees nothing at all.

The servants' stairway lets out onto the hallway just outside the upstairs parlor, and every night on her way to her bedchamber on the third floor, Sally Hemings has to walk past the parlor door. One night Thomas Jefferson looks up from his reading and sees her standing in the doorway, candle in hand. As soon as their eyes meet, she makes a tiny noise and is gone.

On another night he looks up and she is standing in the doorway again. He looks at her for what seems a very long time, but she doesn't move.

"I'm sorry, Mr. Jefferson."

"Is something wrong, Sally?"

She doesn't answer. She is as still as a painting of herself. He wonders if she is looking at him. He tries to determine where her eyes are focused. One instant he thinks she is looking at him, the next instant no. Her eyes glitter in the firelight.

"Not really," she says. "I just wanted to say good night."

"Good night, Sally."

. . . *All the while I told myself that Mr. Jefferson's struggle with his darker nature was entirely sincere and that he was sure to win, because he so thoroughly regretted what he had attempted that night, now months in the past, and he entirely understood how frightened I had been. But even as I worked so hard to deceive myself, I understood that the longer I failed to say no, the more my silence would come to seem like assent and that if I remained silent too long, my apparent assent would ultimately make this dreaded eventuality inevitable.*

Every night when I lay in bed, I would remember the weight of Mr. Jefferson's huge body lying on top of me and his smell—repulsive in memory—filling my nostrils. I would go rigid all over again, and cold with dread. Often I would surge upright amid my covers or even leap out of bed and pace the floor, devising elaborate speeches to Mr. Jefferson, in which I insisted upon my virtue and condemned his dishonorable inclinations.

And yet when I would once more be lying with my covers to my chin, my mind would race with assertions that directly contradicted my imaginary speeches. I would remind myself that this eventuality I so feared was the signal act of womanhood, that far from loathing it, many women smile with a private satisfaction as they talk about it or laugh loudly. My own mother made no secret of her enjoyment of what she always called "a little poke." She had had three husbands in addition to my father, and at the time I was leaving for France, she seemed to be contemplating a fourth. I could hardly imagine ever feeling as my mother and so many other women so obviously did, and I could only assume that, in my profound ignorance, I was unaware of something essential in the carnal act—the very thing that evoked those loud laughs and private smiles. There were times, in fact, when I would despair at what I took to be my utter unfitness for womanhood.

I simply could not stop such bewildering suppositions from streaming through my brain. I had absolutely no intentions of ever acting upon them, but still they filled my head, leaving me deeply confused and afraid.

It is also true, however—and this strikes me now as loathsome and pathetic—that I did sometimes think that if I were only able to endure whatever it was that Mr. Jefferson wanted of me, I might one day, like my sister, become his wife. . . .

Thomas Jefferson looks up from his book when he hears Sally Hemings's footsteps on the stairs. As her candle comes into view just outside the door, he calls, "Good evening, Sally."

She stops and smiles, something in the way the powdery gold of the candlelight falls upon her cheek and gleams in her eyes making her look so like Martha that he feels a sudden falling in his chest that is both sorrow and yearning.

"Good evening, Mr. Jefferson."

"Everything all cleaned up downstairs?"

"Yes, at last." She has taken a step into the room and is standing just inside the door frame. She seems faintly distracted, maybe restless. Her eyes dart about the room.

"I hope you are not too tired."

She crumples her lips and gives the ceiling a comically askew glance. "Oh, no. Not too tired. But it will be good to sleep."

"Good," he says. "Thank you."

She smiles and looks embarrassed . . . or maybe not embarrassed. He has the feeling that if he asked her to come into the room and sit down, she would.

"Sally?" he says.

"Yes." She is waiting for him to speak, her smile maybe slightly hesitant, her eyebrow lifted, alert. Again he feels that falling of sorrow and yearning.

"Oh, well," he says. "Never mind."

She looks at him quizzically a second but doesn't say anything.

"Good night, Sally."

"Good night, Mr. Jefferson."

As she turns and leaves, he feels that he has disappointed her.

Then he is on his feet and hurrying toward the door, where he sees her receding along the dark corridor, her sage green gown deepening toward hemlock, then black, her head silhouetted against the wavering glow of her candle. In an instant she will reach the stairs, turn and be gone.

He knows that he should go back to his chair by the fire and continue to read (a treatise on flight in birds), but something has just happened between him and this beautiful girl, something totally unexpected. He tells himself he is mistaken. Nothing has happened. It couldn't have. But it did happen. He knows it did. And he would be a fool to deny it.

He is afraid as he steps into the hallway. Her name is on his lips, but he doesn't speak it, only hurries after her, until with a rush of crinoline she reels around, her eyes wide, her open mouth a warped O.

"I'm sorry," he says, drawing next to her. "I didn't mean—"

"Oh!" She touches her lips with the clutched fingertips of one hand.

"Please excuse me." He feels stupid. He is blushing and is thankful that the corridor is so dark. "I was just wondering . . ." He has no idea what to say. "I'm sorry I startled you."

"I didn't hear you coming." She lowers her hand, open now, to the base of her throat.

"It's my fault. I should have said something."

Sally Hemings's eyes are still wide, though her lips have contracted to a small pucker of uncertainty. She is breathing heavily. He can see her chest rise and fall.

"It's just . . ." He still doesn't know what to say. "There's something I forgot to ask you. I'm wondering if you might come back to the parlor for a moment. It won't take a second."

She swallows. "All right."

He turns and walks back toward the parlor door, which is flickering orange in the firelight. He has no idea what he is going to do, but he is almost certain he will make a fool of himself.

"Do you mind if I close the door?" he asks once she has followed him into the room. He sees that the question disconcerts her, but he closes the door anyway. "It's a personal matter. I think it best if we are not overheard."

She backs against the wall, just beside the door. She looks worried, but so terribly beautiful and alive, like a doe in the instant before it bounds into the forest.

He gestures at the couch just beside her. "Please sit down."

Her head makes a barely detectable shake, and her back remains pressed against the wall. He should tell her to go, but he can't. He just wants to see what will happen. His mouth is dry. He runs his fingers through the hair on the top of his head.

"I don't know how else to do this," he says, "than to be completely honest." He licks his lips. "I know that I behaved like an utter fool . . ." He is silent an instant. ". . . *before*. Worse than a fool."

There is a faint twitch at the corner of her mouth, but he cannot tell what it means.

"As I hope you understand," he says, "I have tried very hard to behave toward you as would be fitting, given the rules of propriety and our stations in life. But as you have probably concluded—no doubt you know this very well right now—I have mostly failed rather miserably."

There is another twitch at the corner of her mouth, just slightly more pronounced, and he allows himself to hope.

"You are so astoundingly beautiful," he says, "and I have fallen completely in love with you. I have tried and tried to resist it, but there is nothing I can do."

All at once that inert expression comes onto her face again: her eyes looking straight ahead, focused in empty air, her lips closed, lightly but with a subtle tension. He is not sure she has even heard him.

"Does that surprise you?" he says.

There is a long silence.

"No." Her voice is soft. She looks into his eyes, then away.

"How does it make you feel?"

"I don't know." She glances at him again.

"You can tell me the truth. I won't be offended. I only want to know how you feel."

Another silence. Then she sighs and says, "I don't know how I feel."

Her gaze moves toward his but then drops to the floor. She has pushed her back against the wall. He has made her afraid.

"I'm sorry, Sally. I've been thoughtless and a fool. Why don't you just go now, and we can pretend that none of this happened."

Her eyes remain on the floor. She doesn't move or speak.

"What are you thinking?" he says.

Once again there is a long silence. Then she sighs and speaks in a voice so soft he almost can't hear. "I still don't know."

He laughs and takes a step back. He wants to put her at ease. He thinks that whatever chance he might have had has passed, and, in fact, he is feeling relieved. Maybe now that he has made his feelings clear, he can finally get past them and there will be nothing more to worry about.

"You are a funny girl," he says.

She is looking at him. "What do you mean?"

He doesn't know why he said that, but he answers, "I just mean that you always know exactly what you want to say, so I am surprised that now you don't."

She smiles. "Some things are just harder to figure out." She shrugs and smiles weakly. She is still looking into his eyes.

All at once Thomas Jefferson realizes that he has not gotten past his feelings, that he never will. Looking into her smiling face, he wants nothing but to pull her into his arms and hold her against the length of his body.

He doesn't know what he is going to do. He doesn't know how he will ever be able to live with her, feeling as he does.

Her smile is gone, but she is still looking into his eyes. Can she possibly understand what is happening inside him?

She doesn't move. Neither does he.

Once again he tells her, "You should probably go." And then he says, "But I am wondering if you might do me a favor."

She doesn't answer. She doesn't look away. She is waiting.

His mouth has gone completely dry again. There is an airy tremble in his voice. "One way we can both find out how you feel is if . . . you let me kiss you."

She lowers her eyes to the floor again and presses her head back against the wall, which has the effect of lifting her lips just slightly toward his.

"Just once," he says. "I promise."

Her eyes are closed now, and she doesn't move or speak.

Her breath smells faintly of garlic and peas. Her lips are soft and warm, but he cannot tell whether she has returned his kiss—and when he finally pulls his head away, he is so overcome with desire he can hardly keep on his feet.

Her eyes are open again, startled-looking. She is still holding her candle, and some of the wax has spilled onto her hand and the floor.

"You'd better go now," he says. "I think it best."

He turns his back and doesn't see her as she opens the door and slips from the room.

The eyeball is as dispassionate as the camera. Spectroscopically speaking, the colors that strike the retina are true. The pale green between the orange and the purple is pale green. It is only in the mind that the pale green becomes gray. Artists depend upon the lies the brain tells the mind to create that muted luminosity of fog out of purple and orange and black and yellow and white, or to turn that cool red, that winter zenith blue, that brown (or is it gold) into the piercing sorrow of joy displaced by loneliness. The eye, like the camera, contains everything within its field of focus, albeit inverted in each of its two dimensions. The magician tucking a card into his cuff is plainly obvious in the eye, though in the mind there is only the card's disappearance from the magician's hand. In the eye the bush on the edge of the campfire glow is clearly just a bush, while in the mind it is making a journey from smoke puff to hovering dove to red dwarf to bush. All too often, however, the mind fixes on the dove or the red dwarf, and that is how the bush will remain in memory for minutes, months or years until the brain goes cold and dark.

Thomas Jefferson does not see Sally Hemings until sometime after eleven the following morning when she passes in front of his study window, walking from the root cellar to the kitchen and holding a basket of parsnips and beets against her hip. It would be natural for her to glance through the window and for their eyes to meet, but she does not do that. She seems lost in thought as she walks, her eyes looking inward more than out, her pink lower lip pushed forward, as if she is about to make a statement after long deliberation. She is gone in an instant, but he continues to see her contemplative expression in his imagination: those eyes fixed on something not in this world, the urgency of her lower lip, the perfect smoothness of her cheek, undulating from temple to jaw.

A goddess in her youth, he thinks.

He can hear the tones and rhythms of her voice as she talks to Jimmy in the kitchen and then a series of pauses and mono- and bisyllabic utterances that indicate the conversation is about to end. He gets up from his desk and waits by his door, hoping to catch her eye as she steps into the corridor on her way to the servants' staircase.

He feels an uneasy sinking in the pit of his stomach, and his tongue sticks to the roof of his mouth. It is utterly ridiculous that a man of his age and position should be waiting in such agitation for a mere girl, but he can't help himself.

It seems to him that he has waited too long, that she must have gone back into the garden or out onto rue Neuve-de-Berri, but then there she is: a mere three yards down the corridor, eyes alert, looking straight at him, faint uncertainty on her brow.

"Sally," he calls, hoping to sound surprised to see her there. And then, more softly, "Do you have a moment? I'd like a word." As soon as she steps in his direction, the uncertainty on her brow intensifying, he backs into his study and waits in front of his desk, feeling dizzy and short of breath.

She enters the room tentatively, as if she expects to be punished. "Yes, Mr. Jefferson?"

Thomas Jefferson smiles broadly, hoping to put her at ease. "You're looking very well this morning," he says. "I hope you had a good night's sleep."

She smiles, perhaps at the patent absurdity of these remarks, shrugs and then says, almost as an afterthought, "It was all right."

He laughs, as if she has made a joke. "Well," he says, and then his expression grows serious and he speaks very softly so that he should not be heard by anyone who might be in the corridor. "Actually, I called you in here because I wanted to be sure I didn't offend you last night. I felt afterward that I had been inexcusably forward."

She doesn't speak, only looks at him with pursed brows and a partially open mouth, seeming abjectly vulnerable.

"You are so very lovely," he says in a low and emphatic voice.

When she blushes and smiles, he smiles, too.

"I'm sorry," he says.

She shrugs. Her smile fades.

He reaches out and takes hold of her hand by only her index and middle fingers. "Sally," he says, barely above a whisper.

He draws her into his arms, and when she presses her face against his chest, he kisses the top of her head. He holds her in his arms for a long time, feeling that what he has just done is wrong. And when she pulls back her head, he is ready to let her go, but she doesn't move away. She waits with her eyes closed, her lips uplifted. And when he kisses her this time, he knows his kiss is returned.

Some minutes later he is the one to break the embrace, all but pushing her away. "And now you really must go, Sally, because in another instant I won't be able to control myself."

She backs to the door, touching her lips with the fingertips of her left hand.

And then she is gone.

That night Thomas Jefferson waits in his chair before the fire in the upstairs parlor with a book in his lap that he only intermittently comprehends. The silver- and gold-faced clock on the mantelpiece wheezes and clangs out nine o'clock, which is when Sally Hemings usually appears. But then it is ten o'clock, and he is certain that she went up to her third-floor bedchamber by way of the front rather than the servants' stairs—yet still he waits. . . .

It is nearly eleven. He closes his book, hammers the cork back into a nearly empty bottle of Ledanon with the side of his fist and separates the charred and glowing logs with a poker.

There is a light knock behind him. Sally Hemings is standing in the doorway, a pained vacancy on her face, one hand wringing the other in front of her skirt.

"Yes, Sally," says Thomas Jefferson, smiling and leaning the poker against the brick edge of the fireplace.

"I'm sorry," she says—mere speech seeming to cost her immense effort. "I think that I lost something. Left it, I mean. My bonnet. I think I left it here. Yesterday. This afternoon."

"I haven't seen it." Thomas Jefferson glances around the room. "But please come in. I'll help you look for it if you wish."

. . . I told myself that I was only yielding to the inevitable, that I merely wanted to get it over with. But even so, I was making a choice. . . .

As Martha had already been married and given birth to two children by the time Thomas Jefferson met her, he had assumed that there would be few impediments to her succumbing to desire in advance of their wedding. And, indeed, whenever he went to see her at the Forest, after his first visit there with John Fairfield, she seemed as eager as he to steal a moment of privacy amid the boxwood hedges, in the closet under the stairs or in a deserted horse stall. Her kisses matched his for passion, and she was happy to let his hands stray anyplace they wanted—insofar as her stays allowed—but only on the outside of her clothing. Whenever he tried to lift up her skirts, or even just slide his hand beneath them, she would grab him by the wrist and say, "Wait." Then she would answer his surprised disappointment with a lascivious smile, saying, "I want you to have something to look forward to."

One day he arrived for a visit, and Martha, laughing, told him that her family was spending the afternoon with some neighbors and that he and she were alone. Her darting and mischievous glances told him clearly that she had made a decision. No sooner did Betty Hemings go off to fetch him some tea than Martha took him by the lapels and kissed him. When Betty returned, Martha told her that she could have the afternoon off.

But once they were alone, she grew restless and pale. When he finished his tea and gave her a smile she could not help but understand, she held out the pot and asked if he'd like some more. He answered by getting up from his chair, kissing her and then leading her up the stairs. But once they were in her bedchamber, Martha broke from his embrace and went over to the window, saying, "Why don't we talk first?" When he asked what was the matter, she replied, "I don't know. I'm just suddenly so nervous." So they sat in two chairs by the window and talked. Then he stood behind her and massaged her neck and shoulders. Eventually he led her to the bed and helped her to remove her clothing one item at a time. But even once they were both naked and under the covers, she wouldn't let him do more than kiss her neck and cheek. In the hope of further relaxing her and evoking her desire, he began to run his fingertips lightly over her body, from her breasts down to her thighs, over and over, constantly approaching but always, in the end, avoiding that one area he wanted most to touch, because every time his fingers drew near, he could feel her whole body tense.

"Ooh, this is lovely!" she said after a while. "Don't you think this is lovely, just lying here like this?"

He did and he didn't, but all he said was, "I love you."

And so it became a habit, throughout the eleven years of their courtship and marriage, for Thomas Jefferson to commence making love to Martha with a massage and a menu of caresses. Although most of the time this prelude did nothing to diminish the ultimate satisfaction of their lovemaking, it is also true that sometimes the prelude was as far as things would go.

Thus, when, some half hour after Sally Hemings arrives late at the upstairs parlor, and Thomas Jefferson confesses breathlessly that he would very much like to lie with her as a man lies with his wife, and she whispers that she would like that, too, he is prepared for the possibility that this first time might consist of nothing more than a massage and patient caresses. He is determined to prove to her that he is not the selfish brute he all too recently seemed, but he also wants (as he did even that first terrible night) to make her initiation into the pleasures of womanhood as gentle and beautiful as it can possibly be.

Thomas Jefferson has never had sex with a virgin. His first erotic encounters, when he was a law student, were with prostitutes, and all three of the women he has loved had already been married when he first slept with them—indeed, Maria Cosway and his first real love, Betsy Walker, were married during the whole of his affairs with them. And so he is not entirely sure what sex might be like for a virgin. How afraid will she be? How much will it hurt? Is there anything special he should do?

Although he has never seen anything more beautiful than Sally Hemings's long-waisted and luxuriantly hipped body, he decides to err on the side of caution and spends much of an hour stroking, caressing and kissing her, breathing in the sweet and musky odors that hover like an atmosphere just above her skin—which itself is so marvelously soft that he feels as if he is running his fingers and lips across a warm and continuous rose petal.

He waits for a sign that she is ready to go further, but the gasps, soft moans and gentle writhing that first accompany his attentions gradually dissipate, and he begins, reluctantly, to contemplate scenarios in which he tells her that he doesn't mind, that he can wait until she is ready, that he has loved what they have been doing, that she is beautiful, oh, so beautiful. . . .

But then her hand closes around his penis. "Aren't you going to put this in me?" she says.

Smiling, he pulls his head back. "Is that what you would like?"

"Isn't that what we're supposed to do?"

He laughs. She is still holding his penis, and it is feeling very good. "Well, that is the usual procedure under these circumstances."

"All right," she says, and rolls from her side onto her back.

He kisses her on her breast, neck and lips. "Are you sure? We can wait if you would rather."

"No. Go ahead. I want to find out what it is like."

It is hard to get into her, in part because she doesn't have a clear idea where the opening to her vagina actually is and so can't help him. But finally, after a fair bit of groping and prodding, he slips into her warm wetness and is surprised that nothing he feels would indicate she is a virgin.

She makes a short, loud cry, however, and grips his arm and back to keep him from moving. She is holding her breath.

"Are you all right?" he asks.

She releases her breath in a quivery gasp. "Yes," she says, though she sounds as if she's in pain.

"Are you sure?"

"I'm fine." She lets out a long sigh, perhaps more to make herself relax than because she actually is relaxed. "So is that it?"

"What?" He kisses her top lip lightly, then her bottom lip.

"Is this all we do?"

"No."

"Well, what then?"

"This." He pulls most of the way out, then pushes gently back into her.

She makes something between a grunt and a moan.

"How does that feel?" he asks.

"It's nothing like I expected. It's . . ."

He is sliding in and out, in and out, in a slow rhythm.

Her mouth falls open. "Ahh," she sighs. And then a little later, "It's just so different."

"Does it hurt?"

"A little."

"Do you want me to stop?"

"No. Keep doing that. I like the way it feels."

"You're wonderful!" he says.

"Why?" She looks him straight in the eye, her expression bemused, but maybe also slightly challenging.

"You just are." He laughs and moves more forcefully inside her.

"Oh!"

"Did I hurt you?"

"No. Not really. Just keep doing that. I don't want you to stop."

And so he doesn't stop, not even after his own orgasm has rushed up inside him and then receded. He keeps going as long as he can manage it, hoping that she, too, will come. Mostly she is silent underneath him. She grips his upper arm with one hand and runs her other up and down his back and has intertwined her legs with his. Every now and then, she lets out an "ah," an "oh" or a grunt, but most of the time she seems to be studying what is happening with the intensity of a scientist.

When at last his penis has slipped out of her and it is too limp for him to get it back in, he rolls onto his side with a happy groan.

"Are we done?" she says, still lying on her back, looking up at the ceiling.

They are in her chamber, which is on a small alcove on the opposite side of the stairway from all the other servants' rooms and thus so much more private than his.

"For now," he says. "We can do it again in a little bit if you would like."

She rolls onto her side and faces him. She smiles. "No. Now that you've stopped, I'm feeling kind of sore."

"It's always like that the first time."

"I know." She puts her hand between her legs, then looks at her fingers and shows them to him. "Blood."

"Yes."

"That's not too much?"

He takes her hand and examines it in the flickering candlelight. "No," he says. "I don't think so." He doesn't really know, of course, but he considers it unlikely that anything could have gone seriously wrong. He puts her hand down on the mattress between them and pats it.

She lifts it up and looks at it again. "Are you sure?"

"Yes." He smiles. "It's not just blood. There are secretions. From you, and from me. They make it seem that there is more blood than there really is." He rolls backward, gropes around on the floor and reaches into the pocket of his waistcoat for a handkerchief. "Here. You can mop it up with this."

"Thank you." She takes the handkerchief and tucks it between her legs. "I'll get up in a minute and use the basin."

"You're beautiful," he says.

"Thank you."

"How are you feeling?"

She rolls onto her back and sighs heavily. "I'm fine but . . . I don't know. I feel strange. Restless."

"Do you feel as if you've changed?"

She lets her head fall to the side and looks at him. Another smile. "Maybe."

He lifts his head and props it up with his crooked arm. He looks into her eyes and smiles.

"How are you?" she says.

He laughs. "I'm happy. Just happy. I am so happy."

"Good," she says.

"I know I shouldn't be. But I am."

"Good."

They lapse into silence for a while, and in a few minutes they are both asleep.

Thomas Jefferson's last words before leaving in that blackest hour of the night: "I must go now. . . . I can hardly bear it! . . . I must go, before birds rouse the rest of the house. But . . . Oh! . . . One more . . . And now— Oh! Oh! . . . And now I really must— No, I must . . . I must."

In the morning Sally Hemings feels hollow. It is not just that the place where she and Thomas Jefferson were one now seems, for the first time in her life, an emptiness rather than just a part of the amorphous interior of her body; it is that all her strength seems to have drained out of her. Also, there is the pain—a dull gnawing that, because of what it signifies, is almost pleasant.

As she descends the back steps from her bedchamber, she has to steady herself against the wall with a tremulous hand. The very world seems to have weakened and waned overnight. The light through the windows is pale. Deep shadows seem places where physical reality reverts to the nothingness from which it sprang. Even the stone walls of the Hôtel seem like veils hanging in empty air.

Thomas Jefferson has clearly been waiting for her. No sooner does she emerge from the back stairway into the narrow passage beside the kitchen than she sees his shadow loom outside the door to his study. He is entirely in silhouette against the light from the dining room, and he doesn't make a sound, but she can tell from the twitching of his shoulder that he is beckoning her.

He withdraws into his study as she approaches and closes the door once she is in the room. He strokes his fingertips lightly across her shoulder and kisses her, not on the lips but on the temple. "You are even more beautiful in the light," he says, then takes a big step away from her, to sit on the edge of his desk. "Please." He points toward the solitary chair in the room not covered by books, papers and mechanical devices.

She does as she is told, then places her hands on her knees and waits. He, too, seems weakened. Restless. Pale. Capable of being stirred by the wind. In the scant instants before he speaks, his eyes do a dance with hers. Their gazes meet, glance away, then meet again.

"I hope you know," he says, "how terribly grateful I am that you allowed me to . . . to take liberties. I will never cease to be . . . I will never forget, I mean." He looks at her firmly now, his mouth a straight line, his upper lip perspiring. "I am not sure what is going to happen. I feel such a terrific . . . I hardly know how to put it . . . *unity* with you, one that I don't dare imagine is reciprocated."

He looks away. Sighs heavily. In the morning light his hazel eyes seem almost golden. Sally Hemings is afraid.

"But I think we both know," he says, "how very wrong . . . how what happened between us ought never to have happened. And, more to the point that . . . it ought never happen again."

She interrupts him with a sharp intake of breath.

He holds up his flat hand, palm toward her. "Dear girl!" he says. "I don't want to speak on that now. That is something"—his mouth turns down grimly at the corners—"for later. I don't think either of us is sufficiently clearheaded to draw any reliable conclusions. I only want to say two things. First, as I am sure you understand, no one must ever know about last night. No one at all, but most especially Patsy and Polly. You do understand that, don't you?"

After a moment Sally Hemings makes a small nod.

"And second, you must understand that however relations may be conducted between us in the future, I will never be able to give my love to you . . . publicly, I mean."

Thomas Jefferson stands and looks at her firmly, as a teacher might look at his reprobate student. He lifts his hands to grasp his coat lapels firmly. "I trust that you also understand why this must be so," he says.

All Sally Hemings can hear in Thomas Jefferson's voice is contempt. And when she replies, her voice, too, expresses nothing but contempt. "Of course!" she says. "Do you think I am an idiot!"

As soon as she has spoken, sounds go tinny and the walls around her start to whirl. She is not sure she will ever be able to get up from her chair. She feels as if her grasp on being has grown so feeble that she could easily, in the next instant or the one after, expire.

. . . Over the years people have intimated to me, sometimes with words but more often with glances and lingering expressions, that they know why I did what I did, that they think I have had a very fortunate life and that they would have done the same thing had they had the choice. But such commiseration, which I have gotten most frequently from my own mother, has always made me sick at heart, because it means people are seeing me in the worst way, as if I am just an animal, living in a world where only the shameless and cruel survive— although I suppose that is exactly what I am and exactly where I do live.

The most effective way of dealing with my hateful sympathizers has always been to concede some of what they say, and so the only part of my association with Mr. Jefferson that I have talked about is our children. And I have to say that even after all that I witnessed today—or is it yesterday?—I do not remotely regret having these four good and kind people in my life. They have been, and will always be, the purest happiness I have ever known. I also do not have one regret that now all of my children are free and that their children and their grandchildren and all the generations that shall follow them will grow up as independent and proud as any citizens of this great Republic and will never have to suffer the humiliation, pain and fear of the cousins left behind in Virginia.

As for the rest of my life . . .

Well, I've said it all. I don't even know why I'm still writing.

What more is there to say? . . .

A week passes, and then it happens again. It seems so simple this time. A glance. A smile. A hesitation. Then a touch. After a while he tells her he wants to do something for her. He wants to give her a gift. "Turn your back to me," he says. And when she does, he places his hand between her legs, and with his finger he touches that place that only he, of all other people, has ever touched, that place where even she had been ashamed to put her fingers. But this time she feels no shame. This time she only feels a delicious heat radiating from that tiny organ into her thighs and up her belly and spine, into her mouth and throat and all along the surface of her breasts. It comes in waves, and then she begins to make noises that sound to her like the cries of deer and foxes and kittens. And when she feels that he has pushed into her, she thinks that she has never known anything so wonderful. And then they are both making those noises together, and they are thrashing and writhing and rocking, and then all at once a feeling starts in that place where he has filled her up and where he has his hand, and it is like a wave surging all through her body and suffusing her head with light and breaking down the walls around her and the ceiling and the floor so that there is nothing but her own body trilling, humming, surging in the midst of a trilling, humming, surging void, and as soon as the huge wave that has taken hold of her seems to recede, it comes back again, and then again, and all the while he is making his noises as she is making her noises, and he is driving his thing into her again and again and again, until finally his noises are so loud the whole house must hear, and he stops moving, and starts again, and stops, then starts, until finally he curls around her back and makes a soft moan into her ear and holds her tight, and this is all like nothing she has ever known before.

Weeks later . . . It's hard to keep track of time here, where the "daylight" comes from nowhere in particular and is little more than a repeating interval of blue dimness amid gloom. . . . So maybe only days later. Or months. But, in any event, eventually I come across a couple sitting on a log beside a low-burning fire. I have, in fact, been walking in their direction for some time now, drawn by the odors of sage, crispy skin and liquid chicken fat. By the time I am close enough to see their slick chins as they each gnaw happily on drumsticks, I am so hungry that my stomach seems to be digesting itself. I haven't eaten in a very long time.

As I approach the fire, the man raises his hand and calls out, "Hello! My friend!"

It is Thomas Jefferson, and the woman sitting beside him is Sally Hemings, though her skin is much darker than I ever imagined it would be—coffee with just a dollop of milk. Perhaps she has spent time in the sun.

"This is my friend," Thomas Jefferson tells her. "The one I told you about. Remember?"

Sally Hemings stops chewing. Her face goes entirely blank.

"I told you about him," says Thomas Jefferson. "There was that terrific wind? I sat down next to him on this very log?"

"Nope," says Sally Hemings. "Gone."

"Sit down! Sit down!" Thomas Jefferson pats the log beside him. "Help yourself!" He points at the half-eaten chicken, still on a spit over the fire. "Take as much as you want."

I rip a handful of white meat off the hot carcass and take the proffered seat. I do so with some reluctance, remembering the potent stench that emanated from Thomas Jefferson's person and clothing the last time I saw him, but now a faint freshness of shampoo and toothpaste settles over me like a tropical drizzle.

For a good minute and a half, I can think of nothing but what is happening in my mouth, throat and stomach.

"Might I have a little more?" I ask when there is nothing else to do but lick my lips and ferret flesh fragments out of my teeth with my tongue.

"Of course!" says Thomas Jefferson. "We're done. Aren't we, love?"

"Just one more nibble," Sally Hemings says, cracking a thighbone off the cadaver. "Okay—all yours."

I pull the chicken off the skewer, and while I hold it between my knees and tear strips of flesh off the gray bones, Thomas Jefferson and Sally Hemings talk to me.

"We've figured it out!" he declares. "Everything is so vague here because our minds are dominated by probability."

"It's like truth being stranger than fiction," Sally Hemings says.

I have no idea what they are talking about.

"The probable world is like a world created by a committee," says Thomas Jefferson. "It's all compromises and averages, guaranteed not to offend anybody, so of course it's vague and boring and doesn't make any sense."

"Whereas in the real world," says Sally Hemings, "probable things happen and so do improbable things, and they are equally real, so everything is much more vivid—"

"Though sometimes a bit harder to take," says Thomas Jefferson.

"Which is *exactly* how you know it is real," says Sally Hemings.

"The point is," says Thomas Jefferson, "it's not vague, only confusing. There's a difference."

Sally Hemings nips a last meat shred off her thighbone. "Now all we have to do is figure out how to get there from here."

"Where?" I say.

"The place where things are actually real."

"The problem is," I say, "that I've seen the place you are talking about"—I can't bear to tell Thomas Jefferson that I have seen it through his own eyes—"and it's not any more real than this place."

"What do you mean?" says Sally Hemings.

"It's vivid, all right. And clear. Maybe too clear. But at the same time there's no meaning there. And nothing makes any sense. Really it's more like a hallucination."

"Fuck you!" She flings her thighbone at me. "You're the hallucination!"

Thomas Jefferson grabs her forearm. "Sally!"

"Go on—get out of here!" She makes a scat motion at me with her free arm and hand.

"Sally!" says Thomas Jefferson. "He's delusional. He hasn't eaten in days."

"Fuck you, too!" she says. Then swings her foot in a wide arc around his legs and kicks me in the shin.

"Go on!" she says. "Beat it! Scram! Begone!"

Reading lessons are no longer possible. The only way that Thomas Jefferson and Sally Hemings can manage being together when anyone else is around is by studiously avoiding each other's gazes and exchanging only the most commonplace remarks. And when they are alone, reading is something less than a top priority. She shows Jimmy the primer that Thomas Jefferson bought and asks if he will at least help her memorize the sounds of the letters, and he just shakes his head and looks away. "Seems to me," he says in a low voice, "that you got too many other things to worry about to bother with reading." When she asks him what he means, he says, "Nothing at all. You just seem like you got a lot on your mind." She decides not to pursue the conversation any further.

Sunday morning, shortly before lunch, Patsy is on the window seat, frowning into a slim pamphlet that she clutches with both hands. Sally Hemings is sitting on a small chair nearby, embroidering one of Polly's pillowcases with a scene of Monticello: Three wide, upside-down green V's representing the Blue Ridge Mountains. A dozen horizontal yellow rows representing August wheat. And to the right a burgundy square with white columns and a low white roof: the great house. She glances at Patsy again and again, and when she catches the girl's eye, she smiles and asks, "What are you reading?"

Patsy lowers the pamphlet to her lap. "Abbé Sieyès," she says.

"Is it good?"

"It's supposed to be." Patsy sighs. "But I think every one of his ideas was stolen from Papa."

"Why did he do that?" says Sally.

"Because Papa is a brilliant man. His ideas have changed the world. And Abbé Sieyès wants to be the Thomas Jefferson of France."

Sally Hemings becomes thoughtful for a moment. Then she says, "I wish I could read."

"You should learn."

"But there is no one to teach me."

There is an odd expression on Patsy's face: irritation competing with some gentler emotion. Finally she says, "I can teach you." She pats the upholstered bench beside her. "Come here."

As Sally Hemings puts her embroidery into a silk-lined basket, Patsy squints at the pamphlet in her hands. She closes it and places it on the seat beside her. "It is better if you learn to read English," she says. "Bring me that book over there." She points to a row of some dozen books atop the mantelpiece.

"Which one?" says Sally Hemings.

"That one," says Patsy. "On the end."

Sally Hemings pulls the indicated book off the mantelpiece and goes to sit next to Patsy. The two girls' eyes are exactly the same shape, though Patsy's are chestnut brown. The girls also have the same high cheekbones and long jaw, though Patsy's jaw is fuller—"more feminine," is how she describes it; she thinks of Sally Hemings's face as "pointy."

"This book is by Papa." Patsy opens the book and points to two words in squarish lettering on the first printed page. "Thomas," she says, and, "Jefferson." Sally Hemings thinks she probably could have figured out what those two words were, but she is not sure whether that would have qualified as reading. Then Polly runs her finger slowly under the six large words on the top half of the page, saying, "Notes . . . on . . . the . . . State . . . of . . . Virginia." She takes Sally Hemings's hand, grasps her index finger and puts it under the first word. Once Sally Hemings has successfully copied the motion of Patsy's hand and repeated the words she has just heard, Patsy says, "Very good. You can read!"

Sally Hemings smiles in a way that she hopes hides her irritation. "Tell me the sounds of the letters," she says.

Patsy complies but has only gotten through "Notes" when Thomas Jefferson appears in the doorway and says, "Dinner, my dear!"

Patsy eagerly closes the book and puts it on top of the pamphlet by Abbé Sieyès. She hurries over to her father and kisses his cheek. "Greetings, Pa-*pah*!"

Thomas Jefferson looks across the room at Sally Hemings with an expression that seems equally likely to become a smile or a contortion of grief.

Sally Hemings can hardly bear to look at him, but she also can't look away. She is standing, but her legs are suddenly so restless she has to fight to keep still.

"What have you been doing?" he asks his daughter absently.

"I've been teaching Sally to read. We're starting with your book!"

Thomas Jefferson laughs in surprise. His expression has become a broad, happy smile, but he is looking at Sally Hemings with such fierce longing that she has to sit back down.

Patsy's eyes move from the very strange expression on her father's face to the dazed, almost frightened expression on Sally Hemings's, then back again. She does this several times.

"That's wonderful," says Thomas Jefferson. He puts his arm around his daughter's shoulders, steers her out of the room and, over the top of her head, gives Sally Hemings one last, lingering glance.

Patsy also casts one last glance over her shoulder, her expression rendering confusion on the verge of becoming a threat.

Whether the black of the Negro resides in the reticular membrane between the skin and scarf-skin, or in the scarf-skin itself; whether it proceeds from the colour of the blood, the colour of the bile, or from that of some other secretion, the difference is fixed in nature, and is as real as if its seat and cause were better known to us. And is this difference of no importance? Is it not the foundation of a greater or less share of beauty in the two races? Are not the fine mixtures of red and white, the expressions of every passion by greater or less suffusions of colour in the one, preferable to that eternal monotony, which reigns in the countenances, that immoveable veil of black which covers all the emotions of the other race? Add to these, flowing hair, a more elegant symmetry of form, their own judgment in favour of the whites, declared by their preference of them, as uniformly as is the preference of the Oranootan for the black women over those of his own species.

—Thomas Jefferson
Notes on the State of Virginia
Written in 1781–82, published in 1787

Afterward he looks at her and smiles. She smiles, too, though there is a dart of uncertainty over one eye. "This isn't real," he says. He looks sad for a moment. Then he kisses her.

I t is June 27, 1789, almost a month since Sally Hemings returned from Madame Gautier's. She is kneeling on a towel in the garden, pulling Virginia carrots for Jimmy, when she notices Thomas Jefferson standing in the window of his study. The reflection of the sunlit building on the far side of the garden is across his face, so she does not see that he is looking at her until he pushes the window open and gestures for her to come.

Her whole body flushes, and she looks around to see if anyone might be watching. Deciding she has picked enough carrots to make leaving the garden seem natural, she nods once at Thomas Jefferson, stands, shakes the earth off her towel and folds it atop the carrots in her basket. Her hand rises involuntarily to tuck a loose hank of hair under her bonnet, and she also glances at the skirt of her gown to be sure no mud clings to it. She could walk down the path between the cabbage and the ankle-high corn straight into Thomas Jefferson's study—its windows being "French windows"—but she is worried that Clotilde or, worse, Jimmy might step out of the kitchen at exactly the wrong moment. So instead she walks toward the kitchen door. Just as she is about to enter, she sees Thomas Jefferson pull the windows to his study shut.

The kitchen is empty, so Sally Hemings just leaves the basket on the table and hurries into the main part of the house, slapping the remaining particles of earth from her hands as she goes. Thomas Jefferson has not merely closed the windows to his study but drawn shut the heavy curtains. In the room's brown dimness, Sally Hemings notices the rigidity of his shoulders and back. He steps away from her as she enters and turns toward the chair where she sat the last time she was in this cluttered, paper-strewn sanctuary of his.

She does not want to sit. She stops in the middle of the room and faces Thomas Jefferson. He takes another half step back and looks around as if he has lost something. She wants to ask him what is wrong, but she can't bring herself to speak. So she just stands there, waiting.

"Thank you, Sally," he says at last. "I want . . . I asked you to come in here because . . . I've been thinking, and I have come to some conclusions that I hope you will see the merits of."

She remains silent, but this time because she knows she won't like what he is going to say, and she wants to make it hard for him.

The fingers of his right hand reach unconsciously into his left coat sleeve and tug a couple of times at the cuff of his shirt. He clears his throat. "I hope you will not think there is any lack of ardor in my feelings for you. On the contrary, the conclusions I have reached are, very definitely, a response to the intensity of that ardor, as I hope will be obvious. You know, of course, what the world would think if our . . . current situation were to become public knowledge. Or, more to the point, if Patsy and Polly—" He stops talking, looking lost at first, but then his gaze turns severe. "We have been very fortunate, but the longer we allow things to continue, the more likely we are to be discovered. Discovery is an absolute certainty, in fact, unless we take action immediately. And since it is clear that neither of us has the power to restrain our unnatural impulses, I think we have no other recourse than that you should return to Virginia ahead of the rest of us—on the very next boat, if possible."

Sally Hemings experiences three incompatible feelings simultaneously: She feels as if she has pitched over a precipice and is falling helplessly. She feels relieved that this exhausting and terribly confusing episode of her life might be over. And she feels outraged. This "current situation" would not have happened if he hadn't pushed himself upon her—yet now he feels justified in dismissing her without any regard for her feelings! She wants to leap on him and put her hands around his throat.

She cannot move or speak. The blood has drained from her face.

Thomas Jefferson has taken a step in her direction. His brow is puckered and his lips parted in grief. "Oh, sweet Sally! This is so hard. I don't want you to think this is easy for me. But it's only temporary. I'll be back at Monticello by August. September at the latest." He is lifting his arms to embrace her. She takes a step back.

"What are you telling me?" Now hers is the severe voice.

Thomas Jefferson's arms drop. She looks down at the floor.

"If you are telling me," she says, "that we're just going to start up all over again when you get home, then what's the point?"

"I just thought . . ." He shakes his head, his eyes heavy, his lips downturned. "Perhaps, after a little time and distance, we will be more self-possessed."

"I'm *not* going." Sally Hemings turns away from him. She places her hands atop a German specimen cabinet that she can only just see over, and she rests her forehead against it. The room is swirling around her. "I'm not a slave in this country."

"Oh, Sally!"

"You can't force me to do anything."

"Oh, dear Sally!" Thomas Jefferson has come up behind her. She feels his encompassing form against the length of her back. He kisses the crown of her head. "Oh, God!" he says. "I don't know what to do." He puts his arms around her. He kisses her ear. Then he kisses her cheek and neck. "Nothing makes sense." She feels his hardness pressing into her, first softly and then with force.

She turns around in his arms.

"Oh, Jesus!" she says. "What has happened to me?" She seeks out his mouth with her own and slips her tongue between his lips.

Thomas Jefferson and Sally Hemings have retreated into a dark stair-way off a foyer at the end of a deserted street, not far from the market where he spotted her contemplating a pushcart heaped with walnuts. His mouth is upon hers. Her apron, skirt and petticoats are in a heap upon her belly, and he has inserted one finger into her liquid warmth. "We must stop this," he says. "This can't go on. It is wrong. It is just wrong."

S ally Hemings and Thomas Jefferson have left Paris and are walking along a yellow dirt path beside the Seine in the direction of Saint-Cloud. They are holding hands—unworried, so far outside the city, about being seen. It is one of those late-June days when the world seems to be made of sunlight, gentle breezes and birdsong. Within the city the river is constrained by steep embankments, but here its waters make liquid clucks and clicks along a narrow, stone-strewn beach. Two swans drift like water lilies near the far shore. A fisherman in a frayed straw hat stands barefoot on a boulder, his line tugged downstream at a forty-five-degree angle. Just past him half a dozen ducks paddle sociably in the shallows and every now and then tip their tails into the air to nibble morsels from the river bottom.

"I've missed walking in the country," says Sally Hemings, giving Thomas Jefferson's hand a swing. "At home I used to walk for hours all by myself."

"I did, too." He smiles at her. "I am never so happy as when I am walking."

"Really?" She has always imagined him as happiest in his study and in discussions with friends.

"As a boy especially. I never felt I belonged in my own family. It was easier when I was off on my own. I could just be myself. I could live in a world that was more in accord with my natural disposition."

Sally Hemings stops walking, her lips parted, as if around an unspoken word.

"What?" says Thomas Jefferson.

"Nothing." She swings his hand, and they resume walking. "It's just that I felt that way, too."

"I suppose everyone feels that way, at least to some extent."

A fenced-in barge loaded with cattle has just emerged around a bend. With no grass to chew, the cattle all hold their heads up and look oddly alert—like a crowd of delegates on their way to a meeting. Two men at the front of the barge push long poles against the river bottom. A third at the rear holds the rudder.

"Why did you think you didn't belong in your family?" asks Sally Hemings.

"Oh . . ." Thomas Jefferson heaves a deep sigh. "We weren't much of a family, really. More like a collection of prisoners forced to live in the same cell. All any of us could think about was escape."

"Why? What made you feel that way?"

He lets go of her hand. They stop walking. "I don't generally talk about that."

"I'm sorry." She searches his face. He seems more thoughtful than upset.

"That's all right. I'm just not used to it."

"You don't have to—"

"No. I'm glad you asked. It shows that you are attentive, that you want to understand. Those are excellent qualities."

Sally Hemings does not know what to say. She is embarrassed—mainly because his words have made her feel so proud.

"It's simple, really," he says. "My mother was mad. She suffered delusions. And my father drank too much." He makes a curt laugh. "That was *his* escape!"

"You poor thing," she says.

"That's all behind me now." He lifts her hand and gives it a couple of meditative pats. "I never think about it." They start walking again, holding hands. The barge with the cattle is out of sight around another bend. "What about you? Why didn't you belong?"

"Oh, I don't really know. Maybe it was my fault. My family just thought everything I said was stupid."

"Why?"

"They were just more practical than me, I suppose. I think I preferred the world inside my head to the one in which I actually lived."

"Why do you speak of that with shame?" He gives her a sideways glance, one half of his mouth smiling. "What is philosophy but the mind's desire to see beyond the world of sense?"

She makes a small laugh but doesn't speak.

"Where would you go in your explorations?" he asks.

"Oh, everywhere! But along the Rivanna mostly. I loved to walk by the river."

"I did, too. There was so much to see. Deer would come down to drink. Once I saw a bear fishing."

"I've never seen that."

"It was most impressive," he says. "I didn't know what he was doing at first. He was completely still, staring at the water. Then he just splashed with one paw, and this silver thing went flying onto the rocks. He lumbered over, picked it up and made a meal of it while the poor thing was still wriggling."

"That's disgusting!" Sally Hemings laughs. Thomas Jefferson's eyes are avid, bright. She can see him reliving his memories. She can see him as the boy he used to be.

"My favorite place was Castle Rock," he says, "though I don't think anybody else called it that. It was a big, squarish rock, about two stories high—like a tower, or really like a *château fort*."

"I know that rock! I've been there." As she says this, she wonders if she is telling the truth. "It's on the east side of the river?"

"Yes."

"Near Shadwell?" This, however, is at least partly a guess. She knows that he grew up at Shadwell.

"Not really. It's about a half mile downriver."

"That's what I meant." And now she has a clear memory of the rock. She is standing at its base, looking up. "I've been there. I love it, too."

"Have you ever jumped off?"

Sally Hemings searches her memory but can only come up with an image of the rock from that one point at the water's edge—although maybe she was actually standing in the river. She thinks she can remember cold water swirling around her knees while she looks up at the rock, squinting against the sun. And now a new memory comes: She is clambering up a steep bluff beside the rock, clinging to scraggly dwarf oaks. "I'm not sure," she says.

"The water is very deep right there, so it's not dangerous to jump. But it took me about a year to work up the courage."

"I think I was always too scared." She is seeing Thomas Jefferson as a boy, maybe nine years old, naked and bone-pale, his eyes and mouth wide with terrified delight the instant before he hits the water.

"I loved it!" he says. "I would jump off over and over again. And when I got tired, I'd climb out onto this slanted rock and lie there until the sun had dried me."

"I used to lie there, too. I remember lying flat on my back and looking up at Castle Rock." In fact, what she remembers, or she thinks she remembers, is *standing* on that rock looking up. Perhaps that's what she

261

was actually remembering before. She was standing on that rock, not knee-deep in the river. But now she does see herself knee-deep in that river, or waist-deep, or perhaps she is even swimming, and she is looking at a pale, redheaded boy spread-eagled on the slanted rock. She is holding her breath so that he doesn't notice her, but she knows that in the next second he will turn his head and see her.

"How amazing," she says, "that we both used to go to the same place when we were children. Wouldn't it have been wonderful if we had been able to meet each other there?"

Thomas Jefferson stops walking and turns toward her, smiling. "That would have been lovely." He kisses her on the forehead and then on the lips.

A little later, when they are walking again and have mounted the crest of a rise, she watches the golden reeds below her bow down in rolling waves as a breeze crosses them and then shivers the glinting, brown-green surface of the Seine, and she feels suddenly happy, so extraordinarily happy. She doesn't know why; she only wishes they could stay in this beautiful place forever and never have to return to Paris.

There are times when Sally Hemings has to fight her revulsion at Thomas Jefferson's naked body and at the things that happen when she is naked with him in her bed—and yet there are other times when those very same things feel as close as she will ever get to heavenly bliss—except that in heaven her bliss will not be followed by embarrassment to meet Thomas Jefferson's eye, or even her own eye in the mirror. *You are the woman who has done these things*, she tells herself when she looks at her reflection in the morning. *You are such a woman.* Yet she cannot tell whether she makes these pronouncements with loathing or a grim pride.

Thomas Jefferson always leaves her room in the middle of the night, and so, awoken at dawn by the shrill whistling of swallows, Sally Hemings is surprised to feel the tilt of her mattress and the warmth of another body against her back. At first she only licks her lips and watches the slow somersaulting of dust motes in the solitary sunbeam crossing her room from the small window above her bed. Then she rolls from her left side to her right.

She has never seen Thomas Jefferson sleeping before, at least not in daylight. It was hot in the night, and a few strands of his red hair are stuck to his pale forehead. His eyelids are closed, but so delicately they make her think of furled flower petals. His long, thin lips are slightly parted, and a trickle of drool gleams at the corner of his mouth, where his cheek is pressed against the mattress.

He is so peaceful and still that it is almost as if the real Thomas Jefferson has fled his body—the thinking, commanding, eternally busy Thomas Jefferson, the man looked up to by half the world. But at the same time, she wonders if this vulnerable, gently sleeping man isn't, in fact, the real Thomas Jefferson, and if, during this tranquil, fleeting moment, she has been granted the opportunity to look not at the man but at his soul.

And now it seems that Thomas Jefferson has left the balcony and is walking back along the gangway, ever deeper into Sally Hemings's invention. For a while his coattails flap on either side of him and his hair whips into his mouth and eyes. But soon the wind subsides and even the violent lurching of the deck resolves, first into a gentle rocking and then into a hum.

And now he is walking between enormous steel flywheels whirling so fast that their spokes are a blur of gleaming blue and now along an avenue of copper obelisks, from the peaks of which bolts of pink and green lightning continually crackle. Tiny sparks snap between his fingers. There is a metallic sourness on his tongue.

Gradually the gangway widens until it is the size of a country road and slopes downhill through a forest of pole-thin trees hung with silver leaves that tremble with a faint ringing sound on a gentle, unceasing breeze. On the far side of the forest, he comes upon fields of brilliant silver wheat and farmhouses, also silver, that glitter so fiercely in white sunlight they make phosphorescent smears inside his eyes. Even the people working in the fields and passing him along the road have silvery faces and hair. And their voices when they speak seem to echo down long pipes.

Thomas Jefferson asks these people how it is possible that this machine, moving so rapidly hundreds of feet above the countryside, should itself be a sort of countryside, but none of them seem to hear, or even to notice him standing upon the road.

M. de Corny and five others were then sent to ask arms of M. de Launay, governor of the Bastile. they found a great collection of people already before the place, and they immediately planted a flag of truce, which was answered by a like flag hoisted on the Parapet. the deputation prevailed on the people to fall back a little, advanced themselves to make their demand of the Governor, and in that instant, a discharge from the Bastile killed four persons, of those nearest to the deputies. the deputies retired. I happened to be at the house of M. de Corny, when he returned to it, and received from him a narrative of these transactions. on the retirement of the deputies, the people rushed forward & almost in an instant, were in possession of a fortification, defended by 100. men, of infinite strength, which in other times, had stood several regular sieges, and had never been taken. how they forced their entrance has never been explained. they took all the arms, discharged the prisoners, and such of the garrison as were not killed in the first moment of fury, carried the Governor and Lt. Governor to the Place de Grève (the place of public execution,) cut off their heads, and sent them thro' the city in triumph to the Palais royal. about the same instant a treacherous correspondence having been discovered in M. de Flesselles, prevot des marchands, they seized him in the Hotel de ville, where he was in the execution of his office, and cut off his head. These events, carried imperfectly to Versailles, were the subject of two successive deputations from the assembly to the king, to both of which he gave dry and hard answers for nobody had as yet been permitted to inform him truly and fully of what had passed at Paris. but at night the Duke de Liancourt forced his way into the king's bedchamber, and obliged him to hear a full and animated detail of the disasters of the day in Paris. he went to bed fearfully impressed.

—Thomas Jefferson
The Autobiography of Thomas Jefferson
January 6, 1821

"B e reasonable," Thomas Jefferson tells Sally Hemings. They are walking along the Seine, just beside the place Louis XV, where, less than two weeks earlier, a crowd had stoned a detachment of German cavalry and the fall of the Bastille had become inevitable. There are small piles of stones all around the square, but otherwise the horse and pedestrian traffic moves with all the tranquil chaos of an ordinary evening in July. The setting sun has turned the buildings on the far shore goldfish bright. The clouds overhead are fire-colored, and the sky behind them is tinged with green. "All I am saying," says Thomas Jefferson, "is that in regard to the issue of slavery, French law is ambiguous."

"But slavery is forbidden—"

Thomas Jefferson shakes his head and speaks in a low, measured voice. "The law also upholds the rights of property owners."

"But how can two laws—"

"The law is not coherent," says Thomas Jefferson. "Laws are enacted by different people for different reasons at different times. But once laws exist, their only function is to give us the vocabulary by which we may conduct our disputes. And when that vocabulary is ambiguous or contradictory, laws can be interpreted to mean almost anything, which is one reason this country—despite having abolished slavery—has made more money from the slave trade than any nation on earth."

Sally Hemings's eyebrows buckle and her mouth falls open. "But the marquis—"

Thomas Jefferson silences her by giving her smooth, soft hand a quick squeeze. She turns her head away and looks out over the river. He feels a deep quiet growing within her, which is answered by an aching weakness within his own chest.

"But the law is not the chief consideration," he says. "Think about the life you would lead were you to remain here."

Sally Hemings swings her head back around and opens her mouth to speak, but he cuts her off.

"What sort of freedom would you actually have? As Patsy and Polly's companion, you have friends and access to the finest drawing rooms. But were you to stay on here alone, you could not continue living at the Hôtel, nor in arrangements even remotely comparable. And do you think that Madame de Corny would invite you to her Sunday afternoons? Who would pay for your gowns and shoes once these wear out? How would you feed yourself?"

Thomas Jefferson licks his lips, which have become dry.

"But I don't want to stay here," says Sally Hemings. "I was only asking why I could not be free."

"What have you to gain by freedom? I have already told you that within the bounds of discretion you will live as if you are free at Monticello. Were I to formally give you freedom and you were to remain at my home, the whole world would know why, and we could have no life together. And were you to leave Monticello, it would be the same in Virginia as it is here: You would have to make your way in the world entirely alone."

With these words Thomas Jefferson knows he has won, that Sally Hemings cannot refute any aspect of his argument. And yet merely by stating the simple facts, he feels he has done her a great cruelty and that the deep quiet within her has grown so big it has become a cold, dark world in which she might dwell but where he can never follow.

Thomas Jefferson has entirely misunderstood Sally Hemings—in part because she would not allow her true meaning to be clear, even only to herself. The real reason she broached the topic of her freedom was that she thought that only if she were free might it one day be possible for her to become his wife. And now she knows that this is one eventuality that will never come to pass.

The eye, like the camera, sees the idiot leers that afflict the lover's lips, the drunken discoordination between his right eye and his left and the puffing of his cheeks in the winds of speech. But all such manifestations of ungainliness and deformity transpire unperceived amid those countless other accidents and expressions that, one after another, are combined within the mind into the lover's perfect beauty.

S ally Hemings holds on to nothing but her book on the roaring sub-way. Every now and then, a shimmy or lurch of the car might cause her shoulder to touch a stainless-steel pole or her back to bump against the door, but she seems oblivious. Thomas Jefferson notices the faint freckling on her cheeks and nose, the fullness of her lips and that distinct line—almost a ridge—where her upper lip meets the skin of her face. He remembers how he used to cover those lips with many tiny kisses. He remembers the taste of her mouth, and her breath, and the feeling of her tongue moving. He remembers how one time when he leaned forward to kiss her, his forehead bumped the stiff brim of her military-style cap, which afterward he took to calling her "chastity cap." He remembers her smiling the first time he said that. He can hear the sound of her laughter.

IV

VI

"Come in!" says Betty Hemings, stepping through the door of her own cabin. "Come in! Come in! Come in!" She is carrying a leather bag, which she puts down on the dirt floor. Sally Hemings stops in the doorway to look around the cabin, with its knocked-together furniture and mud-chinked walls.

"My Lord!" says Betty, stepping back and putting her hands on her hips to really take her daughter in, now that they are finally alone. "Look at those fine clothes you wearing! Anybody think you Mr. Jefferson's daughter, they see you wearing clothes like that!"

Sally Hemings steps into the cabin and smiles weakly. "I can't believe it," she says, almost under her breath.

"Come here, girl. Let me put my hands on you!"

Sally Hemings doesn't move.

Betty flings out her arms and wraps them around her daughter. "My baby girl is home! My baby girl is home!" After a long hug, she stands back, holding Sally Hemings by the shoulders with her arms straight. "Look at you! I send you off a little girl and you come back a grown woman! I guess they treated you fine over there. You all filled out and grown up. Must have treated you like a princess! You probably too good for all the rest of us now."

"Oh, no, Mammy. I'm so happy to be home."

"Don't sound like you happy."

"I'm sorry."

"You must be bone tired!" Betty pulls a chair away from the table. "Sit down. Sit down."

Sally Hemings sits, shrugs her cape off her shoulders and lets it hang over the back of the chair. "That's better."

"Must have been hard, all that traveling. How long it been? A week?"

"A month—since we left Norfolk, I mean. But it's been three months since we left France."

"Lord! No wonder you so tired!"

"I'm not so tired."

"Don't tell me you ain't tired. You yellow as bread dough! You got big gray circles under your eyes. You sit right there. I got some biscuits I can give you."

"Do you have any water? I haven't had anything to drink since we stopped in Charlottesville."

"Course I got some water! You just sit right there. I'll get you some water."

Betty takes a pitcher off a shelf and goes out to the rain barrel. She comes back in and puts the pitcher down on the table. "You learn how to talk French over there?" she asks as she takes a cup off a shelf in the corner.

"*Oui.*"

"'We'!" Betty laughs. "*We'!*" She places the cup on the table beside the pitcher. "You call that French! Lord, if that's French, I been speaking French my whole life!"

Sally Hemings smiles weakly.

Betty smiles. Then her smile goes away. Softly, she says, "Oh, my Lord!"

She crosses the room and places her hand on Sally Hemings's belly. "Oh, my Lord!" She takes a step back, clutching her hands together. "Don't tell me you let some French nigger have his way with you!"

Sally Hemings's voice is so quiet that Betty can hardly hear her. "There aren't any Negroes in France, Mammy."

Betty just stares at her daughter, but Sally Hemings keeps her eyes on the pitcher in front of her and doesn't speak. A tear runs down her cheek.

"Oh, my Lord!" says Betty. "Mr. Jefferson! Don't tell me it's Mr. Jefferson!"

Sally Hemings looks at her mother, her eyes red, tears spilling down both cheeks. When she tries to speak, she can't. She covers her face.

"Oh, my sweet baby girl!" Betty kneels on the floor with her arms around her daughter. "There's nothing wrong with a baby! Babies is nothing but a joy!" She pulls her daughter's head onto her shoulder and smooths her hair. "I was just about your age when I got pregnant with Mary."

Sally Hemings begins to sob.

"There, there, baby girl. There ain't no reason to be so sad. It's a good thing to bring babies into the world. Be fruitful and multiply. That what the Lord says. Babies ain't nothing but a joy. Every one of you been a gift to me." Sally Hemings continues to cry. Betty rocks her back and forth on the chair and strokes her hair. "He's not rough with you?" Betty says.

Face swollen and wet, Sally Hemings sits up and looks at her mother.

"Your father," says Betty, "he was rough with me sometimes. Mr. Jefferson's not rough with you, is he?"

"No," says Sally Hemings. "No, no, no, no!"

Then she is sobbing again, and Betty resumes rocking her and stroking her hair. "Then everything's all fine. You got a baby coming, and there's nothing better than a baby. And it's a good thing to have a baby with the master. That just about the best thing can happen to a colored girl, except freedom. Especially if you got a master like Mr. Jefferson. It's only you got to keep your feelings out of it. You keep your feelings out of it, everything be just fine."

Sally Hemings buries her face against her mother's shoulder, and her sobs become grinding wails.

Red is a lie, as are blue, gold, alizarin, sage, cyan, indigo and brown. These words are lies we tell ourselves, because we want to mean something definite and real by them, but we can't. No single color can be described by red, only an infinite and borderless spectrum of hues whose profound and essential differences are obscured by the word. Likewise with the names we call every other color. All we can have of color is the color before our eyes, which is both itself and never itself, which exists only in that split instant we define as now, and never again, nor ever before, but which also does not exist, insofar as it is ungraspable, unreliable, always hurtling away from us and never more than a complexly enticing and beautiful void.

S ally Hemings is ashamed, because while she was in France, she forgot that nothing she experienced was real. The Patsy and Polly she knew there, the Thomas Jefferson and, maybe most of all, the person she believed herself to be—none of these people were real, or at least none of them has survived the weeks at sea and the month on the road from Norfolk to Monticello.

Well, maybe Jimmy was real. Maybe Jimmy was the only one who always knew about the huge gaps between the way things seemed, the way they actually were and the way they ought to have been. And maybe that's why he's always so sad. Jimmy is sad all the time now, and she doesn't know what she can do to help him.

. . . There was a time, not long after our return from France, when I saw Mr. Jefferson as he truly was. I remember that moment with a nightmarish vividness, and yet it had no more effect on me than if it had never happened. How is this possible? How is it that from that very moment I did not become an entirely new woman?

That return was very hard on us all. After Paris, Monticello seemed a gray heap of lumber, brick, blurred china and boredom, where no truly beautiful gown had ever swirled and where no silk-shod foot had ever danced. Our spirits were buoyed by the fact that through significant glances, shared reminiscences and by simply speaking French, we were able to pay homage to the beauty, intelligence and grace that we each saw as the essence of Paris. But in the end, all of our nostalgia could do little to preserve us from the knowledge that we were living on a tiny island in the midst of a vast wilderness populated by the brutish and the dim.

Things between Mr. Jefferson and me had grown very distant. We had never been alone during our travels so never had an opportunity to be anything to each other apart from master and servant. Matters were not helped by the fact that everybody in our party—Miss Martha, Miss Maria and Jimmy—suspected, at the very least, the true nature of my association with Mr. Jefferson. Not a word was said by anyone, but every now and then I would find myself the object of an emphatic gaze, or of a double entendre—for example, Miss Martha's remark that it was a "perfect bore" the way young women would throw themselves at her father. "One would think they had no sense of their own dignity," she added, without ever even glancing in my direction. And neither did Miss Maria, her solitary auditor apart from me. There was very little of friendship between the three of us now, although at the same time the sisters seemed to find it extremely difficult to treat me as their servant. They were incapable of issuing me a direct request, and so, to keep the peace, I did my best to anticipate their needs.

Everything was made more complicated by the fact that I was enceinte during our travels—three and a half months by the end. I hoped that people would attribute the new puffiness of my cheeks and bosom to my having been too fond of French pastries, but anyone so disposed could easily have recognized my condition for what it was—and, of course, it would not be very long before I would be unable to hide the truth from anyone.

This latter fact was a particular source of discomfort to Mr. Jefferson. While he was never less than considerate with me, his uneasiness about what people would think grew more palpable every day, and it was equally clear that his ardor for me had diminished significantly. Gone were those breath-stopping glances filled with longing that had made the charade of our last months in Paris such a delight and a torture. The contrast was so striking that his merely friendly consideration seemed coldness to me.

Everything became worse upon our arrival in Norfolk, when Mr. Jefferson received General Washington's letter asking him to be secretary of state in the new government. He proclaimed loudly that he would not accept the offer under any circumstances and that if he were to remain in this country (he had left France with the assumption that he would be returning once the revolution there was over), it would only be as a farmer; he was done with public life. And yet it was clear to everyone—himself included—that this was an honor he could not turn down. From then on, his brow was perpetually crimped with irritation, and he kept to himself, writing letters. During the entirety of the two weeks we stayed with Miss Maria's dear Aunt and Uncle Eppes, with whom she and I had lived before her father sent for her from France, Mr. Jefferson confined himself to a dark room, suffering one of his periodical headaches.

We arrived at Monticello just before Christmas, and from that moment on, Mr. Jefferson became entirely absent from my life, once again locking himself in his chambers for most of every day and then spending the holidays with, as he put it to me, "my family."

Given that I was carrying within my person the youngest member of that family, I could not help but take affront, even if none had been intended. And yet, at the same time, I was becoming more and more aware that my association with Mr. Jefferson was unnatural and untenable. I began to dwell, in particular, on a fact I had known since childhood: that when Mrs. Jefferson was on her deathbed, he had promised her he would never remarry. He had never mentioned this promise to me, but maybe that was because he knew there was no need—my mother had been right there in the room when he'd made it. In any event, during our first days home that promise came to seem the nail in the coffin of my association with Mr. Jefferson. I spent much of my time telling myself that I had been a fool to have imagined any other outcome, that whatever affection my celebrated master might have felt toward me had been only an artifact of our time abroad, and wrong from the beginning, and that I would be better and happier when it was behind me. I was, in short, looking for reasons to hate Mr. Jefferson, and so it was not long before fate answered my call.

One morning, after I had been home less than a week, I woke from a night riddled with grotesque dreams and bouts of feverish anxiety and decided to take a long walk, in the hope that it might restore my peace of mind. I had not gone more than a half mile before I came upon a gang of Negro men rebuilding a stretch of road that had fallen away in a mud slide. They were singing as they worked, a slow song that sounded like the very exhaustion I could see in their bent backs, in their hanging heads and in the wrists they dragged across their sweating brows.

This was the first time since my return from France that I had come across a work gang, and so, to a considerable extent, I saw this once-familiar sight with a foreigner's eyes. During my three years in Paris, I never encountered another slave apart from my own brother—and, of course, he and I were not slaves either, at least from a legal point of view. More important, we dressed better and lived better than many of the French—including some shopkeepers and most of the people working barrows in the market squares. Although I never forgot that I was a slave during those years, for most of that time my enslavement was a mere detail, lacking urgency or the solidity of fact. And so, oddly perhaps, my unconscious assumption on first catching sight of these men bent over their shovels was that they were free—and thus my instantaneous correction hit me like a hammer blow, or like several in succession:

They were not free.

Neither was I.

We were all the victims of a grotesque crime perpetrated by white people—and by Mr. Jefferson in particular.

As I happened on the scene, an overseer was shoving one of the men—or, in fact, a boy who looked to be about fourteen, though most likely he was sixteen. He had huge brown eyes and bone-thin limbs and was clearly incapable of working like the other men. With every shove, and in the most repulsive and obscene language, the overseer asked the boy if he was a girl, an old woman, a lazy sod. And even as each shove nearly knocked him over, the boy kept trying to do his work but was too tired to scoop more than a handful of soil onto his shovel, and even that would be spilled by the overseer's blows. What most shocked me was that none of the men did anything to help him. There were eight of them and only the one overseer, but they just kept shoveling and chanting as if completely oblivious. The overseer was unarmed, but he did have a cowskin coiled on his belt—a symbol so potent it seemed to entirely emasculate all of these tall and strong men.

And then something very strange happened. One moment I was wondering if Mr. Jefferson might actually have been the one to hire this overseer, and if he might even have placed that cowskin into the overseer's hand, and in the next I was running back up the road in abject terror, feeling that I was being borne down upon by some doom so malevolent and vast as to be unimaginable. Only once the stable roof came into view over a copse of locust trees and my breaths began to burn in my lungs did I slow to a walk and think again and again that this man who had just appeared to me in so hateful a form was the very man whose child was growing within my body, the man who had run the back of his finger so tenderly along my cheek, looked so fondly into my eyes and told me that I was beautiful, that there had been a time when he had wanted to die, but that now, because of me, his life was a joy.

"Such a joy," he had said so very tenderly. "Such a joy." . . .

On Slavery (Private)

On January 26, 1789, only three months before the commencement of his sexual relationship with Sally Hemings, Thomas Jefferson wrote to Edward Bancroft, "As far as I can judge from the experiments which have been made, to give liberty to, or rather, to abandon persons whose habits have been formed in slavery is like abandoning children." Up until this point, Thomas Jefferson had advocated for the emancipation of slaves almost exclusively on the basis of their fundamental rights to equality, justice and freedom, but from now on, in his private letters, he would argue that captivity had so destroyed the independence of spirit and habits of industry in slaves that they could not be freed until these virtues had been reinculcated through training and more humane treatment.

Like many other forward-thinking white people in the north as well as the south, he also worried that were slaves freed en masse, their outrage at past treatment combined with the bigotry of whites would inevitably result in race war—a catastrophe avoidable only if emancipation were held off until a "probable & practicable retreat" could be found for newly freed slaves, possibly in Canada or Ohio but most likely in the West Indies, West Africa or Latin America, which were already inhabited by "people of their own race & colour" and had climates "congenial" to the African constitution.

The primary personal implication of these new arguments was that he could relax. There was no longer any moral urgency regarding the emancipation of his own slaves, and while he may have been obliged to treat them in such a way that they might regain their virtues of industriousness and independence of spirit, it was possible for him to argue to himself that he was already doing just that—as, for example, with the top-flight culinary education that he had provided James Hemings, whom he also allowed to travel great distances in France on his own, often carrying a considerable amount of money.

In the years after his return to Monticello, Thomas Jefferson trained many of his slaves to be carpenters, furniture makers, blacksmiths, chandlers, cooks and pastry chefs—with the primary beneficiaries of this policy being members of the extended Hemings clan. It should not be forgotten, however, that by having so many skilled craftsmen working for him Thomas Jefferson was able to build one of the most beautiful houses in the United States, and to fill it with excellently made furniture (often of his own devising), and to enjoy coq au vin, bouillabaisse, ratatouille, crêpes and bûche de Noël.

Those slaves who needed to be literate for their work were also taught to read and write. Unlike at other plantations, no one at Monticello was forbidden to acquire these skills. Indeed, in 1796 Thomas Jefferson even advocated for the establishment of public schools for enslaved and free black children. And in later years he encouraged his grandchildren to give reading lessons to any house slave who showed an interest, though it is also true that he worried that literate slaves could forge manumission papers for themselves and others (his writings on slavery are filled with such contradictions).

Some slaves were paid for their work (though only a fraction of what white workers received), some received a share of the profits their work helped generate, and a few were made overseers, most notably at a small nail-manufacturing plant, which for roughly a decade beginning in 1794 was by far the plantation's most profitable venture—though, in general, Thomas Jefferson was not a skilled farmer and made very little, if any, profit most years from his vast plantation. Slaves were also allowed to have their own small gardens and to raise chickens, and could sell whatever they grew or raised to neighbors, including the Jeffersons.

It is hard to know how many people benefited even marginally from these comparatively liberal practices, but most likely no more than a hundred, which is to say only a small proportion of the more than six hundred human beings whom Thomas Jefferson owned over the course of his lifetime and whom he famously referred to as both his "family" and "those who labor for my happiness."

S mall as her fist. Its own fists like the pistils of daylilies, curling in front of the blue bulges where its eyes would have been. Not it—*her*. *Her* eyes. *Her* fists. Mere wrinkle between her legs, which are smaller than the front legs of tree frogs. Gigantic head that reminds Sally Hemings of nothing so much as the tip of a man's thing—though she is ashamed to even think that.

Her mother says, "That head's why the Lord let her go. The Lord always has his reasons."

Sally Hemings hopes so. But to her it seems that most things don't happen for any reason at all. She washes the little one herself. La Petite. Puts her into the jam jar herself. The one he got her that time in Paris. Apricot preserves. The time he wanted her to think better of him. She seals the jar with grease paper and twine. She wraps the jar in burlap and ties the burlap in twine, too.

She told him when she was going to do it. He nodded and looked as if he were made of sorrow, but he did not say he would come.

He is not here.

She holds the jam jar against her belly. Her mother is with her. And Thenia and Critta. And Jimmy. Jimmy is carrying the pickax. Peter has the shovel.

The sky is filled with snow, but the snow is not falling. The earth is pink and hard. Tow-colored grass. The bare trees are the many colors of bruises. She looks back toward the house, but he is not there.

She walks first; the others follow. When they get there, he is not waiting.

Jimmy thinks what they are doing is sacrilege. Witchcraft. Only those who have lived should have funerals. But he has come anyway. And when they arrive, he holds the pick with both hands and asks where she wants him to dig.

"No," she says.

She gives the jam jar to her mother and takes the pickax. The first time she strikes the frozen earth, the vibration snaps like a cowskin lash up her arms to the center of her spine. She has made only a knuckle-shaped dent in the earth amid splayed grass blades. But she hits again and again and again, feeling it is right that she should suffer for this poor creature to whom she could not give life.

He still has not come when, at last, she lays the jam jar at the bottom of the knee-deep hole and covers it over with the chips of frozen earth and tangled bits of the tow-colored grass. On top of it all, she puts a squarish flag of stone that Peter removed from the wall along Mulberry Row.

"*Au revoir, ma petite*," she says. She also wants to say, "*Je t'aime*," but she can't. The steam of her breath dissipates in the frigid air.

When she starts to walk away, her mother grabs her arm.

"No!" Sally Hemings says. "Let me go!"

Jimmy says, "She'll be all right."

Her mother just stands there, ash-faced, looking.

Down the hill. Down. Down. Not along the road but through the woods. Hands skin-stripped and blistered, crammed into the pockets of her greatcoat. Lifting her skirts over fallen trees. Shoving aside or ducking under face-level branches. Feet making a constant *shush, shush, shush* in the pale-copper leaves.

It is good to get away. She feels nothing but good. Her burning hands throb in her pockets, but the cold air is sweet in her lungs.

Down past the lake, which is sealed beneath a dull-glinting sheet of ice: black and mottled gray, shifting yellow reeds along its shore. She crosses the path where he takes his daily rides. She wills herself not to look for him. She wills herself not to hope she will see him hurrying home, distraught because some accident kept him from her side. Or hurrying *from* home, filled with sorrow and anxiety, wanting only to find her, to get down on his knees and beg her forgiveness. She has resolved to hate him. She will be as cold and hard to him as the earth beneath her pickax.

First she hears a gentle ticking on the fallen leaves, and then she sees the snowflakes, millions of them, drifting between the upreaching branches of the hickories and oaks. Then she is standing by the black river, dank mustiness filling her sinuses, the hissing roar of water over stones filling her ears. The snow is heavier now, obscuring the far shore in its diagonal sweeps and swirls. The world is whitening. Her shoulders are shrouded with snow, and the upper surfaces of her sleeves.

When she felt the warmth trickling down her legs, then saw the blood, she entered into a sort of fog and a numbness that was less grief than a terrific confusion, a profound lostness. But that's all over now. Her mind is utterly clear. Here in the cold beside this loud river, she feels more alert and alive than she ever felt in Paris. Here in this wild land where she was born—the only place where she can feel that she is truly herself and in the living world.

Some hour later, almost back to Monticello, she stops on the edge of a sloping field, now entirely white with snow. The wind has stilled, and the flakes are bigger now, the size of feathers. Rocking. Drifting left, then right. Endless numbers of them, falling all around her in perfect silence. And as she watches, she feels that what she is watching is the settling of grief upon grief upon grief that has been occurring, without relent, for all the centuries since creation.

The glasses in the hands of the guests are like balls of fire, each reflecting the hundreds of candles that Sally Hemings has been replacing constantly ever since the white sun touched the iron clouds over the western hills. That was at four-thirty; it is now after ten.

"Love," says Thomas Jefferson, his face red, candlelight glinting in his eyes, "is our greatest gift."

The guests are being served champagne from bottles carried around the room by Jupiter, Thenia and Critta. Some of them sip from their glasses immediately; some are waiting for Thomas Jefferson to finish.

"Without love," he says, "our homes would be as comfortless as caves. Our labors would have no purpose, for what is the point of straining our backs and going exhausted to bed if not to bring happiness to those we most want to be happy?"

Some of the guests gaze with fixed grins into empty space, as if they hear and see nothing of what is happening around them. Old Mrs. Randolph is seated in the corner, her chair entirely concealed beneath the lavender heap of her skirts, her head against the wall, her eyes closed. Her son, Tom, is standing beside her, shifting restlessly from foot to foot, constantly looking down into his glass. And between him and Thomas Jefferson, her cheeks bunched into shiny pink balls from the huge smile that has not left her face all day, stands Patsy—although she has announced that as a married woman she wants to be called only by her Christian name: Martha. She is seventeen. Not to be outdone, Polly, eleven years old, has announced that she only wants to be called Maria, although the name she was given at birth is Mary. She is not in the room, however. Sally Hemings has not seen her for more than an hour.

"Without love," says Thomas Jefferson, "the word 'home' would have no meaning, for what else makes our homes places of solace and joy than the love that we find in them?"

A candle is guttering on the sideboard just behind Thomas Jefferson, but Sally Hemings is not going to replace it. She remains on the opposite side of the room, staring directly at him, although he has yet to notice her.

"But love," he says, "is not merely a gift we are given; it is a gift we give. Our labors in office, field or manufactory are not meaningless, because they are the gifts we give to our wives and to our children—to the people we love—and their labors in the home are their gifts to us."

Sally Hemings has not moved. She is waiting. But Thomas Jefferson has not looked her way.

"When Tom," he says, "first visited us in France, I loved him already as the son of my dear cousin." He glances at old Mrs. Randolph, but seeing she is entirely unaware of what he is saying, he continues. "But when I noticed the looks he turned toward my dearest Martha and I saw the blushes those looks engendered, my love for him redoubled, not merely because he is, as everyone in this room knows, a fine and responsible young man but because he had the power to give dear Martha the greatest happiness in life—by meeting her love with an equal love of his own."

Tom Randolph lifts his gaze from his glass and trades an embarrassed glance with his ferociously grinning bride.

"And on this day, when the feelings they share have been sanctified before God and in the hearts of all in this room"—Thomas Jefferson lifts his glass, as do all the guests—"I want to make a toast to the sentiment that binds these two young people and without which none of us could bear to spend a day on this bleak earth."

As he raises his glass above his head and says, "To love!" his gaze at last turns to Sally Hemings, who holds it for a long instant before turning her back and leaving the room.

The guard bangs her billy club against the bars of the prisoner's cell. He is lying on his cot, the side of his head swollen—purple and red, capillary laced. She speaks.

—Morning! Rise and shine!

— . . .

—Don't worry. I'm in a much better mood today.

— . . .

—What's the matter? You look so glum.

—I don't see any reason why I should talk to you.

—Well then, maybe you haven't learned your lesson.

—What lesson?

—That you have no rights.

—It's not in your power to deprive me of my rights.

—On the contrary. I can do absolutely anything I want to you.

—I won't deny that you can treat me any way you want to, but that doesn't mean you can deprive me of my rights. My rights are given by God and exist independently of anything you do. You may make it impossible for me to enjoy my rights, but that doesn't mean I don't have them.

—Don't get all academic on me.

— . . .

—If you can't exercise your rights, then you don't have them. End of story.

— . . .

—You idiot! You haven't learned a fucking thing. You still don't know that you're a fucking piece of shit. A disgrace to humanity.

—Leave me alone.

—Hah! Fat chance! I'm your judge, jury and executioner. You got that? And I am not going to let you get away with one fucking thing. You won't be able to touch your dick or pick your nose without me seeing it. I'm going to catch you out on your every lie, your every evasion, your every attempt to escape your own conscience.

—Leave me alone, I said!

—No way. I'm with you to the end.

—You're a fucking lunatic! This is so fucking insane!

—Of course it's insane! Justice is relentless. And monomaniacal. It has to be. I mean, do you think that once you commit an evil act it can ever be undone? Give me a fucking break!

The guard laughs. She speaks.

—You can do a thousand good deeds and make a thousand apologies, but the evil is still there. It never changes, and it never ends, and you can never escape it. Justice, too. Justice never ends; it is eternal, universal and implacable. That's the lesson I'm teaching you. I'm going to strip you of every shred of dignity and pride until you are so desperate you fall on your knees and beg forgiveness. And guess what? There will be no forgiveness. But you know that, don't you? You always have. That's why you trembled when you thought that God is just. And actually, that's the beauty of all this. You are condemned, not merely by your most evil acts but by your finest words, those self-evident truths of yours that created a whole new world—a world that will never forgive you for your sins.

Maria is halfway through embroidering an image of a ship at sea for a pillow cover and has run out of all three of the shades of blue thread she is using for the water and the sky. Sally Hemings is walking down to the stable, a list of the needed shades in hand, hoping to catch Jupiter before he heads into Charlottesville for provisions.

As she nears the stable, she sees Thomas Jefferson's horse rear its head, then leap out into the yard, as if over a snake stretched out in the doorway. Thomas Jefferson pulls the horse's reins tight to steady it, then leans forward, strokes its neck with a gloved hand and murmurs a brief consolation into its ear.

Sally Hemings veers off the road and strides across the crusted snow beside the stable, although she could have no possible business in that direction. She keeps walking even after Thomas Jefferson calls her name but then stops because she realizes her ruse is transparent and she is only humiliating herself.

He calls her name a second time and says, "Could you please come here for a moment?"

She turns about-face and retraces her footsteps without ever lifting her head high enough to meet his eyes. She stops close enough to the horse to smell its breath and keeps her gaze on the red mud, ice and snow beneath the horse's hooves.

Thomas Jefferson's voice is gentle. "Sally, please." She can feel him looking at her. She knows, even, that his expression is tender, in that way she once thought she loved. "I only want to inquire as to how you are doing," he says. "I know these last weeks have been . . . especially with Martha's wedding—"

"Fine," she says.

"I'm sorry?" He is not apologizing.

In a soft but trembling voice she says, "I said I'm fine."

"Oh, Sally." He speaks her name so tenderly. "You're not being fair."

"I'm *fine*, I said!" Her voice is sharper now, though still trembling. "I know *exactly* what I am to you, and I don't care! Not that I have any say in the matter."

She won't lift her eyes above Thomas Jefferson's shoulder, but she can tell by his silence and by the way his hands clench the reins that she has shocked him.

"Sally," he says, but it is a moment before he can speak. "You are being entirely unfair—to me and, worst of all, to yourself."

She, too, is silent a moment, then says firmly, "I don't think so." Now she looks into his mud-and-gold eyes and sees that his tenderness has given way to anger. "I don't believe in telling lies, Mr. Jefferson, *especially* to myself."

He says nothing, but she is no longer looking at him, so has no idea what expression he may have on his face.

"Excuse me," she says. "I am on an errand for Polly." She cuts a wide arc behind his horse and makes for the stable entrance.

He calls her once, but she doesn't reply or look around. Only after she has entered the stable does she hear him make a double suck-click in his cheek, and horse's hooves begin to drum out of the yard.

Jupiter is standing toward the rear of the stable, buckling Lulabelle into the cart harness. His skin is dark enough that his features are hard to make out in the dimness, but she can tell from the weary set of his eyes that he has heard every word of her exchange with Thomas Jefferson and that he doesn't know what to say.

"Polly asked me to give you this." She hands him the list. "*Maria*, I mean." And then she starts to cry.

Sally Hemings is down in the kitchen early the following morning with her mother and Ursula when the bell, attached by wire to a brass ring beside Thomas Jefferson's bed, jingles. Betty casts her daughter a worried glance. She saw Sally Hemings's red eyes at supper yesterday. And she heard her sighing all night long and filling the cabin with the hisses and whispers of dried corn husks as she turned again and again on her tick. Betty is pretty sure she knows what's wrong, even though her daughter has been protesting that it is only her monthly.

Betty climbs the steep staircase to the hall outside Thomas Jefferson's chambers, and when she returns, there is worry on her face and in her voice. "He wants his molasses tea. And he says you the one got to bring it to him. He says you and no one else."

Betty gives her eyes a weighty roll and goes over to the fire, where a bucket-size copper kettle is always on a low boil.

Minutes later Sally Hemings is standing in the dark hallway knocking on Thomas Jefferson's door. Her first knock is too soft, so she knocks again.

"Come in," she hears from the other side of the door.

Balancing the tray bearing the teapot, cup and bowl of molasses in her left hand, she lifts the latch with her right. Thomas Jefferson, who always rises with the sun, is seated at his desk in shirtsleeves and waist-coat. Pen in hand, he seems preoccupied. "Thank you, Sally." He clears a space amid his papers so she can put down the tray. When she has done so, she notices that he is looking right at her.

"I'm wondering," he says, "if we might have a word."

She neither moves nor speaks.

He gestures at a chair. "Please sit down, Sally."

She feels as if she is falling as she sits—falling through the chair, through the floor, falling and falling.

Thomas Jefferson's brow is wrinkled. He meets her gaze, then turns away. As he speaks, his eyes are on the pen that he has placed beside the letter he was writing. "You told me yesterday that you do not lie. So I am not going to lie to you. I think it best, given that we will continue to occupy the same house whenever I am not called away by my duties, that I am completely honest with you regarding my thoughts about what has passed between us."

His eyes lift. He holds her gaze. Her mind is reeling, and she is hardly aware of her own words. "I think that is good."

He looks down again. "You understand, of course, that what has happened between us is wrong. I accept full responsibility for it. I took advantage of you . . . of your innocence . . . to an extent that I had never thought myself capable of." He sighs. "And everything that happened afterward was, in a sense, my attempt to convince you, and myself, that my feelings that first time had been more honorable than they seemed." He looks at her again, smiles sadly, then makes a small laugh. "But I'm lying again! You are a good and caring girl, Sally. And one day you will make some man a fine wife. Soon, I hope. I have never been insensible to your virtues, and nothing would have happened between us had I not had such a high opinion of you. But that is no excuse. In fact, your many virtues only compound my transgression. Especially since my attempts to make good the first wrong I did you only caused you further injury. The fact that my own actions nearly resulted in the issue of a child so troubled me that I was incapable of . . . well, of behaving toward you as I ought."

He looks straight at her again, and she has to fight to hold back her tears.

He pinches the bridge of his nose between thumb and forefinger, then gives his head a shake. "I took the coward's way out. I know that. I pretended that what had happened was no concern of mine. I somehow believed that if I acted like a man who had done no wrong I would actually be such a man. That was cruel. A grave wrong in itself. And I am deeply, deeply sorry."

He looks at her under a folded brow, waiting.

She is filled with rage.

He continues, "But my multiplying transgressions only make more clear how wrong our association is and thus why that association must end, especially now that we are home. In France, distance and the custom of that place gave us a certain freedom. But here in our United States, especially as I am about to participate in the first administration of this new country . . ." He frowns. His hand twitches, as if he is about to reach across his desk for hers. Instead his words spill out all in a rush. "Please understand, Sally, that I like you very much—too much. I think you are an utterly wonderful girl. And I have had to struggle mightily with my own feelings to reach this resolve. What we have been doing is wrong, and so it simply must stop. That is our only choice. I hope you understand."

She doesn't reply, and she hardly hears anything he proceeds to tell her—that he has informed Mr. Lewis that from now on she will have no other duties than to attend to Maria's personal needs. He seems to feel that these arrangements are adequate compensation for all that she has lost—or that *he* has taken from her. He jokes about her having lots of free time, in which she might teach herself to read or find a husband.

At last he falls silent.

As she, also silent, gets to her feet, he reaches across his desk and grabs her hand. "Dear Sally," he says. He kisses the back of her hand, then, looking ill and old, tells her she'd better go.

She stands for a long time in the dim hallway, then straightens her apron, and, willing herself to manifest none of the feeling in her breast, she grips the railing of the steep stairs and descends to the kitchen.

"Well, you know how it is with men," says Betty Hemings. "White men in particular." She is sitting at the table, letting gravy soften her biscuit, sipping a glass of cider. "They only think with their little head. You know what I'm talking about? Right? You know what I mean. They say all kinds of things with their big head, but their little head makes all the decisions. Little head's the master. So you can count on it; he ain't done with you yet. You'll see. Meanwhile you got it good. Most days you can go back to bed after breakfast, sleep till noon if you want. And when he comes back, the fact that he been so hard on himself most likely means he'll go easy on you. Most masters act like God gave them you so they can do what they like. And if you object, they say you got the Devil in you and they got to punish you. Mr. Jefferson's not like that. He treats you like a lady. So you lucky, and I wager you'll be luckier when he come back. And meanwhile you get to live like a princess."

On Slavery (Public)

In 1770, when he was twenty-seven years old, Thomas Jefferson served as a pro bono attorney in two suits for freedom by mulatto teenagers and argued in one of the cases, "Under the law of nature, all men are born free, everyone comes into the world with a right to his own person, which includes the liberty of moving and using it at his own will. This is what is called personal liberty, and is given him by the author of nature, because necessary for his own sustenance." These sentences were Thomas Jefferson's first public articulation of principles he would express so memorably six years later. He lost both cases.

In his instructions to the Virginia delegation to the first Continental Congress in 1774, he represented the abolition of slavery as one of the primary goals of the American colonies, and in his original draft of the Declaration of Independence he asserted that George III had "waged cruel war against human nature itself, violating its most sacred right of life and liberty in the persons of distant people who never offended him, captivating and carrying them into slavery in another hemisphere, or to incur miserable death in their transportation hither." This passage was struck from the final document in response to objections from representatives from the southern colonies.

Thomas Jefferson's first draft of the Virginia constitution, which he wrote in Philadelphia just before the Declaration of Independence, stipulated, "No person hereafter coming into this country shall be held within the same in slavery under any pretext whatever." This draft arrived in Virginia too late to have an effect on the version of the constitution adopted on June 29, 1776—although it is doubtful that its antislavery provision would have been adopted even had it arrived in time, given that the constitution his fellow Virginians did approve denied slaves any guarantee of civil rights by declaring them not a part of civil society.

In 1777 Thomas Jefferson proposed a bill to prevent the importation of slaves to Virginia, which decreed that anyone brought into the state for the purpose of enslavement after the passage of the bill would "thence-forth become free and absolutely exempted from all slavery or bondage." That bill was passed in 1781, during his term as governor.

In a new draft of the Virginia constitution, which he wrote in 1783, he extended his original ban on the enslavement to include not just those "coming into" the state after 1800 but anyone born in Virginia after that date, and once again this provision was struck from the document finally adopted.

In 1784, as a member of the Continental Congress, he developed a plan for the government of the western territories that declared, "After the year of 1800 of the Christian aera there shall be neither slavery nor involuntary servitude in any of the said states," but this provision met the same fate as its predecessors, and for the same reasons.

On December 2, 1806, during his second term as president, he denounced the international slave trade as a "violation of human rights" and called on Congress to make it illegal. The resulting law, which passed on March 2, 1807, and took effect on January 1, 1808 (the first day on which it was constitutionally possible to outlaw the slave trade), was the most unambiguously antislavery initiative of the federal government prior to the Emancipation Proclamation. Unfortunately, the law was never adequately enforced, and over the course of the next fifty years (until the start of the Civil War) more than a quarter of a million Africans were brought to the United States and sold into slavery.

The blue of the sky before sunrise makes the earth blue. The air is cold, sharp on the tongue, but there is a dry-grass sweetness in it that tells Thomas Jefferson it will be warm by noon. Lots of sun. A good day for traveling, if the roads are not too muddy. He is seated in his landau, which, with the lanterns mounted on either side, is good for night travel. He hopes to make it to New York in less than a week. Jimmy is hunched against the cold on the box in front, and Bob is at his side, holding the whip upright, like a fishing pole.

Thomas Jefferson told everyone who would listen that Washington would have to throw him in irons to get him to serve in this administration, yet now he is looking forward to assuming his duties. Now he is wondering if government isn't, in fact, the life that he was born for, and not farming. Yet no sooner does he resolve this question in the affirmative than a hollowness seems to open inside him.

He is passing the cabin where at this very moment Sally Hemings is asleep beside her mother and sister. She is angry at him, and the rift between them is what makes him feel so empty and alone. Still, it is better that he has concluded their intimate relationship. He hopes she will soon realize that her life will be happier this way. He wants nothing for her but her happiness. She is a good girl, and he will never be able to give her the happiness she deserves.

In Sally Hemings's dream, she is wrestling a bear, although at first she does not know it is a bear. It seems like a wall of fur: dense, soft, warm and enveloping. But then she understands that what she is actually doing is trying to get the bear to put on a frock coat and a pointed hat. In the end it is the bear's very astonishment that anyone should want to do such a thing that causes it to go still and let her manipulate its enormous paws down one sleeve and the other and then put a red hat—something like an elongated flowerpot—atop its head. And now, at this very moment when it would seem certain that she has succeeded in clothing the bear, she is suddenly unsure of what she has done. She knows that a crowd has gathered—a crowd of old women and men with the glossy, toothless mouths of infants—and they are all staring at something at the center of a cobbled square, and leering, and making low hooting noises that would seem to be laughter but that might just be something else. She doesn't know what, but maybe something obscene.

For a long time after La Petite's death, Sally Hemings has trouble staying asleep and so falls into the habit of leaving her bed at the faintest hint of pink in the eastern sky and going for a walk, partly to talk herself out of a roiling tangle of bitterness, sorrow and longing that come to her in a different configuration every day and partly to lose herself in the movement of her muscles, the sweet chill of the air in her throat and the thrum of the wind in bare branches.

There is a new building on Mulberry Row. The cockeyed, rain-grayed log cabin that everyone called the "toolshed" (in fact, it was where Thomas Jefferson and a team of workers lived while constructing the first section of the great house) has been replaced by a tall white clapboard building with a stout stone chimney on one side—a smithy.

Most mornings, as Sally Hemings sets out on her walk, she can hear the urgent huffing of the bellows as the blacksmith gets his fire going and, as she returns an hour or so later, the clink and clang of a hammer on steel. She has seen the blacksmith from time to time, resting on a box in front of his shop at midday or lumbering with his head lowered toward his cabin somewhere down the East Road. He is in his thirties, she thinks, though with a patch of completely white hair above his left eye. His shoulders are massive and his forearms as thick as her calves. His skin is middle dark—the color of glazed stoneware—and he has a round, heavy-cheeked face with large, weary eyes. She has never said a word to him. Her mother tells her he is "simple."

One day in early March, just after Thomas Jefferson has left for New York City, Sally Hemings is coming back from her walk and notices that for the first time (perhaps because the weather is warm) the smithy's front door is open. Peering into the dark interior, she sees what looks like a red-hot bar of iron floating in midair and gracefully twisting itself into a knot. She wants to walk up to the door to get a better look, but she is too self-conscious so keeps walking. The next day, however, when she sees the door open again, she feels less timid.

The heat of the forge warms her nose and cheeks before she is even an arm's length from the door. At first all she can see inside the building is the glow of the burning coals, but then a low, merry voice calls out, "Don't be shy, pretty lady," and an orangish smear in the darkness coalesces into the round-faced blacksmith looking straight at her and smiling. "Come on in!" he says. "Ain't nothing to be afraid of in here."

"I don't want to disturb you," she says.

"Pretty girl like you can't never disturb nobody! Come on in. Come on in. *Je vous en prie!*" He laughs. "I know you know what that means! *Je vous en prie!*"

The air inside the smithy is so hot it dries out her nostrils and the back of her throat. She wants to take off her coat but doesn't think that would be proper. The blacksmith is in shirtsleeves, with his collar open to the top of his greasy leather apron. The skin on his neck and chest is glossy with sweat.

"I bet you know all kinds of French after living in Paree," he says. "My mammy came up to Virginia with a family from New Orleans, so I been speaking French practically since the day I was born. *Je vous en prie! Je vous en prie!*"

The blacksmith's name is Sam Holywell.

When Sally Hemings starts to introduce herself, he cuts her off. "I know who you are! Everybody talking about Miz Sally this, Miz Sally that. You pretty near famous around here."

"Oh, I don't know about that," she says, rather unhappy at the news.

"Oh, no! That's a fact!" He laughs. "You just about famous as Mr. Jefferson."

She coughs, in part because of the dryness in her throat. "I was wondering if I might watch you work for a moment."

"Sure," he says. "Make yourself at home. Most likely you'll get bored, though. Ain't been making nothing but horseshoes the last two days." He nods at the jumbled heap against the wall behind him, then picks up a hammer and a pair of tongs. "You best stand back, now. Sparks be flying. Wouldn't want to spoil that beautiful coat!"

Sally Hemings takes a step back and half sits on a barrel.

The work is nothing like what she thought she saw through the door. It's all banging and flipping and banging some more. No graceful twisting in midair. Nothing graceful at all, in fact. And so noisy she has to keep her fingers in her ears. But even so, she is amazed by how rapidly and precisely all that clangorous hammering knocks the bar into an arc and then tapers that arc into a perfect horseshoe.

After a final inspection, he flings the still-glowing shoe into a barrel of water, where it hisses and sends up bubbles of steam as it sinks to the bottom. "So that's it," he says. "Not much of a show."

"I thought it was amazing," she says. "You make it look so easy, but it must be so hard."

He smiles shyly as he puts down his tools, and Sally Hemings decides he has a lovely mouth. "Thanks," he says, glancing at her in the eye. "It's not all that hard, but it sure makes a body thirsty!" He mops his forehead with the back of his arm, then dips a ladle into the same barrel where the horseshoe is still sending white bubbles to the surface. He lifts the ladle to his lips, slurps the water down, then dips the ladle in again and holds it out to Sally Hemings. "Want some?"

"Oh, no, no," she says. "Thank you."

"Ain't nothing wrong with it!" He smiles. "Tastes a bit from the iron. But that's good for you. Makes you strong. Go ahead."

She takes a sip and gags at first but manages to swallow it. "Thank you," she says. The water is warm. It tastes like ash.

"My pleasure!" He smiles at her happily, his large, dark eyes aglint with the daylight pouring in through the open door. "You sure is a pretty woman! Hope you don't mind me saying that!"

Sally Hemings blushes and looks at her feet. "Well, I guess I better be going. Got my own work to do." As she moves toward the door, she smiles and says, "That was wonderful. Thank you so much."

"*Je vous en prie!*" he says, with a big grin. "*Je vous en prie!*"

"*Merci bien,*" she replies, stepping sideways out the door. As she turns toward the great house, where it is time for her to wake Maria with a cup of hot chocolate, she feels a surprising pang of sorrow. *Sam's not simple,* she tells herself, *he's just kind.*

The next day, on her way out for her walk, she carries a tin pitcher of fresh water over to the smithy. No one answers her knock, so she leaves the pitcher on the ground. By the time she comes back, the door is open and the pitcher is gone. She knocks again, sticks her head in the door and says, "Morning, Sam!"

"That you, Miz Sally?" He glances over his shoulder as he dumps a shovelful of coal into his forge. Then he leans the shovel against the wall, wipes his hands on his apron and walks toward her.

"I just wanted to make sure you got that pitcher I left you." She looks over his shoulder but can't see the pitcher anywhere.

"I figured that was you!" He laughs. "I surely did! And thank you very much. Nothing wrong with my water here, but it don't hold a candle to water straight from the well." The pitcher is on a shelf just beside the door.

Sam is looking right at her with his big dark eyes and smiling so appreciatively that she feels another pang in her breast, but this one is warm, and it makes it hard for her to talk. "Well, all right," she says. "Maybe I'll come by for it later in the day, so I can bring you some more tomorrow."

"Ah, you don't have to do that!"

"It's nothing." She blushes. "See you later."

When she stops back at the smithy on her way to have supper with her mother, Sam hands her the pitcher and tells her, "Now, you hold on a minute! Don't you go anywhere!" He hurries over to the water barrel, rolls up his sleeve, plunges in his arm nearly up to the shoulder and pulls something out that he immediately wraps in an old rag. As he walks back toward her, he pats and rubs the rag over the object it conceals. "You know what this is?" He pulls back the rag and holds up what look like two horseshoes joined tip to tip so that one shoe opens to the right and the other to the left.

Sally Hemings is stumped. "A hook?"

"It's an *S*!" he says proudly. "The letter *S*. And do you know what name starts with *S*?"

She laughs. "I know one name that does!"

"I bet you do!" he says. "And the other one is Sam. Sally and Sam! Thought you should have something to remember me by!"

She wants to give him a hug, but doesn't dare. So she just shrugs her shoulders and smiles. "Thanks, Sam. That is so kind of you!" As he hands her the *S*, she gives his thick, hard hand a quick squeeze. "I'm truly touched."

That night at supper, as she is telling the story of her encounters with Sam, her mother frowns smugly and starts shaking her head.

Sally Hemings cuts herself off in midsentence. "What?"

Her mother just keeps shaking her head.

"What?"

"Nothing," says Betty. "Just don't let yourself get all sweet on him."

"I'm not!" Sally Hemings declares, though her face turns crimson.

"Well, that's good. One thing I know about this life is you ain't never gonna be happy if you let yourself want things that just can't be."

"What's that supposed to mean?"

"You know *exactly* what that means." Betty folds her arms, tilts her head to one side and gives her daughter a hard stare. "Men gonna keep talking their sweet talk. Nothing they can do about that. That's just the way they is. But no man with half a brain's gonna let himself get caught plowing the master's field—that's one thing you can count on." She gives her head a firm, slow shake. "And I *know* what I'm talking about."

"You don't know anything!" Sally Hemings snatches the *S* off the table and grips it in her lap.

"Oh, baby girl," her mother says sadly.

"Don't talk to me!" She leaps up from the table, knocking the chair over backward. "My life is nothing like your life!" She is at the door before she has even realized that is where she is headed, and then she is striding away from her cabin, still not knowing where she is going but thinking she might walk down the East Road.

Her mother is a spineless fool. She always talks about herself as if she is strong and wise and independent, but, in fact, she is constantly collaborating with her own enslavement. Sally Hemings is never going to let herself be like that. She is done with Thomas Jefferson. She was stupid enough to let herself be swept along by *his* sweet-talking, his sentimentality and his white-man's blindness to the realities of slavery. But never again! If he comes back to her on his knees, she's just going to turn her shoulder and say she is finished with him, and she'll keep on saying she is finished until he finally gives up and goes away. And she knows he will go away. Because he's not one of those men who's led around by his little head; he's led around by his heart. And that's why she has a power over him. And that's why—in this one way, at least—she is free. People may not know it now, but they will soon. They'll see that she's not the master's woman. Not anymore. And then everything will be different. That's when her real life will begin.

When she sees Sam Holywell the following morning, he smiles at her, tells her how pretty she is, but when she stands close to him, he backs away. And when she looks him straight in the eye so that he might know all the feeling that is in her heart, he looks right over her shoulder. And that is when she understands that he was only flirting with her because he wanted to feel like a big man—a man who isn't afraid to get back at the master through his woman. The problem, of course, is that he *is* afraid—and knowing that, Sally Hemings loses all respect for him.

S ally Hemings is cleaning out the bottom drawer in Maria's dresser when she finds the very same primer that Thomas Jefferson bought for her in Paris. How did it get here? Why would Maria have bothered to pack a child's book? And why would she put it at the bottom of her dresser under all of her outgrown petticoats?

The thin volume is partially wedged under the board at the back of the drawer, and as Sally Hemings slides it out, she feels that the paper is far softer than when she was reading it with Thomas Jefferson. The pages turn without resistance and fall flat upon one another without even a whisper. There are dark stains on some of them, and next to the picture of a dog biting a man there is a child's pencil drawing of an angry face with big teeth. Clearly this is *not* the primer she had in Paris but perhaps the one from which Maria learned to read, and Martha too, and possibly even their mother before them, or even Thomas Jefferson himself. She is touched that he sought out this particular book for her in Paris, but she is also excited to discover that she remembers almost all of the couplets on the first two pages.

She brings the primer back to her cabin, and that night, by the light of a pine knot burning in a tin bowl, she tries, once again, to read the title of *Notes on the State of Virginia*—the very volume that Martha employed in her hasty reading lesson and that she subsequently gave to Sally Hemings as a gift. Almost immediately, however, she encounters two formidable obstacles: The first is that she no longer remembers what the book's title might be, except that one of the words is Virginia. And the second is that almost all of the letters that she will need to read the title's first word would seem to belong to the couplets that Thomas Jefferson skipped over because they contained biblical names.

Since Jimmy and Bobby are both away with Thomas Jefferson in New York, the only person she knows who can help her read is her half brother John, whom Thomas Jefferson arranged to have tutored while they were in Paris, so that he could make sense of treatises on carpentry and joinery. John opens the primer on a table in the joinery shop where he is an apprentice and reads off the mysterious couplets one after another as easily as if he were reciting a prayer. He has Sally Hemings repeat them with him until she, too, is able to rattle them off as if she is actually reading. He also explains that some of the letters—which Sally Hemings thinks he calls "owls"—can be pronounced in many ways, and these he rehearses with her until she, too, has mastered the pronunciations of all five "owls."

For some reason she is able to absorb John's lessons far more easily than Thomas Jefferson's, and as she senses this new knowledge expanding within her mind, she feels as if she is experiencing a revelation on the magnitude of Eve's when she first bit into the apple. John tells her that Thomas Jefferson's book is far too difficult for her and offers to give her the very first book he ever read, but she is determined that by the time Thomas Jefferson has returned from New York, she will have mastered his book.

Back in her cabin, she finds that the title's first three letters (corresponding to Noah, Oak and Timothy) reveal their secrets to her instantly. She has more trouble with the fourth letter (corresponding to Eagle), because she thought the first word was "Note," but now it seems to be "No-tee," a word she has never heard of before. (It turns out that the full range of sounds designated by the "owls" did not last in her memory the length of time it took to walk from the joinery to her cabin.) The final letter (one she knows very well) solves the problem. The word is "Notice," though she thinks it strange that it should be spelled as if it is pronounced "No-teese." The next word is easy: "own"—though she is not sure how that word might connect to "notice," a secret she hopes will be revealed by the following word. That word, however, utterly flummoxes her. She can think of no way the sounds for Timothy, Hat and Eagle might be combined into a word. The same is true for the next word: "Staa-tee"—what on earth is that? She thinks she understands the following word—"oaf"—but when she adds all the words together—"Notice own ??? Staa-tee oaf"—she sounds like a madwoman muttering on a Paris street. So now she experiences a new revelation on the magnitude of Eve's: that she is utterly stupid, that reading is much too hard for her and unimaginably boring.

She wants to tear Thomas Jefferson's book into tiny pieces, but instead she flings it into the hidey-hole under her bed, flings the primer after it and covers the hole with the trunk containing all of her fine clothing from France.

Heaps of creamy clouds fill the sky from horizon to horizon, hazy sunbeams fanning diagonally between them. It is September, the season of goldenrod and fat cattle, of orange dust, balmy afternoons and faintly tarnished skies; a time when the orioles and bobolinks are gone and the cries of the jays and crows grow louder.

Thomas Jefferson has been in New York for six months, serving as secretary of state, and the first Sally Hemings knows of his return is when she sees Goliah carrying a pair of scuffed and mud-splattered riding boots down to the stable to be cleaned and polished.

A little later she is hanging her own wet gowns and shifts on the line in front of the kitchen and hears the clatters and clinks of china and silverware coming from a porch that looks down onto the yard.

She turns her back to the porch and sings as she works, softly, her voice hardly more than a vibration between palate and tongue. Once the last shift has been pegged to the line and is shedding droplets into the red dust, she puts her basket against her hip and turns toward the kitchen door.

There is a darkness overhead.

"Good afternoon, Sally," Thomas Jefferson calls out heartily. He is resting his elbows on the porch railing, and their faces are not more than three yards apart.

"Good afternoon, Mr. Jefferson." Her voice is flat, merely polite. She circles the basket with both arms and pulls it tighter against her pelvis.

He seems to be waiting.

"Welcome home," she says.

"It's good to be home." He smiles broadly, looking directly into her eyes.

She turns away for an instant, toward the sun-mottled eastern plain. "Beautiful day," she says.

"Yes! Very beautiful."

He is still looking into her eyes, but his smile is more vulnerable.

"Well . . ." She lifts her empty basket, as if to signify some urgent duty, then turns her back and enters the kitchen.

A brown darkness presses on her eyes once she is out of the daylight, and she waits just inside the door as the obscurity slowly sorts itself into the fireplace, the wall and the rose glints on the copper pots.

Her entire body is gripped by something between trembling and alertness, as if she has just been slapped or has heard some terrible news. Yet she feels as if she has acquitted herself well.

Thomas Jefferson got nothing out of her.

Not one thing.

The following morning she is seated beside Maria in the back of a carriage. Jupiter is driving. Maria has just turned twelve and has grown three inches over the last year. Sally Hemings has been stitching lace frills to the ends of the girl's sleeves and skirts, but now the buttons on the backs of her gowns can no longer be fastened, and she can only keep decent through the use of brooches and shawls. She is on her way to see Mrs. Mickel, the mantua maker in Charlottesville, to have a new gown made and her old ones let out. She wants Sally Hemings to help her choose the best materials and design.

The carriage is not moving.

Thomas Jefferson hailed them as they were departing from the great house, and now he is giving his daughter strict instructions not to order a gown in green or red. The former color, he says, will make her "Welsh complexion" seem pallid, while with the latter the slightest infusion of color in her cheeks will make her seem feverish.

In the presence of his daughter, Thomas Jefferson can do no more than glance intermittently at Sally Hemings, and so she is able to examine him at length in daylight, something she has not done for a very long time. There are bluish bags under his eyes, and the first puckering of an insipient dewlap beneath his chin. So much gray has filtered into his hair that there is a streak just over his left eye that seems more yellow than red. And during the rare moments when he listens to rather than lectures Maria, his long, thin lips form a straight line across his face that seems simultaneously pompous and weak.

How is it, Sally Hemings wonders, that she could ever have wanted to cover that deflated face with kisses? Or yearned to pull that lank and bandy body between her thighs? All of the cravings, worries and delicious aches that had once filled her every minute apart from him now seem a sort of insanity.

This is good, she thinks.

When Thomas Jefferson gives her one last inquiring glance after bidding his daughter good-bye, she tells herself, *I am free now. Finally free.*

She looks him straight in the eyes, hoping he will intuit the words she is speaking inside her head:

Free.

I am free.

"Ah, Sally—come in!" Thomas Jefferson is seated at his desk, in that strange chair of his own devising in which she once spun until she became nauseated. (She has kept well away from it ever since.) As he watches her cross the room from the door, he sways slightly from side to side, his chair making mouse squeaks.

"Please sit down." He gestures at an ordinary chair in front of his desk.

"I'm all right standing," she says.

Thomas Jefferson makes a laughlike noise, but his expression is serious. "Well," he says. He looks down at his hands. "Yes." He stares into the middle distance for a long moment, as if he has forgotten what he means to say. At last he looks at Sally Hemings. "I'm wondering if we might have a frank discussion about Maria."

He pauses, as if waiting for a confirmation.

Sally Hemings neither moves nor speaks. She blinks to disengage her gaze from his.

"I understand entirely that, as her maid, you must have certain . . . I don't know . . . *confidences* with her, young though she may be—things that you should feel under no obligation to mention. It is not right, after all, that a father know everything about his daughter's affairs."

Thomas Jefferson attempts something like a smile, which Sally Hemings does not return.

"I do hope, however, that in our shared affection for Poll we might be able to help her in what I feel may be a difficult period for her."

Again he looks to Sally Hemings for confirmation. She gives her head a slight nod and says, very softly, "Yes."

"So you agree that she's not happy?"

"I didn't say that."

He leans back in his chair, puts his hands together as if praying and rests his fingertips momentarily against his upper lip. Then he leans forward again.

"What do you think, Sally? I have no idea what to make of Maria. Sometimes I tell myself that I am ridiculously oversensitive, other times—"

He flings his hands, palms up, signifying helplessness. "*You're* with her every single day. Do you know if there is anything wrong?"

Sally Hemings shrugs.

"What?" he asks, his voice and brow expressing frustration. "What are you thinking?"

"Nothing, just . . . you know: Sometimes people get sad."

"So you agree that she is sad?"

"Sometimes."

The fingertips of Thomas Jefferson's pressed-together hands are touching his lips again. He lowers them.

"Listen, Sally, let me tell you why I'm worried. The entire time I was in New York, Maria hardly wrote to me. And when she did, her letters were models of filial decorum, but they were so brief—none even a page long—and they contained not one single word expressing anything like true feeling. All I could gather from them was that she was trying to conceal from me how seriously remiss she was being in her studies. And since I've been home, I've found that the situation was even worse than I had intuited. I don't think that in six long months she's read more than two chapters in *Don Quixote*, and she is unable to utter a single grammatical sentence in Spanish. She even seems to be losing her French. But none of that really matters. The main thing is that I have yet to see a hint of joy, or even of childish enthusiasm, in her countenance. Her gaze is always on the floor, she hardly speaks above a whisper and she prefers the solitude of her room to all other occupations."

Thomas Jefferson's entire expression is tremulous with worry—so much so that Sally Hemings wonders if he might shed a tear.

All at once the rigidity goes out of her body. She sinks into the chair in front of his desk—but not out of sympathy. She knows something—something she can never say, and yet that, at this moment, she wants desperately to reveal. The terrific intensity of her desire to speak is what has taken the strength out of her legs.

Thomas Jefferson looks at her, then smiles sadly. She senses that he is about to reach out and touch her arm, which is resting on the edge of the desk. She pulls the arm away.

"I'm sorry, Sally." The worry has returned to his face. "I know that I am putting you in a difficult position. But I am concerned for other reasons as well." He takes a deep breath, leans forward and speaks in a low, emphatic voice. "The truth is that there is a tendency toward melancholy on both sides of our family. As you may know, Maria's dear mother was very delicate and sometimes so exhausted by sorrow that she could not rise from bed in the morning. I have often thought this susceptibility of hers contributed to her early death. And on my side . . . well, on my side there is an even more pronounced tendency. And I can hardly bear to think that poor little Polly may be laboring under a similar affliction."

What Sally Hemings knows but cannot say is that during the weeks after Lucy's death Polly came to hate her father, partially for leaving her behind when he went to France but mainly because, when she needed him most, after little Lucy's death, he didn't care enough to come to her side. During the three years before Polly boarded the ship to London, she waited every day for a letter from him telling her that he was coming home. When at last she woke from her drugged sleep and found herself miles out at sea, her first coherent words were, "I don't want to go live with Papa. I *hate* him!" And she expressed exactly the same sentiment every day until Monsieur Petit escorted them down the gangplank and onto French soil. After that, Polly allowed herself to love her father again with an almost pathetic servility, but Sally Hemings knows that the hate has never left her heart and that she was, in fact, very sullen and unhappy throughout his stay in New York.

And this is what she wants to tell Thomas Jefferson—because he has no idea of it and because he has no idea how enraged she herself is this very moment, sitting across from him at his desk.

But she doesn't speak the words that have gathered on her tongue. Instead she says, "I don't know if you have to worry about that. Everybody gets sad from time to time. The world is a sad place—that's all. You get sad for a little bit, then you get happy. I've seen Maria happy plenty of times."

"So you think"—Thomas Jefferson smiles wryly—"that I am just being a worried old fool?"

"Not exactly," says Sally Hemings. "But maybe."

Thomas Jefferson laughs out loud and flings himself back into his squeaking seat.

"You're not just saying that to make me feel better?" he says.

"No." Her face grows pale, and when she speaks again, her voice is trembling. "But there is one thing I am going to say to you. You've got to stop thinking so much about yourself. And you've got to think a great deal more about how the things you do affect other people."

Sally Hemings can no longer speak, because anger has choked off her voice. Her eyes are fixed and hard, her mouth a yellow seam.

Thomas Jefferson looks thoughtful but says nothing for a long time. Then he gives his head a barely detectable shake. His voice, when he speaks, is so low it is almost a moan.

"Oh, Sally."

Sally Hemings stands up, then steps away from the desk. "I've got things I should be doing."

"No, wait!" He leans across his desk, one hand extended.

She doesn't move. She doesn't speak. Her blue-gray eyes so filled with fury and yet so beautiful.

Thomas Jefferson's hand falls to the desktop, and he leans back again.

"I'm sorry, Sally." He covers his nose and mouth with both hands, then lets them fall into his lap. "I'm so sorry. And if it is any comfort to you, I, too, have been suffering—"

"I'm not talking about that!" she says. "You made perfectly clear how wrong all of that was, and I agree with you. So that's over. You don't even have to think about that anymore."

This last sentence is spoken as she turns toward the door, which she pulls open so rapidly it flies from her hand and bangs a chair against the wall. She walks straight out into the dark corridor and leaves the door swaying behind her.

"Well, all right," Betty says to her daughter. "You do what you got to do. I just hope you don't make things worse, that's all. Mr. Jefferson's not a bad man. There's lots of worse men out there, colored or white."

"Stop it!" shouts Sally Hemings. "You don't know anything about Mr. Jefferson! You don't know one single thing! Everybody around here talks about him like he's some kind of saint or god or Jesus Christ himself! But I won't do that! Thomas Jefferson can roast in hell for all I care!"

"Hush, child! Somebody'll hear you, talking so loud."

"I don't care who hears me! I hope he hears me himself! I hope he roasts in hell! And when he dies, I'm going to dance on his grave! I promise you that! And I hope he just heard every word I said!"

. . . I could insult Mr. Jefferson, I could hate him, I could reject his overtures and acts of kindness, I could cast him cold stares for weeks on end, but in the back of my mind I always knew that these were mere pretense and nothing that would actually satisfy my rage or quell my pain. The only way that I could be truly rid of Mr. Jefferson would have been to flee Monticello, but that would have meant leaving all the people I loved most and abandoning myself to a future that at the very best would have been decidedly uncertain.

It is possible that I could have convinced Mr. Jefferson to sell me, as had my sisters Mary and Thenia when they wanted to be with their husbands and children. But I had no husband to go to, and I had buried my only child under shards of frozen earth. And from a purely practical point of view, it was almost impossible to imagine that I might find a more comfortable situation with another owner and very easy to imagine that I might end up subjected to the sort of barbarities that every southern Negro dreads and that for too many are simple facts of life.

I did often think about running away, however. Between my appearance, my Parisian clothing and my accent—to say nothing of the fact that I was almost fluent in French—I could easily have passed for white, at least once I had put sufficient distance between myself and this place so that no one could recognize me. But I had no illusions about how a penniless woman might fare, even if all the world saw her as white and even in so enlightened a city as Philadelphia. I had heard the tales of deception, sorrow, shame and lonely death told by Reverend Hodder. I had even seen such women standing on the streets of Paris with their rouged cheeks, their all-but-naked bosoms and their bitter, alcohol-dimmed gazes. When, many years after this time, we sent off our Harriet, it was with fifty dollars, a coach ticket and a letter of introduction to Mr. Jefferson's dear friends the Wentworths. Even had I known when I was seventeen that he could do such a thing, I would never have dared hope that he would want to so facilitate my northern migration.

Many times during the months after I lost La Petite, I had raged at the *injustice of my life and endured many a moment of strangled panic, as if I had been sealed up inside a wall. Such feelings certainly contributed to my rage at Mr. Jefferson, the arbiter of my confinement, but at the same time, the human heart being impervious to reason, the pain and anger I suffered after our departure from France were also evidence of how desperately I still needed Mr. Jefferson, though less perhaps for his physical consolations than for his mind. In our conversations I had felt as if I were in a vast palace and he was constantly opening up doors onto strange and beautiful rooms, corridors, gardens and garrets through which I could wander in endless fascination. . . .*

ELIZABETH: Why do you say Sarah?

Q: [Silence.]

ELIZABETH: Nobody ever called her Sarah. I didn't name her Sarah. Jack— Well, it's true that Jack wanted to name her Sarah, after his daughter who died. But I wouldn't hear of that. I thought that was bad luck. So the closest I would come was Sally. So that's what her name was, and nobody ever called her different.

Q: Sorry.

ELIZABETH: That's all right. I was just wondering.

Q: I just thought—

ELIZABETH: That's okay. I was just . . . you know . . .

Q: Still . . . can we go on?

Elizabeth: Sure.

Q: So . . . one thing I've been . . . uh . . . that I think people will be curious about is . . . uh . . . why you encouraged your daughter to continue her affair—

ELIZABETH: Did she tell you that?

Q: Yes. I'd have to take a look at my notes, but . . . well, yes.

ELIZABETH: That's not how it was. No. I don't remember that.

Q: What do you remember?

ELIZABETH: Maybe I just didn't want her to feel bad. It wasn't like she had a whole lot of choice.

Q: Do you mean that Mr. Jefferson . . . *Thomas* forced himself on her?

ELIZABETH: No. Well . . . at first I guess he did. But it wasn't really like that.

Q: What do you mean?

ELIZABETH: Things were just different in those days. Men just presumed.

Q: Presumed?

ELIZABETH: Right. If you were a woman—*especially* if you were colored—you didn't have a choice. Men just presumed you were there for whatever they wanted.

Q: That can't always have been true. What about courtship? I mean, at least for the upper classes . . . for white—

ELIZABETH: Oh, yeah. Men had to do their song and dance. There was always a little bit of song and dance. But basically they just presumed. And the women presumed they presumed. So that made it easier for everybody.

Q: For the women?

ELIZABETH: Absolutely. Take, for example, Martha Jefferson. Martha *Wayles*, I mean. Sally's sister. She used to talk like she wished she had absolutely nothing between her legs. Just blank there, like a field on a snowy day. But, of course, she didn't really want anything like that at all. So it made her happy that Mr. Jefferson presumed. That way she could just lie back and enjoy it and feel like it was all his doing.

Q: So what you mean is that Sarah, *Sally* felt that way, too?

ELIZABETH: No. Not really. Well, maybe a little bit, but not really.

Q: I don't understand.

ELIZABETH: Well, it was easier for all women, sometimes, to just put it on the man. But Sally wasn't really like that.

Q: [Silence.]

ELIZABETH: She wasn't really like Mrs. Martha.

Q: I guess what I still want to know is if Thomas forced himself upon Sally.

ELIZABETH: Of course. But not really. He wasn't really the forcing kind.

Q: I'm still confused.

ELIZABETH: Well . . . look at it this way: Jack—now he was the kind of man who forced a woman. I had been married for eight years when his third wife died. And one day he called me in and he told me he was going to sell Lonny. (Lonny was my husband.) He was going to sell Lonny to Bath Skelton. (That was his ex-brother-in-law. And later on he married Mrs. Martha, before Mr. Jefferson.)

Q: That's terrible!

ELIZABETH: You mean Lonny?

Q: Of course. That must have been awful for you! What did you do?

ELIZABETH: Yeah. It was . . . in a way. But it's not like Lonny was a saint among saints. In a lot of ways, selling Lonny was the answer to all my problems. I think Jack knew that. I think that was part of what it was about.

Q: But Jack, Mr. Wayles—you said he was the "forcing kind." What did you mean by that?

ELIZABETH: Look at it this way: No woman ever has a choice. But the first thing she has to do is make it clear that she *does* have a choice. For herself, I mean. It's a matter of dignity.

Q: [Silence.]

ELIZABETH: Dignity's the most important thing.

Q: So when Mr. Wayles said that he was going to sell Lonny, what did you do?

ELIZABETH: I told him he couldn't do that. I told him Lonny was the father of my children. You know. The whole song and dance. I told him he couldn't force me.

Q: What did he say?

ELIZABETH: Oh, just what they always do: I was his property. I didn't have any more say than a mule. He could do anything he wanted with me.

Q: That's horrible!

ELIZABETH: [Shrugs.] Yeah.

Q: What did you do?

ELIZABETH: I kicked him. If I was a mule, that meant I was going to kick, so I did. And then I spat in his face.

Q: [Laughs.] Weren't you afraid?

ELIZABETH: Not really. I knew what he was up to.

Q: What did he do?

ELIZABETH: He pushed me down on the floor and he had me right there.

Q: [Silence.]

ELIZABETH: [Silence.]

Q: I'm sorry . . . uh . . . so sorry.

ELIZABETH: It was nothing. I knew he was going to do that.

Q: Nothing? Do you really mean nothing?

ELIZABETH: Oh, course it wasn't nothing. I just meant it didn't bother me. I knew he was going to do it. He was just doing his song and his dance.

Q: I . . . I don't know . . .

ELIZABETH: Look, the problem is that you keep thinking there was some sort of better way. That's not how it was in those days. And the truth is, it's not that different now. So, you know: You've got to keep that in perspective.

Q: Of course—

ELIZABETH: Just think about it from my side. First of all, I knew I was going to be his concubine, or whatever you want to call it, from the minute the last Mrs. Wayles got her fever. I could tell just by the way he was looking at me. Second of all, Lonny presumed all kinds of things. And one of those things was that he could knock me down anytime he got drunk. Which was almost all the time. I'd been trying for two years to figure out how I was going to get away from him, and I didn't see how I could do it as long as he was at the Forest. Unless I was willing to kill him. Which I wasn't. But I *was* thinking about it. I was even talking to one of the old mammies about poison berries, hexes—you know. But I wasn't really going to do that. I just couldn't do that. So when Jack did to me what he did, I knew he was just doing his song and dance. Just like I was doing my song and dance. We were just working out the rules of how we were going to be together. And after that we pretty much had it figured out. You have to remember that I had been the maid to all three of his wives. So I knew how he treated a woman. He was English. You know? He lived in England until he was almost a grown man. So he was kind of old-fashioned. He believed in rules. And as long as everybody behaved by the rules, everybody was happy. He wasn't a cruel man. He wasn't exactly tenderhearted— though he was that, too, sometimes. But he definitely wasn't cruel. And, of course, I knew that as his . . . well, as his *wife* really, things would get pretty easy for me. And they did. Pretty much. After that, everything was much better than it had been before. Or mostly.

Q: So is that why you encouraged Sally—

ELIZABETH: Of course!

Q: So what did you mean by Thomas not being the "forcing kind"? How was he different?

ELIZABETH: Oh, he and Jack were exactly the opposite kind of people. Exactly the opposite. Jack didn't apologize for everything. He just assumed he had a right to anything he wanted. Mr. Jefferson—it was like he assumed he didn't have a right to anything. Sometimes I used to laugh at how afraid of him people were. Most of the people who came to see him, they were so nervous they could hardly talk when he was in the room. I mean, of course Mr. Jefferson was famous and everything, and, you know, once he got started talking, most people felt like they didn't know anything at all. Like they were just idiots. But inside, he was always saying, "I'm sorry, I'm sorry, I'm sorry." He kept trying so hard to be a good man because inside he thought he was so bad. That's the honest truth. That's how he really was.

Q: But he *did* force himself on your daughter. So if he wasn't the forcing kind . . .

Elizabeth: You mean in Paris?

Q: [Nods.]

Elizabeth: I never figured out what happened in Paris. Sally would never be straight with me about that. Most of the time, she told me nothing happened in Paris. Well, not nothing, but not what you mean either. But then sometimes— The only way I could figure it was that maybe something *did* happen. I mean, you've got to think that any man who goes around saying "I'm sorry" all the time— especially a man like Mr. Jefferson who knew, somewhere in the back of his mind, that there was no reason for him to apologize to anyone, that he could have had pretty much anything he wanted and people would have thought he deserved it. You know what I mean? I mean, not only was he smarter than just about anybody, and so famous everybody wanted to get a look at him, he was also this great big tall man and strong as a horse. So when a man like that is always saying "I'm sorry, I'm sorry" and humiliating himself all the time, you got to figure he's getting pretty angry inside. He's building up this whole mountain of anger. So, of course, every now and then he's got to let that anger out. And maybe that's what happened in Paris. I don't know. But all I can tell you is that that's not who he was. He was definitely not the forcing kind.

Thomas Jefferson is an ape. He lumbers apelike through the Great Ape House, mostly on his handlike feet but sometimes on the knuckles of his actual hands. His knuckles are particularly effective whenever he wants to pivot or to swing his feet through empty space. They turn his body into a projectile. They transform his tremendous weight into force.

The air of the Great Ape House is dense with the penetrating sweetness of ape shit. The light in the Great Ape House is the color of watery milk. The hillside on which Thomas Jefferson and the other Great Apes spend their days is the color of mice, and the logs, which constitute the Great Apes' only furniture and playthings, are the color of logs with the bark peeled off—a color you might call Sunset on Snow.

Thomas Jefferson disdains his fellow apes but at the same time depends upon them: for nitpicking, for consolation during his ape-house jitters and for the delights of intimate union. He is the biggest of all the Great Apes, and so he is always first in line when the lesser apes come through the rectangle with the food bucket. And if he should miss the bucket because he is napping, he just takes the food of any ape he chooses. Ditto their mates.

He sees nothing wrong with this state of affairs, and neither, apparently, do any of the other Great Apes. They don't like giving up their food, of course, or their mates. And sometimes the mates seem to take less delight in intimate union than Thomas Jefferson does. But that is not the same as wrong. There is nothing any of the other Great Apes can do to stop Thomas Jefferson, and so there is nothing to be gained by thinking he is wrong. In general, Great Apes are much more interested in harmony than in wrong or right. When Thomas Jefferson is happy, everyone is happy. He will leave them the food he doesn't want. Ditto the mates. He will even nitpick. And when it comes to ape-house jitters, there can be no greater consolation than Thomas Jefferson's gigantic embrace. This is harmony. And as long as no one thinks Thomas Jefferson is wrong, the harmony is total. Or as close to total as anyone can imagine.

One day Thomas Jefferson happens upon a system by which he might cross the gulf from the hillside to that other hillside where duplicate apes perfectly copy every one of his gestures and those of the other Great Apes. They do it in absolute silence. No sound ever crosses the gulf from that other hillside. The duplicate apes seem to worship the Great Apes in the same way as the Great Apes are worshipped by their shadows. The system involves a log tipped off into space and slamming to rest against the end of the duplicate log that has been tipped off into space by the duplicate Thomas Jefferson. The two logs make a sort of bridge between the hillsides. And as Thomas Jefferson walks upon his log, he sees his duplicate walking toward him upon his own. Then something strange happens. The closer Thomas Jefferson gets to his duplicate, the darker his duplicate becomes, until finally the duplicate ceases to duplicate Thomas Jefferson and instead seems to be embarked upon a project of total erasure, which is to say the replacement of everything within the borders of his being with darkness.

But that's not the really strange thing.

The really strange thing is that within the darkness of what once was his duplicate, Thomas Jefferson can see moving things. And when he gets to the end of his log and to that place where he ought to have been able to wrestle with his duplicate and throw him into the gulf, the air suddenly becomes hard—so hard he cannot even touch his duplicate or put one toe onto the duplicate log. But now he can see the moving things clearly. At first he thinks they are spots, like the spots that dent his vision when he rubs his eyes or when he stares at the milky lights too long. But then he sees that the spots are apes. Or they are apelike.

In fact, they are lesser apes.

And as he presses his face hard against the hard air, some of the lesser apes are leaping in fear. And some of them are baring their teeth. And pointing. They seem to be making noises. Maybe he can hear them. A muffled honking. A hooting. There are so many of them. Not just three. Many. *Many.* More than all of the Great Apes. A lot more.

There is something about this that should not be. Something disharmonious—even, perhaps, wrong. Thomas Jefferson bellows. He pounds on the hard air. He is waiting for everything to go back to the way it was. To the way it should be.

It is November 8, 1790, and not yet dawn when Sally Hemings is awakened by shouting. As she looks up into a charcoal dimness, she hears Jimmy's voice: "Underneath the knives!" He shouts that exact phrase three times in a row, giving the last word a strange emphasis. Then someone farther away—a woman or a boy—calls out something indecipherable, which is immediately followed by Thomas Jefferson shouting more loudly than anyone else: "Time's a wasting!" At the sound of his voice, a shiver passes through Sally Hemings's entire body, and she has to roll onto her side and draw up her knees to quell the cold.

This is the morning when Jimmy, Bobby and Thomas Jefferson go north again—to Philadelphia this time, because the capital has been moved there from New York. Jimmy told her last night that they might be gone for a whole year. She said good-bye to him then but intended to get up early so that she could give him one last hug. She woke up several times during the night, in fact, but always too soon. Now she contemplates throwing on her greatcoat and running out to give him, at the very least, a parting wave, but the idea of venturing into the frigid air is more than she can bear.

She is awakened an hour or so later by her mother, who is shaking her shoulder and saying, "Let's go, baby girl. Her Majesty's waiting on her chocolate."

Sally Hemings is so deeply asleep that it is close to a minute before she has any idea what her mother is talking about. She doesn't know how she will be able to get out of bed. Her head feels like a boulder; she can hardly turn it on her pillow. And as soon as she has thrown off her covers, she starts to shiver so violently her teeth clatter.

Her mother is looking at her as if she has just done something shocking. "That you, baby girl?"

Sally Hemings can't answer. She pulls her blankets back up tight around her shoulders, but her teeth won't stop clattering.

Her mother is a darkness bending over her.

Icy fingers touch her cheek.

A low, quiet voice: "Oh, Lord! You burning up."

Her mother goes away and then is back. The odor of a tin cup coats the inside of Sally Hemings's nose.

"Drink this," her mother says. "Water's the best thing when you got a fever."

"No." Sally Hemings squeezes her eyes shut and covers her face with the blanket.

Her mother sighs and then is silent.

The particulate whisper of a stool being dragged across a dirt floor. Clank of cup on wood.

"I'm leaving this here for you," her mother says. "I'll go take care of Her Majesty. You drink this when you ready."

Sally Hemings expects to see her mother standing in front of her when she opens her eyes, but the cabin is entirely empty and it is full daylight—midmorning by the slant of the beams coming in the window.

Now she truly is thirsty—desperately!—but her hands feel so ill-coordinated as she reaches for the cup that she is afraid she will drop it. The room is still so very, very cold. As she grabs the cup and presses it against her lips, every fluff of air seeping under the covers is like ice against her skin. And once she has put the cup back on the stool and has pulled the covers up to her neck, she is colder than ever before. Hard shivers rack her shoulders and grind down through her abdomen. Her feet feel cased in snow. She wants to get up and take the covers from her mother's bed but can't bear to cross the cold room. She is too weak. Her teeth are clattering again. She will wait until her mother returns.

There follows a long period during which she is not really awake but not entirely unconscious. For much of that time, she feels she is lying naked on the hard floor of a dark and frigid cave, her shivers so violent they are painful. Sometimes the cave floor is like the deck of a ship in a heaving, blowing storm. Grunting beasts shamble past her from all directions, and she knows that one of them will step on her with its huge, clawed feet. *That will be the end of me*, she thinks. She is afraid but does nothing to stop those huge, shambling beasts—because, of course, there is nothing she can do.

When next she wakes, it is because her mother is covering her with her own blankets, though Sally Hemings doesn't remember asking her to do that.

The blankets are not enough.

"Cold," she says. "So cold."

Her mother pulls the trunk out from under the bed and covers her with all the gowns, petticoats and shifts that she wore in France and tops the heap off with her greatcoat and cape. The weight of all that clothing is good. Sally Hemings feels comforted. But still she is shivering.

Time has passed. She has awakened to the sound of her mother's urgent murmuring and realizes that the poor woman is praying with her face to the wall.

"Mammy," Sally Hemings calls from the bed. "Mammy, it's all right. You don't have to worry. I'm getting better."

"I know you is," says her mother turning around. "But it don't hurt to ask the Lord for help." She turns back to the wall, and her urgent murmuring continues.

As Sally Hemings slips back into sleep, she thinks that she really is getting better. A while ago she felt so very terrible that she was sure she was about to die, and she didn't actually care. But now things are different. Now she is not so cold. Now she is almost comfortable under all her covers and clothes.

It is late in the night when she wakes. She is so hot she can hardly breathe. She flings off all her covers and lies on her back in her sweat-soaked shift, savoring the coolness of the night air.

She feels as if she has been in the grip of a giant and now she has been released.

The chilled air on her ankles, feet and arms feels good. So does the layer of cold cloth clinging to her body. There is no light in the cabin. She looks toward the window and sees only black within black. So quiet. No birds. No human voices. Not even a breeze shifting the yellow leaves on the ground.

Then, from somewhere down the hill, a weird and echoing cry that would be laughter if only it weren't so very attenuated and sad. Then silence. Then exactly the same cry all over again.

At some point, much deeper into the night, when she has pulled the covers back over herself and is lying there, content in her solitude and happy in the knowledge that she will not die (not yet), memories that she has not allowed herself for many months come back to her all in a rush.

She remembers the time Thomas Jefferson said, "I don't know how I have ever lived without you," and a time when he looked into her eyes, put his hand softly against her cheek and told her, "You are so beautiful!

I want to draw your face!" and the night he pressed his head against her belly and wrapped his arms tightly around her waist and said that he couldn't bear to let her go, because if he did, the moment would end and he never wanted that moment to be over.

For months such memories have been far too painful for her to allow into her thoughts, but now, in her solitude and quiet, they are a comfort, and she finds herself imagining that when, in the bluish morning, she steps on her unsteady legs out onto her porch, intending to make her way around to the outhouse, she will find Thomas Jefferson waiting in the road. His expression will be so terribly sad. And when he comes to her, his touch will be so very gentle.

The prisoner is holding the bars of his cell door, looking at the guard. His mouth is open. His eyes are heavy with grief. The guard is sitting in her wooden chair, holding a fork with a yellow blob of scrambled egg on the end of it. She puts the blob into her mouth, chews, swallows, speaks.

—Delicious! Man, was I hungry!

The pink tip of the prisoner's tongue moves along his lower lip. The guard mops up the buttery smears of her egg with a piece of toast and pops the toast into her mouth. She chews. She speaks.

—Oh, God!

She puts the plate down on the floor and picks up the paper coffee cup that has been waiting on the opposite side of her chair. She wraps the cup in both hands, warming her fingers, leans back in her chair and rests the cup on her belly. She speaks.

—That was fabulous. I was starved.

The prisoner is looking at the tray. He can see a shred of egg that she didn't mop up. She pulled the crusts off her toast before she ate it, and they lie like a heap of tiny timbers on the tray beside the plate. The prisoner doesn't speak; the guard does.

—Did you ever think about whose nightmare this is?

— . . .

—I mean, who's dreaming this: you or me?

—I'm not dreaming anything.

—That's what I was afraid of.

— . . .

—I guess what I'm really asking is, which of us is the illusion here?

— . . .

—Because if only one of us is real, the other one must be an illusion. That's simple logic, right?

—What the fuck are you talking about?

—Are you deaf? Or are you just being an asshole? Jesus!

— . . .

—You're *my* nightmare! That's what I'm talking about!

— . . .

—It's simple logic, right? I mean, if I wasn't here with you, I could be lying on a beach somewhere. Or maybe I'd be studying impressionist painting in Paris. Or I could be a pediatrician with a tiny plastic monkey climbing up my stethoscope. You know?

— . . .

—But because of you, I don't have any choice. I am morally compelled to spend my life underground and behave like a barbarian, just because you're such an evil piece of shit. You see what I'm saying? It's like the nightmare you created never ended, and now I'm stuck in it.

— . . .

—I should hate you all the more for that.

— . . .

—What the fuck. Today's the day I'm supposed to make you stand on a carton of dog food and hook your dick up to a car battery. You're going to love that.

V

C lose to a year has passed. Clouds tower in the burnished sunlight of an unnaturally warm September afternoon. First deep stillness, then a wind gathers in the trees and rushes across the lawn and into the house. Doors slam. Someone inside cries out "Oh!" The treetops hiss and thrash. The clouds darken. The sound of shattering glass.

Sally Hemings, coming up from the orchard with a basket of peaches for Ursula, thinks that before going to the kitchen she should check Thomas Jefferson's chambers to make sure none of his windows are open and that none of his precious objects have been damaged.

She is just about to enter his doorway when she hears a voice in the front hall. Unable to believe she has heard right, she takes a few steps down the hall and sees a tall, slim man in a sweat-soaked yellow riding jacket. It is Thomas Jefferson, who was not expected for another two weeks.

His back is to her, and he is talking to Monsieur Petit, whom she hasn't seen since Paris. Jimmy and Bobby must also be home, though she can't see them or hear their voices.

As she hesitates in the hallway, torn between the desire to flee and another desire she can't define (she tells herself it's to see Monsieur Petit, whom she didn't even know was coming to this country), Thomas Jefferson turns suddenly and looks right at her. "Sally!" he exclaims. His face is radiant. His hair is windswept from the road. He looks as if he is about to laugh. Just then there is a cool rushing of air through the house, and the front door slams with a bang. "It seems we're in for a big storm!" says Thomas Jefferson, still looking straight at Sally Hemings. And then he does laugh.

It is night, and Sally Hemings, candle in hand, is descending the narrow staircase from the second floor, where she has just put away Maria's clothing of the day, laid out her gown, shift, stays and petticoats for the morning and bade the girl herself sweet dreams.

Her candle just barely illuminates the white balusters and a moving sphere of bare wall, so she makes her way downstairs more by memory than sight. Just as her foot touches the floor at the bottom of the stairs, the door to her left cracks and opens. Another candle hovers in the darkness, accompanied by a crimped thumb and the knuckles of a forefinger, and then she sees Thomas Jefferson's temple, cheek and the rightmost plane of his nose. "Oh!" he exclaims under his breath, and starts to push the door closed. Then he pulls it open again.

"Sorry, Sally! I didn't know anyone was there."

She has stopped at the bottom of the stairs. "Good night, Mr. Jefferson."

He, too, has stopped, with one arm, shoulder and leg through the doorway. "Yes," he says. "You, too." And then he smiles. "Sweet dreams, Sally."

This morning is as steamy and hot as every morning of the last week, but the air is restless, and so it feels cooler—as if something like ordinary life might be lived again.

Sally Hemings steps out of her door, barefoot, in nothing but her shift and a shawl, on her way to fetch some water from the rain barrel. Thomas Jefferson, just passing by on his favorite horse, Eagle, calls out, "Morning, Sally." Giving her a smile and a curt wave, he continues down Mulberry Row, toward the western woods and the riding trail that winds north, then down along the Rivanna and back along the East Road.

Later that morning, Maria's beloved Aunt Eppes and her son Jack arrive for a visit of several days. After lunch, on Thomas Jefferson's recommendation, they, too, go for a ride, and Sally Hemings decides to make the best of her free time by taking a walk down to the lake. She has only just crossed the field and begun to descend the steep, wooded path when she hears footsteps coming up rapidly behind her.

She turns and sees Thomas Jefferson striding down the path. His cheeks are flushed, his eyes bright, his step loping and strong.

"Good afternoon, Mademoiselle Sally," he says cheerfully, doffing his hat. "A beautiful day for a walk."

"Yes," she says, then blushes and is silent, as he falls into step beside her.

"I have spent my morning," he says, "devising ways to keep that petty Caesar, Hamilton, from handing our government over to bankers and speculators."

"Why would he want to do that?" she asks.

"I don't want to talk about it!" He smiles at her as if he is about to break into laughter—but in the next instant he is scowling and his voice is loud. "That man wants Congress to serve no one but his wealthy friends! He intends to establish a national bank, and I am certain that his entire purpose is to make beggars and sycophants out of the people's representatives. He doesn't care a fig for democracy, and won't be satisfied until a king has been crowned in this country!" Thomas Jefferson falls silent a moment, then shakes his head and smiles. "I'm sorry. This morning I wrote a dozen letters to President Washington warning him about Hamilton, but consigned every one of them to the fire, and now I feel as if I am on the verge of another of my periodical headaches. I was, in fact, feeling no small degree of despair on that account when I saw you walking past and then I thought, 'That's exactly what I should be doing!'"

"Oh." Sally Hemings doesn't look at him. Her step quickens without her realizing it. But he keeps pace.

After a moment he says, "I think there is no better way to relax the brain than walking. The trick is to empty the mind and to give oneself over entirely to the landscape and to the physical exercise of the body. In my observation, people who walk at least two hours a day lead happier and longer lives."

Sally Hemings is silent awhile. Then she says, "Is it working?"

"I'm sorry?"

"Your headache. Has it gone away?"

"Oh." He crumples his lips and shakes his head. "No. Not really. Well, maybe a little. But at least it's not getting worse."

They both fall quiet, and after a while some of the vitality seems to drain from his step. Sally Hemings wonders how long he plans to walk beside her and if she shouldn't make an excuse to go back to the house.

Finally she says, "I didn't know Monsieur Petit was coming."

"Oh, yes. He's going to be my chief of staff."

"When did he arrive?"

Thomas Jefferson is silent a moment, then says, "A while ago." After another moment he adds, "July, I mean. He arrived July nineteenth."

The corners of his mouth turn down, and his brow rumples with consternation.

Sally Hemings doesn't know what to say, and neither, apparently, does he.

They walk along without talking, and then he stops abruptly, and she does, too. He is smiling, but it is the sort of smile that is used to cover uneasiness. He seems about to reach for her hand but ends up clasping his own.

"I am afraid," he says, "that you are going to think me the most incoherent of men." His smile has shifted, almost to a boyish earnestness. "But I have a confession to make. I suspect you already know what I am going to say."

Sally Hemings's own head has begun to ache. A heat floods into her cheeks. "Then maybe there is no need for you to say it."

"I want to," he says. "I have to." He looks into her eyes. "It's just that over these many months I have been away, I thought of you constantly. I tried to stop myself, but there was nothing I could do."

Sally Hemings wants to be angry, but all she feels is a tightness in her head. She cannot look at him. Her eyes are on the muddy toes of his boots. "Mr. Jefferson," she says, "I don't think it is wise to talk like this."

"No," he sighs. "Not wise at all."

Now some of her desired anger begins to rise within her. "Maybe you better think about all the trouble this has caused us."

"I have been thinking," he says.

"Maybe you better think some more."

He takes her hand.

"Mr. Jefferson, please." A rod of pain runs from one temple to the other. Her whole body is filled with an urgent feeling that is half a desire to run and half a desire that makes her body go hard and immobile.

"Oh, Sally." He lifts her hand to his lips and kisses the knuckles of her middle and ring fingers.

The gentle suction and the warmth of his mouth are more than she can bear.

"I'm sorry!" she says. "I have to go!"

She turns and hurries in long strides back up the path.

He doesn't follow.

All the way home, she repeats to herself, *I have to be free. I have to be free. I have to be free.*

During the afternoon bulbous heaps of cloud loom out of the flatlands to the east and drift toward, then over, the mountaintop, going from cream to gray to blue-gray and finally to green. The air beneath the clouds seems to tremble, and then the leaves in the trees hiss and turn up their pale undersides. Winds come from all directions at once. They bludgeon and seethe. There is a massive thunderclap, and then the rain falls with such ferocity that it snaps in spikes off the rooftops, roads and puddles. Freshets race from gutter pipes. Small ponds rise in lawn dips, and branchlike bolts of pink and purple lightning cross the whole sky—so many at once, sometimes, that they are like enormous nets of stutter-blasting light.

And then, after hardly more than an hour, the air goes dead still and oven hot. Roof edges and branch tips drip. The returned sun cooks clouds of steam, first off the roads and then out in the fields. It is hard to breathe. People begin to sweat inside their rain-moist clothes. Buttons are undone, waistcoats and underskirts dispensed with. By suppertime the dogs are lying in the shadows of the houses with their tongues hanging out.

Then it is night, and Sally Hemings is waiting for sleep in the still, steamy heat. She kicks off her blanket, then draws her shift above her knees, then to the tops of her thighs, then to midbelly. Finally it is bunched in a hot lump under her armpits, and she wrestles herself out of it and flings it to the floor. She lies back down but experiences no relief.

She is thinking about freedom.

She is thinking about the freedom she felt when she and Thomas Jefferson were naked together in bed. She is thinking about how that was not really freedom and yet how for instants and even for whole nights it very definitely was.

She wonders if it might be possible to be with him like that again—or rather, if she might be able to give him the whole of her body but absolutely nothing of her soul.

Sally Hemings says, "I have loved this man I should never have loved. My love was like a disease from which I thought I would never recover. And yet when this disease ravaged my soul most fiercely, I was the happiest I have ever been. I knew joy."

. . . I don't think I have ever had a simple thought or feeling about Mr. Jefferson, one that didn't contain its opposite or which—more to the point—wasn't radically intensified by having to do constant battle with its contrary. The day before yesterday, when I had almost nothing to do but wait and worry, I decided to take advantage of a thaw by going for a long walk. The roads were slick with mud, but the wooded paths were rich with that springlike musk of old leaves. The only birdsong to keep me company was the abrasive squawking of jays and crows, but even so I felt the anguish passing out of my muscles and mind, and I moved with an easy contentment that I have not known for months. The sun was a yellow-white flare and the sky forget-me-not blue. It wasn't long before I was able to loosen my scarf and open my cloak.

I hadn't set out with any destination in mind, but once I found myself down by the Rivanna, I knew that I was headed for the lodge. It has been four years since the last time Tom and I visited that small house, and my heart rose into my throat as I rounded the bend and saw it atop a rise just beside the river. As I drew closer, I could see that the porch railing had gone askew, and that the white clapboards had grayed from rain and dust, and that a mist of green moss was spreading up the walls. I expected to find that the house had been broken into again and reduced to a shambles by vandals and by time, but the door was solid, the key was still in the tiny cabinet Mr. Jefferson had built for it underneath the porch and the lock turned easily.

Somehow the fact that nothing whatsoever had changed inside the lodge since we last locked the door behind us only made the passage of time more clear. The bed was neatly made, the kettle was on the hob, a single spoon lay on the mantel, where it had been left by Mr. Jefferson or by me after it had been used to scrape the last of some soup off the bottom of a bowl or stir some sugar into a cup of coffee. But the spoon had gone dark with tarnish, and a layer of whitish dust lay over every item in the room, including the counterpane.

There was a book beside the bed: Diderot's Lettre sur les aveugles, *of which*

Mr. Jefferson had had a very high opinion. I was the one to bring it to the lodge, however, having foolishly concluded that such a slender volume would be perfect for teaching myself to read French. I had probably left it behind out of sheer frustration and had so forgotten its existence that I was startled to discover it on the night table. As soon as I saw it, I snatched it up, clutched it to my breast and sank down upon the bed, suddenly overwhelmed by memories of all the afternoons and nights that Mr. Jefferson and I had spent in this small house.

I sat rocking back and forth on the edge of the bed, tears streaming down my face, crying, "No. No. No. No." For what did this book represent but my own selfishness? Even then, the day before the brutality of this world was revealed to me in such stark relief, I understood that whatever I might have gained from reading and my conversations with Mr. Jefferson had served only for my own enjoyment, and to advance my own opinion of myself, and, most repellant of all, to legitimize my fantasies that I was an exception, that I could somehow live in this world without being either colored or white. I had done nothing to help anyone else, nothing to correct the manifold injustices on which my own privilege depended. I could hardly have been more selfish.

I placed the book back on the clear rectangle amid the dust haze covering the top of the night table. I wiped away my self-indulgent tears and straightened the bodice of my gown. As I leaned forward to get to my feet, I noticed a gleam. Bending over, I found an old shoe buckle resting against one of the night table's legs. I picked it up and polished it with my sleeve. It had to have been Mr. Jefferson's, though I had no memory of his ever having ridden home with a loose shoe. I held the buckle in my hand as I left the lodge and locked the door. I didn't know what I was going to do. It occurred to me that by rights I ought to just throw the buckle into the river. But I didn't. I clutched it tightly in my fist as I walked away from the little house. Sometime later I slipped it into my pocket. It is still there. . . .

"The roof is still solid," says Thomas Jefferson. "It would be easy enough to bring a pallet out here, and other necessaries."

The river makes its rustles and clicks just outside their open door. He and Sally Hemings are lying on a horse blanket and their heaped clothes. Flies buzz, settle, suck the sweat off their bodies and then buzz some more. He admires the blue sheen of indirect daylight spilling through the door across her thighs and belly and the small darkness of her mussed pubic hair. Her head is on his shoulder. With his fingertips he can feel the smooth, soft weightiness of her breast. He circles his middle finger around the tip of her nipple and feels it grow hard. He is not sure he has ever known moments more beautiful than these. "How did this ever happen, Sally?"

Sally Hemings heaves a long sigh.

The cabin they are in—built by Thomas Jefferson's father as a hunting lodge—stands on a high, wooded bank of the Rivanna River and is entirely overshadowed by ancient oaks and beeches, amid which sunbeams illumine brilliant emerald clusters.

"I just want to lie here," she says, "and let this be the whole world."

Thomas Jefferson also sighs. "You're right. This is perfect." He sighs again and for a long moment is silent. Then he says, "I'm happy, Sally. Are you happy?"

She doesn't answer.

There are rapids just in front of them. As the water clatters onto itself, its sound echoes off the trees on the far bank. A small animal rustles in the leaves beside the porch. A catbird runs through a stream of liquid whistles—its song, too, echoing off the trees on the far bank.

Thomas Jefferson slides his shoulder out from under Sally Hemings's head and sits up cross-legged on the blanket. His neck is stiff, his head having been pillowed only by his shirt wadded against the wall. He cranks his head right, then left, feeling muscles cracking down the length of his back.

Sally Hemings rolls onto her left side and supports her head with her crooked arm, watching him as he stretches. Pursing her lips in discomfort, she pushes herself into a seated position. Her breasts wobble, then still.

That vacant, lost expression is on her face again—and it hurts him, even as he feels he has never seen anyone more beautiful.

"I wish we never had to leave here," he says.

"We don't." She smiles weakly, then sweeps her long brown hair away from her face and looks out the door. A jay makes its cold, piercing cry.

"A week ago," he says, "as I was climbing the hill toward home and that big storm was brewing, I promised myself that I would not even think of doing this. I simply would not allow it. And now—" He shakes his head. "I don't even know how this happened!"

What happened was that Sally Hemings came to his chambers shortly before lunch to tell him that Maria would be having a picnic with her cousin Jack in the copse at the top of a bluff above the South Road. Thomas Jefferson thanked her for the message and asked if she wouldn't mind bringing his laundry down to the kitchen for Nance. As she crouched to pull the basket of soiled clothing out from under his bed, he pretended—to himself, mostly—that he was entirely engrossed by his reading and that he hadn't even noticed her lithe back stretching beneath her bodice nor how her gown, clipped tight between the floor and her knee, revealed the long arc of her thigh. Nothing might have happened had she not, as she got to her feet and shifted the basket onto her hip, cast him such a shy and knowing glance under her lowered brow—at which point he threw his book onto the floor and raced to take her hand.

He doesn't remember their speaking a single word, only that they kissed for a very long time. When his hand strayed under her skirts and he discovered how ready she was for him, he murmured into her ear with a quivering voice that she should meet him on the bridle path to the lake in twenty minutes. And then, as a sort of promise, when he withdrew his hand, he put his middle finger into his mouth and sucked it clean. Twenty minutes later she was waiting exactly where instructed. He pulled her up onto the back of his horse and took her to this cabin—a place where he had imagined being with her since they were first together in Paris.

"I made those same promises," she tells him now. She shakes her head and gives him another of her knowing smiles. "But . . . well, the truth is, Mr. Jefferson"—her smile broadens, and Thomas Jefferson, still sitting cross-legged, feels his penis stretching in spurts along the instep of his right foot—"that Miss Maria never told me to let you know where she would be eating."

Sally Hemings laughs. She leans forward, and as they kiss, she places her hand between his legs.

A little later he is sitting up again and she is still lying down. He puts his hands to his temples and says, "I think I am insane."

"You are." Her smile is obliterated by a sigh.

"This is serious, Sally. What are we going to do?"

She doesn't say anything. She looks up at him from the floor, her narrow eyes suddenly weary.

"I am the secretary of state," he says. "I am President Washington's representative and the representative of this country—the world's first true democracy. The monarchs of Europe are watching us and want nothing but to see us fail. And the revolutionaries in France are looking to us to give them courage. What this means is that every one of us in the government must be beyond reproach, not just in our political lives but in our private lives."

Sally Hemings rolls away from him, onto her belly, her head pillowed on her folded arm, her face toward the floor. "If you want to stop," she says, her voice reverberant against the floorboards, "just stop."

She doesn't look around at him. She doesn't move.

His eyes run the length of her body. There are two pink ovals of unequal size at the top of her buttocks, where her pelvis was pressed against the floor.

"I can't stop," he says. "You know that."

She neither moves nor speaks.

"I live in fear," he says. "All it would take—" He doesn't finish.

Sally Hemings rolls onto her back and looks up at him ruefully for a long time. Then she sits up.

"Why does anyone have to know?" she says. "I can keep a secret, and so can you. Up at the house, you are the famous Thomas Jefferson and I am just your servant—one of a hundred and seventeen. All we have to do is be careful. We never do anything dangerous there. We never do anything that will attract anyone's attention. That's not so difficult. We can just wait until we are here, alone. This will be our own little country. No one will see what we do here, because no one will even know it exists."

She leans forward, smiling, and puts a hand on the inside of each of his thighs, just above the knee.

"Oh, Sally Hemings!" He shakes his head, but he, too, is smiling. "You are a most wonderful and persuasive girl!"

Y*ou will make me hate you.*

They are lying on a horse blanket on a bed of mint. They are wearing no clothes. A waterfall pours like a leaden fog off a broken rock into the cold pool where they have just been swimming. Thomas Jefferson laughs. "I cannot end slavery all by myself."

Sally Hemings refills his tin cup from a tin coffeepot. He says, "The sentiment against emancipation among the general public is so strong that we can only proceed in small steps. The first is to end the importation of slaves from Africa, so that the crime may not be enlarged. The next is to outlaw the practice in all states added to the Union after 1800, so that eventually the southern states will be so outnumbered that they will not be able to oppose the will of the majority. And then we must work upon the consciences and pocketbooks of the masters—" *So you are saying it is impossible.* "Not at all. I am saying the opposite." *You are saying that we must wait so long and meet so many conditions that it cannot possibly happen.* "Be reasonable, Sally. There is no other way. I am only telling you how it must come to pass. And it will!"

It is midnight on Christmas, and Thomas Jefferson has arrived at Sally Hemings's cabin (drunk), having just had a fight with Martha because he thinks her husband, Colonel Randolph (also drunk), is showing signs of insanity. "Oh, you must detest me, Sally. I am a fool and a bully, and I believe almost nothing that I write or say."

S he waits to put it to him until she is naked and he, too, is naked. They are sitting face-to-face, and his thing is sticking up between them like a gooseneck. A fire is blazing in the hearth.

It has been two months since their first visit to the lodge, and she has been thinking about this for days. She rehearsed her words all last night.

"I want you to promise me," she says, "that if we have any children, they will be free."

Thomas Jefferson's eyes narrow. His sultry smile is gone. His thing begins to droop.

"I'm not asking for anything for myself," she says. "I will stay with you as I am. But I want my children—*our* children, *your* children—to be free. That's all I ask."

Thomas Jefferson's mouth seals tight. His expression says he is being taken advantage of.

"You have to promise me," she says.

He pulls away from her. "I need to think. That's a complicated—"

"No," she says. "There's nothing complicated about it. Our children must be free. Why do you have to give that even one second of thought?"

"I'm just thinking about what Martha and Maria—"

She, too, pulls away, then shifts onto her knees. In a moment she might be standing.

"Don't." He puts his hands on her thighs. "You are right. Of course, you are right."

"Good," she says. But then she does get to her feet. She walks over to the dust-hazed windows and looks out at the many grays of the leafless trees.

He has come up behind her. He is kissing the nape of her neck. He runs his hands up her belly to her breasts. After a while she lets herself be led back to the bed.

The falling is so sudden and swift that it takes Thomas Jefferson a moment to realize what he is seeing: the earth careening away beneath the clouds, which themselves seem to be spiraling into an abyss. Clinging to the arms of his chair so that he might not also tumble down through the empty air, he feels something warm and smooth sweep along his clutching fingers and then settle atop his hand. It is the hand of Dolley Madison, whose eyes partake equally of the brilliance and blackness of this strange theater and whose mouth is stretched wide with delight. She is speaking to him, but her words are lost in the roaring throb of a thousand cellos, violas and violins.

The earth and sky have stopped falling, and now Thomas Jefferson has the impression that he is coasting between clouds the size of mountains. The roaring strings have resolved into a dithery waltz but are still so loud that their vibration in his hair and against his cheeks seems something like a breeze. Gradually his coasting accelerates into a gently arcing dive toward a particular cloud that darkens and looms as he approaches. For an instant all he can see is fog gray and the knoblike heads of the people seated in front of him, but in the next instant he has zoomed past the silver-feathered edge of the cloud and can now see an orange-and-red balloon, emblazoned with a huge yellow sun face, drifting from behind a different cloud.

At the bottom of the balloon is a sort of balcony on which three people stand, looking out at the landscape beneath them. As he dives (or feels he is diving) like a hawk straight toward them, they grow ever larger and ever more recognizable. The nearest of the three is a man in an enormous hat with an even more enormous panache that bends like a fountain of fluff over the hat's brim. His facial hair consists of three black spikes arrayed about his mouth, and he is looking straight at Thomas Jefferson, smiling with what would appear to be immense self-satisfaction. Directly behind the man is the actress with the golden skin and the gold-frosted, tightly curled hair, who is not looking at Thomas Jefferson but at the actor in the copper-colored wig, who is also looking at her, his face a beacon of adoration.

All at once Thomas Jefferson seems to be on the balloon's balcony him-self, but behind the three passengers. He sees that the couple are squeez-ing each other's hands in the very narrow space between their thighs and that the man in the enormous hat has leaned back far enough to see exactly what they are doing. He looks again at Thomas Jefferson and winks.

And now Thomas Jefferson is flying in a long, ascending arc around behind a cloud and then back, right over the top of the sideways-drifting balloon. As the violins, violas and cellos accelerate into another roaring throb, he feels as if he is shooting right toward the blue edge of the sky, and he so wishes that he had actually been able to take Sally Hemings up in a balloon or that somehow he had been able to fly as he is flying now, with her at his side.

I t is August 5, 1792. Sally Hemings has just returned to bed after drawing back the curtain on one of the lodge windows to let in some daylight. She is nineteen, and Thomas Jefferson is forty-nine.

"What?" she says as she lifts the sheet, their only cover this hot afternoon.

Thomas Jefferson doesn't answer.

She slides into the bed, and, supporting herself on one straight arm, she rests her other hand on the center of his chest. Her head is tilted sympathetically. "What's the matter?" she says.

Thomas Jefferson blinks, as if rousing himself from a dream. He gives her a wan smile. "Nothing."

She grunts dubiously and lowers her head to the pillow but keeps her hand on his chest. "Really?" she says.

"Nothing." He lifts his eyebrows toward the window. "It's a beautiful day."

"Then why do you look so miserable?"

He smiles, but also seems to wince. "I don't know. I'm just feeling a little sad."

She rolls onto her back and lets her hand slide off his chest and onto her belly. But then, with her other hand, she takes hold of his under the sheet. "Are you missing Mrs. Bolling?"

He sighs heavily. "I suppose."

"I missed my sisters terribly when I first arrived in France. Critta especially. I was so lonely those first few months."

He squeezes her hand but doesn't say anything.

"Although I did have Jimmy, of course."

Thomas Jefferson gives her hand a second, more urgent squeeze. "What did you think of Mary—Mrs. Bolling?"

Sally Hemings sighs. "I could tell that she loves you."

"Yes. But what else?"

Sally Hemings sighs again, heavily. She lets go of Thomas Jefferson's hand. "I didn't like her husband."

"Why not?"

"I think he's stupid, and he doesn't love her."

"Well . . ." Thomas Jefferson smirks thoughtfully. "You're probably right. On both accounts."

"I also think he only married her because of you."

"That, alas, may be equally true." The branches outside the window sway in a gentle breeze. Dollops of sunlight rise and fall on the leaves. A hermit thrush makes its lonely, crystalline cry. "But I don't think it is bad that she is married."

Sally Hemings rolls onto her side and faces him, her head pressed into the pillow. "The main thing is that it is hard for me to believe that she's your sister."

"She has more of my mother in her, I suppose."

"That's not what I mean." Sally Hemings squashes more of the pillow under her cheek, so that her head is higher. "It's the same with your brother. Neither of them seem anything like you. It's hard to believe you come from the same family. But Mrs. Bolling especially."

"Well . . ." Thomas Jefferson's mouth hangs open for a long moment, but he doesn't say anything.

"Did something happen to her?"

Thomas Jefferson grunts.

"What?" says Sally Hemings.

"Why do you ask?"

"I don't know. She seems to carry around this heavy weight."

"You mean she's slow?"

"Well . . . Yes. But more than that. I just feel this deep sadness in her. And that terrible scar—"

Thomas Jefferson rests his fingertips on her thigh and stops her talking. "You're right." He makes a noise in his throat as if he is having trouble swallowing. "Mary wasn't always the way she is now. When she was a girl, she was so full of life—so courageous and strong. . . . Now—"

He doesn't finish his sentence. He rolls toward Sally Hemings and gives her a hug and a kiss on the forehead. Their faces are so close together that there is a crisp echo when she speaks. "What happened?"

"Oh—you know: My mad mother." He gives Sally Hemings one more kiss on the forehead, then rolls away. She puts her hand back at the center of his chest and stirs her fingers amid the sparse hair there. "My aunt once told me," he says, "that my mother was pretty and charming when she married my father, but I have no memory of her like that. Around the time she began to have children, a number of manias took hold of her. She became obsessed with the idea that someone was trying to poison her, and she would go for weeks without eating anything except pickles and preserves that she had made herself and kept in a locked box under her bed. The problem was that my father never recognized her madness for what it was. He would try to reason with her. And placate her. Which he could never do for long, because her manias kept changing. For a while she believed that whoever wanted to poison her had begun poisoning the animals, and she told my father that the only way to get the poison out of a hog was to strangle it with a rope before slaughter, and he went so far as to erect a sort of gallows in the barn for that purpose. And whenever she got it into her head that one or another of our servants was her poisoner, she would insist that my father give the servant a lashing . . . and . . ."

Thomas Jefferson sits up in the bed and lowers his head into his hands. His back is to Sally Hemings. "I'm sorry. I shouldn't be telling you this."

Sally Hemings gives his back a reassuring pat, then gets up onto her knees and crawls around in front of him and puts one hand on his shoulder and the other on his knee. She waits for him to look up at her, but he doesn't.

He covers her hand with his own and grips her fingers. "It was terrible," he says. "My father did terrible things. In truth, I think that's what killed him. And after that my mother's madness only became worse. And there was no one to protect—"

Thomas Jefferson's voice thickened just before he cut himself off, and now Sally Hemings can feel a cold sweat coming onto his shoulder. She doesn't know what she will do if he should start to weep.

"I'm sorry," he says, his voice sounding perfectly normal, although he is still looking down.

"It's all right," she says. "Really."

"I'm just so ashamed." Now he lifts his head, his features loosened by sorrow, but his voice matter-of-fact. "We all protected ourselves from our mother in our own ways, and mine was to lose myself in books. I learned to read with such concentration that when I had a book open in front of me, I could forget the whole rest of the world. Also, I could sit for hours in the window of my chamber when I read, not making a sound, hoping my mother would forget I was even there. But I was the only one who chose reading for protection. My brothers took up boxing and carousing with their friends and so were rarely at home. My sisters became obsequious church mice. All except for Mary. Mary was the only one in the family who would stand up to my mother and tell her that what she was doing was evil. Or mad . . . And so . . . of course—"

Again he stops talking, and after a moment he turns to Sally Hemings, wraps his arms around her and lowers his head again, placing the top of his forehead against her shoulder, just beside her neck, as if he means to keep her at a distance. He speaks into the enclosure created by their two bodies. "One time, when Mary . . . when she . . . I don't know what she said or did. . . . But one time my mother became so enraged that she beat Mary . . . savagely . . . with a rake. . . . That scar . . . that's why . . . the rake . . . And I heard what was happening . . . but—"

And now Thomas Jefferson does seem to be doing something like crying. Sally Hemings hears him swallowing again and again, and breathing heavily. And she feels the heat building up in the space between them, and his shoulder going slick with sweat.

"That's all right," she says. She shushes him gently. "Everything's all right. You don't have to worry."

"No." The word comes out as a gasp. "I heard what was happening, but I didn't *do* anything. . . . I went out to the barn . . . and she was still beating Mary. . . . Her eye was filled with blood . . . and I thought she was dead . . . but I just *stood* there. I didn't do *anything*."

He lifts his head, and Sally Hemings can see that although his eyes are red, they are completely dry and that the expression on his face looks less like grief than a panicked restlessness.

He hugs her close and speaks into the air behind her head. "And after that," he says. "And after that," he repeats, and has to repeat the phrase twice more before, all in a burst, he says, "She was never the same."

And then he goes limp and falls over sideways, and Sally Hemings falls with him. She kisses his temple and cheek. She strokes his hair and says, "Oh, Thomas. My poor Thomas. My poor, poor Tom."

And then he puts his arm around her and pulls her tight against his body, and they both lie side by side in silence for a very long time.

"**I** am worried you will get into the habit," says Thomas Jefferson.

"I'm not in the habit," says Sally Hemings. "I've never once made a mistake."

"But still, if you continue . . . If Martha were to hear you even once . . ."

"That is never going to happen. I am a completely different woman when we are around other people. But here . . . in these moments . . . everything is different. I am your Sally, and you are my Thomas. My Tom. I can't think of you any other way. . . . And this fellow here, he is our friend, Little Tom. . . . Oh, look! He was asleep, but now he seems to be waking. . . . Yes! Look! He's getting up and he's stretching. . . ."

You have to stop talking or you will make me hate you.

Every day I hear of Negroes who have gone north and made fine lives for them-selves as ministers, blacksmiths, musicians. "But that's exactly what I'm say-ing! You, yourself, have agreed that we should keep our children here until they have so thoroughly mastered a craft that they might have just exactly the successes you describe. Why should it be different for any other slave? Those able to make a satisfactory living as free men and women and who desire to be free can be freed posthaste. But as for those who have not ac-quired the necessary training or the habits of industry and foresight, I think it is far better to inculcate these virtues through encouragement and example than to abandon such people among a populace who mean them only ill, who will never pay them adequately for their labor and will clap them behind bars at the least excuse."

So you are saying it is impossible.

Sally Hemings sometimes believes she is many people—which is to say that she possesses within her brain and breast the capacity to lead many lives. Sometimes the other lives seem so familiar she feels as if she has actually lived them: She is walking along a street in Philadelphia, a city where she has never been but which is indistinguishable in her mind from Paris. It is a sunny spring afternoon, and her gown is a deep pine green, but made of satin, so it shimmers in the sun as she passes along sandy yellow paths beneath trees cut into the shapes of cones and boxes. Or, in another life, she is sitting at Thomas Jefferson's side, at a table of raised glasses, and she herself is raising a glass, and there are glints everywhere—on the lip and camber of each glass, on the silver candlesticks and tableware, in the eyes of the many guests, in Thomas Jefferson's eyes and her own. And sometimes the other lives could hardly be less familiar and yet feel terrifyingly easy for her to live: She is running through the great house in the darkness of night, and she is carrying an ax, which she swings at everything she passes: tables, chairs, wardrobes, the walls themselves. The ax penetrates and stops, and as she wrenches it free, a wild, guttural cry escapes her throat. Or she is herself wild: an animal dashing on all fours through the underbrush on the edge of an enormous wood. It is raining. She is hungry and cold. She hears human voices and runs from them ever faster, thorns ripping at her shoulders and ribs. And then there are all those lives she can hardly make sense of: She is a sea captain perhaps, at the helm of her ship, an infinity of air and water all around her, the wind blowing her hair off her forehead. Or maybe she is flying, but not like a bird, like a cannonball. She arcs through the clouds on a trajectory that never ends. Or she is in a loud room. There is the shriek of a hawk hurtling out of the sky. There is thunder. The floor heaves and trembles beneath her feet.

The lodge is filled with sunlight, birdsong and river noise. "Oh!" says Thomas Jefferson. His voice is husky, low, almost a grunt.

"What?" says Sally Hemings, who has only just this instant discovered she has been asleep.

"Oh, God!"

"What?" she says. Her eyes are open, but she wants to close them again.

"Come here." He slips his arm under her pillow and across her back.

As he draws her near, she rolls onto her side, puts her arm across his chest and touches the silky skin along his ribs with her fingertips. She slides her thigh across his thigh.

He speaks into her hair. "I had a terrible dream."

"Oh?" she murmurs, and looks up at his face, but he is looking out the window. She kisses his sleep-fragrant chest.

"I dreamed you and I were walking on a bridge over the Seine. Only the bridge was very high, hundreds of feet above the water. Something had happened on it. A battle, I think. There was broken stone everywhere, and parts of the bridge had fallen away. 'Be careful,' I said, and you smiled at me sweetly, the way a mother smiles at the foolish fears of a child. I took hold of your hand so that you wouldn't fall. But then something happened, and you did fall. I was lying on my belly on the bridge, still holding your hand as you dangled in empty space. Only the bridge wasn't over the Seine anymore. It was over a rocky canyon, with a small stream at its bottom, hundreds of feet below. I remember thinking that everything would be all right because I was still holding your hand. But you were terrified. Your legs and your free arm were flailing as you tried to grasp on to something, but there was nothing there. 'Don't worry,' I said. 'I'm going to pull you up.' But then you were falling. I don't know how that happened. I just watched you falling away from me. You had such a look of terror on your face, and you were falling and falling. There was nothing I could do. I just watched you get smaller and smaller as you fell toward the rocks."

. . . That lodge! How it haunts me. When we were there, we seemed in a different world, one not ruled by a cruel or incompetent God, a world in which we hadn't been created master and slave, in which slavery itself had never perverted the human heart or was, at worst, a faint rumor of a distant time and place; and in this better world, our tender murmurings, our delight at touching and being touched, our jokes, our hopes, our conversations and even our fights, our domestic tedium, our aging—all of these things were only themselves, never the means by which we betrayed our souls or those we loved; and we were simply one woman and one man, whose sorrows and joys together were only the product of their intermingled humanness, unprofaned by botched grace. . . .

T wo tin plates, heaped with steaming carrots and parsnips, a bowl of salt, a bottle of wine and two glasses. The wavering orange glow of a burning pine knot. "What would you have me do, then?" *I don't see why you can't just free everyone and let those who want to leave take their chances. They are human beings, capable of making their own decisions. Why should you feel responsible for the decisions they make?* "Everything would be ruined." *Why do you say that?* "Everything would be ruined." *Stop saying that! And besides, I'm not finished.* "Finish, then." *You have often told me that people work harder if they feel that it is their choice to work and that they have something to gain by their labor. So if you were to pay Negroes at the same rate you pay whites, you would have the best Negro workers flocking to you from miles around, and they would work far harder for you than your present laborers, not merely because they would be choosing to work and getting adequately paid for their efforts but because they would be grateful to you for doing what is right. That is the main thing. You would be doing what is right. There would be no need to wait for a general emancipation. Tomorrow, with the stroke of a pen, you could transform Monticello into a beacon of justice and good fellowship for the whole of Virginia.* "That is a beautiful dream. But should I tell you what would really happen? I have thought this through many times. Monticello, as we know it, would collapse in a minute. The curse of slavery is that it makes itself indispensable. There are no farms such as this north of Chesapeake Bay. We have our own world here, not just laborers in the ground and house servants but coopers, blacksmiths, carpenters, furniture makers. Were I to run Monticello as you propose, I could not employ the eighth part of these people, and I would lose, first of all, the craftsmen, who—as you know—are the very men best trained to make good lives for themselves in the event that it is practical and desirable for them to be free. And by losing them I would also be losing the ability to train others, so that they, too, might have valuable skills and a means of making a living in freedom." *But they could be apprenticed to the white craftsmen.* "I would have to let the white craftsmen go, too. There simply wouldn't be enough money to pay them. Yet that is nothing. The most immediate tragedy would befall the seventy laborers in the ground whom I would also have to let go, because I couldn't pay them either. Yes, some few of these might escape north or find a way of eking out a living in Virginia, but what proportion do you think would end up reenslaved, in prison or dead? Almost all of them, I would wager. So what would be the gain? A few effectively imprisoned on a northern-style farm here, a few more finding uncertain futures in the north and the rest condemned to fates far worse than they enjoy now. Is this what you want? Is this what you think would be 'right'?" *So you are saying it is impossible.*

. . . For a while I had a joke. Whenever he and I fell into a discussion about slavery or race, I would put it to an end by shouting, "Stop! You will make me hate you!" I would always smile as I made this remark; sometimes I would laugh, and he would laugh, too. I used to think that this was a clever way of keeping the peace—which it did, to an extent; Mr. Jefferson always heeded my implicit warning, and we would move on to more congenial topics. But it was nevertheless the case that I was, in fact, already hating him even as I smiled, and the hatred would take a while to go away—if it ever truly did.

And so the hatred silenced me.

Because I thought my anger would destroy my life. . . .

I t is September 14, 1792, and Sally Hemings is nineteen years old. She is standing beside the counter of the dry-goods shop owned by her sister Mary and Colonel Thomas Bell. Mary worked for Colonel Bell while the Jeffersons were in Paris and had two children with him. Five months ago, at her request, Thomas Jefferson sold her and the children to Bell, who freed them and married Mary. Now she looks after the shop while Bell spends most of his day managing the plantation he owns east of town. Her two oldest children, Joey and Betsy, remain at Monticello.

Sally Hemings has come to the shop to buy ribbon for a nightgown she is making for Martha's two-day-old first child. She is trying to choose between two ribbons—a satiny rose pink and a coarser but more beautiful pale lavender—when she hears her name called and looks over to see Mary, standing in the doorway between the shop and her house, a troubled expression on her face. Mary gestures for her sister to come and begins to back away from the door. Sally Hemings holds up the lavender ribbon and tells the girl who has been helping her, "I'll take a yard of this." No sooner has she spoken than she decides the pink would have been better, but it is too late.

"Tilly," Mary calls to the girl. "Wrap that up for Miss Hemings, would you. And make sure you cut it straight."

The girl lowers her head in a semi-curtsy. "Yes, ma'am."

Sally Hemings follows her sister out the door, across a breezeway and into a laundry room. Mary closes the door behind them.

"I'm sorry," she says. "I heard you was out there, and I couldn't wait."

"What's the matter?"

"Oh, Sally! I just don't know what I'm going to do!"

Mary collapses onto a bench beside a long table, and Sally Hemings sits opposite her. "What?" she says, reaching across the table to take her sister's hands.

Mary is forty, with twists of silver beginning to infiltrate her dark brown hair. Her plump cheeks and habitually merry gaze have always made her seem more girl than woman but now her cheeks are drawn, her golden brown skin has gone slack and crinkly and in her gaze there is the desperate intensity of someone who feels all alone in the world.

"It's about Joey and Betsy," she says. She looks down at the table and lets go of Sally Hemings's hands. After a moment she speaks. "You know how grateful I am to Mr. Jefferson. You know how kind I think he is, on account of what he done."

"He's always liked you," says Sally Hemings.

Mary casts her sister a quick, timid glance. "I was very grateful when— you know: I told him what Colonel Bell and I wanted, and he just said yes straight out, and then he said that Bobby and Sally could come with me. I didn't even have to say a word. 'Of course you're taking your little ones.' That's just how he said it. And I said, 'Thank you, Mr. Jefferson. I am so grateful!' And I really was grateful." She sighs heavily. "I never been anything but grateful to Mr. Jefferson. But the thing is, I think I made a big mistake."

Sally Hemings takes hold of one of Mary's hands again and gives it a squeeze. "I'm sure you didn't."

"No, I did. I really did. Because I was afraid."

"Of what?"

"Well, I also wanted Joey and Betsy to come with me. But when he said that about Bobby and Sally, without my even having to ask, I thought he'd be angry if I asked for Joey and Betsy too."

"Why would he be angry?" Sally Hemings lets go of her sister's hand and folds her own hands in her lap.

"Well, I don't know. I reckon I just thought I might seem greedy." Mary covers her face with both hands. When she lowers them, her eyes are red and she has to wipe away a gloss of tears. "Did he tell you about yesterday?"

"No."

"That's what I'm talking about, really. Ever since I left, I been trying to work up the courage to talk to Mr. Jefferson, and I just couldn't do it. But finally, yesterday, I got so I couldn't stand living without Joey and Betsy no more, so I walked up to Monticello first thing in the morning. And when I got there, Mr. Jefferson was coming out of the stable on Caractacus. So I just walked right up to him before I lost my courage."

Mary's lips part, but she doesn't speak. The loneliness in her expression gives way to something more fierce.

"What happened?" says Sally Hemings.

"Well, he *did* get angry. He told me he couldn't do nothing less I talked to Colonel Bell first. And I told him Colonel Bell already told me he loved my children and he wanted me to have them with me."

Sally Hemings sits back with a furrowed brow.

"What?" says Mary.

"Did Colonel Bell really say that?"

"Of course he did! He said, 'I love you, and I love your children, and I want you to have what makes you happy.' That's exactly what he said."

Sally Hemings makes a dubious grunt.

"What?"

"Well, Mr. Jefferson told me that Colonel Bell said that since Joey was Mr. Fossett's son, and Betsy was Mr. Fairchild's, he didn't see why he should have to bear the expense of raising them."

"He wouldn't ever say something like that!"

"Are you sure?" asks Sally Hemings.

"Of course! He never said that. I know that for a fact."

"Not even to Mr. Jefferson?"

Mary is silent a long time. When tears begin to stream down her face again, she doesn't bother to wipe them away. "I don't care about that!" she says. "I just can't stand not having Joey and Betsy here with me. I think about them all the time. I just can't stand it. I tried. Been five months, and it only gets worse and worse. Sometimes it's so bad I want to kill myself."

I t is almost a week before Sally Hemings has a chance to intervene on Mary's behalf concerning Joey and Betsy. Congress is about to begin its winter session, and Thomas Jefferson has been in daily communication with James Madison about how they might make the most of the near collapse of Colonel Hamilton's newly established national bank. Also, for reasons that Sally Hemings does not fully understand, the Marquis de Lafayette has been declared an enemy of the French Revolution. Fearing for his life, he fled France, hoping to make his way in the United States, but before he could get onto a boat, he was arrested by the Austrians, who are now threatening to execute him. Thomas Jefferson has been writing to everyone he can think of who might possibly intercede on his dear friend's behalf, but he is terribly afraid. He hardly sleeps at night and keeps telling Sally Hemings that he feels utterly helpless. And as if all of this were not enough, every corridor at Monticello is blocked by baskets, trunks and heaps of laundry. Martha is getting ready to return to Edgehill now that she has recovered from giving birth to her daughter, and Maria is packing to spend the year in Philadelphia with her father.

Sally Hemings is in Maria's chamber, folding clothing and placing it in a trunk, when eight-year-old Davy knocks on the door and informs her that Mr. Jefferson has gone for a ride and wants her to tidy his study. This is a signal that she should put on her riding boots and proceed directly to the stable, where Jupiter will have Goodfellow saddled and ready for her. She glances at Maria, who meets her eye for half a second, then looks away, continuing her ongoing pretense that she doesn't know what Davy's messages actually mean. When Maria comes back from Philadelphia, Critta will be her maid, and Sally Hemings's sole responsibility will be to take care of Thomas Jefferson's chambers.

Some forty-five minutes later, she meets a very weary-looking Thomas Jefferson on the western shore of the lake. The first quarter mile of their journey down to the lodge is along a road broad enough for them to ride side by side, and this is where Sally Hemings decides to fulfill her promise to her sister. Hardly a word is out of her mouth before Thomas Jefferson interrupts her.

"I've already been through all of this with Mary," he says, "and I don't know what else there is to discuss."

"She's in a terrible way. She's been missing Joey and Betsy so dearly she says she's not sure she can go on living."

"What nonsense! Tell her she's free to visit the children anytime she likes. And they can join her at Colonel Bell's on Sundays and holidays."

"But she wants them to live with her! And so does Colonel Bell."

"Well . . ." Thomas Jefferson is silent a long time. Then he says, "I think that's something she'll have to take up with her husband."

"But she has! He told her straight out that he would love for the children to live with him."

Thomas Jefferson gives Sally Hemings a skeptical glance. "I think it's best not to meddle in other people's private affairs."

"But she's miserable. And you are the only one with the power to reunite her with her children."

"I'm sorry, Sally, I've given this matter all the attention I have time for. I have every sympathy for Mary. You know that. I know perfectly well what it is like to miss one's child. But even so, a time comes when children must be allowed to make their own way in the world. I went off to school when I wasn't much older than Joey—"

"But Betsy is nine years old!"

"Indeed, but that is older than Maria was when she journeyed across the ocean."

Now it is Sally Hemings's turn to cast a skeptical glance. She does not bother to say what she is thinking, because she can tell from the exaggerated attention Thomas Jefferson is paying to the reins of his horse that he knows—after all, one of the reasons he is bringing Maria with him to Philadelphia is to compensate for having abandoned her when she was so young.

"At the very least," she says, "why don't you have another talk with Colonel Bell?"

Thomas Jefferson gives her a beleaguered glance. "I'll do what I can." Then he kicks his horse's flanks and moves in front of her as the wooded road narrows down into a path.

She doesn't make it into Charlottesville for nearly two weeks, at which point Thomas Jefferson, Maria, Jimmy and Bobby are long gone. The very first thing she does is go over to Bell's Store, but Mary is not comforted by Thomas Jefferson's suggestion that she is free to visit her children and to have them visit her, and she has seen no indication that he spoke to her husband before leaving for Philadelphia.

"He's been very busy." Sally Hemings explains about Alexander Hamilton and the Marquis de Lafayette and ends by saying, "I'm sure that Colonel Bell will be receiving a letter on the matter any day now."

Sally Hemings knows perfectly well that no such letter will ever arrive. But she tries to believe that it will for as long as she is with her sister and for some days afterward.

When, at last, she feels she has no choice but to face the facts, she comforts herself by resolving to speak to Thomas Jefferson as soon as he returns—at least if either of the two children seem truly to be miserable by then.

She watches them over the course of several months. While neither seems especially happy, she sees no evidence whatsoever that they are unhappy. Joey, in particular, strikes her as an entirely ordinary twelve-year-old boy—loud and rambunctious but never sullen or tearful. Betsy does seem a bit subdued, but perhaps she is only thoughtful. Both children, in any event, are being schooled in useful trades: Joey in blacksmithing and Betsy in sewing and child care. And what is more, neither child seems appreciably happier when their mother comes to visit. They are not rude to her by any means, nor are they joyful. As far as Sally Hemings can tell, their demeanor does not alter one jot in the presence of their mother.

Mary's demeanor, on the other hand, alters dramatically as the months pass—at least in regard to her sister. At first she will greet Sally Hemings with nothing more than a baleful glance, but after a while not even that. On her part, Sally Hemings tries to look cheerful when she spots Mary and will raise her hand and call out a greeting, but her sister keeps her eyes to the ground and walks past as if she hasn't seen or heard a thing. Ultimately Sally Hemings decides that Mary is simply not being realistic, neither about the malleability of Thomas Jefferson's will nor about the true situation of her own children. As winter turns into spring and spring into summer, Sally Hemings becomes increasingly inclined to see her sister's enduring misery as a matter of choice. Mary could choose to make the best of the situation, but she simply refuses to. Over the course of the year, Sally Hemings also notices that Mary's hair goes from silver-laced brown to completely gray.

It is September of 1793, and Maria has been back in Monticello for nearly a month. She has been sent home early because a plague of yellow fever has struck Philadelphia and her father is worried for her health. Critta is still down at Edgehill helping with Martha's baby and won't be back for a couple of weeks, so Sally Hemings is on her knees in the washroom, scrubbing bloodstains off the back of Maria's sky blue riding gown. Earlier that afternoon Maria, who is fifteen, took a solitary ride around the mountaintop and did not realize that her period had commenced until she climbed down from the gig and felt her shift sticking to her legs. And now Sally Hemings is, herself, so intent on what she is doing that she does not notice the knock on the jamb of the open door behind her and is startled when she hears her own name called out by— she realizes in half an instant—her brother.

"Jimmy!" she cries, getting to her feet and hugging him with her forearms, because she does not want to wet him with her hands.

"Hey there, Cider Jug!" He lifts her off the ground and spins her in a circle.

She shrieks as the room whirls around her, and she is still laughing when he sets her back on her feet.

"What are you doing home so early?" she says.

"Oh, all the white people decided to clear out of Philadelphia because of the fever."

"I know," she says somberly. "Maria's told me about it. I've been so worried about you."

"No need to worry about me! Colored people don't get yellow fever, only whites."

"Really?"

"That's what Mr. Jefferson says."

Sally Hemings finds that hard to believe, but before she can query Jimmy any further, a big grin comes onto his face. He puts his hands in his pockets and swells out his chest.

"So?" he says. "Haven't you noticed anything different?"

He is wearing an elegant gray frock coat, cream breeches and black shoes with plain silver buckles. His clothes look remarkably clean for someone who has just spent ten days on the road, but Sally Hemings has seen them all before.

"New stockings?" she suggests.

Jimmy doesn't say a word, just continues to grin at her.

"What?" she says.

"You mean you really can't tell?"

"What?" she says emphatically.

"You are looking at a free man!"

"What!" she shouts. "You did it? You finally did it?"

Jimmy replies only with a broader, happier grin. Sally Hemings is so happy she bursts into tears. "Oh, Jimmy! Oh, Jimmy! Praise the Lord!" She throws her arms around him, and he gives her another whirl.

Jimmy has been talking about asking for his manumission ever since an evening in Paris when the Church family came to supper at the Hôtel de Langeac. He prepared a blanquette de veau that all of the guests found so delicious he was called in to accept compliments. Amid the general praise, Kitty Church cried out, "You should open a restaurant!" and Thomas Jefferson interjected, "Not until he trains a replacement!" Everybody laughed, but in the middle of it all, Thomas Jefferson shot Jimmy a glance that made him wonder if the remark had not been partly in earnest. Over the four years since that time, Jimmy primarily considered the possibility that he might be freed as little more than a pipe dream, but then, when Thomas Jefferson granted Mary's and Thenia's requests to be sold so that they would be with their husbands and allowed Martin to buy his own freedom, Jimmy began to be more hopeful.

"So how did you do it?" Sally Hemings asks.

"I told him Adrien and I want to open a French restaurant in Philadelphia."

It takes Sally Hemings a moment to realize that Adrien is Monsieur Petit, who has been Thomas Jefferson's chief of staff in Philadelphia for the last year. "What did he say?" she asks.

"He said he thought that was an excellent idea, and he drew up the papers on the spot."

"Just like that! It was that easy!"

"Just like that," he says.

"Oh, Jimmy!" She gives him another hug. "So you're free now? Actually free? I can hardly believe it!"

"Yes," he says. "Free as a bird." He takes a celebratory leap into the air, but when he lands, his smile has slackened and he speaks in a lower voice. "The papers have been drawn up, but they don't take effect until I have trained my replacement."

"How long will that be, do you think?"

"Not too long, I reckon. But it depends on how fast a learner he is."

"Who?"

"Peter."

"Peter!" Peter, the brother in between Jimmy and Sally Hemings, has remained at Monticello; she sees him almost every day. "Why didn't he tell me?"

"He doesn't know yet." Jimmy laughs, but when he is finished, he is no longer smiling.

Sally Hemings remembers that it had taken Jimmy a good four years to truly master the art of cooking, and he had been studying with some of the best chefs in Paris. She gives Jimmy an encouraging pat on the shoulder. "Peter's a hard worker. I bet he'll pick it up in no time."

"First he's going to have to learn to read."

It is cold in the lodge—the sort of cold that in a couple of months' time will seem balmy but that now leaves Thomas Jefferson expecting to see the steam of his breath. He is naked, crouched in front of the fireplace, putting a couple of logs on top of the skeletal remains of the fire he started when he and Sally Hemings first arrived. He is fifty years old, and while he is still muscular and lean, he is aware that the skin on his belly has lost much of its resilience and makes crinkly folds when he bends over like this. He suspects that other parts of his body might be similarly flaccid. As he prods the logs into place with his fingertips, he wonders if Sally Hemings, waiting in the bed, thinks he looks old.

"You're cold!" she says when he has rejoined her.

"You're warm!" He pulls her toward him, and presses his chest and belly against hers, and slides his leg up between her thighs until he can feel her pasty wetness. He thinks for a moment that they will make love again, but then she kisses him on the cheekbone and rolls away.

That's all right. He is satisfied. More than satisfied.

Her head is on his shoulder, and they lie looking up at the beams and boards of the lodge's loft. It is the late afternoon of the day following his return from Philadelphia and still full light, though the sky above the trees is winter gray.

"Have you spoken to Jimmy yet?" he says after a bit.

"Yes."

"Did he tell you?"

"Yes."

"What are your thoughts?"

She cranes her head backward and smiles. "I'm very happy. Thank you." She kisses him on the cheek. Then she sighs heavily and looks back up at the ceiling. Her feet are moving restlessly under the counterpane, and Thomas Jefferson wonders if she is about to get up.

"No," he says, "I mean, what do you think about Jimmy?"

She looks up, an irritated expression on her face. "What else can I think? This is what he's wanted for a very long time." She looks away again.

"Well, yes but that's not—" Thomas Jefferson falls silent. He sighs. "I suppose what I'm wondering is if you think it is wise."

Sally Hemings raises her head off his shoulder and lifts herself over his left arm, which has been embracing her. She faces him on her side, elbow crooked on the mattress, hand supporting her head. She is glaring at him impatiently. "I don't know why you are even asking that question. Is it 'wise' that you are free? Is it 'wise' that anyone is free? That question doesn't make any sense."

"That's not what I mean," he says. "I am not going to stand in the way of his desire. I told him I would give him his manumission as soon as he has trained Peter in his stead, and I will. But still, I'm concerned about him."

"There is a great deal of cruelty in this world." Sally Hemings is sitting up now, clutching a corner of the sheet across her breasts. "But does that mean that all the people who might suffer from it should give up their freedom?"

"That has nothing to do with it!"

"It has everything to do with it! You yourself said people should be free to *pursue* happiness, but you didn't say anything about their actually having to get it!"

"You're not letting me say what I mean." Thomas Jefferson is sitting now, too. He puts his hand on her knee. "What I really want to know is if you think Jimmy is all right. Did he tell you about Hoff?"

There is a skeptical wrinkle at the center of Sally Hemings's brow, but her voice is low and uneasy. "No. Who is Hoff?"

"You remember the beating Jimmy gave Monsieur Perrault?"

She nods. Monsieur Perrault was their French tutor in Paris. Jimmy thrashed him with a parasol one afternoon when the old man told him that Negroes were incapable of mastering the subjunctive because, as he put it, "There is no subjunctive in the African language."

"Well, something similar happened twice in Philadelphia. The first time it was only a beggar boy who ran in front of his horse, and there was perhaps some justification to that. The boy needed to learn not to run heedlessly into the street. But Hoff was a different matter. Hoff is the servant of Mr. Clagget, the butcher Jimmy patronizes on Market Street. Hoff is the one who makes deliveries. So one day he arrives with a leg of lamb. I happened to be in my study at the time and could look right down at the back gate, so I saw the whole thing. The first I knew of it was when I heard Jimmy shouting, 'This leg is crawling with maggots! How dare you insult me with this piece of rotten flesh!' When I got to the window, he was brandishing the leg over his head like a club. 'Do you think I am stupid!' he was shouting. 'Do you think I'm an absolute idiot!' As it happens, Hoff is Dutch and has very little English. I'm not sure if he understood a single word of what Jimmy said to him, nor am I sure if any of his defenses were intelligible to Jimmy. All I know is that Jimmy became so enraged that he grabbed Hoff by his hair and started to beat him with the leg of lamb. I could see that the poor man was more startled than injured at first, but then Jimmy landed a blow that may well have broken a bone in his shoulder. He staggered and fell to the ground, and then Jimmy started to kick him—"

"Stop!" Sally Hemings is clutching the sides of her head with her hands.

"That's all there is," says Thomas Jefferson. "By the time I got down to the yard, Jimmy's fit had passed. He pointed at poor Hoff, whom he called a swindler and a criminal, but he was clearly already beginning to think those charges were absurd."

"The poor man was only the servant," Sally Hemings says plaintively.

"Exactly. Although once I was in the yard, it was clear that the meat was anything but fresh. In any event, Hoff took advantage of that moment to run out the gate, and we never saw or heard of him again. Jimmy, of course, was filled with remorse. I think he had been drinking even before Hoff arrived, because as soon as we were alone, tears started to spill from his eyes. 'I know there is a Devil,' he told me, 'because I can feel him inside my brain.'"

"Oh, no!"

Sally Hemings gets out of bed and starts looking for her clothes.

"From that day until we left, he was his kind and temperate self," says Thomas Jefferson. "I think he was deeply shocked by what he had done, and chastened. Though I fear his drinking is beginning to get the better of him. One morning, not three days before we set off to come here, Petit and I searched the entire house and couldn't find him anywhere, until finally I went out into the garden and discovered him lying there unconscious in a pool of his own vomit."

"Oh, poor Jimmy!"

Sally Hemings gets down on her knees and lifts the counterpane so that she can look under the bed. "Where is my shift? We've got to go back up to the house. What did I do with my shift?"

A swallow of wine. A mouthful of warm parsnip. "I have never said that it is impossible—if by 'it' you mean emancipation—only that it must be pursued methodically and with patience. Two things are required: first that, by moral argument and political pressure, southern landowners are persuaded to give up the practice of slavery; and second that a homeland be established in Portuguese South America or in Sierra Leone, where all the freed Negroes might be transported at the public expense and provided with sufficient acreage, animals, seeds and money to begin new lives for themselves and to found a new society. Only by the geographical separation of the races might we avoid the commencement of a cycle of assault and revenge that could last centuries and reduce all the beautiful dreams of this nation to charred rubble and pools of blood." *Stop. You are going to make me hate you.*

The floor beneath Thomas Jefferson's feet bucks and wobbles, and the heads of the seated passengers rock all in one motion. From the set of Sally Hemings's shoulders and the grace with which she rides the heaving floor, he can see that she is more confident than she used to be, and more capable. *She has come into her own*, he thinks, and that fills him with both a warm appreciation and a sorrow that he has missed so much of her life.

VI

IV

Thomas Jefferson is an artist of silence. Into the midst of whinnies, susurrant poplars, catbird shrieks, jingling harnesses, cicada drones, coughs, field chants, foot thumps, fox cries and thunder rumbles, he introduces silences, some of them lasting half a breath, some as vast and enduring as the silence between stars. Silence is a form of freedom. In silence "ought" need never be contaminated by "is," and what *is* is, simultaneously, *not at all*. Silence is our agreement that the world is more than we can bear. When the silent people in the silent room close their eyes, they are utterly alone. A solitary word in the midst of silence has no meaning.

It is six in the morning of May 1, 1795. Thomas Jefferson has already taken an hour's walk along the Rivanna and has returned to the lodge with sleeves and smallclothes chilly in patches from the dew. He is sitting on a wooden footstool in front of the fireplace, pouring boiling water from a copper kettle into a tin coffeepot balanced on two bricks just beside the fire. He hears a murmur and a rustling of bedclothes.

Looking around, all he can see of Sally Hemings is the underside of one half-closed hand resting against the headboard just beside her pillow. She is four months pregnant, though the only obvious signs are a certain thickening under her jaw and the taut enlargement of her breasts. He has known of her condition for just over a month, and so far neither Martha nor Maria knows—or, at least, neither has said a word to him about it.

He is happy, but he has unhappy thoughts.

Sometimes he worries about how he will manage once the child has come into the world and there will be no plausible way to deny that it is his own. More often, however—though usually only in the darkest hour of the night—he remembers his wife's suffering during and after childbirth, her helpless grief at the loss of Jane, their second child, and then of their third, their one and only son, who never mastered the art of breathing and never received a name. But those griefs, as unbearable as they felt at the time, came to seem innocent and even mild. It was after their lovely little Lucy Elizabeth went crimson with fever and then so pale and still that Martha succumbed entirely to despair. "Why is God so cruel?" she cried out one day. "He laughs at our hopes. He fills our life with misery." Thomas Jefferson was shocked to hear his good and kind wife speak so bitterly, but he found himself unable to argue with her, especially as that was a moment when the British seemed to be winning the war. When she again became pregnant not four months later, he hoped that her spirits would revive, but she remained listless and melancholy, and following the birth of their second Lucy, she only grew weaker and weaker, until finally the mere weight of existence was more than she could bear. And then, of course, two years later poor Lucy herself expired in the very home where he had believed she would be most safe.

He picks up a bowl from the floor, pours the just-brewed coffee into it and brings it over to the bed. "Here you go, sweet Sally—a little liquid daylight." He puts the bowl down on the chair that serves as a bedside table, and she makes a noise that he interprets as a sleepy thank-you. Her face is turned to one side, her eyes closed and brow pinched, as if from pain.

"How is your back feeling?" he asks.

She turns and looks up at him through squinting eyes. "How am I supposed to know? I'm not even awake!"

"Sorry," he says. "I was just worried that it had hurt you all night."

She closes her eyes and doesn't respond.

He backs away from the bed and turns toward the fire. But then he looks around again. "It was just an expression of concern," he says. "Why do you always mock me when all I am doing is expressing my concern?"

In his not-sleep, Thomas Jefferson, invisible, walks from room to room, though not always bothering with the doors. He steps so lightly as he crosses lawn and field that the grass does not bend beneath his feet and the wheat does not hiss against his shins. The hearts of those he loves and of those he does not even know are as open to him as his own, though often the feelings arising from those hearts are profoundly mysterious and thus disturbing, disorienting.

That is Maria's cheek in the moon's gray brilliance. He knows by the faint oval of a chicken-pox scar and by how, at the edge between moonbeam and blackness, the convexity of the cheek undulates into the concavity beside her upper lip. The feeling that comes to Thomas Jefferson is loneliness as a form of agony. It is like the howl of a wounded animal, cut off from its pack, helpless and exposed on a slope of scree.

Thomas Jefferson himself is so wounded by his daughters' pain that he is taken by a whirlwind madness and only comes to himself half a mile away, in a cabin down the hill occupied by two families of field laborers, where a five-year-old boy in his own not-sleep is moving his lips to words voiced inside his head: "They not gonna take my pappy. They not gonna take my pappy. I got to tell them. They not gonna do that. I got to build him a house out of branches and leaves, with hay for a floor. I got to make him come back and stay in that house and not do nothing bad no more, and I got to keep him for my own till I'm old."

And then Thomas Jefferson is walking again until it is a tiny heart, a mouse's or a vole's—beating like an elfin drumroll—that opens inside his own, and he is possessed by a firm, fixed innocence that wants merely to persist from this instant to the next and the next and the next, without end.

And then he is in the kitchen of his own house, vault-black, where Jimmy Hemings sleeps upon a pallet in the corner in the posture of a man who lost consciousness while crawling. There is a bed for him in the cabin where his brother John lives with his wife and child, but Jimmy refuses to stay there. He will not say why. He is a man possessed by powerful antipathies that he will never explain. Jimmy's heart is a mansion with a broken roof. Rain warps the floorboards and embroiders the couches and beds with mold. Every room has its shameful history, and the people still dwelling in them never come out. You can hear their feet dragging in the night, and their groans.

And then Thomas Jefferson is walking upon a breeze, into the heart of Sally Hemings, who sleeps beside her mother in the cabin he might see from his bedroom window were he to rise from his not-sleep and part the curtain. Her brow, in the gray moonlight, is darkened by a cluster of V-shaped dents, and her heart is entirely occupied by the desire to get something right. It is her invention, which is constantly falling apart, and must constantly be reconstructed. The parts slip between her fingers and roll across the floor. She darts after them, sweeps them up, but she is never sure she has gotten all of them, so is never sure if her invention, once it is reassembled, will actually work. But it is never reassembled, because as she works to bolt one part to the next and the next, still other parts are falling to the floor and rolling into corners. Always. Always. Always.

And then Thomas Jefferson has passed through her heart into another within her body that although it has only just commenced beating is already possessed of a yearning so relentless it might destroy the world.

This is what Thomas Jefferson thinks: Sally Hemings has no African in her, except perhaps in the barely noticeable fullness of her upper lip and in the rondure of the tip of her nose—though, indeed, precisely these traits can also be found in people of the purest British stock. The blood of Captain Hemings and, even more so, that of Thomas Jefferson's own father-in-law, John Wayles, has entirely overwhelmed the necessarily less robust African blood to which she might have been heir. As a result she has inherited none of the less savory traits of the race.

Although she has had no formal education, her mind is as sharp as that of any woman Thomas Jefferson has ever known, particularly in regard to her judgment of people. Her assessment of Tom Randolph, for example, has proved sadly accurate. He is just exactly as unsure of himself as she hypothesized during his first brief visit in Paris and exactly as prone to countering his weakness of character through a spiteful coldness that he fancies as dignity. There is also something vengeful in his indulgence of cider and whiskey, and poor Martha seems to be the one who most has to suffer from it. But Sally Hemings is also a shrewd judge of people she has never met. Thomas Jefferson had hardly said ten words about Alexander Hamilton before she'd pegged him as having the conscience of a rattlesnake, and Carter Braxton as a buffoon and a would-be confidence man.

Needless to say, Sally Hemings also lacks that sluggishness of the kidneys that inclines Negroes toward indolence and excessive sweating, and her skin is no more sable than a bowl of milk into which a tincture of molasses has been diffused.

This temperate evening in mid-September, Thomas Jefferson is the one who is sweat-drenched and black of face and hands, while Sally Hemings is seated in the open air outside her cabin, taking advantage of the waning sun to embroider a tiny nightcap.

He has decided that the proportions of his house are entirely lacking in grace and that he must extend it on both the north and south and replace the top floor with a dome. For six weeks he has been attempting to come up with the right combination of clay, sand, water and heat to produce durable bricks, and just this afternoon he made the first batch that neither exploded in the kiln nor turned to grit on the application of the least weight. He is happy as he walks, soot-blackened and smelling of charcoal, along Mulberry Row back toward his house. When he has amassed a suitable number of bricks—by the spring, ideally—the new construction can begin.

Sally Hemings is so immersed in her work that she does not see him, even though he is only a few steps away. She is seated with her back partly turned to the sun so that it might better light her sewing. Her cheek and shoulder are gilded with it, and her loose dark hair is streaked with auburn glints. She is seven and a half months pregnant, and her forearms rest lightly on the sides of her enormous belly.

He stops walking. He will stand in the road until she looks up and notices him. Every time she pushes her needle through the gathered cloth, she purses her lips, and as she pulls the thread through, she tilts her head slowly to the left, then straightens it and repurses her lips as she prepares to jab the needle into the cloth another time. It is true that these little motions make her look ridiculous, but even so, Thomas Jefferson has never seen her more beautiful.

As Thomas Jefferson contemplates the identity of color, which can never be separated from the relationship between colors, he also contemplates the relationship between horror, consolation and beauty. Since his arrival in New York City, he has been thinking about Rilke's notion that beauty is "nothing but the beginning of terror," which he interprets to mean that we feel beauty most intensely in the presence of that which, if only by its transcendent magnificence, would seem capable of destroying us and yet does nothing of the kind. Our fear combined with our sense that we have nothing to fear translates into the sort of elevation we call beauty.

For most of his adult life, he has applied this notion primarily to the beauty of such things as mountains and dazzlingly starry skies. But lately he has been thinking about those instances when he has experienced joy of such terrific intensity that it is barely distinguishable from sorrow. In every case the joy has arisen out of the simultaneity of two contradictory impressions. The first took him years to recognize, because it is so at odds with the sort of person he has always wanted to be and who, even now, he tends to think that he actually is. He wants to be an idealist and an optimist, but, in fact, at the deepest level of his being, he sees ideals as nothing more than sad delusions and existence as the theater in which we are shown our utter selfishness, perversity and insignificance. And thus when he perceives, against the backdrop of this grim conviction, even the smallest instance of human decency—an act of simple kindness, for example—he experiences such an upwelling of joy that it is all he can do to hold back tears. Every time it's exactly the same: our earthly loathsomeness intersecting with a minute or fleeting suggestion that we might not be entirely damnable—nothing else fills Thomas Jefferson with such joy or seems so profoundly beautiful.

This beauty is, of course, consolatory—but not falsely so. An instance of beauty endures only so long as it seems manifestly real and true. At the faintest tremor of doubt, it reverts to sad delusion or to hypocrisy. And so as he walks the streets of New York City and rides in metal boxes underground, among glum and oblivious strangers, Thomas Jefferson has come to define beauty as that which gives us joy without blinding us to truth.

But what about the beauty of color? When we get lost in that deep red, which is also red next to zenith-blue, and red and blue together beside a matte gold-brown—do we secretly feel ourselves to be truly lost and so become afraid? And do we then experience a sort of consolation insofar as we know that we are not, in fact, lost, that a mere blink is enough to liberate us from that complex red and restore us to our world of nothing much, in which we feel at home? Or is the beauty of color only the product of color's simplicity, of the fact that it is entirely uninflected by selfishness and perversity, or by morality and meaning, and that when we are lost within it, it is only itself and we are only ourselves, happily, childishly and deeply alive in our being? Is color so beautiful simply because it is perfectly innocent and pure?

. . . I engaged in a constant debate with myself, arguing that Mr. Jefferson merely suffered from the white man's constitutional incapacity to speak sensibly on matters of slavery or race, but that even so he was a good man, a brilliant man, a sad and kind man, and he loved me deeply. I am lucky, I would tell myself. I am very lucky.

And I was lucky, of course, in many ways, but there were aspects of my good fortune that I could not bear to face—privileges that had been granted to me not by fate but by Mr. Jefferson, privileges that I did not truly deserve but that I worked hard to maintain by taking his attentions only at face value and by living in an incomplete world.

I didn't, for example, merely avoid conversations about slavery, I did my best not to see or comprehend proofs of the institution's cruelty, injustice and pain that were manifestly evident near at hand. When I could not turn away from them, I tried to find ways in which Mr. Jefferson might remain untainted and pure—in which he did not fully comprehend what was being done in his name and in which none of it was what he intended. And so I became a wretched paradox, filled with fury at what I knew to be the willful blindness and indifference of the man with whom my life had become so inextricably tied and yet adopting that very blindness and indifference myself.

I am only a woman, I would tell myself. I am only a slave. What can I possibly do? I don't understand. Nobody understands. There is nothing anyone can do. That's just the way things are. I have to accept it. I have to be realistic. I can't be blamed. . . .

James T. Callender says, "Mute! Mute! Mute! Yes, very mute!"

July 12, 1797. There is a moan from the corner. Sally Hemings leans back from the table and pulls a curtain aside just enough to see almost two-year-old Harriet flopped on her back, legs and arms akimbo, as if she has fallen out of the sky. Sleeping next to her, brown legs drawn up under her bunched-up shift, single pigtail lying across her neck, is eight-year-old Aggy, the servant Thomas Jefferson sent to live with Sally Hemings so that she might have help with Harriet at all hours of the day and night. Aggy is the one who moaned. Her legs give a doglike twitch. A wince flickers at the corners of her mouth and eyes.

"Just dreaming," Sally Hemings says to Thomas Jefferson, who is seated across the table from her, his cheek and temple a soft yellow-green in the lamp glow, tiny bent lamps in each of his eyes. He is fifty-three, and Sally Hemings is twenty-three.

She leans forward and lowers the wick, in case the light is what disturbed Aggy.

Thomas Jefferson arrived unexpectedly twenty minutes ago, with a crooked-necked bottle of wine, asking if she would like a bit of company, and now the bottle is half empty and so is her glass. She finishes it and puts it down on the table with a firm smack.

"Anyhow," she says, "that's wonderful that the Republican side is finally publishing lies about Colonel Hamilton."

"They're not lies."

"Articles, I mean."

Thomas Jefferson refills her glass, then his own.

"It's good that you are fighting back," she says. "That's what I mean."

"What's especially good is exactly that they are not lies. There is no question whatsoever that Colonel Hamilton was behaving improperly with his Mrs. Reynolds. He's admitted it. And it is certain that he has used secrets that have come to him as treasury secretary to make his friends and himself rich, and that he has thereby not merely cheated the American public but stolen from it as well."

"Can't you throw him in jail for that?"

Thomas Jefferson laughs. "That will never happen."

"But it should! He's broken the law." Sally Hemings also laughs. "He's broken all kinds of laws—human and divine."

"Hamilton has far too much influence to ever end up in prison." Thomas Jefferson smiles wryly and looks directly into her eyes. "And, of course, one of his transgressions is perhaps just a bit too common for people to get up in arms about."

Sally Hemings sips from her glass, and Thomas Jefferson sinks down in his chair. He slides one foot a few inches across the floor.

"In any event," he says, "I think this may put an end to his chances of ever becoming president."

"Is this man going to write some more articles about Colonel Hamilton?"

"Callender?"

"Yes."

"Perhaps. I don't know. I've had very little communication with him."

"You should get him to," she says. "Maybe he could sink Hamilton with one more article. Or President Adams. You should get him and other journalists to expose all the lies and corruption of the Federalists. If the journalists do the dirty work, the public will finally understand the evil that has been done in their name, and *you* will only look better for having stayed above the mud fight."

"We shall see," says Thomas Jefferson. He is smiling broadly as under the table he presses the inside of his right knee against the outside of Sally Hemings's left. Now she is smiling, too. They fall silent and only look at each other. In the lamplight her eyes seem twin disks of steel.

. . . *Of course, I could not entirely avoid discussing such matters with him. But when I did, my arguments—so potent in my mind—would come out as a series of peevish complaints or feeble suppositions. Only as I lay sleepless in a dead, dark hour of the night would my arguments come back to me in all their clarity and force—but too late, and so they would only fill me with self-loathing and a sense of helplessness.*

I hated myself when I spoke, and I hated myself when I was silent—so I labored to lose myself in the pleasures of Mr. Jefferson's company. Throughout my twenties and thirties, he was almost childishly attentive to me whenever he was home, or at least whenever we could evade the alert and judging eyes of his daughters and much of Albemarle society. And his attentions were not only physical—though he could be both energetic and tender in that regard. We talked more than anything else, and as time went by, he increasingly sought out my advice on matters of government. I was more practical than he and was better able to reduce some of the complex dilemmas he faced to their most essential elements. He often joked that I was the natural-born politician while he was a natural-born parson—or he would be, were it not for his congenitally equivocal faith. . . .

Thomas Jefferson says, "We must be patient, Sally."

He says, "Our enemies are determined, united and strong, and the immoral practice is so well established in the southern states that it would not end in a generation, even were it outlawed today."

He is standing on the porch, where the rain, atomized by fierce wind, coats his cheeks in trembling droplets. He is shouting, "All right, you are free! I will give you your papers as soon as we get back to the house. Then go off into this world ruled by vicious and bigoted whites and see how precious your freedom is!" *But I am white! Look at me! Who would not think that I am white!* "You are not so white as you would like to believe." *I hate you! You are a monster!* "I am sorry. I am sorry. Forgive me. I am sorry."

He refills her glass. "You are right. I can't disagree. You are absolutely right."

For a while Sally Hemings thinks her secret life is not only her best life but her real life. Then things change.

At first she thinks it is her fault. Thomas Jefferson is the vice president and so must continue to be away at least half the year, especially as President Adams, despite having been a dear friend, now seems to want to ascribe many of the powers of a monarch to himself—in particular the power to jail his political enemies—an ambition Thomas Jefferson is combatting with every tool he can muster. She is lonely when he is away, and she worries from time to time that he might have another woman in Philadelphia or New York. But on the other hand, the fact that he is such an important man has always loomed so large in her sense of him that she cannot object when he is doing the very work that has *made* him important. And there are still days when it thrills her to remember that this man known all over the world has held her in his arms and that he is the father of her little Harriet and of the new baby inside her.

Often she thinks that Thomas Jefferson loves her, but this thought is not reliably comforting, because while he sometimes confesses his love when they are alone, his pretense in the company of others that she is a mere servant can be so convincing that she will feel as if he has spit at her. He is never cruel, only indifferent. "That will be all," he will tell her. Or, "My riding boots need polishing." Or, "The hamper in my chamber is full." She believes—or sometimes only wants to believe—that this pretense is merely another part of their secret life, that his false indifference is his way of ensuring that he might love her freely when they are alone. She consoles herself by remembering how he calls her "sweet girl" and "Senator Sally," and the tenderness of his fingertips on her cheeks or breasts, and all those times when he cannot bear to leave her bed, or simply those times when he is reading on the porch of the lodge or writing at his desk and his casual glance in her direction is lit with all the world's kindness.

The change comes, she thinks, because of her pregnancy. She is not vomiting, but she is nauseated almost all the time and is always tired, even when she first rises from bed. Also, Thomas Jefferson does not want to be with her once she starts to get a belly. He says that it is bad for the baby and that he and Mrs. Jefferson lost their only son because he couldn't exercise proper restraint, and he will never forgive himself for that. Sally Hemings takes his desire to protect their baby as a particularly important indication of his love, but still, she is lonely now in a way that she hasn't been for years.

Harriet is two, and the sweetest of babies—laughing constantly, giving her mother tender, glossy-lipped kisses on the cheek, taking delight in every little thing: sparrows hopping in the dust, sneezing horses, flowers. All summer long, every time she sees a flower, she runs up to it and gives it a noisy sniff, after which she always says, "Pur-ty!"

But once the cold weather arrives, the little girl seems to become perversely willful and heedless of peril. Sally Hemings need only forbid her to do something and she will run straight off to do it, no matter how dangerous. One time she picks up a knife and runs her finger on the blade until the blood starts to flow. Another time she tries to climb into the pigsty, even though just the day before she saw the puddle of blood and the bits of bone and hoof left after the sow ate her own baby. And then there are her fits. Sometimes she starts to scream and thrash and kick for no reason, and all of Sally Hemings's hugs, kisses and consoling coos only make her scream louder and thrash more ferociously, with such a wildness in her eyes that she doesn't seem to know her own mother.

Sally Hemings can't help but think of Jimmy, and she worries that her beautiful child might have a lifetime of pain and rage ahead of her. But her mother says, "When a baby's two, that's when the Devil tries to wrestle her soul from God. You got to seal up your heart to her and be so hard on her it makes you sick. 'Cause you let her get away with one little thing, the Devil going to get her, and then he'll have her for the rest of her life."

In between Harriet's struggles with the Devil, she is exactly the sweet, happy girl she has always been. She sings constantly, just like her father. And she loves to play a game she calls "Booteefoo Mammy," during which she runs a comb through Sally Hemings's hair over and over and then washes her nose and cheeks and forehead with a kitchen rag. So most of the time it is easy for Sally Hemings to love her little girl and yet be both strict and fair when she starts at some devilry.

But the weather only gets colder, and after three months, instead of her pregnancy nausea going away, it gets worse. Also, at the start of December, Thomas Jefferson must go to Philadelphia again to resume his duties as vice president, and most likely he will be there until after her baby is born. Sally Hemings is terrified that something will go wrong while he is away. She worries that she has been too lucky with Harriet and that God will not allow her so much good fortune.

And then one rainy day, the wood is wet and Aggy is useless at keeping the fire going. Sally Hemings has to rekindle it herself while also making Harriet her porridge and feeding it to her, because the little girl says she doesn't like Aggy; she only likes Mammy. But then she says that she also doesn't like the porridge, and when her mother pointedly pays her no mind, she sweeps the bowl off the table, and it shatters on the floor into a dozen pieces and splatters gray muck up the wall. There is a moment of roaring silence, and then Sally Hemings slaps her daughter across the face and starts to scream as if *she* is the one whose soul the Devil has snatched. Only the sight of a droplet of blood running down from the little girl's nostril brings Sally Hemings back to her right mind. She crushes Harriet against her chest and weeps onto the top of her sweet-smelling little head. All the while Aggy is crying in the corner.

The very next day, a bright red pimple comes up on the side of Harriet's nose that the blood ran from. And the day after, the pimple is bigger and enflamed. Sally Hemings treats it with a mix of mud and birdlime. But the following morning it has grown shiny and purple and so swollen it encompasses Harriet's nostril and the end of her nose. The little girl is fretful and asks her mother to make her nose stop hurting, but when Sally Hemings tries to salve it with another layer of mud and birdlime, Harriet howls with pain.

Later that day her eyes have gone glassy, and although she doesn't feel hot, Sally Hemings still worries that she has a fever. Then, at bedtime, her cheek is sticky with sweat and her neck is so hot it could burn Sally Hemings's fingers.

She puts the little girl into her own bed and sends Aggy to fetch Betty Hemings, who has been given her time and lives in a small, white clapboard house of her own, in the neighborhood reserved for the white mechanics and their families. Betty arrives with a bottle of feverfew wine that, miraculously, Harriet drinks as if it were honey milk. But it doesn't do any good. Aggy curls up on Harriet's empty bed and is the only one who gets any sleep that night. Sally Hemings and her mother sleep on the floor, taking turns attending to Harriet, whenever she whimpers or wails.

The following morning, when Thomas Jefferson comes to say good-bye, Sally Hemings begs him not to go and tells him that she is terrified something awful is going to happen. "Harriet's a good, strong girl," he says. "A little fever is nothing to fret over, as long as she doesn't have a cough." He looks her long in the eyes, as if to convince her that she has no need to worry, but what she sees is his own worry, doing battle with his obligation to his office. He bends and kisses Harriet on her burning forehead, and then he kisses Sally Hemings on her cheek. "It will be fine," he says, squeezing her hand. "I will tell Martha that if the fever should get worse, Dr. Cranley should be called."

It is raining when Thomas Jefferson leaves. Sally Hemings does not go up to the house to wave good-bye from the veranda, even though her own mother is there, and Critta, Ursula, Jupiter and Tom Shackelford, along with Martha, Mr. Randolph and little Anne, but she does see the landau pass by her doorstep, with Jimmy driving, shoulders hunched under an oilcloth hat and cape and Thomas Jefferson snug and dry under the leather roof. From the shape of his silhouette, she thinks he is looking at her cabin as he passes, but she is sitting in the dark, Harriet cradled against her breast, so there is no way he can see her.

Martha and her family go back to Edgehill that afternoon, and thus, late that night, when Harriet's temperature rises so high that Sally Hemings cannot quell her shivering, even by covering her with several blankets and lying on top of her, Jupiter has to ride through the night and rouse Martha from sleep so that she can write him a note to bring to Dr. Cranley.

By the time the doctor arrives late the following morning, Harriet's shivering has turned into violent shudders that culminate with her back arching and the whole of her little body going rigid before she gasps and collapses into unconscious exhaustion. And then, after less than a minute, the whole process starts over, and so it has gone since long before sunrise. In an effort to keep her temperature down, Sally Hemings has stripped the little girl naked, despite the cold weather, and bathes her body constantly with rags dipped in water straight from the rain barrel. But the fever stays high and possibly gets higher.

It is clear that Dr. Cranley has no idea why he has been summoned all this way to treat a nigger girl—even though her skin is as white as his own and her sweaty curls are red. As soon as he walks in the door, he shakes his head pathetically and makes a *tsk* that is like a blade of ice plunged into Sally Hemings's heart. "Put some water on to boil," he tells her. Without bothering to examine his patient, he sets his satchel on the table, removes a mortar and pestle, into which he dispenses some dried herbs and a white tablet and begins to grind them into a powder.

When the water has boiled, he pours a little into the mortar, stirring it into the powder. Once he has turned the ingredients into a gray syrup, he pours it into a tin cup that just happens to be sitting on the table. "Let this cool," he says while wiping out the interior of his mortar. "Give her a mouthful every four hours until her fever passes."

"But how can I do that," says Sally Hemings, "when she is either unconscious or grinding her teeth in her fever?"

Something like a smile comes into the doctor's eyes before he looks away. "Well, if you can't get her to take her medicine," he says wearily, "I am afraid there is no hope."

He packs up the rest of his belongings and puts on his oilcloth overcoat. Just as he passes through the doorway, he looks back and says, "God be with you."

Then he is gone.

Sally Hemings closes the door and leans her head against it, her hands clutching her own shivering shoulders. For a long moment, she feels as if she cannot move, as if she might never move again. But when at last she turns away from the door, she finds her daughter watching her patiently, neither convulsing nor unconscious.

"Hey, Little Apple," Sally Hemings says. "You feeling better?"

Harriet only looks up at her mother with her large, dark eyes that seem so deeply lonely and filled with longing.

Sally Hemings puts her hand across the little girl's forehead and finds her temperature unchanged. She is no longer shivering, but her pulse is visibly beating with a birdlike rapidity at the base of her neck.

Sally Hemings pulls the covers up over the child's bare body, and goes to the table, where she pours a little of the gray syrup into a spoon. Returning to the bed, she eases her daughter into a semi-seated position. "Here," she says, holding up the spoon, "this will make you better."

Harriet turns her face away, grimacing as if in intense pain.

Sally Hemings sniffs the syrup, which smells like day-old urine.

Lowering Harriet back onto her mattress, she dumps the medicine into a bowl, adds a bit more from the tin cup, then stirs in a spoonful of molasses. "Here," she says, holding another spoonful to her daughter's lips, "all sweet and delicious!" But the mixture is met only by an averted face.

When Sally Hemings tries to force the mixture into Harriet's mouth, the little girl pushes the spoon out with her tongue and then spits out the trickle of medicine that managed to pass her lips.

"Come on, Little Apple, you have to eat this! It's good for you."

Again and again Sally Hemings tries to get her daughter to take the medicine, but either the child grimaces and turns away or she spits out whatever her mother manages to force between her lips.

Eventually Harriet falls into an exhausted sleep, and Sally Hemings uses her fingertip to smear a bit of the syrup inside her mouth, hoping that some of it will trickle down her throat. The little girl sleeps quietly for a couple of hours, and Sally Hemings begins to wonder if the medicine has actually begun to do some good.

She drifts into a light sleep herself, lying on the floor beside the bed, but after only seconds, or so it seems, she is awakened by a howl and finds Harriet gripped by a new kind of convulsion—one caused by or causing agonizing pain.

Sally Hemings sends again for the doctor, but Jupiter returns saying the doctor is busy with other patients and will return when he can.

Harriet's convulsions go on almost without interruption for two more days. She howls so relentlessly that eventually her voice gives out and she can only emit a ragged hiss. She will neither eat nor drink—not even a mouthful of water—and soon goes yellow and gaunt, looking more like a tiny old woman than a child.

Sally Hemings cannot imagine how the girl has the strength to endure such racking agony. Many times, even as her voiceless screams rip from her throat, she will look right at her mother as if asking to be put out of her misery.

At dawn of the second day, Sally Hemings sends once again for the doctor, and at noon Jupiter returns with the same message as before (on neither occasion did he see the doctor himself but had only been given the message by the doctor's wife).

Sally Hemings has not rested or even closed her eyes in three days, and finally, near dusk, while her mother, Critta and Aggy keep watch, she falls into a deep sleep.

When she wakes, the cabin is dark in that way it can only be after midnight, and utterly silent, apart from the whispery riffling of Aggy's snores. A solitary candle burns on the table where her mother and sister are sitting wordlessly and have clearly been waiting for her to rise.

They don't have to speak.

Thy will be done.

The first thing Sally Hemings feels is relief.

And then she knows that she has killed her daughter—that because she could not restrain her rage, disease took possession of this sweetest and most innocent of creatures. Little Harriet is dead, and Sally Hemings doesn't know how she herself will continue to live. She is an evil woman.

M artha does not come to the funeral. But when, the following day, Sally Hemings walks the four miles to see her at Edgehill, Martha greets her at the door herself and invites her into the parlor.

"My dear Sally," Martha says over and over. "My dear, dear Sally."

While Sally Hemings sits, Martha remains standing, rubbing one hand over the other as if she is washing them. "I am so sorry," she says. "I wanted to come to the . . . to the . . . to your—" She cuts herself off with a swallow before continuing. "But I was kept here by pressing concerns. I hope you can understand."

Martha does not wait for a response before telling Sally Hemings that Mrs. Maria (who, at nineteen, has married her cousin Jack and moved to Eppington) sends her consolations and apologies.

"Would you like some tea?" Martha asks after a moment of silence.

"No, thank you." Sally Hemings looks down into her lap. "I am wondering if I might ask a favor of you. Would it be possible for you to write to Mr. Jefferson, and—"

Martha's teeth flash white in a relieved though still anxious smile. "As it happens," she says, "I have already written to Papa. I will be sure to give you his reply the instant it arrives."

As this is all Sally Hemings wanted to hear, she stands up.

"Are you sure you won't have some tea?" asks Martha.

"No, thank you."

Martha escorts Sally Hemings to the door and gives her hand a quick, forceful squeeze before saying good-bye.

A week and a half later, Mr. Richardson, the steward, comes to Sally Hemings's cabin with a letter from Martha, which he reads aloud, in total: "'Sir, Could you convey at your earliest opportunity to Sally Hemings my father's expression of sorrow at her recent misfortune—to wit, "Please tell Sally I am sorry to hear of the loss of her child." Yours, Mrs. Randolph.'"

"Is that all?" asks Sally Hemings.

Mr. Richardson shrugs. Before he leaves, he looks at her as if he has something more to say. In the end he only mutters, "Sorry," and walks out into the daylight.

Sally Hemings is alone, sitting on the edge of her bed.

Her child, she thinks. Her *child?*

"No point getting angry at Mr. Jefferson for that," says her mother. "Might as well get angry at a mule 'cause he stubborn."

"But he's not a mule," says Sally Hemings. "He's a man. And a man has a choice about what he says and does."

"I didn't say he ain't got no choice. All I said is that anger won't get you nothing. You got a choice, too, and you got to do what's good for you—that's all I'm saying."

"You mean whatever he does, I'm just supposed to shut up and take it? What kind of choice is that?"

"All I'm saying is you do what's good for you. He's a man, and men don't think about nothing in a woman except pussy. That's just a fact. Nothing you can do about that. But Mr. Jefferson—seems like, long as you let him get a little every now and then, you in the catbird seat. That's not so bad, far as I can see."

"I'll kill myself first!"

Betty shakes her head wearily. "Oh, baby, ain't no one ever said being a woman is easy—a colored woman especially."

It is nearly midnight, and Thomas Jefferson is stretched out in his bed, fully dressed except for stockings and shoes, his legs under the covers and his portable wooden desk in his lap. His fire has burned down to cinders, and his breath is making a bronze fog in the light of the candelabra on his night table. Two letters lie drying on the covers beside him, one to Aaron Burr, asking for his aid in keeping President Adams and the Federalists from launching a full-scale war against France, and the other to James Madison, concerning the deeply troubling rumors that Adams is planning to pass a so-called Sedition Act that would allow him to imprison for treason anyone who published, wrote or even uttered criticism of his government. While the former is the more pressing issue, the latter is by far the more serious, and a clear violation of the most sacred principles articulated in the Declaration and the Constitution.

What Thomas Jefferson feels is more sorrow than outrage. It is beyond his comprehension how Adams, someone he had once so admired and thought a dear friend, would want to arrogate unto himself the powers of a monarch. Not merely is such an ambition a complete repudiation of the most passionate and noble struggle of both their lives, it would seem to indicate that no human being, not even the most idealistic and pure, is immune to the corruptive influence of power.

How might the nation be preserved from the weaknesses of human nature? Only, apparently, through the constant vigilance and fervent efforts of the truest believers in the ideals of democracy and republican government. But if Adams can be so compromised, where are such true believers to be found? Is simple human nature the greatest enemy of government by and for the people? Is democracy even possible if the representatives of the people yield so easily to self-interest? Or is the concentration of power in the hands of the corrupt and greedy few the inevitable and most natural form of human governance? Is this why there have been no true democracies since creation? Is the entire American venture doomed?

Such thoughts have been eating away at his own will to fight ever since his arrival in Philadelphia a week and a half ago. He has found it impossible to sleep for more than two or three hours a night, and whatever he eats passes almost instantly through his body, causing painful turbulence all along the way. He has been alternating almost daily between despairing lethargy and frenzied, not entirely rational or well-coordinated efforts to combat his opponents, solidify bonds with his supporters and gain new allies. This entire day has been devoted to such efforts, and now, even as the fire and his candles burn low and the December cold seeps under the door and through the window sashes, he feels so restless that he can't imagine going to sleep.

The letter on the wooden desk in his lap is the one from Martha he received three days ago telling him of the death of poor little Harriet. When he first read the news, his head reeled and it seemed minutes before he could breathe again. Of the eight children whom he has sired, Harriet is the sixth to die. For days he has been seeing images of her trying to catch dust motes in a sunbeam, making her satisfied *gnar-gnar-gnar* moan at Sally Hemings's breast and taking great effort to articulate her every syllable when, two days before he left Monticello, she told him, "I want to ride with you on your horsey." How is it possible that this sweet little girl should be gone? He remembers all the dear little ones he has lost, their fluffy heads, their dewy cheeks, their delicate smiles. He remembers Lucy, the second Lucy, who, only two years old, had no comprehension of what he was saying when he went to bid her good-bye before leaving for France. She had looked up at him with those huge, dark brown eyes of hers, some sort of consternation at what he was telling her brewing inside them, but not enough to amount to real understanding. They were the eyes of trust. She was trusting him never to do anything that would bring her sorrow or put her in harm's way—and he had done both, by turning his back and walking out the door to his carriage loaded with trunks and boxes.

It was the same, he feels, with little Harriet. When he left, he had told himself that her illness was only *la grippe*, that in a day or two she would be outside again, squealing happily as she ran after squawking chickens. But now it seems to him that he actually knew she was going to die and that the reason he had not postponed his departure for Philadelphia was that he could not bear to witness her death agony or to see her bright and avid little face go pale and permanently still. And thus it was that he had betrayed not only her but also her mother.

His first thought on hearing of Harriet's death was to write to Sally

Hemings directly, through Jimmy. He had even begun the letter but had hardly gotten through his second sentence before he realized how disastrous it would be were so incriminating a document to be intercepted by Adams or Hamilton—especially at this particular juncture. So he tore up the letter and threw it into the fire. There followed a day of despondency, during which he could not bear to even think of the news Martha had conveyed to him. Yesterday he wrote several different letters to Martha, all of them containing descriptions of Harriet's sweet and lively face—but then, knowing the unpleasant thoughts such description would put into his eldest daughter's mind, he tore up each letter as soon as he had finished it and threw it into the fire.

And now, as one of his candles has already guttered and gone dark and as, even under his greatcoat, both of his shoulders are shaken by a chill, he decides that the simplest and least lugubrious message is the best: "Please tell Sally I am truly sorry to hear of the loss of dear little Harriet." Excellent reader of character that she is, Sally Hemings will, he hopes, intuit all the sorrow and sympathy behind his words.

But as he folds the letter and slips it into an envelope, he thinks that should she not understand his true meaning, that might not be so bad. At this moment, when he is in such despair over the corruption of so many of his onetime allies and friends, perhaps it would be best if he were able to transcend his own human weakness, even at the cost of hurting a lovely and kind young woman.

The day after Mr. Richardson reads Martha's letter, Sally Hemings drags the trunk containing her Paris clothes off the hidey-hole under her bed and pulls out the primer. That night she goes to Thomas Jefferson's chambers, where, taking his pen in hand and opening his inkwell, she copies out onto several sheets of foolscap every letter of every word in all the couplets. She works until long after midnight, and the result of her efforts looks more like an assemblage of broken twigs than actual writing, and the muscle between her thumb and first finger has grown so hard and painful that she has to sit on her hand before she can open it flat. But this time she knows that she has actually *read* every word she copied rather than recited it from memory or simply guessed what it might be. And she also knows that her marks will become more and more like real writing with every new attempt.

The next night she makes two copies of the couplets and the following night three, and with every repetition she feels the sounds the letters signify rising more naturally within her mind and the forms the letters take flowing more naturally from her quill. She repeats the exercise for two more nights, and on the third she brings *Notes on the State of Virginia* with her and copies out its first page, a much more arduous labor that takes her two long nights, not because there are more words but because the words are much more difficult to sound out and comprehend—especially since there are no rhymes. But even so, by the time she has copied the whole page, she feels that she has mostly understood what she has read: that Thomas Jefferson is explaining the circumstances under which the book was written and apologizing for its flaws, which he ascribes, in part, to "the want of talents in the writer."

Sally Hemings is surprised that even Thomas Jefferson should worry about his writing, but at the same time his confession is a comfort, because it tells her that writing is difficult for everyone, and so she feels less alone.

With this thought in mind, she closes the book, and just below the last sentence she has copied, she inscribes:

"I am Sally I can red and writ"

By the time she finishes these eight words, her heart is pounding as if she has just climbed a mountain, and a strange, uneasy thrill is running all through her body. It takes her a long moment to understand why she should feel as she does, but then the thought comes to her that she has just acquired a dangerous skill. She isn't sure how she is going to use it or if she should let anyone know that she possesses it. She is proud of herself—very proud. But she is much more afraid than she is proud, and she isn't sure why she should be afraid at all.

James T. Callender is hated because he sees people exactly as they are—and they know it, even when he keeps what he sees entirely to himself. But since the truth is a weapon, and one that gains potency according to the wealth and influence of the man it concerns, many people are willing to pay Callender to put the truth into words. Almost all of these people are either cowards, who are actually paying him to say what they dare not say themselves, or hypocrites, who desire nothing more than the brutal evisceration of their enemies but who rely upon Callender's perspicacity and impeccable journalistic reputation to give them license to proclaim, at the first twinge of guilt or hint of condemnation, "But it's the truth!"—as if paltry factuality were an unassailable guarantor of virtue.

While the clarity of his vision is what has kept Callender in meat and drink for decades, it is also the primary source of his despondency. There is not, for example, another man on the American continent whom Callender admires more than Thomas Jefferson. Again and again, on reading Jefferson's remarks on the natural rights of man, the corruptions of monarchism or the evil of concentrated political or economic power, he has had the uncanny sensation that he is reading his own thoughts. And so, when his Philadelphia publisher brings a tall, redheaded man into his office and introduces him as Vice President Jefferson, Callender staggers as if a thunderbolt has burst within the room. Were Jesus Christ standing before him, he could not have been more cowed by awe. But then he shakes Thomas Jefferson's soft, perspiring hand and knows the truth: The man is both coward and hypocrite, animated solely by a desire for revenge. There follows a brief moment during which Callender is enraged that Thomas Jefferson should turn out to be so abjectly human. But in the next moment, Callender realizes that his former hero's weakness amounts to his own strength.

Thomas Jefferson says nothing of his real motives, of course, but, on parting, Callender intimates that he understands them perfectly. Making a gesture that combines a deferential bow with a knowing wink, he says,

"Should you ever have need of my services, I am entirely at your disposal." And, indeed, two days later Callender receives a message from Thomas Jefferson asking for a private conference at the home of their mutual friend, Thomas Leiper.

While secretary of state, Thomas Jefferson rented Leiper's house, and as has been the case in every house he has rented, he substantially renovated it during his tenure. The stately room where he and Callender meet, with its mauve walls and brass chandelier, was once divided by a rough wooden partition into the work and storage rooms for a hat manufactory. Leiper was extremely dubious when Thomas Jefferson suggested that he might renovate, but so satisfied with the results that he moved into the house after his illustrious tenant departed and now rents out his former home instead.

After the briefest exchange of pleasantries, Leiper places an open bottle of burgundy and two glasses on the table and leaves the room. The bottle poses a question: Which of the two men will pick it up and serve the other? Callender decides to answer this question by remaining perfectly silent and still. When, at last, Thomas Jefferson reaches over and begins to fill one of the glasses, Callender raises his hand, palm forward. "That's for you." Thomas Jefferson glances at him, perplexed. "I've brought my own." Callender pulls a silver flask out of his pocket. "Don't have much taste for wine, actually." He fills the empty glass with brandy, then taps its base against the glass Thomas Jefferson has already filled. "To your health." He smiles. Clearly disconcerted, Thomas Jefferson returns the smile uneasily, then begins to chatter compulsively about President Adams's proposed Sedition Act, his monarchist tendencies and the betrayal of the Revolution by the Federalists in general. But finally, after pausing to moisten his dry mouth with a sip of wine, he comes to the point. "I am wondering if this might not interest you in a professional capacity, which is to say if you mightn't make some of these points in an essay or a pamphlet?"

"I am at your service," says Callender. And then he says, "I've met Adams on a number of occasions. The man is a clear sodomite."

Thomas Jefferson glances down into his wine.

Callender smiles. "I'm sure it would be no trouble to come up with incontrovertible evidence of his proclivities, although our best sources might be his neighbors in Braintree."

"I don't think that . . ." (Thomas Jefferson's mouth hangs open indecisively for a long moment.) ". . . will be . . ." (Another long pause.) "Well, let's just say I'm not sure that would be a productive avenue of inquiry."

Callender doesn't respond, only stares straight into Thomas Jefferson's eyes, smiling all the while.

"My concern," says Thomas Jefferson, "is entirely for the continuance of the Republic."

"Of course! Of course! You know that no one has greater respect for you or is in closer accord with your political philosophy than I."

Thomas Jefferson crosses one leg over the other and finishes his wine in a single swallow. His contempt for Callender is palpable, but so is his helplessness.

Callender lifts his index finger admonishingly. "Given how critical it is that we quash Adams and the Federalist traitors, we must pursue our every advantage. Anything less would show both a lack of backbone and a profound underestimation of the dangerousness of our enemies."

"I agree that we should stop at nothing to defeat the Federalists, but it is my firm belief that we will be most likely to succeed if we pursue only *necessary* efforts. Irrelevant or unsubstantiated attacks will make us seem indifferent to moral and political principles and to care for nothing but the maximization of our own power, and so could undermine rather than advance our cause."

"Mr. Jefferson?" Callender is holding out the bottle of wine.

Thomas Jefferson seems at first not to understand the significance of the gesture but then extends his empty glass.

Returning the bottle to the table, Callender sits back in his chair. "No one holds moral principle in greater estimation than I," he says.

Thomas Jefferson recrosses his legs and takes a sip of his wine, his gaze turned entirely away from Callender.

"But in all due respect," Callender continues, "you must bear in mind that our friend Colonel Hamilton was not brought down by the actions of the courts nor by any investigative body but by my revelations concerning his callous disregard for his wife's reputation and feelings and his sordid exploitation of the poor Mrs. Reynolds."

Thomas Jefferson takes another swallow of his wine but still does not look at Callender.

"I would ask you, then," says Callender, "to consider which efforts were, in fact, *necessary* to rid the nation of so corrupt an influence as Hamilton."

"Mr. Callender, I would not be here if I did not have immense respect for your capacities as a journalist." Thomas Jefferson speaks with bitter irony, and he looks Callender straight in the eye, as if to underline that fact.

"Exactly," says Callender. "And I trust, then, that you understand that as the journalist *I* will be taking full responsibility for what I write. What this means is that anything you have to tell me about Mr. Adams, Mr. Jay or about any other matter will be held in strictest confidence. My readers and the nation as a whole will benefit from your wisdom, but not a soul will even suspect that you were the one to advance my understanding."

"Yes," says Thomas Jefferson. "Good."

He is weakening. James T. Callender smiles and refills his own glass with brandy.

"But at the same time," he says, "since I am the one taking responsibility for what I write, I am the one who will determine what that might be. You may speak to me about Mr. Adams or not, as you choose. But if I determine that a trip to Braintree is merited, I am entirely within my rights to undertake it. Mr. Leiper has informed me of the gracious contribution you have made toward the care of my ailing wife and my poor children, and I am immensely grateful. I thank you, in fact, from the bottom of my heart. But nonetheless I must still insist upon my journalistic freedom. If you have any misgivings in that regard, I will immediately return your moneys to you, with interest."

Thomas Jefferson has finished his second glass of wine. He is looking out the window. His voice is low. "That won't be necessary."

"I assure you that I hold myself to the strictest standards. My investigations will be exhaustive, and I will not make one assertion unsupported by fact."

"Good," says Thomas Jefferson.

Callender is holding out the bottle of wine once again. "Mr. Jefferson?"

Thomas Jefferson looks at the hovering bottle, then offers his empty glass. Callender fills it, then refills his own with brandy. He smiles and lifts his glass. "We are on the verge of great things!"

Sally Hemings says, "Is it possible that we will grow old together? That we will be purified by age? Is it possible that I will own enough of my heart that I might give it to you?"

Sally Hemings says, "I accept your kisses, your caresses, the blunt shoving of your veined member, not because I like any of it but because you so clearly want me to like it and I don't—that is my revenge."

Sally Hemings says, "You are more than a man. Other men are mere beagles sniffing your boot heels. How is it I am allowed to see your flesh float in bathwater? How is it I am allowed to make you great?"

Sally Hemings says, "I want us always to be as we are here, where we are only our eyes, our hands, those parts of us made for each other by nature, where our only words are the ones we whisper in the little caves we make between pillow, cheek and lips."

Sally Hemings says, "My hope is so simple: to sit opposite you at a table we share with our children and friends. My hope is only pain. It is a mountain, airless at its peak, so it kills us. Love kills, too—that love, I mean, which is a variety of hate."

Sally Hemings says, "Such hopes as I have are like orphans along the byway. They are beautiful, and they will die."

Sally Hemings says, "Oh, I am black, I am white. I am stained to the bones by hate. Would that I had only been your trollop."

S ally Hemings hears Thomas Jefferson's landau drive up to the house before dawn. His rooms were prepared for his arrival two days ago, so she is not surprised. It is March 7, 1798, exactly three months since Harriet's death, and Sally Hemings is eight months pregnant. Her head is throbbing. She has had the most painful headaches of her life these last weeks, but today is the worst. She feels as if her head is being crushed between two pointed stones. The sun has risen a fist's width above the trees, and she is still lying in bed when she hears Thomas Jefferson's footsteps passing along the muddy road outside. He is singing, just above a whisper, "'He is no gypsy, my father,' she said, 'but lord of these lands all over. . . .'"

An hour or so later, she has just pulled her chamber pot out from under her bed when she hears Thomas Jefferson returning. She doesn't dare squat over the pot until he has passed, so she stands with her legs pressed tightly together, clutching the front of her shift and winding it tightly around her fist. His footsteps slow as he approaches and stop just in front of where she is standing. For a long time, she hears nothing but the repeated screech of a catbird, but then there are quick steps on the mud and the thump of a shoe on the porch. There is a knock on her door.

"Sally?"

She doesn't move or speak. She hopes he will go away. The urging of her bladder is unbearable.

Another knock. "Sally?" With a soft thud, the door loosens from the jamb and opens. His hand still poised in midair to knock, a tremor of discomfort passes over his face as he watches the door swing inward. But when he spots her standing beside her bed, he breaks into a big smile. "Good morning. I'm not disturbing you, am I?"

She does not answer, but, letting go of her shift, she makes a shooing gesture with her hand that she realizes he will probably construe as an invitation to enter.

"One moment." He backs out the door, and she hears him scraping the mud off his shoes on the edge of the porch. He stamps a couple of times, and then he is in the cabin. "Look at you!" he says, happily regarding her belly, which holds the front of her shift a good foot in front of the tips of her toes. "Clearly you've been hard at work! Do you think it's a boy? It looks like a boy to me."

Just at that instant, he glances at the chamber pot resting in the middle of the floor.

"One moment," she says, then brushes past him and out the door, so desperate now that she can't even make it all the way to the outhouse. Around behind the cabin, she half crouches, bracing her back against the wall, hikes her shift and pees, knowing she is perfectly audible inside the cabin and taking a sort of pleasure at the affront she might be causing.

"I'm sorry," she says once she is back inside. "These days I can't even wait a second." She pushes the chamber pot back under the bed with her foot.

His smile is both wry and uncomfortable. "Of course," he says, then looks away for an instant. When he looks back, his expression is earnest, if not entirely at ease. "I hope I'm not disturbing you."

She doesn't respond.

He pulls a chair away from the table and sits down. Since her only alternatives are to sit at the table with him or to sit on the bed, she remains standing.

"I've been thinking about you the whole way here," he says. "Hoping that you haven't suffered any—" He cuts himself off, but his words send a jolt of complex pain through her breast.

"I've been fine," she says.

"Good," he says. "Good. I hope you've been eating well. And getting plenty of sleep."

"I know how to take care of myself, Mr. Jefferson."

"Yes, of course." His lips tense. He searches her eye a moment, then looks away. "You are looking very well."

"Actually, I have an awful headache." She turns away from him and walks to the window that looks southeast, out over the fields and across the purple-and-gray flatlands. She is hoping that he will understand that she wants him to leave.

"Maybe you shouldn't look out the window," he says. "Is the light hurting your eyes?"

"No," she says, though, in fact, she does feel a painful pressure on the sides of her eyeballs.

She turns away from the window and sits down on the farthest corner of the bed from Thomas Jefferson. Neither of them speaks for a long moment, then he says, "I suppose you must be feeling stirrings?"

He is looking at her belly.

She takes a deep breath and gives him a severe stare. It is a long while before she can bring herself to speak the words she has formulated. "I don't see why you are troubling yourself about my well-being, Mr. Jefferson."

Weariness comes into his eyes and hurt to his lips.

She speaks again. "Or maybe I should say that I don't see why you should think you actually care."

"Sally," he says plaintively.

"Don't lie to me," she says. "And don't lie to yourself. You are clearly indifferent to my suffering and to all of my feelings."

"How can you say that!"

"I would rather you leave right now, Mr. Jefferson. My headache really is very bad, and I need to sleep."

"Sally, please."

"I don't want to talk. I think it would be better for both of us if you would just leave."

"For God's sake, Sally, would you just listen—"

She stands up and sweeps her arm in the direction of the door. "I am asking you to leave me alone." Her voice is firm and low. "I know that I have no right to ask you anything, that I have no rights of any sort. But if, in fact, you care at all about how I am feeling, I hope that you will heed my request."

Thomas Jefferson slowly gets to his feet, his expression promising revenge. When he is standing outside the door, his face livid, he says, "You are completely wrong about me."

"I don't think so."

She closes the door. She trembles as she stands inside her dark cabin, listening to his footsteps retreat toward the house. She feels a sort of elation but at the same time a cold dread. She suspects that what she has just done is profoundly foolish and that she will soon regret it. All at once a spike of pain shoots through her skull and into her right eye. She hurries to the window and vomits into the weeds outside.

The following morning Thomas Jefferson leaves to inspect his Poplar Forest plantation, three days distant, and he is gone two weeks. At the end of the first week, a letter from him arrives for Mr. Richardson, containing numerous recommendations and requests regarding the management of Monticello, among them that Sally Hemings be given a double food ration and that she continue to be exempt from all of her normal duties at the plantation. Thomas Jefferson also instructs that if she should go into labor before his return, Dr. Cranley should be summoned immediately.

Spotting her in the hallway, Mr. Richardson delivers this news to her in a low, diffident voice, but when he has finished, he winks, smiles and says, "Good afternoon, your ladyship."

"I want us to understand each other," says Thomas Jefferson. He has been back from Poplar Forest for two days, but this is the first time he and Sally Hemings have actually spoken. He arrives at her cabin long after dark, carrying a bottle of wine. It is clear that he has already had at least one bottle himself. He doesn't seem drunk, but his face is flushed and glossy in the lamplight, and he has forgotten to bring a corkscrew with him, so he has to push the cork into the bottle with a rock and a twenty-penny nail. Sally Hemings drinks a cup of the wine, but alcohol has made her flushed and nauseated ever since she got pregnant, so she resolves not to touch the cup in front of her that Thomas Jefferson has just refilled. He has had two cups and is starting on his third.

"I want you to tell me what I have done to offend you," he says.

Maybe he *is* drunk. Now, at least. His face has grown bleary, and some of his words are slurred. He and Sally Hemings are sitting directly across the table from each other, and she doesn't know how she can tell him the truth.

"You haven't offended me," she says.

"I have, but I think only through a misunderstanding."

She makes a barely audible grunt but says nothing. Then she takes a swallow of the wine.

Thomas Jefferson speaks: "I wish that I'd been able to be here when Harriet—"

She cuts him off. "That's not it."

"I've told you from the beginning that my responsibilities to the Republic must come first."

"That's not it, I said."

"Everything is in the balance now. If we cannot make this government work, we will live in either chaos or tyranny."

"I know that. Don't you think I listen to you?"

"What is it, then?"

Sally Hemings looks away. "It's too much." Tears are falling down her cheeks. "I can't tell you."

Thomas Jefferson flings himself back in his seat, the disarray of his arms and legs showing a restless irritation but his face chastened and worried.

The phrase "her child" repeats in Sally Hemings's mind over and over. It was so unnecessary. If Thomas Jefferson had merely wanted to maintain secrecy in a letter to his daughter, he could simply have said he was sorry and left it at that. And if he had truly cared about her, he could have made some private reference that would have revealed his love and his own grief only to her.

"*Her* child."

Every time the phrase repeats in Sally Hemings's mind, she grows more wildly furious.

But she also finds her fury misplaced, or at least undignified. She can't imagine scolding Thomas Jefferson for not loving her, especially considering all the warnings he has given her about his inability to love her publicly. She now realizes that all of her hopes and beliefs concerning their "secret life" had never been more than desperate fantasy or, worse, outright self-deception. She will not say a word about her feelings. If Thomas Jefferson truly loves her, he will understand, and if not, *damn him to hell!*

He leans forward, putting both arms on the table, extending his hands toward hers. Now she is the one to lean back. She puts her hands in her lap, placing them flat against the underside of her belly.

"Dear Sally," he says. "I wish there were a way that we could avoid such pain."

"What pain are you talking about, Mr. Jefferson?"

Weary sympathy comes onto his brow. "Yours," he says. "Mine. There are times when it seems that we are made to bring each other joy. But then . . . always . . ." He sighs. His smile is sad. He stops talking.

Sally Hemings only looks at him without speaking. There are so many things she wants to say, but it seems to her that the best revenge is simply to keep silent.

"Oh, Sally," he says, "tell me what is troubling you?"

"Nothing," she says. "You needn't worry about me." And, indeed, her tears have stopped. If she ever loved him, that is over now.

"I do worry about you." He is smiling—stupidly. His hands still rest on the table, palms upward, waiting for hers. He sighs again. "Well, I suppose we simply have to become philosophers."

"What do you mean?"

"We have to be Stoics. If we can accept that our moments of pain are an inevitable part of life on earth, as well as of our own particular situation, they will be easier to bear and they will pass more quickly."

"Will they?"

"Of course. They always have. We're not miserable all the time, are we?" He smiles broadly, apparently thinking that what he has said is funny.

He doesn't understand at all. He is so utterly convinced of his own virtue and importance that he is blind to the sufferings of others, and most especially to the suffering caused by his own actions.

He is a fool.

"You're beautiful," he says. He twitches the fingers of his right hand, an invitation for her to lift her left hand and place it in his. She doesn't move. His face is puffed and red, the gazes of his eyes don't quite meet, and he has that easy, self-satisfied smile that means he is about to ask her for a kiss, and maybe to relieve his desire with her hand or mouth.

She is staggered by the degree to which he misunderstands her. How could she ever have loved such a vain and blind man?

"We'll be fine, Sally," he says. "We may be fools, but we'll be fine."

He twitches his fingers a second time, and at that very instant she feels a change. She gets up from her chair and walks around to his side of the table. She lifts the front of her shift and places the palm of his hand flat on her bare belly. "Do you feel that?" she says.

He looks up at her, uncomprehending but happy.

"Do you feel how hard it is?"

He presses her belly slightly with his fingertips. "It's like stone," he says.

"That means the baby is coming. When my stomach gets hard like that, it means the baby could come anytime. Tonight. Tomorrow. A week from now. But soon."

She sees his face grow serious. For an instant she smiles—a cruel smile. Then she grows serious, too.

She takes a step away.

Before leaving Sally Hemings's cabin, Thomas Jefferson promises that he will stay until their baby is born, but the very next day a courier arrives with a letter from Philadelphia, and the following morning he is gone. Their baby, or *her* baby—a boy—is born two days later, after a mere six hours of labor. Harriet was named after Tom Randolph's sister, who lived for a while at Monticello and whom Thomas Jefferson found endearingly earnest and full of life. Before he leaves, he asks Sally Hemings if she would name their child Peter or Jane, after his parents, although Jane is also the name of his older sister, to whom he had been very close before her death. Sally Hemings is tempted by Peter, which, after all, is her own brother's name, but in the end, as the bloody little boy lies across her deflated belly and takes his first tugs from her breast, she decides to call him Beverly.

Bev-er-ly.

When she was a little girl, she thought that was the most beautiful name in the world. Whenever she thought of it, she saw honeybees on a sunny day, sipping from yellow flowers.

Bev-er-ly.

She loves the way the first syllable buzzes on her lips and how the second comes from deep in her throat and how the last can only be said with a smile.

It is a happy name. Whenever people say it, they will be happy, which means that her little boy will be surrounded by happiness all his life.

Thomas Jefferson's dreams are a catalog of failure and shame, histories of a world that contains no joy and can only be endured, an endless twilight of sorrow. In this dream he is sitting on the porch of the cottage at Poplar Forest looking out over the meadow. The trees are the color of shadows, and they have deeper shadows beneath them. In the obscurity under one tree, he sees a smear of darkness that might just be a human figure. No, he concludes again and again, it can't be. But again and again he changes his mind.

Finally he descends from the porch and walks out into the high grass. It is raining, and the longer he walks, the farther away the shadow within the shadow becomes. But then he is underneath the tree, and the shadow within the shadow is Sally Hemings. She is dressed in her most beautiful gown—the yellow one he bought her for Princess Lubomirsky's ball—but she is sitting in mud, which seeps up through the gown and its underskirts the way blood seeps through layers of gauze.

"Why are you sitting here?" says Thomas Jefferson.

"Because I was only a ghost to you," says Sally Hemings. "And now I am a ghost in reality, and you are the one who has killed me."

"How can you be dead if you are speaking to me?"

"I am dead, I am dead," she says. "And I wish I had never lived."

All at once Thomas Jefferson is so overwhelmed by sorrow that he wishes he, too, had died.

"I didn't know," he says. "I wish I had known."

"He's beautiful," says Thomas Jefferson. "Such a perfect little boy. And look: You see that little dent? Right there, between his nostrils? He got that from you. I noticed you had that the first time I saw you."

"Well, Mrs. Martha has it."

"Yes, she does. And her mother had it, too, but he got it from you!" Thomas Jefferson lifts the three-month-old in his arms and smells the top of his fluffy head. "He's a beautiful little boy, and he looks exactly like you!"

Sally Hemings smiles. "Would you like something to drink? Cider? I could make some coffee."

"No, thank you. I'm having breakfast with Martha in a few minutes. I just wanted to see my little boy." Thomas Jefferson glances at Sally Hemings, who is smiling so tenderly at their son, her gray eyes lit with such happy relish. It has been a long time since Thomas Jefferson has seen her so at ease. And between her pregnancy and his being away for most of the year, he had forgotten how very young she is, how her skin seems so moist and resilient, like a mushroom just sprung from loam.

He straddles the tiny boy across his knee, which he bounces up and down, as he chants, "Beverly, Beverly, Beverly!" The little boy squeaks, makes a huge toothless grin and sticks his wrist into his mouth. "Beverly, Beverly, Beverly!"

"He's my first son," Thomas Jefferson tells Sally Hemings. "Mrs. Jefferson had a boy, but he was not meant for this world."

He turns back to the little boy. "Beverly, Beverly, Beverly!"

Then he says, "My father had a friend named William Beverly." He smiles at Sally Hemings, but uneasily. "How would you feel about adding William to his name?"

Before Thomas Jefferson's return, Sally Hemings swore to herself that she would fight to the death over the name Beverly, but right now that doesn't seem to matter—and not only because she knows that the name she chose has fused so firmly with her baby's identity that no one will ever call him anything else.

"All right." Her smile is generous. "Whatever you wish."

"Excellent! William Beverly it is." Then Thomas Jefferson bounces the little boy to a syncopated rhythm, like the trot of a horse with an injured leg. "William Beverly! William Beverly! William Beverly!" More squeaking and a happy grin. But when Thomas Jefferson reverts to a more emphatic and bouncy version of his original chant, "Beverly, Beverly, Beverly!" the little boy bursts into a happy chortle.

"He laughed!" cries Sally Hemings.

Thomas Jefferson looks at her.

"That's his first laugh!" She claps her hands.

"Really?"

She answers with her own delighted laugh.

"How wonderful!" says Thomas Jefferson.

More bouncing, more chanting, and the tiny boy keeps laughing and laughing, as if he has always laughed and there is nothing he loves to do more.

"Beverly, Beverly, Beverly! Beverly, Beverly, Beverly!" Thomas Jefferson and Sally Hemings chant together.

The guard: vertical. The prisoner: horizontal, on a yellowed foam-rubber mattress. The guard: smoking. The prisoner: breathing (just barely), pale and grease-glossed, eyes closed (twitching). The guard: exhales a blue cloud, turns about-face, exits and locks the cell, sits. The prisoner: motionless. The guard speaks.

—You feeling better now?

— . . .

—I mean, of course you are! So make the most of it. Right? You got eight hours, then we start all over again.

The prisoner's eyes flutter, open, shut again. The guard exhales blue smoke through her nostrils. The guard speaks.

—Actually, I was thinking about you in there. Mostly it's pretty boring, so I have time to think. In between, I mean. And I was thinking about how they say that we only live in the present. One instant at a time. And I was thinking about how that was literally true for you. Every one of those instants seemed like it would never end, and maybe like you never lived any other life. Right? And I was thinking about how tomorrow, when you're back, these next eight hours—the hours in between— are going to seem like a glance out the window, like nothing.

—Nnynnyaygnahnn . . .

—Absolutely! And that's the problem. That's why you're in here. Or, more to the point, that's why you think you don't belong here.

The guard's lips close around her cigarette. It crackles. She sighs two long blue plumes through her nose. The guard speaks.

—The problem is that every instant of life is like an eternity. The world is just so *present*! There's so much of it, pouring into us through every sense, from every direction. Even from inside our own bodies. It's overwhelming. I mean, we're used to it and all. But if you actually think about it, it's overwhelming. And that's why we always feel like, *This is it. I'm here. This is real. Me. Who I am. Living in a world that really is.* Right? And you keep on feeling like that. Instant after instant after instant. You know what I mean?

— . . .

—That's just natural, isn't it? But the truth is, it's all bullshit.

The guard's lips close around the cigarette. Her cheeks are sucked against her teeth. Hiss. Sigh. Her head is enveloped in blue. She speaks.

—Ever notice how in the movies, when the bad guy is playing with his kid, he's never just playing with his kid? It's always ironic. Or he's being sadistic, and the kid's just too stupid to know. Or maybe there's this one second where the kid gets this tiny confused look on his face. But then he's laughing again, even when his dad bounces the rubber ball right off the top of his head. And they've got that scary music playing. You know, that music they always play in scary movies. Only in this scene, it's very quiet.

Crackle. Sigh. Smoke. The guard speaks.

—And that's how we know we're not evil. You follow me? I mean, when *we* play with our kid, we're *really* playing with our kid. And when we're taking a shit or doing the dishes, same deal. We go up in the mountains and we're like, "Wow! This is so beautiful! The air is so fresh! I feel so alive!" There's no scary music playing. There's nothing ironic. It just is what it is. You know, *innocent*. And that's how we know we're not evil. Because we have these innocent moments and the evil guy in the movie doesn't. His life is monolithic. All-evil-all-the-time.

Crackle. Sigh. Smoke. The guard studies the end of her cigarette: down to the filter. She drops it on the floor. Steps on it. The guard speaks.

—But, of course, that's not how it is at all. A real evil guy's life is practically nothing but innocent moments, just like anyone's. When he's taking a shit, he's just taking a shit. He's up in the mountains, and he can hardly believe the world could be so beautiful. When he's playing with his kid, he thinks his kid is the cutest kid who ever walked the planet. And then he goes off and . . . I don't know, pilots a drone over some country ten thousand miles away and blows the shit out of a wedding. Or he talks some old lady out of her life savings. Or he discovers that his wife is cheating on him, and he goes psycho for an hour. But even so, his life is made up almost entirely of ordinary moments: cutting his toenails, having drinks with his buddies out on the patio, ordering a bale of peat moss at the garden store.

The guard knocks another cigarette out of her pack. Click. Hiss. Odor of lighter fluid. Crackle. Sigh. The guard speaks.

—You know how that is, right? You see where I'm headed with this? I mean, there you are, screwing your sixteen-year-old girlfriend, and you're thinking, "Oh, my God! I just love this girl so much! She's the most wonderful thing that ever happened to me!" And then you're saying, "All men are created equal," and you're calling slavery an "abominable crime," and you're wholly sincere. You mean that one hundred percent. Every word. And you're thinking, "I am the kind of person who thinks such things and who says them. That's who I really am." And you are. That's true. But then you discover that you're short of cash, so instead of selling a few acres of land, or some hogs, or just doing without a shipment or two of French wine, you sell a bunch of human beings. You tear them away from their homes, everyone they know, and you consign them to a future that could well include torture and rape, murder even—the sort of things you would never perpetrate yourself. Right? Because that's not who you are. You don't do that sort of thing. And after that you go back to work designing this gigantic clock, or you're cutting open a kernel of wheat, thinking, "How wonderfully complex! How extraordinary that God should give us this miraculous vegetable."

— . . .

—The problem is, there's no scary music in life. And we don't actually live irony. The irony gets added later. And nobody out there is monolithic, all-evil-(or whatever)-all-the-time. And since every instant that comes along overwhelms us with its presentness and its complexity, and since we're always feeling, "This is really me being real in the real world; this is who I am," and since almost every one of those instants we live through being who we really are is an innocent instant, all of that added together makes it easy for us to lose track of the fact that we also live through not-so-innocent instants, when the me-I-really-am is a not-so-innocent me—though we almost always lie to ourselves about that fact. And so it is easy for us to pretend to ourselves that we are nothing like the evil guy in the movie. And we can allow those instants in which we are not-so-innocent to be overwhelmed by all the completely innocent ones, until they become insignificant. Or they almost don't exist.

— . . .

The guard exhales blue smoke through her nostrils. The guard speaks.
—You know where I'm going with this, right?
— . . .
—That's why no one ever thinks they belong here.
— . . .
—Except the murderers, sometimes.
— . . .

Sally Hemings's invention grows and grows, until it stretches to the horizon in all directions. Tendrils ascend from its glittering fields, smokelike, vinelike, at once vegetal and mathematical in their proliferation; intertwining, interlocking, growing ever higher, ever denser, ever more rectangular and gray. And as they rise, the sky contracts, now to a rhomboid of blue, rose and gold, now to a wedge, now to a crevice and now a glimmering crack.

And the people!

There are so many people!

As Sally Hemings's invention grows ever more vast, ever more unruly, dirty and loud, more and more people crowd its streets; they filter out of alleyways and doors; they stream down boulevards, assemble on plazas and in parks; they arrive in roaring steel boxes and boil up stairways out of the earth. Teeming. Roiling. Millions upon millions. Sand-colored, peat-colored, the color of Virginia's iron-rich dust; moseying, marching, strolling, striding; so intent, so lost in life's prolixity, so redolent of human odor—of perfume and sweat, of tooth rot, worry and sex.

VII

While the colors of light are pure—which is to say that, spectrographically measured, each designated color is itself and only itself—each reflected color, the colors we see when we look at a painting, a wall, a flower, contains all the other colors—which is to say that that cool red is also yellow, magenta and green; that gold is also indigo, brown and carmine; and that bluebird blue is also orange, verdigris green and burgundy; which is to say that we can never see what is actually before our eyes. Not ever.

Thomas Jefferson's first sign that he is becoming unbelievable is a certain hesitancy among even those people to whom he is closest. Something he has said or done will be met by a shift in attention, an instant of silence, a glance toward, or away from, him—some indication that whomever he is with will have noticed something wrong but not feel it significant enough to remark upon. The effect is very subtle. If Thomas Jefferson perceives it at all, it is mainly as a slight strain entering the conversation or a coolness—sometimes even as a literal drop in temperature.

After a while, though, people start making noises and gestures of disbelief: *tsks*, gasps, shakes of the head or disparaging grunts or guffaws. He has difficulty grasping the true significance of these responses, however, partly because they are first made by his political rivals—Alexander Hamilton, John Adams and their Federalist henchmen—and so are not surprising and partly because they so often follow his expression of those feelings or ideas he holds dearest and thus that seem least susceptible to ridicule.

His barely conscious disconcertion begins to verge on alarm when the people closest to him start manifesting signs that they no longer take him seriously. One time, for example, he is talking to James Monroe about public education as the foundation of democracy, when he notices that Monroe is shifting restlessly in his chair and looking impatiently out the window. When Thomas Jefferson asks if something is wrong, Monroe rolls his eyes and throws his hands in the air. Assuming his good friend must be distracted by some personal matter, Thomas Jefferson suggests that perhaps it would be better to continue their discussion the following day.

"Finally!" Monroe exclaims as he gets up from his seat and leaves the room.

Another time Thomas Jefferson is exhorting Maria to practice her French by reading French books.

"Oh, Papa!" she says with a mocking smile.

"What?" Thomas Jefferson is utterly perplexed by his daughter's response. When Maria only begins to laugh, he says, "What! What is so funny?"

"Oh, come on, Papa! Stop pretending!"

"Pretending what? French is the language of Voltaire—"

He stops talking, because Maria is laughing—so hard she bends over halfway to the floor. During a momentary lull, she regains enough self-possession to tell him, "I can't believe you are actually saying that!" And then she is lost once again to laughter.

Thomas Jefferson wonders if his daughter has gone mad.

He doesn't begin to recognize the pattern in what is happening until a couple of days later, when he and Sally Hemings are returning to Monticello from the lodge. They are riding side by side along a wooded path, and he reaches over to give her hand a squeeze. "I so wish that we could marry," he says.

She gives him an arch glance and pulls her hand away.

"I do," he says. "I'm so sick of all this surreptitious—"

"Stop!" she says.

He just stares at her, not understanding what she could possibly be objecting to.

"Do you think that you have the right to mock me?" she shouts. "Do you think I have no feelings? I don't know what's come over you lately. You never mean a single thing you say anymore. You're just an imitation of yourself!"

"But I *do* mean what I say. I *do* wish we could—"

"I'm sick of you!" she shouts, then gallops ahead.

Thomas Jefferson brings his horse to a stop and, in a state of profound bewilderment, watches Sally Hemings grow smaller and smaller, then disappear around a bend in the path.

By the time he has ridden back into the stable, he has figured out that people no longer seem to believe in his sincerity, no matter how clearly and passionately he expresses himself.

As he dismounts, Jupiter, who has been loading a wheelbarrow with dung-matted hay from a vacant horse stall, leans his pitchfork against a post and comes to take the reins. "Thank you, Jupiter," Thomas Jefferson says distractedly, and straightens his hat, which was knocked askew during his descent along the horse's flank. He takes a step toward the door—then stops and turns around. "Jupiter?"

"Yes, Mr. Tom?"

"You're not having any trouble understanding me now, are you?"

Jupiter seems momentarily taken aback by the question, but then he smiles and shakes his head. "No, Mr. Tom, no trouble at all."

"And if I tell you that I have always valued your service, you under-stand that I am being entirely sincere?"

Jupiter's mouth hangs open a long moment. And when he says, "Oh, yes, sir. Of course, sir," he sounds as if he himself does not mean what he is saying.

"And I seem to you to be the same person I have ever been?"

Once again Jupiter is silent. Sweat begins to glisten on his dark brow and nose. "If you mean, do I think you look like yourself, then yes I do." He makes a laughlike noise in his throat.

Thomas Jefferson chooses to be comforted by this response. He bids Jupiter good day and walks slowly back to the great house.

As he crosses the lawn to his own chambers, he sees Lucy, Bet and Nance standing by the laundry and hears one of them hiss, "Here he is!" They begin to shift restlessly from foot to foot and touch their head scarves and the hems of their aprons, as if in preparation for going some-where, but none of them budges.

"Excuse me," says Thomas Jefferson.

The three women only stare at him silently with faintly aghast ex-pressions on their faces.

"How are you today?"

Again there is no response, and Thomas Jefferson is so puzzled by their behavior that it is a while before he himself can say anything.

At last he asks, "Is something wrong?"

The three women exchange glances and lick their lips, but none of them actually speak.

"I assure you," he says, "that I am not the least bit angry. I only want to find out what might be disturbing you."

"Who are you?" Bet asks sharply. At fourteen she is by far the young-est of the three. The other two shush her instantly, and Nance shoves her away.

Thomas Jefferson is so disconcerted by this entire exchange that he simply turns and walks to his chambers, a sinking hollowness in his chest.

That night, when he rings the bell to have a cut of ham and some bread and wine delivered to his chambers, no one responds, although not long afterward he does hear whispering and a shoe scuff outside his door. He attempts to cross the room in perfect silence, but when a floorboard creaks beneath his foot, he dashes to the door and whips it open, only managing to catch sight of a hunched shadow in the dark to his right disappearing atop a thunder of footfalls down the kitchen stairs. Straight ahead he hears the *thump-thump-thump* of someone running barefoot across the entrance hall and then the slam of the front door.

When additional tugs on the bell cord evoke no response, Thomas Jefferson descends to the kitchen himself, which he finds utterly deserted and dark, except for the ash-dimmed orange of coals smoldering in the hearth and the flicker of his own candle in the night breeze. He pulls a linen-wrapped smoked ham out of the larder and hacks off a slice, which he eats with his fingers while rat talons click back and forth across the bare floor along the wall just opposite.

At four-thirty in the morning, he saddles a sturdy horse and rides off to visit James Madison at Belle Grove and arrives at the plantation just before sunset, a journey that ought to have taken two days but feels as if it transpired in a matter of hours. He doesn't bother with the approach road but cuts across a field and mounts the lawn, tying his exhausted horse to a juniper bush at the back of the mansion, just outside the doorway to Madison's library. He is already in the middle of the room when Madison, investigating the unexpected noise, emerges from his adjoining office. No sooner does he catch sight of Thomas Jefferson than his face goes gray and his mouth hangs open. "No!" he gasps.

"Jim," says Thomas Jefferson, holding out both open hands in a calming gesture.

"This can't be!" says Madison, staggering a step backward and grabbing hold of the doorjamb.

"Jim, please!" Thomas Jefferson takes a step forward and turns his palms upward in supplication.

"No! You have to go!" says Madison. "I can't talk to you. I must not. You don't make sense. You are a fantasy of my youth, a cloud of impossibility and hypocritical sanctimony. Please go, Tom. You must go. If I even allow my eyes to stray toward that place you still seem to occupy I feel utterly mad."

With that he retreats into his study and slams the door.

This is when Thomas Jefferson finally understands that the nexus of perception, emotion, action and belief that has always seemed so simply and obviously his self no longer makes sense to other people, and so he has become unbelievable. After a moment of shocked contemplation, during which his pulse whooshes loudly in his ears, he leaves Madison's library by the door though which he entered. As he steps outside, his lungs are filled with the sweetness of warm hay and dust. A yellow-orange sun is just touching the treetops on the hills to the west, and he can feel a new coolness rising out of the lengthening shadows.

His horse stands with its head low and eyes closed, clearly asleep. For some reason Thomas Jefferson doesn't feel the least bit tired. On the contrary, he feels as if he has just risen from a restorative nap after a day of good exercise. He leaves the horse where it is tethered and walks across the lawn, with no particular destination in mind. After a while he finds himself wandering along a dirt road between two wheat fields. A dozen laborers being marched back to their quarters by an overseer squint at him with the uncertainty with which one might contemplate an optical illusion or an incipient hallucination. But as the light goes blue and particulate, the few stragglers he passes along the road hardly even glance in his direction and perhaps don't even see him.

The longer he walks, the more Thomas Jefferson begins to suspect that the final stage of his unbelievability might be nonexistence—just as the flat world (once a matter of common sense) has ceased to exist and those giants who once roamed the countryside snacking on maidens and knights are now confined to fairy stories told to lull children to sleep.

And yet Thomas Jefferson doesn't see how this can be possible. He is as filled with desire, hope and dread as he has ever been, and the night air is so fresh in his lungs, and breezes buffet his hair and cool his cheeks, and pinprick glints, one by one, appear in the metallic blue over his head. How is it that a man who seems so fully alive and complexly real to himself might fade from existence as rapidly as a lie exposed by truth?

I t is October 1798.

In the warm weather, Moak Mobley tends the vegetable garden. In the cold he helps Ursula around the kitchen and splits wood for the fires. His eyes are huge and black, his skin a coppery brown, and when he smiles, he seems so merry and content that it is hard not to smile with him. He is married to Patty, and they have a little girl. Although Sally Hemings knows she shouldn't, she can't help paying attention to the ropelike muscles rippling in his arms whenever he lowers a load of fragrant wood onto the brick apron of the kitchen fireplace, and when he smiles, she smiles, too.

Moak is five years younger than Sally Hemings—which is to say that he is twenty-one—a man doing a man's work but not quite done yet with being a boy, and that is something Sally Hemings particularly likes about him. She has been aware of him all his life, though she had almost no contact with him prior to last summer, when Mr. Richardson transferred him from fieldwork to the garden. At first he seemed too shy to even look at her, but as the summer wore on, he went from giving her surreptitious glances whenever their paths crossed to smiling and saying, "Morning, Miz Sally!" or "Afternoon!"

One morning, not long after Thomas Jefferson has gone to spend a fortnight with James Madison in Belle Grove, Sally Hemings is sitting in the kitchen with six-month-old Beverly, who is screaming and purple-faced with rage. She offers him her breast, which he sucks for a few seconds, then spits out. She checks his clout, which is hardly even wet. She tries bouncing him on her knee and walking him around the room. Ursula is muttering to herself as she butchers a chicken on the hacked table-top. After a while she starts casting pointed glances over her shoulder. Sally Hemings knows that she should go outside, but it is cold and she doesn't want to be alone in her cabin with the miserable boy.

Finally Ursula reels around from the table and almost shouts, "Why don't you feed him?"

Just exactly at that instant, Moak kicks open the door and comes into the kitchen with that day's supply of wood.

"I have been," Sally Hemings tells Ursula, "but he doesn't want any."

"Well, maybe your titty's gone dry."

Sally Hemings knows by the weight and the ache in her breasts that they are anything but dry, yet there is no point arguing with Ursula. So as Moak stands motionless just inside the door, a sling of wood across his broad back, she wraps Beverly up in a blanket, pulls him close to her breast and walks out into the cold. By the time she gets to her cabin, the little boy is asleep, and when he wakes two hours later, whatever was troubling him is long past.

The next day she is once again at the table in the kitchen when Moak walks in. "Morning, Miz Sally," he says, giving her a particularly broad smile.

"Morning, Moak."

He lets the wood clatter-thump to the hearth apron, then comes back to her, still smiling and holding his hand in his pocket. When he reaches the table, he pulls out his hand, which is holding a plum-size gourd with a whittled piece of wood sticking up out of it. "This here's for Master Beverly," he says. "Make him happy next time he feel so bad!"

"What is it?" she says.

Moak holds the stick toward Beverly. "Show your mammy, Master Beverly!"

The little boy's fingers wrap around the stick, and as he pulls it away, a hissing sounds within the gourd. Open-mouthed, open-eyed, pensive, he holds the gourd still for a couple of seconds, then shakes it and smiles when it hisses again.

"A rattle!" says Sally Hemings. "Where did you get it?"

"I made it!" Moak smiles happily, and Sally Hemings joins him. "Just had this little old gourd lying around," he says. "So I put in a pinch of creek sand and stuck in the stick."

"Thank you!" She looks away because she can feel her cheeks going red.

He nods and says, "Anything to oblige."

Another morning when Moak comes into the kitchen, Sally Hemings asks him if he would like some tea. "It'll help keep you warm out there," she adds.

He slips the canvas sling of wood off his shoulders and lowers it ponderously to the dusty brick apron. "Don't mind if I do."

As he takes the wood off the sling and stacks it beside the hearth, Sally Hemings pours boiling water into a pot.

Ursula gives her a dubious glance and walks out of the room.

Beverly is lying belly down on a blanket on the floor, working hard at turning over. He hasn't yet figured out that he needs to keep his arm at his side when he rolls, and so every time his wriggling legs get him most of the way onto his side, his outstretched arm flips him right back onto his belly. He is clearly frustrated and has been fussy all morning. Sally Hemings hopes he will stay quiet long enough for Moak to have his tea, but no sooner does she place the cup and a pot of molasses on the table in front of Moak than Beverly starts to wail.

She bends and picks him up, but he doesn't stop wailing.

She bounces him on her hip—"Beverly, Beverly, Beverly!"—and his cries yield to fussy grunts, as he buries his head in the gap between her breast and her upper arm.

"I don't know what's the matter with him," she says. "He's been like this for the last three days."

Over the top of his cup, Moak says, "Look at his mouth."

Sally Hemings looks down but can't actually see Beverly's mouth.

"It's all slobbery," says Moak.

She looks down again but doesn't quite understand what Moak is trying to tell her.

"He got teeth coming in," says Moak.

"He's too young for that."

"No he ain't." Moak gets up from the table and walks around to Sally's side. "His gums red? Take a look at his gums. See if they red."

Moak is standing so close that his manly muskiness is a cloud enveloping her nose and lips.

She rocks Beverly back, so that his head is resting in the crook of her elbow, and she pulls down his lower lip with her thumb.

"Nope," she says. "Just pink."

"Don't matter. He teething." Moak smiles and nods to emphasize his certainty. "And I got just what you need."

Ursula is back in the room with an apron full of potatoes. She is glaring at Sally Hemings, but she doesn't say a word.

The next morning Moak holds out a piece of goldish brown wood, whittled and sanded into the shape of a smooth, blunt spear blade, with a short handle at one end. "Here you go, Master Bev!" Beverly grabs the handle and sticks the blade right into his mouth.

"There! See!" says Moak, looking at Sally Hemings with a big, satisfied grin. "Didn't I tell you? He got teeth coming in, all right. Look at that!"

Indeed, Beverly is gnawing on the blade with particular intensity. But then again he puts absolutely everything in his mouth—so who can say for sure?

"It's made out of sassafras wood," says Moak. "Babies just love sassafras! If you want, you can always put a little molasses on it. That good for babies, too. But the best is rum!"

"Rum!"

"Oh, yes! Mix some rum in with the molasses, babies just love that! Make them so happy! They chew on that for a while, they have sweet dreams all night through!"

Moak seems so pleased with himself that Sally Hemings can't help laughing right along with him.

"Well, thank you," she says.

"Happy to do it! I like making things. I make all kinds of things!"

"Like what?"

"Oh, all kinds of things!" He screws up his mouth and looks toward one corner of the ceiling, as if there's a list tacked up there. "Baby toys, drums, banjars—"

"Banjars?" says Sally Hemings. "What's a banjar?"

"You don't know what a banjar is!" Moak's eyes go round, and his jaw hangs open in mock astonishment. "Girl, what you doing for fun? Ain't you ever danced to a banjar? Banjars is the finest instrument there is for playing a dance tune. Banjar and a fiddle. I'll bring it sometime and play it for you."

"I'd love that."

When Thomas Jefferson returns from his stay at Belle Grove, there are bluish bags under his eyes and his skin is flaccid, cod-flesh gray. Apparently he and James Madison were up late every night writing letters and briefs—the beginning of a major campaign to undermine the Sedition Act, which was passed by Congress over the summer.

Thomas Jefferson is sitting at his desk in his chambers, taking papers out of his satchel. Sally Hemings is kneeling on the floor, transferring laundry from his trunk into a basket.

"I'm destroyed," he says. "In spirit as well as body."

Tossing the last item of clothing into the basket, Sally Hemings gets to her feet.

"If we are not successful in our efforts," he says, "I don't see how this Republic will stand."

Sally Hemings rests the edge of her basket on the corner of his desk, smiles and tells him she is sure everything will be fine.

He laughs and flings himself back in his chair, a boyish smile on his face. "Oh, Sally! You're making me feel like a human being again!"

When he suggests that they spend the night at the lodge, she says, "But you've just been two days on the road. Don't you think you ought to rest?"

"I don't want to rest!" He leans forward and, smiling happily, pulls her hand away from the basket rim. "I need to feel that I am made for arts other than deception, blackmail and bribery!"

She wants to jerk her hand back, but instead she lets herself be drawn down for a kiss—and with that their spending the night at the lodge becomes a settled decision.

In the end, however, the night goes well—or mostly it does. She is a little self-conscious, but no more so than she has been on other occasions—which fact she takes as an indication that she need not worry about Moak. He is just a gentle and bighearted man. Her friend . . .

Two weeks pass, but Moak never brings the banjar. And something in his manner makes Sally Hemings feel that she shouldn't ask him about it.

Ursula doesn't like him—a fact she makes clear through manifold disapproving glances and, one day after Moak has left, by sitting down next to Sally Hemings and proclaiming, as she jabs the air with a rigid index finger, "I'm not gonna tell you this but one time. That Moak ain't nothing but a sweet-talking, low-life nigger. You be too nice to him, he gonna make you pay the price, I swear as the Lord Jesus is my Savior. So you best stay away from here in the mornings, if you know what's good for you. And that all I'm gonna say on it."

Telling herself that Ursula is just a jealous old biddy, Sally Hemings is determined to keep coming to the kitchen for her morning tea in time to catch Moak—but not only do Ursula's stares and brow-grumbling continue without relent, after a day or two Moak stops smiling at Sally Hemings and meeting her eye. Clearly she's not the only one who has gotten a talking-to—though when she confronts Ursula about it, the old woman only says, "I told you I ain't talking about that no more."

Finally Sally Hemings decides that meeting Moak in the kitchen is just too unpleasant, so she has her tea alone in her cabin and waits to run into him where she won't have to contend with Ursula. As it happens, she doesn't have to wait at all. The very first day that she has her tea alone, she looks out her door and sees that Moak has taken the long way around after dropping off the wood for Ursula and is walking, sling draped over his shoulder, right along the road in front of her cabin.

In her hurry to get to the door, she spills a big dollop of tea on her dress, just above her knee, but she is careful to actually step through the doorway as if she were merely coming out to check the weather.

Moak gives her a big-toothed smile the instant he sees her. "Morning, Miz Sally!"

"Morning, Moak. Just wondering if it's going to rain."

They talk about the weather long enough for Sally Hemings to feel she has convinced him and—to some extent—herself that she really only did come out to look at the sky. It is definitely not going to rain, they both agree. No, no, always dry this time of year. Finally Sally Hemings asks, "So why didn't you ever bring your banjar around to show me?"

"Oh, I couldn't do that." Moak shakes his head slowly and gives her a sly smile. "Because you hear the banjar, you have to dance, and the kitchen's no place for dancing, especially not with Ursula staring all the time."

Sally Hemings can't bring herself to say the thing that is in her mind, but that ends up not being necessary.

"Of course," says Moak, "I can always play it for you someplace else—somewhere we wouldn't have to worry about Ursula staring."

Feeling breathless and dizzy as she speaks, Sally Hemings allows as it might be possible to meet in another place, and Moak suggests that she come to the old tobacco barn near Iron Field at about sundown.

She will only be out for an hour, she tells herself. Should Thomas Jefferson turn out to have sent for her, she will simply say that she went for a walk. "My head was hurting," she will tell him. "I thought the night air would do me good."

S ally Hemings leaves Beverly in Aggy's care and makes her way to the East Road via the vegetable gardens, a route that keeps her well downhill from the great house and entirely out of sight. She sees her breath in the orange glow as the sun eases down, and then a shimmer of blue mist rises over the dark fields and the scant yellow leaves in the woods turn pale gray.

By the time she catches sight of the tobacco barn, just up a short path to the left of the road, she is so cold that she is shivering, even with her cape from Paris pulled tight around her shoulders. She stops at the bottom of the path and decides that she should turn around immediately. But in the next instant she is telling herself she would be a fool to have come all this way for no reason. She stands in a state of shivering paralysis for close to a minute and then hears the nasal *plink-plonk* of what must be a banjar.

"Too late now," she says aloud, and starts up the hill.

The instrument sounds to her like a cross between a harpsichord and a lute—nothing like she's been imagining—and Moak is clearly not playing it so much as plucking at individual strings, maybe to tune it or maybe just to fill the silence.

The entrance to the tobacco barn faces the field, on the far side from the road, so she doesn't see him until she is actually in front of the door and they are less than a yard apart.

"Good evening, Miz Sally," he says, standing up from a bench. The barn is empty and hasn't been used for several years, but even so, the air inside is still dense with tobacco's acrid pungency—so dense that Sally Hemings feels something swirl inside her head as she comes to a halt in front of Moak.

She doesn't know what to say, and for a few seconds, it seems, neither does he. Then he presents the instrument to her, holding it horizontally with both hands. "So here she is!"

The first thing Sally Hemings thinks as she takes it from him is that it is a giant version of the rattle he made for Beverly—a broad stick, flattened on one side and almost as long as her arm, stuck into a gourd slightly larger than her head. The front third of the gourd has been cut off, however, and some sort of animal hide has been stretched across the opening. Gut strings run from wooden pegs at the top of the stick across the stretched hide and are knotted at the gourd's base.

"Go ahead," says Moak. "Give it a strum!"

"No. *You.*" She tries to hand the banjar back, but he pushes it away. "Come on!"

He is smiling so sweetly that Sally Hemings can't resist. Holding the instrument vertically by its neck, she runs her fingernails across the strings, producing a sound much louder than she expected. She laughs and feels sweat prickling out all over her body, even though she is still cold.

"Now you do it." She gives the instrument back. "Play me a song."

"All right." He puts one foot up on the bench where he had been sitting and rests the gourd on his thigh. "But you have to dance."

She laughs again, nervously.

"You won't be able to help yourself," he says. He gives the strings some preliminary plucks, and tightens the pegs at the end of the neck. "That's how it is with the banjar. You hear it playing and your feet just got to move."

At this suggestion Sally Hemings experiences another prickling sweat and feels her feet anchor themselves to the ground. She doesn't move when Moak starts to play, and after a while he nods encouragingly. "Come on!"

The truth is that the jangling music doesn't make her feel like dancing at all. She had been imagining that the banjar would be much more soulful, a sort of baritone guitar or maybe something like a viola. But Moak's tinny twanging is far more comical than soulful, and the rhythm is too fast and regular for dancing. She had been expecting something like a reel or a waltz.

"Go on," he says, giving her another nod. "Just let yourself go! You'll see. Your feet already know how to do it."

Out of sheer pity, Sally Hemings takes a few steps to the left, and then to the right, but only grows more embarrassed. After a while she slows to a sort of sway, which gradually diminishes to something less than toe tapping. Moak's disappointment in her only makes things worse. He serenades her for a few minutes, then stops abruptly.

"You want to play?" He holds out the instrument.

"Oh, no!" she cries. "How could I do that?" These words aren't even out of her mouth before she is feeling like a coward and a fool.

"It's easy! I'll teach you."

He gives her the banjar, then moves around behind her, so that he can position the fingers of her left hand on the neck. She likes the feeling of his strong, callused fingers on her own and the warmth of his body running all down her back. She realizes that she is not cold anymore and has not, in fact, been cold for quite some time.

Once he has shown her how to hold down a single string with the middle finger of her left hand, he presses the thumb and forefinger of her right hand together and then makes her strum, up and down several times. "Now let go of the string," he says. He helps her strum a couple of times more, then tells her, "Now press your finger down again." After a few mistakes, she manages to do what he tells her, and then, as she lifts and lowers the middle finger of her left hand and allows him to strum a complex rhythm with her right hand, he sings a *dee-deedly-dee* melody that actually makes what she is doing sound like music.

She laughs again and again during all this and leans back into his warmth, becoming ever more alert to the contours of his body and to that manly muskiness she smelled in the kitchen and which is somehow potent enough to be distinct even amid the heady smell of the tobacco. Sally Hemings is just beginning to think that maybe she could dance to the banjar after all when she notices a new hardness behind her. After only a moment, he begins to press that hard part of himself against her, and all the strength goes out of her hands. He stops trying to move them, and he stops singing, too.

He presses himself against the whole length of her body and sways slightly from side to side. "I'm wondering," he says softly, and has to lick his lips before continuing, "if you thinking the same thing I'm thinking."

Sally Hemings also has to lick her lips before she can speak. "I don't know." Her breath is trembling.

"You want to go find out?"

She doesn't move and doesn't speak for a long time. But then she pushes the banjar aside and steps away.

"I can't," she says. "I'd like to, but I just can't."

The more Sally Hemings reads, the more she becomes aware that the difficulty she has making sense of words is not just a matter of her own ignorance but also of certain weaknesses of the alphabet. She finds it particularly illogical that two letters should combine to make a sound entirely unrelated to the sounds each letter makes on its own, with *th* being the worst example, but *sh* being almost as bad. She is also bothered that the letter *c* can sometimes make the same sound as *s* and other times as *k*, and she is of the opinion that *c* is an entirely superfluous letter that should simply be dropped from the alphabet.

Be that as it may, her skill at decoding letters and the tiny marks in between them has progressed to the point that she has little trouble reading newspapers and has become particularly adept at spotting the name Jefferson. The newspapers keep her up to date about what Thomas Jefferson does while he is away, and they portray him as leading a heroic battle against the Federalists and the Alien and Sedition Acts. While she is never sure that she fully grasps all she reads, she finds it hard to believe that John Adams is truly the villain and fool that the newspapers declare him to be. She very much liked Mr. Adams during the fortnight she lived with him and Mrs. Adams in London. One time he came into the house carrying a tiny white rose that he had just picked in the garden. "For you, my dear Miss Sally-Bump," he said as he handed her the flower. He always called her "Sally-Bump," though she never understood why. At the time she thought that he was referring to a pimple on her chin, but now she can't imagine that could be true.

Despite her progress with the newspapers, Sally Hemings still finds *Notes on the State of Virginia* almost entirely impenetrable, not so much because it is difficult to read—although she does have trouble with words like "latitude," "commonwealth," "suffrage"—as because it seems to consist only of long catalogs of geographical features, plants, animals, products, laws and so on, all of which she finds entirely boring. Nevertheless, she remains determined to finish this book before moving on to others, and so every now and then she will pull it off the shelf over her bed and open it to a random page, in the hope of finding something she might actually want to read.

During one such attempt, she flips the book open to the middle and instantly spots three words that interest her very much indeed: "emancipate all slaves." She glances over the succeeding pages to see if Thomas Jefferson is, in fact, advocating emancipation and happens upon a passage where he seems to be comparing Negroes and whites, in the midst of which she reads: "in memory they are equal to whites; in reason much inferior." She snaps the book shut, her head pounding, a nausea whirling in her stomach and radiating up her throat.

Over the next month, she is constantly seeking out and avoiding Moak, flushing with delight in his presence or going cold with anxiety. Finally, one afternoon two days after Thomas Jefferson has gone to Philadelphia, she lets Moak raise her skirt in a locked storage closet and have his way with her. They start out with her back against the wall, but after only a few moments he lifts her into the air without pulling out of her and stretches her atop Polly's sea chest, where he pounds into her with a speed and a force she finds so thrilling it is all she can do to keep silent.

When he finishes—far sooner than she would have liked—he bends over, wraps his arms around her and—still panting—murmurs into her ear, "I always wondered what white pussy felt like."

For some reason this statement doesn't bother her in the least.

"How was it?" she asks.

"Good," he says. "Deep and tight."

Deep and tight. She smiles. And she smiles again and again over the next few days, whenever those words come back into her head. She doesn't know why they please her so. Maybe it's just the notion that she can satisfy so young and good-looking a man. Maybe it's because there was something in the way he spoke those words that made her feel like she was his possession, and somehow she welcomes being his possession—a feeling she has never remotely had in connection with Thomas Jefferson.

They meet three more times over the next week—once more in the storage room, once in a woodshed and once in the cloakroom. And every time he uses her with the same delirium-inspiring vigor but then quits just as her own orgasm approaches. On each occasion she is left in such an agony of desire that she can hardly wait to be alone in a privy or her bed, where she might satisfy herself with her fingers. But that never really satisfies her, and she only grows more desperate for the moment when she will have her orgasm with him.

Often, when she is alone in her bed, either after they have made love or late in the night when she needs to relieve herself simply so that she can sleep, she imagines saying to him, "I want you to give me a gift," and that is the very instant when her orgasm surges from that slippery nub beneath her fingers all the way up into her throat and cheeks and head.

S ally Hemings feels people's eyes linger on her as she moves about Monticello. But at the same time, she thinks that people are avoiding her—most obvious is Patty, Moak's wife, whose head jerks around as if she's been punched whenever she sees Sally Hemings approach. But even people with whom Sally Hemings would normally stop and have a quick chat avoid her gaze or walk past with only a grunted greeting or a somber nod. Ursula tells her straight out, "I'm not talking to you no more!"

She knows why, of course. And she tells herself she doesn't care. She tells herself she wouldn't care even if Thomas Jefferson were to find out. Sometimes she worries that he might sell her, but on the whole she thinks that possibility highly improbable. He could banish her from the great house perhaps, but most likely he would act as if she were so far beneath his notice as to be invisible.

She imagines what life would be like if she were Moak's wife. She'd have to work harder, of course, but she wouldn't have to feel so out of place all the time. She could just be herself. Patty is a pretty woman. She'd find herself another man. There'd be bad blood between them for a while, but in the end it would all work out.

S ally Hemings is in the storage room again, this time belly down over the sea chest, and Moak is grunting behind her. When he finishes, she grabs his thigh and says, "Don't stop."

He pushes her hand aside, pulls out of her and bends to grab his breeches, which are collapsed around his ankles. "Sorry, baby, that's all I got."

"Use your fingers, then."

"What's the matter?" he says, pulling up his breeches. "My willy ain't good enough for you?"

"Please." She turns around and grabs his hand. "I want you to give it to me." She pulls his hand between her legs, but he yanks free.

"I thought white women was crazy for black willy," he says.

"Only my skin is white."

"How come you so stuck up, then?"

Moak is not so much angry as contemptuous. Sally Hemings is so shocked that she cannot speak.

"That's what everybody say about you." He gives her a smug, close-lipped smile. "You know that, don't you? Everybody say you so stuck up 'cause you think you white, when really you just a black nigger, same as the rest of us."

Sally Hemings's period is only a couple of days late, but there is an unusual fullness in her breasts and a sensation in her belly that she thinks of as an opening-up, as if her womb were a flower within a bud and on the verge of bursting. She is sure she is pregnant. She knows there is no way she can be certain, but she is certain anyway—and filled with dread.

As soon as Thomas Jefferson has returned from Philadelphia, after being away for three months, she knocks on the door to his chambers and kisses him before he has completely closed the door behind her. She tells him how much she's missed him. She caresses his cheek and runs her hand across his chest. Clearly he is surprised by her behavior, and equally clearly he is exhausted and is not really in the mood, so she slides her hand down his belly and, in a matter of seconds, knows that she will get what she wants.

But it repulses her. He is still redolent of the road: horse, dust and sweat, and once she has gotten him out of his clothing, he is so pale, mottled and flaccid-fleshed that he seems diseased. His muscles creak. The bones in his wrists and shoulders feel as if they are rolling against each other. As soon as she gets him inside her, she cups her hand over his testicles because she knows he loves that and that it will make him come almost instantly, which he does.

And once this has happened, she finds herself repulsed by the very trait she found so lacking in Moak. Thomas Jefferson's unhappiness that she has not had an orgasm now seems fawning and unmanly to her, and it fills her with such a visceral abhorrence that she cannot bear to have him inside her or to be touched in an erotic way by his hands.

"That's all right," she tells him. "I'm not really in the mood," assertions that clearly disconcert him, given her previous behavior. "Let's just lie here together," she says. "This feels nice. It's good to have you back."

In fact, even lying there beside him doing nothing at all makes her skin crawl, and she does not see how she will ever be able to make love with him again.

U rsula has fallen ill, and Sally Hemings is in the kitchen garden gathering feverfew to make tea for her. As she stuffs a handful of the ragged leaves into the pocket of her apron, she notices a shadow on the ground at her feet. Reeling around, she finds that Moak is standing not one foot behind her.

"Afternoon, Miz Sally," he says, lifting his straw hat off his head.

"What are you doing?" Her voice is low, but furious.

He smiles, her anger only seeming to amuse him. "I was just passing—"

"How dare you come up behind me like that!"

She tries to step around him, but he moves directly in front of her. "Aw, come on, Miz Sally." Still smiling, he reaches for her hand.

The stalks of feverfew are as fibrous as ropes, so she has had to use a knife to cut them. Now she is holding the knife between her face and Moak's.

She is shouting.

"Don't you touch me!"

"Hey!" Moak takes a step back, laughing.

Sally Hemings cannot believe that she is actually brandishing the knife in front of him. The gesture makes her feel more weak than strong. She worries that he will snatch the knife out of her hand.

"I'm sick of you!" She takes a step back. "I don't ever want to see you again!"

"But, Sally, I just—"

She slashes the knife in the empty air, then turns and runs toward the kitchen.

"You stay away from me!" she shouts. "You just stay away from me."

She glimpses Moak as she slams the kitchen door. He has not followed her. He has stopped smiling. He is standing exactly where she left him, his hands open, outturned and slightly lifted.

On Power

Thomas Jefferson's primary political objective throughout his career was to limit the power of any one group—including the very government he helped found. In 1778 he opened a Bill for the More General Diffusion of Knowledge by declaring, "Whereas it appeareth that however certain forms of government are better calculated than others to protect individuals in the free exercise of their natural rights, yet experience hath shewn, that even under the best forms, those entrusted with power have, in time, and by slow operations, perverted it into tyranny."

Nearly a decade later, he was in a decided minority among the Founding Fathers in not being troubled by the Shays' Rebellion, a revolt by poor farmers that led to the suspension of habeas corpus by Massachusetts's governor. "God forbid we should ever be twenty years without such a rebellion," he wrote from Paris in 1787. "What country before ever existed a century & a half without a rebellion? & what country can preserve it's liberties if their rulers are not warned from time to time that their people preserve the spirit of resistance? . . . The tree of Liberty must be refreshed from time to time with the blood of patriots & tyrants. It is it's natural manure."

His bill for the Diffusion of Knowledge concerned the establishment of a public school system, which, along with a free press, he saw as essential for the preservation of democracy—a linkage made clear in one of his most famous (or infamous) statements, also written in 1787: "Were it left to me to decide whether we should have a government without newspapers or newspapers without government, I should not hesitate a moment to prefer the latter. But I should mean that every man should receive those papers and be capable of reading them."

His idea was that grammar schools should be paid for by the state and open to all economic classes. Latin (or high) schools and universities would charge tuition, but poor students who showed exceptional promise would be eligible for full scholarships. Public education didn't gain much traction in the United States until the the mid-nineteenth century, but Thomas Jefferson sought to help it along in the Land Ordinance of 1785, a plan for the development of the western territories. The ordinance decreed that all newly settled land should be divided into a grid of townships, each measuring six miles square, which in turn should be divided into a grid of thirty-six sections, with one of those reserved for a public school. The effects of this grid system can be plainly seen by anyone flying over the Midwest and the West, and, indeed, to this very day the public schools in many localities are in exactly the section of the grid (number 16) that Thomas Jefferson reserved for them.

The only element of his education plan that he saw through to fruition in his home state was the University of Virginia—a project with which he was involved on every level, including as architect. Perhaps nothing more clearly distinguishes this university as the product of his ideals than the fact that its campus, unlike those of all other American universities of that era, is centered on a library rather than a church.

Thomas Jefferson's religious views were always controversial, with his critics commonly denigrating him as a "confirmed infidel" and even as a "howling atheist." While he probably did believe in God—at least most of the time—he was decidedly not orthodox and wanted to put strict limits on the ability of any one denomination to wield governmental power or dictate the conscience of individuals. In 1777, during an era when the Anglican Church had such sway over Virginia society that children not baptized in the faith could be taken from their parents, he wrote the Virginia Statute for Religious Freedom, both to prohibit the establishment of state religion and, as he put it in his *Autobiography*, to protect the rights of "the Jew and the Gentile, the Christian and Mohammedan, the Hindoo and the Infidel of every denomination."

Believing commerce to be governed by "a selfish spirit" that "feels no passion or principle but that of gain," Thomas Jefferson also sought to minimize the power of business, especially within government, an agenda at the heart of his opposition to the policies of Alexander Hamilton, which he felt would enslave Congress to the ambitions—and bribes—of New York bankers. He strongly preferred temporary local militias to a standing national army, because he believed that the latter could all too easily be deployed against the people by a tyrant. And, lastly, he was an advocate of the dispersal of governmental responsibility to the states as a check against the power of the federal government.

Thomas Jefferson rarely hewed to any of his ideals with perfect consistency, however. He became rather less sanguine about freedom of the press once he was subjected to vicious attacks by the Federalist papers, and he asserted entirely unconstitutional executive authority when, as president, he pushed the Louisiana Purchase through Congress. Nevertheless, he remained skeptical of institutionalized power to the very end of his life.

In the epitaph he composed only weeks before he died, he said nothing about having been president, governor of Virginia, ambassador to France or about any of his official positions within government. Instead he wanted to be remembered only as the author of the Declaration of Independence and the Virginia Statute for Religious Freedom and as the "father" of the University of Virginia.

It is September 1, 1799. Sally Hemings is twenty-seven years old, and the northern wing of Monticello is in ruins. The roof lies in heaps among the weeds a small distance from the foundation. The walls are naked brick, penetrated at intervals by rectangular holes that lack doors, jambs, casements or windows. The floors inside the wall, on which once stood mahogany tables, silk-upholstered chairs, dressers and bookcases, are warped and grayed by the rain and in some places not safe to walk on. A substantial honeysuckle vine has commandeered the fireplace and rises up the whole of the chimney like a frozen cloud of dark green and yellow butterflies.

Thomas Jefferson had intended the demolition of this wing of his house to be completed in March and for construction of a new wing to have progressed all summer, but he has been too busy with his struggles in Philadelphia to direct his mechanics, and now that he is considering standing for president, he has even less time.

Sally Hemings, six months pregnant, is sitting in a straight-backed wooden chair under the shade of the very copper beech where some two decades earlier Martha Jefferson asked her if she wanted to be little Polly's companion. She is repairing the skirt of one of her own gowns, which she accidentally stepped on and ripped as she was climbing the stairs. Seventeen-month-old Beverly is asleep on a blanket beside her, twitching his legs and arms like a dreaming dog, occasionally uttering tiny cries and moans as delicate as pigeon coos.

The door to the southern side of the house opens, and Thomas Jefferson walks out onto the terrace to pace in his shirtsleeves and riding boots, with head lowered and one hand clutching the other behind his back. He passes briskly up and down the terrace eight, nine, ten times, then goes back into his study. A moment later he is out again, with a dented and frayed yard-wide straw hat on his head. He crosses the terrace, trots down the steps into the ankle-high grass of the lawn and strides off, in exactly the posture in which he has just been pacing. At the edge of the woods, he reverses direction and recrosses the lawn, his hat brim wafting lazily on either side of his head like the wings of a great blue heron.

All at once, halfway to the house, he makes an oblique left turn, walks directly toward one of the outdoor privies, mounts the two steps in front of it, opens the door, takes off his hat, backs through and closes the door behind him. He emerges a few moments later, puts his hat on again, straightens his clothing and, hopping down the steps, seems possessed by new vigor.

At just that moment, Beverly stirs on the blanket. His little face reddens, and he makes the first stuttery cracks of his usual post-nap hunger cry. In a moment Sally Hemings will have to bring him into the kitchen for some porridge, but for the moment she settles him at her breast. Just as he begins to suck, she looks up to see Thomas Jefferson, only three yards off, walking straight toward her.

"Beautiful day!" he says as he comes to a stop. The sun reflects off the yellowing lawn, turning his eyes a buttery brown. "Can't understand how anyone can keep inside on a day like this."

And with that he lifts the crown of his hat, turns about-face and strides off toward the woods, left hand clutching his right wrist behind his back, his hat brim wafting.

Two weeks before Christmas 1799, Jimmy comes to see Sally Hemings. "Now that you can read," he tells her, "I'm going to write you letters, and you have to write me letters back."

Jimmy is free. The previous day their brother Peter completed his first week as Monticello's cook, and Thomas Jefferson, pronouncing himself entirely satisfied, signed Jimmy's manumission papers and gave him twenty-five dollars. Jimmy's plan is to move back to Paris, or maybe to Spain, but first he is going to Philadelphia, where he can earn enough money cooking in taverns to pay for his transatlantic passage. His plans to start a French-style restaurant with Adrien Petit are long forgotten—Petit having returned to Paris some five years previously, under a cloud of disgrace that neither Jimmy nor Thomas Jefferson would ever fully elucidate to Sally Hemings.

"Why do you have to leave now?" she asks.

"I just do. I feel like if I don't go today, I'll never leave. And then what's the point of being free?"

Sally Hemings is sitting in a rocking chair by her fireplace. Her belly is so large she can't see her knees, but the baby inside her isn't moving. This baby has never moved very much, not like Beverly or little Harriet. She thought the baby would be born in mid-November, and here it is a week into December and nothing is happening. Can babies suffocate, she wonders, if they stay inside too long?

She doesn't tell her brother what she is thinking.

"Don't worry," he tells her. "I'll be back. I just have to see the world a bit."

She doesn't tell him that she is not sure whose baby is inside her. She doesn't tell him that she thinks the baby has been killed as a punishment.

"Maybe I'll go to Africa," he tells her. "I think I should see Africa, find out what it's really like. You hear all kinds of things about Africa—about lions and savages and kings with golden palaces. I wonder if any of that is true."

She doesn't tell Jimmy anything she is thinking because she thinks he should already know. Or if he doesn't know, he should ask. But Jimmy will never ask, because he is too lost inside his own head. His head is a deep, dark cave, and he doesn't have a light to find his way out. She doesn't tell him any of this either.

"I'll be back," he says. "You can count on that! I'll always come back and visit you."

"I hope so," she says.

"Someone's got to watch out for you, right? Make sure you don't get into trouble!"

Sally Hemings makes a smilelike grimace, but says nothing.

Jimmy throws his arms around her. "I love you, Cider Jug."

She speaks into the empty air behind his back. "I love you, too."

The morning after Jimmy's departure, Sally Hemings's water breaks. She is all alone in her cabin with Beverly—her mother and Aggy having gone to fetch a sack of cornmeal from Mr. Richardson. "Mammy peeing," says the little boy as soon as he sees the fluid leaking through the chair bottom and splattering onto the floor. "Why you peeing, Mammy?" Beverly is twenty months old.

"I'm not peeing," she says. "That just means your baby brother is coming. I'm all full of water, and he's been swimming around inside me, but now he's coming out."

Sally Hemings is terrified. Her water has broken before she has felt a single contraction. Also, the movements of Harriet and Beverly had only become more noticeable once they were no longer cushioned in a balloon of water, but she feels no movement from this baby at all.

She leaves the mess on the floor for her mother to clean and pulls her drenched gown and shift over her head so that she can dry herself and change. The first contraction hits her when she is completely undressed, and it is so powerful that all she can do is fall onto her bed and pull her cover over her.

This is where her mother and Aggy find her when they return twenty minutes later. Betty sends Aggy to the great house to tell Mr. Jefferson what is happening and to ask him to send for Dr. Cranley and Mrs. Coombes, the midwife. He does, and Mrs. Coombes comes within the hour, but Dr. Cranley doesn't arrive until midafternoon.

The contractions come hard and fast all afternoon and evening and into the night. When he heard that Sally Hemings was delivering, Thomas Jefferson requested that Aggy come get him the instant the baby is born, but, in fact, he spends hours pacing up and down in front of the cabin, periodically approaching the door to ask for reports. He makes his last visit at midnight and is back at the cabin at five in the morning, wild-haired and unshaven, clearly having slept in his clothes.

He is startled by Sally Hemings's transformation during the few hours since he last saw her. The flush has gone entirely from her cheeks, and her forehead is glossy, not so much with sweat as with the slime of illness. But worst of all are her eyes, which squint at him unseeingly and make her seem more animal than human.

Betty Hemings is standing next to her daughter's bed, one hand clutched fiercely in the other, a scowl upon her brow but her eyes too frightened to even meet Thomas Jefferson's.

"Sally is strong," he tells her. "We must have faith."

"Lord's will be done," says Betty, so softly he can only tell by reading her lips.

Dr. Cranley also left at midnight and hasn't returned. Thomas Jefferson sends Davy to him with a message saying to come immediately.

Once the cabin is sufficiently suffused with dawn light, Mrs. Coombes asks Thomas Jefferson to wait outside. As soon as he has gone, she draws back the covers, pushes apart Sally Hemings's legs and then sees at once what the problem is. The baby is breeched.

Mrs. Coombes and Betty help Sally Hemings turn over and get onto her knees and elbows. The heel of one of the baby's feet is just visible, pressed against its buttocks, and as Sally Hemings rocks back and forth with her contractions, more and more of the little foot becomes visible until finally, with one contraction, the whole foot appears, and with the next the entire leg pops out. Mrs. Coombes glances over at Betty Hemings and shakes her head once. Betty puts her folded hands to her lips and begins to pray. It takes three and a half hours for a tiny girl to slide into Mrs. Coombes's hands. Her skull is gourd-shaped and her face swollen and purple from the brutal labor, and her right leg (the second to come out) is broken or dislocated.

Dr. Cranley arrives just exactly as the baby makes her first, bleating cry. Determining that her leg is only dislocated, he pulls and twists, causing the baby to shriek. But afterward she instantly falls into a deep sleep, and he declares the procedure a success. He waits until the afterbirth has been completely expelled, then puts on his hat and coat and orders Sally Hemings to drink nettle tea at least twice daily for a week. Just before leaving the cabin, he looks down on the poor, battered infant and shakes his head. He neither meets Sally Hemings's eye nor says a word.

Thomas Jefferson has been sitting on the porch with his head in his hands ever since Mrs. Coombes asked him to leave the cabin. He stands as Dr. Cranley comes out the door, but he doesn't dare ask what has happened. The doctor gives him a long, disapproving look, fully understanding his relationship to both mother and child. "The mother will live," he says, "but the infant . . . she's in the hands of the Lord." With that he turns and makes his way back to his carriage.

Thomas Jefferson straightens his clothing and hair, then knocks on the door. Betty Hemings, her face sallow and deflated, lets him in without a word. Glancing at the infant, whose skin has a decidedly brownish cast, she ushers Aggy and Mrs. Coombes outside, then exits herself, pulling the door shut behind her.

Sally Hemings is sleeping when Thomas Jefferson draws a chair up beside the bed, but as he sits down and leans forward, she opens her eyes. "Well, you did it, Sally Girl," he says. "That was a hard one, but it's over."

A feeble smile comes to her lips and fades almost instantly.

"How are you feeling?"

She meets his eye and shakes her head. Then she looks up at the ceiling, and he wonders if she is praying.

He is silent until his thoughts become more than he can endure.

"So you've got a fine little girl!" he exclaims.

Again Sally Hemings meets his eye but seems not to have comprehended what he said.

"Have you chosen a name?" he asks.

"Thenia," she says, barely above a whisper.

He's surprised at first, but then he nods. He sold Thenia to James Monroe so that she and her children could live with their father. But a year hadn't passed before she contracted pneumonia while walking to church in a snowstorm. She died in a matter of days.

"That's a good name," says Thomas Jefferson.

Sally Hemings's lips twitch into another feeble smile, but her eyes are closed.

He looks at the swaddled infant, her eyes so purple and swollen that she has yet to open them. He, too, has noticed the brownish cast to her skin but attaches no particular significance to it, knowing that mulattoes can be almost any color, even after multiple generations of mixing only with whites. The little girl is deeply asleep—though it is hard to imagine that her injuries are not still causing her terrible pain.

"I'll let you rest," he tells Sally Hemings as he gets to his feet.

But when she opens her eyes and looks at him, he bends down again and kisses her.

"I'm so glad you're still with me," he says. "I had such terrible thoughts during the night. Such grim, awful thoughts."

Her eyes are closed again. Very possibly she did not hear a word he said. He pats her hand, stands and leaves.

At dawn the following morning, Betty notices that her new grand-daughter is ashen and not breathing.

A little later, lying in bed beside her weeping daughter, she murmurs, "It's for the best. There was just too much pain in that poor baby's life."

But Sally Hemings has other thoughts.

Two weeks after Thenia's tiny coffin is placed into the ground, Thomas Jefferson returns to Philadelphia, less to resume his duties as vice president than to garner support for his plan to challenge Adams in the upcoming presidential election. Madison, Monroe, Burr and half the editorialists of the Republican newspapers have been saying that Thomas Jefferson alone can stop Adams and Hamilton from reestablishing the monarchy. The night before his departure he protests to Sally Hemings yet again that he has no taste for government and would much rather remain at home, attending to his family, his books and the construction of his house.

She shakes her head ruefully and pats his cheek. "Do you actually believe that you might be happy here when you can have the love of a nation?"

"Do I seem so vain as that?" he says. "Is that what you truly believe?"

She answers only with a gently mocking smile.

No sooner has his carriage lumbered out the gate and turned toward the South Road than Sally Hemings has gone to his library and stands staring at his bookshelves, her arms folded across her chest. She has no idea how many books there are in this room. Hundreds? Thousands? She breathes deeply, her sinuses filling with a thin sweetness that reminds her equally of dried oats and mice.

She has decided that she will take advantage of Thomas Jefferson's long absences to read as many of these books as she can—until, perhaps, she will have read them all. She has absolutely no idea where to begin, however, so simply walks up to the nearest shelf and pulls out the first book that catches her eye. It is black and shiny, with red bands across its narrow spine, but the letters on its pages look like tiny knots, twists and curls of string—not a one of them intelligible. She snaps the book shut and picks up its neighbor, only to find that it is written in an entirely different and equally incomprehensible alphabet—this one dark and jagged, like an army of tiny, heavily armed soldiers standing row upon row upon row. It has never occurred to her that there might be more than one alphabet. Could there be a different alphabet for every language? Will she have to learn two, three or ten new alphabets in order to read every book that Thomas Jefferson has read?

This thought exhausts her and makes her left temple throb. She thinks of giving up and going back to her cabin. Instead she decides to try the books on the shelves on the opposite wall. But these are all filled with numbers, diagrams and drawings of buildings—none of which make any sense to her, though the words at least are written in familiar letters.

Several books on the neighboring shelf are filled with pictures of flowers, and she spends a long time looking at these, even though the drawings make the flowers look crotchety and old. But she does not want to look at pictures, she wants to read—she wants, in fact, to learn to read every word in the English language, and possibly in French, too. She wants words to flow through her eyes and into her mind as easily as air flows into her lungs.

The next book is a treatise on the art of war, which she thinks might be interesting, though grim and sad. She puts it back. Then she notices a book lying across the tops of other books, perhaps because there is not enough room on the crowded shelf. She feels sorry for this book, which is squat and brown and reminds her of a brick. It is entitled *The History of America* and by a man named William Robertson, D.D., whose picture is on the facing page. He, too, appears crotchety and old, but his eyes look straight into hers.

She closes the book and presses it against her chest, where it seems to have the effect of speeding up her heart and making it just a little hard to breathe. Suddenly she is frightened. She puts the book back in its lonely spot atop all the others, then pulls it out again and hugs it to her chest a second time.

She lifts her head and closes her eyes as if she is praying. But she is not praying, only waiting for something to feel right. In the end maybe it does or maybe it doesn't. She can't say for sure. But she slips the book into the pocket of her apron anyway, hurries to the door and steps out into the dark hall.

After an unimaginable length of time, the prisoner has been reduced to a barely human mass—less a man than an insect without a carapace. To a casual observer, it would not be clear whether he is conscious, or even alive. The guard, too, is exhausted. Gaunt. Gray of hair and complexion. She is chewing gum. She speaks.

—You know how this is going to end, don't you?

— . . .

—I finish you off.

— . . .

—Terminate you. Cancel you out. Right? What other ending is there? It's inevitable.

— . . .

—Though I guess that means I'm not God, right? Because nothing is inevitable for God. I mean, God, absolute freedom, all-powerful—aren't those just three ways of saying the same thing?

— . . .

—So it's a paradox. And one of the many things that makes me think this is *my* nightmare and not yours.

— . . .

—Maybe I'm just dreaming you. Maybe you're nothing but my own sick delusion.

— . . .

—Never mind. I'm tired of fucking with your head.

— . . .

—Actually, I take that back. Because now I am *really* going to fuck with your head. Although some people might call it grace.

— . . .

—Grace! Do you hear me, fuckface? Grace!

— . . .

—Get the fuck up!

— . . .

—Get up! Do you want me to come in there and step on you, you fucking cockroach? I can always do the inevitable. I mean, that is a choice I have. Is that what you want?

—...

—Look, just get the fuck up. I'm setting you free.

—...

—Do you hear me? I'm setting you free.

—Fuck you!

—What?

The guard laughs. The guard speaks.

—I suppose you think this is too good to be true. Well, it *is* too good to be true! But even so, I'm still setting you free.

—...

—Get the fuck up! You hear me? Get the fuck up! Now! You've got two choices: Either I come in there and put you out of your misery forever or you get the fuck up and go free.

—Leave me alone.

—That's an improvement. Look.

The guard pulls the keys out of her pocket. Unlocks the cell door. Opens it. She takes the gum out of her mouth and rolls it into a ball on her finger. She speaks.

—I'm sticking this into the latch hole.

She sticks the gum into the hole where the tongue of the lock goes. The hole is filled. She flattens the gum inside the hole with her index finger and covers it with a folded-up piece of the foil gum wrapper. She speaks.

—Okay. So you stole this gum from me. Right? Because that's the only thing that makes sense. Because why would I give it to you? So you stole it. And look.

She opens and closes the cell door twice. She speaks.

—It looks like it's locked. But it isn't. So you can get out anytime you want.

—...

—Only here's the deal: You do it on somebody else's watch. You get me? You wait till that fuckface Quinn comes on. Or Rex. I don't give a shit. Just wait until I'm long gone, and then you can do whatever you like.

The prisoner crawls to the front of his cell, then pulls himself up on the bars until he is balanced unsteadily on his knees. The guard speaks.

—You wondering why I'm doing this?

—Yes.

—I told you already: I'm fucking with your head. Although, actually, the truth is that I'm sick of you.

— . . .

—This hasn't exactly been a picnic for me. I mean, the way I see it, I'm just living out your sins. And after all this time, what's the point? You know? My life's a fucking nightmare.

— . . .

—So now I'm really free. Free to exercise my absolute freedom. If that's not too much of a tautology. Or is it actually a contradiction?

The prisoner lifts his hands over his head and takes hold of the bars. He groans. Trembles. He stands. He speaks.

—Thank you.

—What are you thanking me for? You don't know what's going to happen yet. You, of all people, should know not to be so trusting. Didn't I just tell you I'm fucking with your head? You'll see. It's a whole different world out there.

—I hardly remember it.

—What you remember doesn't exist anymore. It's gone. All of it. You've been here much longer than you think.

—How long?

—An eternity.

— . . .

—So I'm just going to give you one piece of advice. Once you get past Quinn, or Rex (whatever; I don't want to know the details), then you've got two choices: You go *this* way, you're still in isolation. You go *that* way, you're in the tunnels. Take the tunnels.

—Where do they go?

—Out. It's a long way. You'll probably think you're never going to get there. But just keep going. There'll be staircases. And people. A whole lot of people. Don't worry about it. They're harmless. Pretend you don't even notice them and they'll do the same to you. But just keep walking along beside them and, eventually, they'll lead you up to the street.

—Thank you.

—I'm not going to say you're welcome, because you're not.

—You're actually going to do this?

—I guess you'll find out. But you'll still be a fucking piece of shit. Don't you ever forget that. I'm not doing this because I think you've re-deemed yourself, or you've been rehabilitated, or transcended your sins, or any of that bullshit. Nothing makes the evil go away. The evil is eternal. Remember that.

—...

—It's a fucking evil world in my opinion. The truth is that most people never get caught. Their lies last. They never have to endure their dark night of the soul. You'll see. Maybe that's why I'm sending you out there. You'll be shocked. Everything is different. That's a world in which you don't make any sense. Believe me: You won't even recognize yourself.

It is October 5, 1800, ten months after Thenia's death, and Thomas Jefferson will stand for election to the presidency at the end of the month. He is fifty-eight, and Sally Hemings is twenty-eight.

She waits for him at the intersection of two paths, just past the lake. As he rides up, he reaches down with one hand and helps her climb into the saddle behind him. It is cold. She wraps her arms around his taut abdomen and squeezes him tight to keep warm. They talk about how they will have to build a fire at the lodge, and he says he's not sure if they will have enough kindling. As they ford the river, she pulls down his collar and kisses him on the back of his neck, where his smell is so rich and savory.

She is happy today. She doesn't know why. The sky is low with steam-colored clouds. Nothing special has happened, or not really. Her period is a month late, but her cycle has been irregular since Thenia, so it is too soon to draw conclusions. She hasn't said a word to anybody about what she is thinking.

She's just happy. She hasn't been happy in such a long time.

The horse shambles out of the rushing water and then along the wooded bank. After a few minutes, the lodge comes into view, on a small rise, shaded by two brilliantly yellow beeches and a crimson-and-burgundy pin oak. As soon as the horse begins to mount the rise, Sally Hemings knows that something is wrong, and in the next instant she knows why: The lodge door is open, and dangling off the porch onto the steps is a red-and-white cloth—her apron.

"Shit," says Thomas Jefferson.

Sally Hemings says nothing.

They stop beneath one of the yellow beeches. As he ties the horse to the porch railing, she picks up the apron, which is crumpled and stiff—as if it has been used to wipe up something messy, though it is unstained.

Inside the lodge the sheets are straggling off the bed and trail across the floor. The blankets are gone, as is a lantern and a hunting knife that Thomas Jefferson left on top of the mantelpiece. Otherwise the room seems undisturbed.

At first Thomas Jefferson merely turns in a circle in the middle of the room, a perplexed expression on his face. Then he gets down on his hands and knees and looks under the bed, then under a dresser on top of which the lantern had been resting. He gets back to his feet and kicks the bedstead.

"Damn it all to hell!" He kicks the bedstead again. "Goddamn it!"

Sally Hemings winces, not so much because his shouts disturb her as because she would still like to make love and thinks that Thomas Jefferson probably won't want to now.

She sits down on the bare mattress. "It's not so bad," she says.

"I know." He sits down on the bed beside her.

"We can replace everything the next time we come." She puts her hand on his knee.

"It's just that . . ." He shrugs. "This was our sanctuary." He picks up her hand, gives it a squeeze, lets it go and stands up again and walks to the window. "I suppose I'll just have to get John to build us some strong shutters and put a lock on the door."

"Do you think that's a good idea?"

"What do you mean?"

She leans back, putting one arm behind her head as a pillow. "If someone wants to get in here, they'll just get in. The only difference a lock will make is that they'll have to do more damage."

Thomas Jefferson looks as if he is going to contradict her, but then he doesn't say anything.

She smiles.

"I'll have to think about it," he says. "Maybe talk to John."

Still smiling, still lying down, she extends one hand in his direction. "Come here," she says.

He does.

A while later Thomas Jefferson is sitting on the porch reading a treatise on astronomy and Sally Hemings is crouched barefoot on a rock at the water's edge, the skirt of her gown knotted around her waist. Her newly cleaned apron is spread on a bush beside her, drying in the intervals of brilliant white sunlight that come and go as the clouds drift over. She is clutching one of the bedsheets in the shallow water and lathering it with a block of soap. Warm fluid oozes out of her onto the rock as she crouches. Her wet feet are cold, as are her hands in the water. And the gusty wind, constantly blowing a loose hank of her hair across her eyes, is also cold. But none of that matters. She is just feeling happy today. That's all. Just happy.

This is what Sally Hemings thinks: She is practical. She sees things as they really are. Thomas Jefferson is a dreamer who doesn't know he is dreaming. Because he is white and wealthy and has so often been lucky, his dream is a beautiful dream, in which he himself is beautiful and his work is to rebuild the world as the beautiful place he believes it has always actually been. He is almost done, he thinks. Every morning he rises convinced that with just a little more effort the world he is building will be perfect. Only the details need to be attended to. The beautiful world exists. In essence. History is on his side.

This is what Sally Hemings thinks: Thomas Jefferson is ruthless, corrupt and completely self-centered. He does nothing that he does not see as advancing his own interests, and he works to maintain a reputation for thoughtfulness and moral backbone only so that people will be less likely to recognize his naked grabs for power. He condemns the aristocracy as corrupt, trivial and effeminate, and yet he wants nothing so much as to possess aristocratic comforts and tastes. And so he is entirely willing to have a pianoforte sent all the way from London for Maria, who shares little of his own love for music, and he is willing to tear down a perfectly good house for no other reason than that he is unhappy with its proportions. And, of course, although he announces to the world that "all men are created equal" and have claim to certain "unalienable rights" and he proclaims repeatedly that slavery is an abomination and a curse upon the nation, he is nevertheless content, at night, by candlelight, to tot up the appreciation of his human property.

This is what Sally Hemings thinks: As a child Thomas Jefferson learned that living is synonymous with pain, and so, for all of his life, he has sought not to live. He has sought to exist in a child's drawing, where each thing is only one color and each color is only a variety of happiness. He has sought to divide the world into that which might be celebrated and that which must be forbidden, and he has worked tirelessly to believe that what he wants forbidden has never actually existed in the first place. For Thomas Jefferson belief is a form of blindness, or paralysis. He is like an infant rabbit, separated from its mother, so demented by fear that it can only tremble in the grass as a hawk circles high overhead or as a dog comes out the back door of the house and sniffs the breeze.

While Thomas Jefferson reads from the pages that tremble in his hands, Sally Hemings notices a plump brown mouse sit up on its haunches and put its front paws to its cheeks. Then, in an instant, it has dropped to the floor and disappeared behind the night table. She says nothing.

Thomas Jefferson says, "'. . . to express my grateful thanks for the favor with which they have been pleased—'"

"Louder!" says Sally Hemings. "I'm sitting right here in the room with you, and I can hardly hear a word."

They are in the lodge. It is a late afternoon at the end of February. The western rims of the trunks and bare branches outside the window seem furred with gold. Sally Hemings is sitting in a plain wooden chair beside the crackling fireplace. Her legs are slightly spread to accommodate the modest bulge of her belly, and her hands are folded on top of it. She will have another baby in less than three months.

Thomas Jefferson reads, "'. . . grateful thanks for the favor with which they have been pleased to look toward me, to declare a sincere consciousness that the task is above my talents, and that I approach it with those anxious and awful presentiments—'"

"I still can't hear you."

"I can't! This is impossible!" His hand falls, and the pages snap against his thigh. There is a wild sorrow in his eyes. His mouth is open and downturned at the corners, as if he can't breathe.

"Of course you can. You are the president of the United States! Reading a speech is nothing—"

"No. I can't."

"Don't be ridiculous! You can talk for hours—"

"With *friends*. I have no problem with friends. But formal addresses—"

"And dinner parties. I've seen you myself lecture a whole table."

"But that's different. In my own home, it's different." He smiles nervously. "And, of course, the wine always makes it easier."

"Then have a couple of glasses before—"

"I can't do that." He drops onto the bed and flings his speech across the counterpane. The pages scatter. "I don't know what I'm going to do."

"You're going to go to Washington, you will be sworn in as president and then you will give this beautiful address."

As she speaks, Sally Hemings sees that the plump mouse has ventured out from behind the night table. It veers suddenly in the direction of Thomas Jefferson's left boot, and then, when it is not six inches from his heel, it darts back toward the wall and disappears from sight.

Sally Hemings says, "How can you possibly worry about it, given all you have accomplished? Remember how afraid Mr. Madison was that there would be open rebellion in the streets?"

"Yes, but—"

"Stop it! Your election is a tremendous accomplishment. Not just because you won but because the government you helped to found is succeeding. You have changed history. *You*, Thomas Jefferson—"

"Please! That's making it worse."

"Why?"

"I don't know. I'm filled with uneasiness. It's as if my arms and legs are crammed with insects." He heaves a sigh and shakes his head. "It's because I'm not that man. The Thomas Jefferson whom everyone in that room will be looking at is a fabrication. It's as if someone has been out in the world doing an impersonation of me, and now I have to live up to his reputation." He laughs and looks sheepishly at Sally Hemings. "It's true," he says.

Sally Hemings gets up from her chair and gathers together the scattered pages of his address. "Here." She puts them onto his lap, and he grabs hold of them before they slip to the floor. "You're behaving like a child," she says.

Thomas Jefferson looks up at her with a child's expression. He takes hold of her left hand by the tips of her index and middle fingers, lifts them to his lips and kisses them.

"It's easy," she says. "The words are here on the page. All you have to do is read them one after the other. And read them in a voice loud enough for people to hear." She pulls her hand away. "The problem is that I've been sitting too close. I'm going to go out on the porch, and you'll have to read loudly enough for me to hear you there."

"It's freezing!"

"No it isn't." She smiles and caresses her belly with both hands. "And besides, I have my little stewpot to keep me warm."

Thomas Jefferson smiles and stands up.

Sally Hemings crosses the room, opens the door and steps out onto the porch, leaving the door open behind her.

In fact, it *is* freezing outside. A sharp breeze blowing across the porch immediately chills her shoulders and neck, even though she is wrapped in a shawl. She won't be able to stand the cold for terribly long.

"Start where you left off," she says. "Read it loud enough that I can hear it out here."

Grim worry comes onto Thomas Jefferson's brow and lips. He lifts the sheets of foolscap covered with his own handwriting, and after clearing his throat a couple of times, he begins to read, "'. . . I approach it with those anxious and awful presentiments which the greatness of the charge and the weakness of my powers so justly inspire. . . .'"

Sally Hemings can hardly make out his words, but she is only half listening. She hears the clattery rush of the river at her back and the thrumming of wind high in the bare branches of the trees. Her baby is stirring inside her. A jay squawks a few feet over her head. A chickadee is balanced atop the porch railing on its toothpick legs, its head shifting in spurts: now left, now right, now up, now down. Then, with another spurt, it reverses its position on the railing. A chipmunk or a squirrel rustles in the winter-grayed leaves on the forest floor just behind her.

How vital and alert she feels—her body filled with life: her own and that of this yet-to-be-known person inside her. From the soles of her feet to her nose and her fingertips—she is made of life, and life is all around her: the birds, the trees, the animals, near and far; even the breeze and the endlessly noisy river—the whole world is alive, and the life of the world is indistinguishable from the life that has always been her own and from the life that is inside that life. She feels this with such purity and simplicity that it is as if her spirit is filtering out into the world and there is no difference between her and every moving, striving, perceiving thing.

"'. . . During the contest of opinion through which we have passed,'" says Thomas Jefferson, but his voice has grown so soft now that she wouldn't know what he was saying had she not read his speech herself.

Thomas Jefferson cannot speak. He is in a gigantic room within the half-built Capitol Building, where barn swallows dart to and from their muddy nests on cornices and gables, copper sunbeams angle through the interstices of labyrinthine wooden scaffolds and pigeons turn in circles on dusty floorboards making their fretful *whurr*s. Thomas Jefferson is the newly elected president. His mouth is moving, but he cannot speak. His eyes pass from word to word—"'the task is above my talents'"—and those same words vibrate in his throat and between his palate and tongue, but they become nothing in the open air. He knows this from the sympathetic entreaty in James Madison's eyes, Alexander Hamilton's happy sneer and John Marshall's buckled brow and open mouth. He knows this from the coughs that echo in a room where his words do not, and from the rainlike rustle of scores of shifting feet, and from the creaking of at least as many chairs. "'A rising nation spread over a wide and fruitful land . . .'" The words echo within Thomas Jefferson's whirling skull, but they cannot pass his lips. His sweating fingers slick the wooden podium and warp the paper when he turns a page. He tries to raise his voice, but his throat only constricts. His voice is a duck's voice, and he can hardly breathe. He knows that the most important words are coming soon: *We are all Republicans, we are all Federalists.* He knows that for the first time in history, the rule of a nation has passed from enemy to enemy without bloodshed and that this is a cause both for celebration and for grave concern, because there is no guarantee that the peace will prevail. And he knows that his primary challenge will be to act according to his own principles without offending too many of those who find his principles abhorrent. The most important words are coming closer and closer. They loom and they loom. Now, here they are: "'We have called by different names brethren of the same principle. We are all Republicans, we are all Federalists.'" But the words do not pass his lips. He knows because the rainlike rumble has grown thunderous, and the coughs are hard to distinguish from guffaws. "'Sometimes it is said that man cannot be trusted with the government of himself. Can he, then, be trusted with the government of others?'" With every word the veracity of his opening remarks—which he had thought merely ceremonial humility—only becomes more clear: Yes, it is true; his talents really are entirely inadequate to the task with which he has been charged. "Equal and exact justice to all men,'" he reads, and '"freedom of religion; freedom of the press, and freedom of person under the protection of the habeas corpus . . .'" These are all mere murmurs in a room resounding with disappointment and happy mockery. He is not even halfway through his address, and he doesn't know how he will ever make it to the end.

O nly days into his presidency, Thomas Jefferson decreed that henceforth he would deliver all official addresses, including the State of the Union, only in writing, a practice that was honored by all succeeding presidents, up until Woodrow Wilson, who reestablished the tradition of orally presenting the State of the Union address in 1913. Over the remainder of his life, Thomas Jefferson would deliver only one more formal address, at his second inauguration, but this address, like its predecessor, was barely audible.

The festive strains of a handful of violins commence as a glowering, white-wigged, bulldog-mouthed man—Chief Justice John Marshall, it would seem—administers the oath of office to the young actor, whose copper-colored wig now has patches of gray at the temples. But almost instantly, the young actor's stoic, handsome face fades into a field of yellow, which turns out to be the wall of a brilliantly lit room drifting from right to left like the hull of a ship leaving a dock. A cluster of musicians looms into view, all of them wearing trim blue frock coats and white wigs, and tilting prissy, V-shaped smiles at one another over the strings of their instruments, and then just as suddenly the musicians shrink and fall away, until it becomes clear that they occupy only one corner of an enormous room aglitter with silver, crystal, hundreds of candle flames and the jewelry of women, whose wedding-cake gowns billow and sway around their invisible legs, as they themselves are swirled around the room by yet other trim, bewigged men in blue-and-gray frock coats.

Now it is the actor in the copper-colored wig who looms into view, and he is clearly the tallest and most handsome man in the room and the only one not wearing a white wig. For a moment his face is so large and the room behind him is hurtling so dizzyingly from left to right that Thomas Jefferson feels as if he is an infant being carried in the man's arms. But then the man's head swings around, and he is revealed to be dancing with a very young woman, who is also very beautiful in a faintly comical way involving a towering hairstyle and a large black beauty dot stuck to her skin a little below and to the right of her perfect mouth. The beautiful woman's eyes gleam as she whirls in the light of ever-multiplying candelabras, and her lips are pressed together in a smile unlike any that Thomas Jefferson has ever witnessed, but one that would seem to indicate her smug certainty that she will bed the widower president once the music has ended, the guests have departed and the last of the candles has been snuffed by a less-than-approving servant.

Just as Thomas Jefferson is becoming alarmed at what might happen next, the woman's towering coiffure looms so large that it makes the whole theater go black, while the notes of a single violin rise above the rest. When, at last, the head whirls away, it turns out to be not that of the woman but of the actor in the copper-colored wig, who is coatless, in an open-necked white shirt, playing a violin—although the balletic movements of his bow are entirely unrelated to the notes resounding in the darkness.

As he shrinks and the room around him grows larger, it becomes clear that he is not dancing with his violin but is seated on a stool at an ordinary wooden table in a mud-chinked log cabin, lit by a solitary candle. Swatches of calico are nailed over the window, and a battered, long-handled frying pan hangs from a rafter.

Finally the room has loomed so large that Thomas Jefferson is able to see that the beautiful young woman with the honey-brown skin is also sitting at the table, smiling guardedly as she watches the actor in the copper-colored wig play the melody he has only just been dancing to. She has no beauty spot. Her loose hair makes a gold-tinged cloud around her face, which is a celebration of convexities and dimples. If the beauty of the woman dancing at the inaugural ball might be characterized by the odor of a very fine French perfume, this young woman's beauty is like the smell of a forest when rain has just begun to fall.

"There you have it, Sal," the actor in the copper-colored wig says as he lowers violin and bow to his lap. "You didn't miss a thing."

The golden young woman's smile momentarily broadens but then all at once shuts off. "You play beautifully," she says as she gets up from the table and turns her back.

She hurries to a window, and now the dark theater is loud with the noises of crickets, peepers and a bullfrog. When the actor in the copper-colored wig comes up to her, his handsome brow furrowed intelligently, she pushes him away. "No," she says, and hurries to a corner, where she lowers her face into her hands.

All at once the actor in the copper-colored wig is standing behind her. He hesitates for a long moment before lifting his hands lightly to her shoulders. "Oh, Sal," he says sorrowfully, and for another long moment she seems determined to reject him. But then, in an instant, she has turned, and, revealing just the faintest flash of a smile, she presses her forehead against his chest.

He wraps his arms around her, shifting her head so that now her cheek is against his chest, and she pulls him suddenly closer, until, in silhouette, they form, together, that classic tableau of masculine protectiveness and grateful female vulnerability.

It turns out that Thomas Jefferson is neither dirigible nor cloud nor breeze, but a bronze monument hundreds of feet high, and all of us are trapped inside him, though some of us claim to have come here voluntarily. "He is a great man," these people argue. "We should be honored to live inside him." But how can any of us know what sort of man he might be? To us he is only darkness and other people. The air in here is dense with the breath of those who do not eat well and with the corporeal emanations of those who do not wash. We do a lot of blind stumbling, sometimes over the bodies of people who are exhausted, or who have fallen to the floor in a drunken stupor, or who, perhaps, will never again get to their feet. There are a lot of curses, mumbled prayers, grumbles, wails and shocked, infuriated and orgasmic shouting. We are a shabby species, capable of gallows humor, perhaps, but little in the way of greatness. We are venal. We are ignorant. Most of all we are terrified. And we are almost always self-deceived. Why should anyone imagine that Thomas Jefferson might be any different? "Because we fabricated him ourselves," say those who wish to be hopeful. "Because we built him out of our desires and dreams and our disgust with who we are."

My brothers, sister Harriet and myself, were used alike. We were permitted to stay about the "great house," and only required to do such light work as going on errands. Harriet learned to spin and to weave in a little factory on the home plantation. We were free from the dread of having to be slaves all our lives long, and were measurably happy. We were always permitted to be with our mother, who was well used. It was her duty, all her life which I can remember, up to the time of father's death, to take care of his chamber and wardrobe, look after us children and do such light work as sewing, and Provision was made in the will of our father that we should be free when we arrived at the age of 21 years. We had all passed that period when he died but Eston, and he was given the remainder of his time shortly after. He and I rented a house and took mother to live with us, till her death, which event occurred in 1835.

—Madison Hemings
"Life Among the Lowly, No. 1"
Pike County (Ohio) *Republican*
March 13, 1873

It is August 16, 1801. Sally Hemings is twenty-eight, and the air this day is so heavy and hot that the sun seems tarnished and the heaps of cumulus, even at noon, are rust-tinged and indefinite through a haze of steam. It is hard to breathe. Evelina, the servant Thomas Jefferson has provided her, has taken three-and-a-half-year-old Beverly down the hill to spend the afternoon with his grandmother, as he has almost every day for the last year. Holding her three-month-old daughter against her shoulder, Sally Hemings crouches on her front porch and, with one hand, lifts the wooden cover off a bucket of greasy water and drops in the baby's soiled clout.

A scrape of a shoe over gritty dust.

Then a voice: "At least this time it's a white one!"

As she reels around, the bucket cover thumps to the porch floor and rolls into the yellow grass. "Jimmy! Oh, my word! Jimmy!"

"Hey there, Cider Jug!"

Jimmy stands in the middle of the road, grinning as if he's just pulled off a very successful practical joke.

"Oh, my word!" Sally Hemings repeats as he steps up onto the porch. "Oh, Jimmy!" She flings her free arm around him. "Oh, Jimmy! Oh, Jimmy!" She hugs him as hard as she can with her one arm, but he remains inert in her grasp and has the acrid funk of someone who has gone weeks without changing clothes or washing.

She lets him go.

"When did you get here?" she says.

"Just this minute. You're the first person I've seen. Been walking from Charlottesville since before sunrise."

Despite the heat he is wearing a frock coat and a linen shirt, buttoned to the neck. His shirt is sweat-darkened and his velvet collar marked by multiple lines of salt sediment. He seems to have shrunk since the last time she saw him—coming on two years ago now (just before Thenia was born, she suddenly remembers). He's gone gaunt, his cheeks look sucked tight against his teeth and there is a deep vertical line on the right side of his mouth. He's only thirty-six, but he looks fifty, or older.

"Come inside," she says. "You must want something to eat."

"No, no, no!" he says. "Nothing for me!"

"Don't be ridiculous, Jimmy! You look like a scarecrow."

"I'm not hungry. I never eat in the morning."

"But it's nearly time for dinner."

An irritated perplexity comes onto Jimmy's face, and he is silent a moment before nodding at the infant on Sally Hemings's shoulder. "At least this one's white."

Now it is Sally Hemings whose expression is perplexed and worried. She lowers her daughter and holds her with both hands so that Jimmy can see her. "Here you go, Little Bug," she says. "Time to meet your Uncle Jimmy!"

The little girl, having been disturbed from sleep, goes red in the face, and grimaces as if she is about to cry. But then, with a gurgly peep, she settles back into slumber.

Sally Hemings laughs happily.

"Beautiful," says Jimmy, though not with any feeling. "A boy or a girl?"

"A girl. Her name is Harriet."

"Harriet!" Jimmy's eyes widen, and the corners of his mouth turn down. "Don't you think that's bad luck?"

"No!" Sally Hemings cries. "I love that name. And I like to feel that the spirit of her sister lives on in her. Mr. Jefferson feels the same way."

Jimmy shrugs. "Well, at least she's white."

Sally Hemings pulls the baby back up to her shoulder. "Stop saying that, Jimmy! Why are you saying that?"

"It's better to be white." Jimmy shrugs again. "That's all I'm saying. Better for the baby and better for you. I heard about the other one." He smiles at his sister as if they are complicit in some evil.

Sally Hemings is so angry her knees are trembling. *The other one!* He never even saw Thenia. How dare he talk about her that way! He'd promised to write, but he never wrote a single letter—not even to say he was sorry she had lost her baby. All this time she'd been thinking he didn't know. But he *did* know—somehow—and he'd never even bothered to write.

"What are you doing here, Jimmy?" she says at last.

"I'm back!" He smiles and holds out both hands, as if he has just materialized before her eyes. "Mr. Jefferson just can't live without me. He's been trying to get me to come back ever since I left. But I just kept telling him, 'No. Too busy!' I was running my own very successful business venture in Baltimore. A restaurant, *à la française*. In the very best part of town. All of my customers were white—and rich. And they just loved me, even though I spat in every plate as it went out of my kitchen. I really did that. None of them ever knew, of course. I'd stir it up. I did that just so I could always remember that I was better than the whole bunch of them. I really did. They loved me, and I didn't give a damn about them. That's the truth. God's own truth. But then I started to get sick of the whole thing. Didn't know why I was doing it. And that's when Mr. Jefferson got in touch with me again. Wrote me this letter saying, 'Please come cook for me in Washington. Peter can't cook worth a damn. Please come cook for me again, and I'll give you ten dollars a month.' I said, 'You give me *twenty* dollars a month and that's a deal.' And he said yes, so here I am!"

Sally Hemings's anger has turned to something much more like fear. She doesn't believe a single word Jimmy has said—especially about being rehired. Thomas Jefferson is due back any day now, and then Jimmy's lie will be exposed and he will be utterly humiliated. And what will that do to him? Is he still drinking so hard? He looks like a man who drinks and does nothing else. But maybe it's good that he is back with his family. Maybe that's the real reason he came home.

"Are you sure you wouldn't like some food?" she says. "I've got some fresh corn bread inside. Or some water? Would you like some water? You must be thirsty."

"No, no," he says, holding up both flat palms as if to keep her at bay. "I'm fine. Maybe I'll have something to eat when I go see Mammy."

And with that he backs off the porch and sets off down the road, without saying another word.

"I heard that he had lost his job at a restaurant in Philadelphia," Thomas Jefferson explains. "So I thought—"

"Why was he dismissed?" says Sally Hemings.

"I don't know." Thomas Jefferson tilts his head and gives a weary shrug. "But I suppose we can both imagine. . . ."

"Yes." She looks down into her glass.

He puts his hand on her shoulder and gives her a reassuring stroke, then pats her lightly twice and pulls his hand away. They are sitting on the porch just outside his chambers, drinking cold cider. The sun set on the far side of the house a few minutes ago, but there are small, rose-colored clouds straight overhead in an indigo sky and faint smears of green along the southern horizon.

"In any event, since I will only be making short visits home as long as I am in Washington and since Peter sometimes has to begin preparing for larger gatherings weeks in advance, it made little sense for him to come with me, so I thought that if Jimmy needed the work, it would be good to enjoy his cooking when I am home. I wrote to him a couple of times and got no response, so I decided he wasn't interested. But then six months went by and he finally wrote to me."

"Six months?" says Sally Hemings. "What was he doing in all that time?"

"He didn't say."

She sighs heavily. Thomas Jefferson holds out his hand in the accumulating dimness, and when she puts her hand in his, he gives her a squeeze and doesn't let go.

"How does he seem?" says Thomas Jefferson.

"I don't know." She heaves another deep sigh. "He seems . . . I don't know how he seems."

He gives her hand another squeeze. "I think it is good that he is home."

"I hope so."

For the first few days, Jimmy manages so well in the kitchen that Thomas Jefferson declares he doesn't know how he survived two years without Jimmy's cooking. But then one night he helps himself so liberally from the wine cellar that he forgets to take a pot of succotash off the fire and burns it to the point that it can only be used for pig feed. The next day he will not leave his pallet in John Hemings's cabin, claiming that he is beset with the same "ailment of the head" as Thomas Jefferson. But Pricilla, John's wife, says that it is only corn liquor that keeps Jimmy in bed, half the time unconscious, the other half drinking. The next day he manages to produce a passable pork dinner, but the following day he burns the trout so badly that its skin is ash and its flesh like wood splinters. The day after that, his "sauce" for the peas is only melted lard—the smell alone so sickening that Maria, who is only weeks from giving birth to her first child, must rush from the table, out into the open air, to keep from vomiting.

The next day Jimmy is once again afflicted by an "ailment of the head," but Thomas Jefferson sends Sally Hemings for him. When brother and sister arrive in his office, Thomas Jefferson folds his hands at the center of his desk and tells Jimmy, in a voice so soft it is hard to hear, "While I had very much been looking forward to both your cuisine and your company, Jimmy, I am afraid that your susceptibility to spirits is making it impossible for you to do your job."

Jimmy's face is slick with sweat, his eyes are red and he is visibly unsteady on his feet. "I'm fine," he says.

Thomas Jefferson continues to speak quietly. "I am only thinking of your own good. And for that reason, I think it best that until you have regained your self-control, Edy Fossett will be the mistress of the kitchen, and you will be her sous-chef."

"Edy!" Jimmy practically spits the name. "That ignorant bitch!"

"Jimmy!" says Sally Hemings.

"I'm just speaking the truth," he says, his voice loud and flat. "She doesn't know anything about cooking! She's never even heard of vichyssoise! She couldn't make a wine sauce if she practiced for a month!"

"Jimmy, please!" Sally Hemings tries to calm her brother by putting both hands on the shoulder nearest her, but he only shrugs her off.

"I think you should taste one of her meals before you insult her like that," says Thomas Jefferson.

Now Jimmy is shouting. "How dare you insult *me* like that! I am a *master* chef! I've cooked for royalty! How dare you tell me that I should be the sous-chef to that ignorant black bitch!"

"Jimmy, *please*." Thomas Jefferson's hands, no longer folded, grip the front edge of his desk as if he is about to stand. "I am only trying to find a way that you can continue to receive your salary while you—"

"I don't want your money!" Jimmy puts both fists on Thomas Jefferson's desk, leans forward and shouts. "Do you think I have no dignity! Do you think I was only put on this earth to serve your pleasure! I am a free man, Mr. Jefferson. I worked hard for my freedom, and no one is going to tell me what to do."

"Jimmy—" Thomas Jefferson's voice is trembling with anger.

"I don't want to talk to you!"

Jimmy turns toward the door. Sally Hemings grabs the lapel of his coat, but he shoves her aside and strides out of the room.

"Jimmy!" she calls after him, her half-closed hands hanging in the air in front of her, as if she were still clinging to his lapel. She turns to Thomas Jefferson, her gaze distraught and afraid.

"Let him go," says Thomas Jefferson.

"I have to talk to him!" She is out the door in two steps. Her running feet resound down the corridor and across the great hall.

Jimmy is gone for two days after fleeing Thomas Jefferson's study. When he returns to Monticello, he serves as Edy Fossett's sous-chef for much of a week, but always sullenly and with the slurred speech and slow-motion lunging of a drunk. One night he cuts his finger so badly that he bleeds all over a bowl of onions, and Edy tells him to leave her kitchen and not come back until he is sober. As Sally Hemings is getting into bed that night, she hears his voice drifting up the hill from where the field laborers live. First he is singing, and then he is shouting in anger.

Sometime during that very silent and black hour that just precedes the first light of dawn, she awakes with a start and realizes that someone has touched her shoulder. She hears panting in the darkness, right beside her bed, and smells the sweet rankness of corn liquor.

Jimmy is speaking, much too loud for so silent and lonely an hour. "You are loved, Sally. I just want you to know that."

"Jimmy, quiet!" she whispers. "The children."

"You are loved," he says as loudly as before. "People love you. That is very important."

"Jimmy, please." She hears Beverly stirring in his bed across the room. Evelina cries out in her sleep, "No!"

"It's because you are good," says Jimmy.

She hears shoe scrapes, thumps and the stretching of cloth. Jimmy is sitting on the floor and resting his hand on her belly. She can't see him at all.

"People despise me," he says. "I can't be good in this world. Because I can't be myself."

"What are you talking about?" Sally Hemings wants to sit up, but she is still too sleepy. She rolls onto her side, and Jimmy's hand slides from her belly to her hip. He squeezes her there as he speaks.

"I can be a black nigger. I can be an African god. I can be a slave. But I can't be loved for who I am. Do you know what I'm saying? Do you understand?"

She feels the weight of his head against her belly and his hand across her buttocks pulling her close. His voice is thick now. He is crying.

"But I can't be myself," he says. "So nobody loves me. I can't be myself in this world."

She reaches behind her back, takes his pressing hand in her own and brings it forward, clutching it against her ribs. "I love you, Jimmy."

He lifts his head away from her belly. He pulls his hand out of hers. "I know you do, but it's not enough."

She can tell from the thumps of his shoes and knees that he has shifted to a crouch.

"I have to go," he says.

Beverly whimpers, then cries out, "Mammy!"

Jimmy is standing. Sally Hemings sits up in bed. "No," she says. "Wait."

"I have to go."

By the time Sally Hemings puts both feet on the floor, Jimmy is gone.

S ally Hemings is sitting on her porch, stitching a bonnet for baby Harriet. She hears a heavy sigh and looks up to see Goliah, the gardener, standing just before the porch step and holding his hat in his hands. "I'm sorry to disturb you, Miz Sally." He shifts from one foot to the other and licks his lips. "But my cousin, Henry, who works over to Grand Pointe, he told me to tell you that he heard word from Baltimore about Jimmy."

Sally Hemings drops the bonnet onto her knees but cannot bring herself to speak. It has been a month since Jimmy came to her cabin in the night and she hasn't seen or heard from him since.

Goliah looks down at the ground. "I hate to . . . Well, I'm really sorry, but Henry said . . . that Jimmy is dead."

The bonnet slips from her lap to the porch floor. "How?" she says.

"I don't know. That's all Henry told me. Jimmy's dead. That's all he said."

When Goliah is gone, Sally Hemings sits for a long time thinking. Thomas Jefferson has told her never to write him a letter when he is in Washington City. His enemies are always stealing his mail in the hope of finding something they can use against him. And for that reason he writes his most important letters—chiefly those to Mr. Madison—in a code generated by a device of his own invention. But Sally Hemings can't think of anyone who might be better able to get the whole story of what happened to Jimmy than Thomas Jefferson. So she leaves her sewing on her porch rocker and walks across the lawn to the great house, where she sits at Thomas Jefferson's own desk and writes, "Sir, Forgive me for writing. I have just heard that my brother J has died in Baltamor. Do you know if this is true? and if it is do you know how he came to take such a despret action? Respecfully yours, S."

She gives the letter to Remus and asks him to go straight to Washington City and give the letter directly to Thomas Jefferson and to no one else. "Put it right into his own hand."

Ten days later Remus returns with Thomas Jefferson's reply: "Madam, I was deeply saddened to learn the tragical news you have had of your poor brother. I have made an inquiry of Mr. E., who lives in Baltimore and was well acquainted with your brother. I regret to inform you that the news you heard was correct. J. took his own life on the 28th of October. It seems that he had been drinking excessively for at least a week, and I am sure he had little comprehension of what he was doing. This is a very, very sad story, and I am, myself, feeling quite bereft, although I think everyone who knew J. understood that something like this might happen. I send my most sincere condolences to you, your mother and to your whole family. I am much occupied by my duties at the present, but will convey more news at my earliest convenience. My thoughts are with you." The letter is unsigned.

When Sally Hemings has finished reading, Remus says that Peter told him to tell her that Jimmy slit his own throat.

For a time Thomas Jefferson can jot notes and do a sort of work involving barometers, yardsticks and magnifying glasses. But soon he discovers that he is no longer independent of the crowd overrunning Sally Hemings's invention, that he, too, is being swept across plazas and parks, down boulevards and streets, along alleys and underground corridors, ever deeper into the interstices of an ever-more-massive city, its buildings rising ever higher into an ever smaller sky.

At first he thinks of all these people as insects: ignorant, soulless, moving mindlessly toward their doom. But then he notices that they are talking—as volubly and variously as any crowd exiting a theater. And it would seem from the rhythms and tones of their speech that some members of the crowd are delivering stern lectures while others are telling jokes, or pleading, or trading gossip in voiced whispers. So many words, near and far, crossing from lips to ears, from mind to mind—yet for Thomas Jefferson they remain airborne packets of mystery. A rippling of lips and teeth. Collages of tiny sounds.

For a while he thinks that the best way to extract meaning from these words is to measure them with his yardstick, but they won't stay still long enough, and he can never quite tell where one word ends and the next begins. And then it seems that he has lost his yardstick, or maybe he never had it. The same is true of his barometer and his magnifying glass. And the last he ever sees of his notes, they are doing loop-the-loops over the heads of the crowd.

Without tools his judgments become ever harder to sustain, or even to remember, and he can offer no resistance to the human tide. And so he is swept ever deeper into Sally Hemings's invention, hoping against his every certainty that he might yet be rescued—by some strange new freedom or by some improbable variety of truth.

And now the hammering car is pierced, yet again, by the screeching of steel against steel. And now, again, it is dark, and the yellow dimness of the incandescent bulbs mounted between the tunnel struts slides stroboscopically down the length of the car, lighting, for an instant, shoulders and flanks and frozen faces and then, an instant later, lighting them again. Thomas Jefferson is on his feet now, rocking as the car rocks, remembering how he never allowed himself to truly love Sally Hemings, when, in fact, he had never loved anyone more, and how she came to hate him, and to close herself off, and how he had lost her that way and had never known such excruciating pain. But now, after all this time, here she is, rocking in the darkness in which he, too, is rocking, in this steel screeching—multitonal, mounting and mounting, like an escalating feedback loop or like an insane fugue performed by an orchestra of metal birds. And then the screeching stops. And the lights are on.

VIII

. . . I don't know exactly how or when it happened, but at some point I simply defined the life I was leading as a good one, which meant that anything I did that allowed me to continue living my good life was also good. And so I became afflicted with an especially perilous form of blindness.

Where I had once seen light and dark, black and white, red, yellow, orange, purple, I now saw only gray. Everything became muted, dim. I lost my ability to feel the pain of others or to be outraged. In order to believe that I lived in a good world, I had to believe that the whole rest of the world was no good— people especially—and that my only obligation was to care for my children, my family, the people I loved.

And so I used little truths and partial truths and sometimes big truths (my love for my children) to convince myself of the very big lie that I need feel no shame, that I was as close to virtuous as I could reasonably have expected to be.

I said yes to Mr. Jefferson and yes to evasions, lies and complicity. But I could have said no. No, you may not kiss me. No, I do not want your hands on my body. No, I owe you nothing. I don't believe you. No, I don't. I won't. I don't love you. No.

Had I adopted that policy, none of yesterday's evils would have been averted, but I would not have been complicit in them, nor in any of the other evils from which I have profited over the last forty years.

No and no and no.

I might have had a purer soul. . . .

James T. Callender is walking up Pennsylvania Avenue toward the president's mansion—although "avenue" is an absurd euphemism for this dirt track passing through swamp and primeval forest, along which a carriage could not travel twenty feet without jolting over a boulder or an insufficiently excised tree stump. So, too, the name "city," when applied to these half dozen unfinished and ill-designed Palladian imitations amid a scattering of shacks and swaybacked houses belonging to trappers and fishermen and to the benighted farmers who supposed this swampland might be made to flourish under their plows.

Almost exactly a year ago, Callender was martyred for his service to Thomas Jefferson and the Democratic-Republican Party when John Adams had him imprisoned under the Sedition Act for the crime of publishing the truth of Adams's own villainy and the villainy of the party he serves. No one could have been happier than Callender himself when his efforts propelled Adams out of office and Thomas Jefferson into the presidency, and no one could have been more justified in the expectation that those efforts and his consequent martyrdom would be amply compensated for by the man who had derived the greatest benefit from them. But this expectation has been revealed to have little more validity than the fantastical notion that this mosquito-infested wilderness through which he is walking might be the august capital city of a great nation.

Although it is early April, the weather belongs to July, and Callender is aware of the rank effluvium being suffused by his own person and wardrobe. He remained naked much of the previous day, as he scrubbed his solitary suit of clothing and then waited for it to dry. He had worn those same clothes every day of his imprisonment and, despite numerous washings, had never been able to rid them of the fetid stench of his cell. This morning, lifting his coat and breeches to his nose, he concluded that his efforts had at last met with success, but now, thanks to the heat of the sun and of his own body, he knows that he will never cease smelling of the jailhouse until he has the funds to purchase an entirely new wardrobe.

But maybe that is a good thing. Maybe nothing would be better than for Thomas Jefferson to experience this mere hint of the suffering that James T. Callender endured on his behalf. Maybe then he will comprehend the rankness of his own failure to live up to his obligations.

Callender's requests could hardly have been more humble: the mere two hundred dollars that Thomas Jefferson has already promised him and an appointment as postmaster of Richmond. Is that too much to ask? The money would only cover the fine he had to pay after his conviction, and the job could hardly be more innocuous, nor easier for a president to effect. The current postmaster is, after all, a Federalist, and it is only in the government's best interests to purge every last Federalist occupying an administrative post.

While Thomas Jefferson seems to have entirely given up answering his letters, Callender does not see how the man could possibly deny the justice of his requests once he has been confronted by them in person.

A hot day indeed, and a brilliant one, especially once he ventures across the muddy plain that surrounds the president's mansion—so brilliant that he can see almost nothing once he has stepped into the building itself. But he can hear Thomas Jefferson's voice echoing down a corridor to his right. And even though Callender can still make out little more than floating wads of darkness and smears of illumination reflected off polished floors, he hurries in the direction of the voice, knowing that Jefferson could well choose to avoid him if given the chance.

Callender has hardly taken two steps, however, when a figure looms out of the obscurity and catches him by the elbow. It is James Madison, Jefferson's lackey and attack dog. "Mr. Callender!" he says. "What a surprise! Might I trouble you for a moment of your time?"

James T. Callender tugs his elbow from Madison's grasp and says, "I have essential business with the president."

"Yes, yes—I'm sure you do. But I need to have a word with you first. It's important."

This time Madison grips Callender's arm with such force that it would be impossible to escape without a struggle. "Right here," he says, and all but shoves Callender through the door into an office, pleasantly decorated with mahogany furniture and gilt-framed paintings and suffused with golden daylight. "Please," says Madison, indicating a chair in front of the desk, behind which he himself takes a seat.

"I have to talk to the president immediately," says Callender.

"I'm aware of that," says Madison. "But I have to speak to you first."

He indicates the chair again, and Callender, thinking better of making a dash for the door, finally sits. He pulls his flask from his pocket and takes a deep swallow but pointedly does not offer any to Madison.

Everything transpires exactly as Callender expects. The corruptive magnetism of power cannot be resisted. Within the precincts of Monticello, Thomas Jefferson was an immensely articulate opponent of all forms of power, and so Callender dared to imagine he might prove truer to his own principles than most. But in the end, words and principles are less substantial than the breath it takes to speak them, and they have no force except insofar as they prettify brutal self-interest. Now that Thomas Jefferson has achieved the most powerful position in the land, his own words and principles are only an embarrassment, because they expose, by contrast, the true nakedness of his greed.

This is precisely what Madison is referring to—although he himself may be entirely unaware of the fact—with all his sanctimonious chatter about "practicality," "indiscretion" and "extremism." And so Callender cuts him off in midsentence by getting to his feet and declaring, "I have no business with you, but only with the president."

In fact, Callender has just abandoned all of the arguments he was formulating over the last several days. Thomas Jefferson may now be insensible to argument, but he will not be insensible to Callender's physical presence, nor to the threats that Callender now realizes he has no choice but to make. Once a man's soul has been infected by power, he will heed only those who might help him increase his power and those who might take his power away. Since Callender is no longer welcome as a member of the former category, he will do his damnedest to occupy the latter.

As soon as he emerges from Madison's office, he makes straight for the corridor down which he can still hear Thomas Jefferson's voice resounding. But Madison, not two steps behind him, calls out to a pair of soldiers, and after some hasty contention involving insults, grunts and an elbow to the cheekbone, Callender's arm is wrenched up behind his back and he is marched out into the brilliant day. Some hundred yards from the presidential mansion, he is let go and told that if he dares to enter the building again, he will be shot on sight.

Callender wants to laugh at the retreating backs of the soldiers, but he can't quite manage it. The reason he wants to laugh is that he knows Thomas Jefferson goes for a ride every afternoon, and so all he—James T. Callender—has to do to have his moment with the president is sit down within sight of the stables and wait. He walks around to the rear of the mansion and finds a comfortable place to sit, on a rock outcropping beside a dirt track designated as New York Avenue.

There is only one thing wrong with this plan: Between his trip from his hotel that morning and his audience with Madison, Callender has already emptied his flask and he is not at all sure he will have the necessary fortitude to confront Thomas Jefferson without another swallow or two.

Even in so imaginary a city as Washington, there can't be very much distance between taverns, so Callender sets off and does not have to walk even a quarter mile before he finds himself sitting at a table, a glass of brandy in front of him and his flask refilled. He would have been back at his lookout point beside New York Avenue within fifteen minutes, but he gets into an argument about the superiority of militias to a standing army and ends up not starting back to his post until the sun is a good third past its zenith. He walks with heavy steps, all but certain that Thomas Jefferson has already returned from his ride. But then, still some twenty yards from the rock outcropping, he catches sight of a tall man on a bay stallion just approaching along New York Avenue. Lifting his coat hems with each of his hands, Callender sprints until he is standing directly in front of the bay and its rider.

"Now you have no choice but to hear me out!" he declares between gasps.

"There's no point in wasting your breath," says Thomas Jefferson. "Randolph has given up his suit, and you will have your money forthwith." He tugs the horse's reins to the right, but Callender leaps again into his path, before the horse has taken half a step.

"Damn the money!" he shouts. "I don't care a pig's prick for the money! I only want my just and deserved recompense for the services I have rendered you!"

Thomas Jefferson yanks the reins a second time. "I will not discuss this matter any further," he says as he passes. "You have been more than adequately compensated for your work. I agree that your imprisonment was a travesty of the law, but I pardoned you as soon as I took office, and now I have seen to it that your fine will be returned to you. I owe you nothing more and consider our association ended."

Callender shambles alongside the horse as Thomas Jefferson speaks. Several times he reaches for the horse's reins, intending to bring it to a halt, but they repeatedly elude his fingers. Only when the horse bucks and grazes his knee with a hoof does Callender leap back and give up his efforts.

"You're fucking arse wipe, Jefferson!" he shouts at the president's retreating back. "You're twice the tyrant that Adams was, and even Washington would be staggered by your self-serving hypocrisy. You're the fucking traitor! Do you hear me? You don't give a rat's arse for democracy! But you can't escape your own actions! Mark my words: Even you don't have the power to change the facts! I know why you're always in such a hurry to get back to Monticello! I know that every word you have ever uttered about niggers is a damnable lie! Rind may have been too afraid to publish what he knew, but I am not! Do you hear me? I am not!"

I t is well known that the man, *whom it delighteth the people to honor,* keeps, and for many years past has kept, as his concubine, one of his own slaves. Her name is SALLY. The name of her eldest son is TOM. His features are said to bear a striking although sable resemblance to those of the president himself. The boy is ten or twelve years of age. His mother went to France in the same vessel with Mr. Jefferson and his two daughters. The delicacy of this arrangement must strike every person of common sensibilities. What a sublime pattern for an American ambassador to place before the eyes of two young ladies! . . . By this wench Sally, our president has had several children. . . . THE AFRICAN VENUS is said to officiate, as housekeeper at Monticello.

—James T. Callender
Richmond Recorder
September 1, 1802

On September 3, 1802, Mr. Lilly sends Tom Shackelford into Charlottesville to dispatch several barrels of nails to Baltimore and London. Sally Hemings goes with him so that she might visit Mickel's Millinery to buy cloth for the quilts she is making for Maria's son, Francis, and for her own little Harriet, who is a year and a half old. But also it is a fine day for a ride: sunny and coolish, one of those days in which the sky seems to have expanded and the breezes to move about more freely—an enormous relief after three solid weeks of nearly one-hundred-degree heat.

She gets off the wagon at the stage office and walks east on Main Street, which is still muddy from the previous day's thunderstorm. A white man in shirtsleeves and a pink waistcoat is sitting on a bench in front of a grocery, smoking a pipe. Sally Hemings's eye is drawn to him more by his perfect stillness than anything else. He is gaunt, with deltas of shadow under his cheekbones. His brow is gnarled, one corner of his mouth is pulled down and his china-blue eyes are staring directly at her. "Yellow bitch!" he says, and spits at her feet.

Sally Hemings is so shocked that she stops in her tracks.

"Abel!" the man shouts through the grocer's door. "Come on out here! Jefferson's nigger slut is right in front of your store!"

"What?" a voice calls from the dark interior.

"Just come on out! That yellow bitch whore is right here! Right on your doorstep!"

Sally Hemings has lifted the skirt of her gown and is hurrying with her head lowered along the muddy street.

"Dusky Sal!" a voice calls from behind her. "Dusky Sal!"

She hears laughter—from two men and a woman.

She doesn't know where she is going; she only wants to put as much distance between herself and the man at the grocery as she can. But other people have heard the shouting and have stopped in twos and threes to watch her go by.

"That's her," one woman tells another as she passes.

"Who?" says her friend.

A man lurches in front of her—drunk, or pretending to be drunk—then gives her upper arm a stinging, three-fingered slap as she dodges past. She hears several people speak the words "nigger wife."

At last she is in Mickel's Millinery, the door shut behind her and its little bell still jingling. She leans her back against the door for half a second, then steps away, trying to regain her self-possession.

Yesterday Edy Fossett told her that an article about her and Thomas Jefferson had appeared in a Federalist newspaper—but Edy had only heard tell of the article, not read it herself. When Sally Hemings asked what it had actually said, Edy replied, "Just silliness and balderdash! I don't know why people trouble themselves with those rags!"

Mrs. Mickel glances at her as she stands by the door but doesn't meet her eye. There are two other people in the store—a white woman and her grown daughter—and Mrs. Mickel is explaining to them that she is all out of baleen and won't have any more until the week after next, but if Miss Clark—the daughter—is in a hurry, the wooden stays are almost as good. There follows a long conversation comparing the virtues of various types of stays, during which Sally Hemings keeps a few steps to the rear, waiting her turn, grateful for the opportunity to calm her hammering heart. She doesn't know what she will do when she finally has to leave—except that she won't go back to the stage office along Main Street, but maybe along Market and Little Commerce, although that would take her considerably out of her way.

Sally Hemings has been coming to this store for close to thirteen years, ever since she got back from Paris. Mrs. Mickel used to love it whenever she brought in Martha's or Maria's French gowns for copying or repair, and she could talk for hours about the quality of their materials and the fineness of the design and the stitching. Even those beautiful dresses became old-fashioned, however, and Mrs. Mickel was close to tears the day Maria asked to have one of Martha's passed-down Parisian gowns altered so that it might look more stylish. Ever since Maria's marriage, however, Sally Hemings has mostly come into the shop on her own business. She and Mrs. Mickel have that placid affection that arises between shopkeeper and customer over years of counter-side chitchat, and of learning bits and pieces of each other's life, and of watching each other age. It is clear Mrs. Mickel thinks Sally Hemings a kindred spirit.

Miss Clark and her mother simply cannot decide whether to settle for the wood stays or hold out for the baleen and hope the latter come in on time. Sally Hemings keeps waiting for Mrs. Mickel to cast her a surreptitious eye-rolling glance, but no such glance is forthcoming.

At last the women reach a decision: They will have the dress made now and perhaps substitute baleen stays for the wood at a later date. Mrs. Mickel tells them she has just exactly the material they will want for the bodice and skirt, and then she calls for Nora, her Irish servant, to bring out the new shipment of silk.

Nora does as instructed, and while Miss Clark and her mother consider the skeins of evergreen, midnight blue and burgundy silk, Mrs. Mickel retreats to the back room with Nora for a couple of minutes. When she returns, she continues to ignore Sally Hemings, even though her two other customers have little need of her attention.

After a couple of minutes, Nora also emerges from the back room and indicates to Sally Hemings with a lateral glance and a hook motion of her hand that she should go out the front door and meet her in the alley.

Nora is only twelve, and as she speaks, she keeps her eyes on the ground. "Mrs. Mickel told me to tell you," she says, "that she is sorry, but she will no longer be able to serve you in her store." After a moment of silence, the girl looks up with her almost-Oriental, coffee-brown eyes. "I'm sure she doesn't mean it," she says. A nervous smile flashes across her face, and then a wince of sorrow and shame.

Sally Hemings's only response to the message is to ask whether Nora thinks it would be possible to make her way to Market Street via mewses and alleys.

"I'm afraid I wouldn't know, miss," says the girl, and Sally Hemings decides to give it a try.

There is nothing in her head. Nothing in her heart. She walks because she has nothing to do. Sometimes she turns in a circle, like a leaf in a breeze, watching a sky full of clouds swirl around her head. Sometimes the yellow fields, buzzing with cicadas, seem to rise and fall as she breathes. We pity her. She thinks her fancies are her real, true life. She thinks she is free. We know that nothing good is ever given, only taken. We know that a master's promises are equal to a snake's hiss. We know that forgiveness is surrender and that the road to freedom runs through hate.

It is normal for Thomas Jefferson to have up to twenty visitors a day when he is at Monticello, but ever since the publication of Callender's articles, his visitors have numbered fifty or more, with many of them not actually wanting formal audiences but only to spot "the African Venus" and "Tom," her supposed child. Every time Sally Hemings steps out of her cabin or the great house, she sees at least one person looking at her, sometimes two or three and, once, a small crowd. So far no one has actually approached or called out to her, but often people point or whisper into one another's ear, and she worries that it is only a matter of time before she is accosted once more, as she was in Charlottesville, or that something worse will happen to her or her children.

When there is no letup in the number of visitors after a week, Thomas Jefferson decides to send Sally Hemings to Poplar Forest, the most distant of his plantations, eighty-three miles southwest of Monticello. He tells her that she will be "more comfortable" there while the scandal is still raging. Not only do very few people know that he owns the property, it is practically on the frontier. Nobody there has much interest in Federalist newspapers, or in any other form of printed matter, so she is far less likely to be troubled by curiosity seekers.

She leaves the following morning, as soon as there is enough light for Tom Shackelford to see the road. In her arms she holds sixteen-month-old Harriet. And seated at her side is nine-year-old Evelina, Harriet's "nurse." Beverly has stayed behind with his grandmother. The journey takes three days. They spend the first night lying on a tarpaulin underneath the carriage and the second in the servants' quarters behind Flood's tavern in Appomattox. They arrive at Poplar Forest just before sundown, and Tom Shackelford heads back to Monticello before the sun has risen the following morning.

There is no great house at Poplar Forest, only the former steward's cottage, built half a century earlier by Thomas Jefferson's father-in-law when the plantation was an acre of stumps in an interminable forest at the edge of the known world. The present steward, Mr. Chambliss, built himself a brick house on a small rise, from which he can survey most of the plantation, and so the original house, unoccupied eleven or more months out of the year, is neglected and moldering. Its roof leaks, and many of its clapboards, especially on the southern side, are paintless and weathered gray. Thomas Jefferson recently had the inside painted teal, sage green and liver pink, but the furnishings are all boxy and rough-hewn—built by farmers rather than a joiner. The whole house smells of termites and mice, and the sheets on the beds feel moist against the skin and have the acrid tang of mildew.

There are no servants living in the house, but Mr. Chambliss sends his cook, Mag, in the mornings to make dinner, portions of which Sally Hemings saves for that night's supper and the following morning's breakfast. Every couple of days, Jemma comes to dust and otherwise make sure the house is, as she puts it, "in fine shape for Mr. Jefferson"—which phrase is only one of the many ways by which she expresses her resentment at having to serve Sally Hemings and her daughter (though not Evelina) as if they were white. Mag feels the same way, as do all of the other Negroes with whom Sally Hemings comes into contact at Poplar Forest. The worst are the field laborers, who never speak to her when she encounters them on her walks but only cast her sullen gazes and seem to be awaiting with a preternatural patience for the first opportunity to take revenge upon her for her privilege. She is lonely most of the day and frightened all of the night. Every creak and thump in the darkness sends her bolt upright in bed, her whole body trilling with the cold electricity of fear.

She has met Mr. Chambliss several times at Monticello, where he struck her merely as bland and unintelligent, and embarrassingly deferential to Thomas Jefferson. Here, however, he is not the least bit deferential, but self-possessed to the point of being imperious. His every motion seems calculated, and his expressions emerge only gradually on his face, as if they are rising from primordial depths. He smiles a lot, but with his eyes averted, and he seems always to be in the process of executing some secret plan that he believes is going exceptionally well. He is unfailingly polite in a superficial sense—he even addresses her as "Mrs." Hemings—but every now and then she catches him looking at her, and she can see in his eyes not only that he has mentally removed every stitch of clothing from her body but that he wants her to know he is relishing everything he sees.

The servants and laborers never meet his eye when he gives orders but listen with their heads bent and don't even glance at his back when he walks away. They do exchange weighty glances with one another, however, and they sometimes lift their eyes to Sally Hemings. Then they just do what they were told.

On their second day at Poplar Forest, when she and the children take a shortcut behind the barns on their way to a duck pond, she spots a post with a rope lashed around it just about as high as a man might reach, with the two lengths of the rope dangling down about a yard on one side of the post. They are twisted and kinked in a way that indicates they have been knotted many times. The lower half of the post is stained a brownish black with what can only be blood. As soon as she understands what, in fact, this post is, she picks up toddling Harriet and grabs Evelina by the hand. "Where are we going?" the older girl says in surprise. "I forgot something," says Sally Hemings. "We have to go back. I have to get something." Once they are all in the house, she slams and locks the door and tells Evelina that she is too tired to go to the pond. Maybe they will go another day.

S he walks. We watch her from the fields, our hands salty, yellowed and stinging from tobacco leaves. We watch her as we swing picks along the road. She walks because she has nothing to do. She holds down her straw hat against the wind, so that she might preserve her precious whiteness. Her step is light. She sings. She is a bauble. She believes that she lives outside the world created by the cowskin, but nothing she believes is true.

In this world—our world—everything is simple. The cowskin is our Devil. The cowskin uses our fear to teach us helplessness. The cowskin uses our rage to teach us silence. It eats our souls as it eats our flesh. It blends our sweat with our tears and causes our blood to run in rivers. And yet it gives us a justice unknown to the white man. It teaches us that in a world of evil, the evil in our hearts is innocence. It tells us that we are angels because we live in hell. We are beatified by pain. We are beatified by hate. Hate is our hope. Even as our lives drip into the dust, we have entered the Promised Land.

It astounds Sally Hemings that Thomas Jefferson could ever imagine that she might be "more comfortable" under the sway of Mr. Chambliss. Sometimes she thinks this just another instance of how incompletely he comprehends the facts of his own existence. He cannot find his spectacles even when they are resting on top of his own head. He can pick up a cup of coffee that has sat on his desk for an hour or more and be genuinely perplexed that it is cold. It has often seemed to her that Thomas Jefferson's brain is so labyrinthine that ordinary human understanding simply gets lost in it.

Yet with every day she spends at Poplar Forest, she asks herself more frequently if the comfort he was talking about was not hers at all but only his own.

As soon as she returned from her awful trip to Charlottesville, she asked Thomas Jefferson to show her the newspaper articles about him and her. "They're just a lot of nonsense," he told her. "There's no need to trouble yourself over them."

"Don't I have a right to see what's been said about me?"

His lips crumpled dubiously. "Really. There's no need."

"You've read them," she said. "So why shouldn't I?"

For a moment he seemed about to argue. Then he just shrugged and pulled a thick handful of newspapers from a drawer in his desk. "You can burn these when you're done with them," he said. "Better yet, tear them up and put them in the privies."

From the newspapers she learned all the nasty and absurd things that had been said about her (among which was a cruel poem by John Quincy Adams, who, like his father had been so kind to her when she was in London), but she also learned that people were saying much more cruel things about Thomas Jefferson. He was being called a disgrace to the nation, an offense to public decency and a traitor to his race; people said that he should be impeached, tarred and feathered, driven out of Washington or locked in the madhouse at Williamsburg.

"I'm sorry to have caused you so much trouble," she said, flinging the last of the newspapers onto the table. When he only met her words with the buckled brows of incomprehension, she added in a more neutral voice, "How are you going to deal with all this?"

He puffed his lips disdainfully. "It's nothing. It will pass."

"Are you sure?" she asked. It was impossible for her to believe that such threats—and the outrage that inspired them—would not cause him considerable political damage, to the point where he might have to retire from the presidency. The outrage in some of the editorials and letters was so ferocious that she could imagine one of his enraged critics challenging him to a duel, or even just shooting him in the street. He had already received death threats, after all, and even had to travel around Washington with an armed guard for a whole week the previous April. Why should Callender's articles not inspire more of such murderous intentions?

"I'm not going to worry until I have reason." He smiled wryly and flicked his hand as if chasing away a fly. But then he became thoughtful. "We shall see what transpires."

The next day he told her about his plan to make her "more comfortable." He also told her that he, too, needed "a little peace and relaxation" before returning to Washington and so would be joining her after five days.

The prospect of soon having Thomas Jefferson at her side has been her one consolation during all her loneliness and anxiety at Poplar Forest. She waits for him in happy agitation the whole of the fifth day. But by nightfall he still hasn't arrived, nor does he arrive the next day or the one after, and he sends her no word of explanation. As time passes, she finds herself increasingly defenseless against her worst fantasies: that Thomas Jefferson sent her to this foul and frightening place not just to hide her away but to get rid of her once and for all; or that Mr. Chambliss has already received instructions to set her to work in the field, where she, too, might become stooped and glowering and possessed of only one hope: revenge; or that Thomas Jefferson simply told Mr. Chambliss to sell her to whoever would be willing to pay for her; or that he should feel free to use her however he pleases.

Such grim possibilities come to her at all hours of the day, but she is generally able to quell them by devoting herself to little Harriet or by reading (she brought half a dozen books with her from Monticello, including Locke's *Conduct of the Mind* and a translation of Fénelon's *Adventures of*

Telemachus). But in the night her fantasies arrive as implacable certainty, and she waits, sweat-glossed and with a pounding heart, for the door to fly open and for Mr. Chambliss to drag her screaming down the stairs and shackle her into the back of a wagon that will take her away from everything she loves and all that she has ever known.

Of all the damsels on the green,
On mountain, or in valley,
A lass so luscious ne'er was seen,
As Monticellian Sally.

Yankee Doodle, who's the noodle?
What wife were half so handy?
To breed a flock of slaves for stock,
A blackamoor's the dandy.

—John Quincy Adams

S he dances on a dust cloud, believing herself outside the evil. We pity
her. She whirls, hand atop her head, believing she escapes black by
being white and white by being black. But there is no escape, and nothing outside the evil. Not one thing. The white people know this—the
real white people—but they know it only in secret. They know it in their
nightmares and in their never-ending fear. They know it in their belief
that all men are born evil and that only the cowskin makes them good.
And the gun. And the jail cell. They know it in the cowskin's bitter whistle and in the snap of splitting flesh. And they know it most of all in their
churches, where love-your-enemy incinerates in hellfire.

I t is the fourth day after the one on which Thomas Jefferson promised to arrive, and Sally Hemings is alone among trees. Sunbeams angle between slender branches and long trunks, and the air is cool and still where she walks—though from time to time there is a seething in the treetops. *This is good,* she tells herself. *This is helping.* Being immersed in the beautiful and the familiar is giving her a measure of hope. And strength.

She has been walking for half an hour and will walk an hour more. She left the house in a frenzy of anger and shame, afraid of how close she had come to doing something horrific.

Harriet had awakened, crying plaintively, every ten minutes all night. She would suckle herself back to sleep but would continue to twitch and grimace and groan, until finally her crying would start all over again. Her clout had to be changed three times during the night. The first time Sally Hemings got Evelina to do it, but after midnight it was more trouble to wake the girl than to change the clouts herself. It was only just before dawn that Harriet finally sank into a sound sleep, but by that time Sally Hemings was hot-eyed, with humming nerves and an endless stream of ghastly and sordid realizations flooding her mind.

Harriet slept later than usual but was awake by eight, and thereafter the day was the same as the night: She would suckle without being satisfied and refused to swallow even a mouthful of solid food. Over and over she would fill her clout with watery muck, which, more often than not, would leak onto the floor or the bed or wherever she happened to be sitting or lying, including, one time, Sally Hemings's lap. Angry red pimples came up on the delicate folds between her legs—but she only shrieked when her mother tried to salve them with melted butter.

While Evelina was outside washing the soiled clouts, Sally Hemings paced between the parlor and the dining room, rocking her little girl in her arms, singing to her, kissing her, stopping every now and then to see if she would eat from bowl or breast—but nothing helped. And then there came a moment when yet another image of her daughter being ripped from her arms flashed into Sally Hemings's mind, but this time, instead of paralytic despair, the image filled her with such terrific rage at the relentless cruelty and injustice of this life that it seemed to her there was no purpose in living, that all the care and work she lavished on her daughter was a sham and that, in fact, the greatest service she could do the little girl would be to smash her skull against the stone fireplace—and as this notion came to seem not a mere supposition but an active impulse taking control of her arms and hands and heart, Sally Hemings burst sobbing out the door, her baby in her arms. She ran around the side of the house to where Evelina was hanging the newly washed clouts on a clothesline. "I am an awful mother!" she said, thrusting Harriet into the girl's arms, saying, "I have to go. I'll be back. But I have to go—now!"

She strode away from the house along the wooded bank of the stream where Evelina had been doing her washing. She passed between several fields, in one of which she could just make out the bent backs and the rough, sad songs of the laborers. When, at last, the stream turned south-ward along the edge of a wooded bluff, she clambered to the top and entered an old-growth forest where, beneath stout and lofty maples, beeches and oaks, the passage was relatively easy.

This is where she has been walking for half an hour. This is where she has heard the wind seething in the treetops and the cries of birds and where she has begun to feel that the worst of her fears about Thomas Jefferson are exactly as unsupported by fact as the most tender of her hopes. She knows *nothing*, neither good nor bad. *Nothing at all.* And so, for the time being at least, her inescapable ignorance seems to be her only problem, the one that she must struggle with and learn how to manage.

Eventually she comes to a trail leading more or less in the direction she has already been going: west, she thinks, toward the unmapped wilderness beyond everything she has ever heard of. The trail is narrow but well trodden. She can feel how it has been worn into the forest floor by centuries of foot traffic, even in those places where it is beginning to be overgrown. This must be an Indian trail, she thinks, here since creation. If she follows it long enough, perhaps she will come to an Indian village, or to a whole country of Indians, where there are no white people at all and no colored. Maybe that would be a better place for her and her children. Maybe that would be a place where they might belong.

She is just beginning to worry about having spent so much time away from Harriet—an hour at least—when there is a furious hissing in the uppermost leaves, the tall boughs around her begin to creak and groan and a current of dank air cools her cheeks and presses her gown against her body. It is still sunny straight overhead, but in the direction she is walking, a part of the sky has gone storm dark.

She wheels around and hurries back down the path, hoping that the sky will be slow in turning, that maybe only clouds will come or that, at the very least, the rain will hold off until she has reached the house. But the sunbeams have already withdrawn from the trees. The winds grow ever more fierce. The light dims, grows dusk gray, then a strangely luminous green. All at once there is a fierce rattling at the tops of the trees, and then huge drops begin to strike her shoulders, cheeks and hands.

The problem is that Sally Hemings did not take note of the place where she turned onto the trail and thus doesn't know where she ought to leave it so that she might make her way to the crest of the bluff and then home along the stream. When, at last, she strikes out on impulse into the trackless forest, she realizes after less than a minute that nothing around her is familiar, that she has no idea where she is going.

It is another two hours before, clothes frigid cold and hanging heavily off her body, she walks out of a field and onto the drive up to the house. For most of the last hour, she has been hoping that all of the cold, confusion and fear she has endured will be rewarded by the sight of Thomas Jefferson's landau at the house and Peter standing at the doorway under an umbrella, watching for her.

But of course there is no landau, no horses, no brother. The drive is a river through which she must splash up to her ankles to get into the house.

Once inside, though, she sees that Evelina has lit the lamps and managed to get a good fire going—in front of which she has draped a row of Harriet's clouts across a bench to dry. And the tiny girl herself is toddling toward her mother in nothing but a shirt, both arms upraised. "Mammy! Mammy! Mammy!"

Wet as she is, Sally Hemings scoops her daughter into her arms and covers her with kisses, the little girl's giggles escalating from throaty glugs to breathless clicks and cackles. As she carries Harriet toward the fire, the child tugs at the neck of her gown, and so Sally Hemings undoes her bodice and slips her cold, wet nipple into her daughter's warm and hungry mouth.

We pity her because she believes in the virtue of white people. Or because she wants to believe. Or because she is lying to herself and she doesn't know she is lying. Or because she is lying to the world and she thinks that she is better than everyone in it. Or because she has become blind to insults and indignity and has learned to celebrate small kindnesses. Or because she worries that she is actually as incompetent and hideous and stupid as her master believes she is. Or because she, too, believes what her master believes. Or because she believes that she is white even though her master treats her as if she is black. Or because she believes that she is better than black even if she is not as good as white. Or because she has learned to feel cuffs as kisses and hear insults as sweet nothings. Or because she believes she is evil and so deserves her enslavement. Or her punishment. Or because she believes that, having turned her back on her people, she is undeserving of forgiveness. And we pity her even if she is right to believe she cannot be forgiven. We pity her because whatever she may think or feel or have done, she is one of us—a Negro and a human being. We pity her because she has become a stranger to herself, because she has lost her soul.

Hours later Sally Hemings is awakened from a deep sleep by the sound of someone moving downstairs. She slides out of the bed where Harriet and Evelina are both filling the air with their rustling snores and picks up the broken table leg she placed in the corner days ago for use as a weapon.

As she feels her way along the edge of the bed, through the darkness, toward the door, she can hear almost nothing above the urgent thudding of her own heart, and there is a moment during which she imagines that there is no one in the house, that she only dreamed those sounds or that they were only the product of old wood shrinking as it cools. But then she hears the curt rumble of a male grunt and the sound of something heavy hitting the floor, followed by the light tread of what is clearly a boot-shod foot.

She pushes her door against its jamb, so that she might lift the latch silently, but as she pulls the door open, a hinge squeaks and silence falls at the bottom of the stairs. She freezes for a long moment. There is another thump, followed by footsteps moving rapidly across the parlor and into the dining room. As she crosses to the top of the stairs, she sees an ocher luminosity wavering on the wall in the entryway.

Now her heart thuds with a different sort of urgency, because she has recognized the rhythm of the movements below and, more particularly, the man's breathing. She is halfway down the stairs when the shadows of the balusters loom and then swing rapidly across the wall. Thomas Jefferson catches sight of her just as he puts his hand on the banister. He lifts his candle so that he might see her more clearly, then smiles and speaks in a voiced whisper, "I hope I haven't disturbed you."

Sally Hemings shakes her head. She takes a step back upstairs, but he scoops the air rapidly with his hand, indicating that she should come down.

As she descends, he sets his candle on a step, takes off his cape and holds it out to her. "What's that?" he says, looking at her right hand.

She lifts the broken table leg and smirks. "I thought you were Mr. Chambliss. I was going to hit you on the head with it."

"Sounds like you don't much care for Mr. Chambliss," says Thomas Jefferson.

"I hate him!" The force of feeling in her own voice surprises her. "He's a very bad man. You should dismiss him."

"Here." He is still holding out his cape.

She leans the table leg against the wall and takes the cape, which is warm from his body and redolent of his familiar smell. She drapes the cape over her shoulders and draws it tight across her breast. Her feet are freezing.

"Come," says Thomas Jefferson. "Peter has gone to get some wood."

She follows him over to the parlor fireplace, where the coals of their evening's fire are still winking and making tiny clicks. She steps right onto the brick apron to warm her feet.

Thomas Jefferson is crouching over one of his bags, and just as he stands and holds up a bottle of cognac, Peter comes into the room with an armful of firewood.

"Sally!" he says, lowering the pile to the floor. He steps over to her, touches her hand and smiles in a way that promises his real greeting will come later.

Sally Hemings finds herself moved almost to tears at seeing her brother again. She has to swallow before, speaking to Thomas Jefferson but looking at her brother, she asks, "Why were you so delayed? You were supposed to have been here on Monday."

Peter's expression conveys both embarrassment and concern.

"I'm sorry," says Thomas Jefferson.

She looks at him coldly. She does not want to hear his apologies.

"To begin with," he says, "we were delayed a day because I had some business to attend to with Mr. Madison in Belle Grove."

"You should have sent a message, then."

"Yes, I suppose I should have. But I thought we would make up the lost time on the road."

Peter, who has begun placing logs on the bed of coals, grunts ironically.

"We've had something of an ordeal, Peter, haven't we?"

"Oh, yes indeed!" he says. "The gods were against us the whole way!" Peter gives her an entreating smile. Then he crouches and blows on the coals beneath the logs. Flames leap up almost instantly.

"The worst thing was that we lost a wheel in Findlay's Gap, and that cost us another day and a half. Then we got caught in a terrible downpour this afternoon, after which the roads were so muddy and flooded that we almost gave up and stopped at New London. But we both wanted to be here so badly that we decided to just keep on going by moonlight. We've been riding since sunup." He puts the bottle of cognac down with a firm smack on a table beside the fireplace. "Which is why we are so in need of a glass of this!"

"But you still should have told me you would be delayed, right at the beginning, when you knew you would have to stay longer with Mr. Madison."

Thomas Jefferson is at the sideboard, where he has gone to get glasses. "I'm sorry," he says again. "I never expected that it would take this long."

Sally Hemings doesn't respond. Peter, standing up and dusting off his hands, gives her a significant glance.

Thomas Jefferson opens the bottle and pours three glasses.

Peter finishes his in a gulp. "I need to go settle the horses."

Sally Hemings takes a sip from her glass. She is very tired. She should go back to bed. But instead she draws a chair closer to the fire and sits down with her feet tucked under her. She takes another sip from her glass and watches the flames leap and vanish against the black fieldstone.

Thomas Jefferson also pulls a chair up to the fire and sits. Out of the corner of her eye, Sally Hemings can see him lift his glass, but she doesn't look at him.

"What's the matter, Sally?" he says as he lowers his glass.

"I told you, Mr. Chambliss is a cruel and evil man."

"He's always struck me as an exceedingly stupid man."

"He's much worse than that," says Sally Hemings. "He should be dismissed. He should never have been hired."

"Let's talk about that in the morning."

Thomas Jefferson finishes his glass and pours himself another. He holds out the bottle toward Sally Hemings. First she shakes her head, then extends her glass to let him top it up. She takes another sip.

"You're upset." He gives her a sympathetic glance.

She holds his gaze for a moment, then turns to the fire. "I don't want to talk about it."

He leans toward her, resting his elbows on his knees, hands wrapped around his glass. "I am truly sorry. I know I should have written."

"You don't know anything!" The words come out in a ripping whisper.

Thomas Jefferson looks both hurt and confused.

She takes a big sip from her glass, then takes another, emptying it. She puts it on the floor beside her chair.

"I thought you weren't going to come," she says.

"Why would you think that?" He shakes his head, incredulous. "Of course I was coming! Why wouldn't I come?"

"I thought you only sent me here to get rid of me!"

"Oh, Sally!" He puts down his glass and comes over to her chair. He crouches on one knee and reaches for her hand, but she pulls it away. "Why would I want to do that?"

"Because of what people are saying in the papers. Because if you don't get rid of me, they'll force you out of office."

"Oh, no! Oh, no! You poor girl!" He reaches for her hand again, and this time she lets him take it. "It's nothing like that! Not at all! I don't have to be afraid of these people. They're all fools, and everyone knows it—even their allies. You don't have to worry." He strokes the top of her hand. "Really, there is nothing to worry about."

With his back to the flickering firelight, she can hardly see his face.

"And besides," he says, "if you want to know the absolute truth, I am already sick of Washington, and I am sick of the presidency. I could walk away from it in a minute if I had to. I am willing to give my country my sweat and my time. I am willing to make every effort to do what I think needs doing. But I am not going to surrender my soul."

It is when he says these last words that Sally Hemings begins to cry. Thomas Jefferson pulls her into his arms, squeezes her hard. And kisses the top of her head.

"Don't worry, Sally Girl. Nothing bad is going to happen. You'll see. Everything will be fine. We'll enjoy ourselves here for a few days, and then we'll go home."

Thomas Jefferson has no idea what Sally Hemings's life is actually like. He thinks her tears are only feminine weakness, and so his consolations mean nothing at all. And yet she can't stop crying.

She lets him pull her close. She lets him lift her to her feet. She puts her arms around him and kisses his neck and cheek and mouth. She feels the strength in his arms across her back, and she feels the strength of his back beneath her hands. She knows that it would be easy for him to lift her into the air. She squeezes him hard and lifts both feet up behind her—and then it is happening: He is holding her in the air as if it were nothing at all.

Dusk dissolves into midnight and midnight dissolves into dawn and Thomas Jefferson is still walking after having fled James Madison's library in a state of delirious perplexity. In fact, he doesn't feel as if he is walking. His progress along roads and even up very steep slopes has become a sort of drifting, as effortless as thought. From a hilltop, he looks out across a green and golden valley in which the improvements of man seem entirely harmonious with the rhythms and proportions of nature. The road along which he is walking, for example, arcs down into the valley and crosses it in a perfect S, with the bottom, or near, part of the S seeming exactly double the size of the top, or far, part, although he is certain that, seen from above, both arcs are equal. And as the road undulates up the far side of the valley, the angles of its incline correspond so exactly to the angle of the hilltop against the sky that they seem the very image of the hilltop's angle and of its inverse. And so, in this valley glinting with dew under a new sun, we have those relationships between the parts and the whole and between the real and the ideal that constitute the highest form of beauty: that beauty which allows us to feel at one with the mind of God.

Who were the people who laid this road with such attention to its aesthetic and symbolic attributes? Why had he never heard of them? How could this beautiful valley exist so close to Belle Grove without Madison ever having showed it to him, or having mentioned one word about it? Could it be that Madison has never been here, that he knows nothing of this extraordinary place?

At the bottom of the valley there is a river, the flood plain of which is quilted with wheat and cornfields, pastures of clover, vineyards and orchards and gardens. And atop rises all across the valley are houses, humble and august, but all constructed according to the classical symmetries of Palladio—clearly the dwellings of a well-educated populace, who have profited from hard work, cooperation and the discoveries of modern agronomy.

As Thomas Jefferson descends into the valley, he is flattered to discover in a field by the side of the road his own invention—the mathematically perfect moldboard plow—hitched to a pair of fine ginger draft horses, their nostrils wide, their muscular haunches shivering with an eagerness to do their work, though the farmer is nowhere in sight. And in the houses he comes to, he sees more of his own inventions: twenty-four-hour clocks, conveyances for ferrying food and drink through rotating doorways or up from basement kitchens, and studies outfitted with his own revolving book rack, his swivel chair and his modified polygraph, as well as with drawing boards, telescopes, barometers, measuring instruments of all kinds and, of course, libraries (every home he enters has its own library)—confirmations all of his supposition that the owners of these houses are inquisitive, hardworking and ceaselessly looking to understand and improve their world.

Yet the owners themselves are absent. In every farmhouse he enters, he hears nothing but his own footsteps and their echoes off the walls. At first he thinks some great celebration or monumental announcement must have drawn the entire population to a meetinghouse or to the village square, but then, as he tours home after home after home and notices not a single scratched floorboard, not a scuff on a wall or a stain on a carpet, not a child's hobbyhorse lying in a hallway, not a solitary dish unwashed or a bed unmade, he begins to wonder if it isn't that the inhabitants of these houses have gone away but that they have never arrived.

And it is the same even in the village, where the columned edifices of the municipal assembly and public school preside at either end of the central square, and where there are more newspaper offices than places of worship, and these latter include not just churches but the temples of Jews, Mohammedans, Hindoos, Buddhists and Jains, and there is not a single bank. Every one of these buildings is open and ready to accommodate the diverse needs of a thriving community, and yet none of them seems to have ever been profaned by a single human breath, apart from that of Thomas Jefferson himself.

It is not, of course, possible to do an emotional taxonomy of color—which is exactly why the idea appeals to Thomas Jefferson and why it might even be important. What he wants is to find a vacant apartment building—or, better yet, an abandoned hospital or asylum—and paint every room a different color and furnish each room with tables, chairs, beds and paintings all exactly the color of the walls, and there would be microphones hidden in every room, recording what people say as they pass in and out. And then this installation could have a second life in a gallery or a museum, where projected video images of the empty rooms would have sound tracks consisting of the words of the people who once passed through them. Or perhaps he could live as a different color every day for a year, dyeing his clothes and his skin and his hair that color, and then have someone follow him around with a video camera, documenting everything said to him by strangers and friends. Or maybe he could give strangers and friends sunglasses with lenses he would color himself, and ask them to spend a day seeing only that color, and then tell him what they did and thought and felt. Or he should put people in a dark room and project ambiguous colors on the wall—bluish green, purplish gray, yellowish orange—and ask them to name the color and then tell him a story, made up or remembered, lived, read or watched. And perhaps every one of these installations and conceptual pieces could have its ultimate life on a Web site, to which people from all over the world would be encouraged to add their own color-related musings and artworks. What he would love most is to have millions of people from all classes and all countries trying to define what cannot be defined and each having an experience of color that only he or she can have, and only once, and never again.

IX

XI

Of my father, Thomas Jefferson, I knew more of his domestic than his public life during his life time. It is only since his death that I have learned much of the latter, except that he was considered as a foremost man in the land, and held many important trusts, including that of President. I learned to read by inducing the white children to teach me the letters and something more; what else I know of books I have picked up here and there till now I can read and write. I was almost 21 1/2 years of age when my father died on the 4th of July, 1826.

About his own home he was the quietest of men. He was hardly ever known to get angry, though sometimes he was irritated when matters went wrong, but even then he hardly ever allowed himself to be made unhappy any great length of time. Unlike Washington he had but little taste or care for agricultural pursuits. He left matters pertaining to his plantations mostly with his stewards and overseers. He always had mechanics at work for him, such as carpenters, blacksmiths, shoemakers, coopers, &c. It was his mechanics he seemed mostly to direct, and in their operations he took great interest. Almost every day of his later years he might have been seen among them. He occupied much of the time in his office engaged in correspondence and reading and writing. His general temperament was smooth and even; he was very undemonstrative. He was uniformly kind to all about him. He was not in the habit of showing partiality or fatherly affection to us children. We were the only children of his by a slave woman. He was affectionate toward his white grandchildren, of whom he had fourteen, twelve of whom lived to manhood and womanhood.

—Madison Hemings
"Life Among the Lowly, No. 1"
Pike County (Ohio) *Republican*
March 13, 1873

Sally Hemings and Thomas Jefferson are dead. The world they inhabit is the world in which they lived, except that they are all alone and things don't seem connected in the usual way. The trees, for example, will be bare one instant, then lush and August green the next, and then outlined with snow, and then hung with whispering, copper-colored leaves. Or it will be a brilliant morning and then—in an instant—a star-crowded midnight. Or Sally Hemings and Thomas Jefferson will be smooth-cheeked and avid-eyed, then toothless and gray. Or they will be standing on the veranda, or in the kitchen, or on the lawn, or they will be strolling along the Rivanna, or amid meadows they don't quite recognize—all within instants or hours (it is impossible to be sure which). But mostly they will be lying side by side in bed. It will be dark. Or it will be that slow moment when dawn becomes a blue possibility around the edges of the window curtains.

"I am not sure I like being dead," says Sally Hemings.

Thomas Jefferson is silent a long time.

"I think I prefer it," he says.

"Why?"

"Because there is so much to wonder at, so much to see. This is all so beautiful." (They are in a rattling coach now, a procession of rust-orange mountains passing by its windows.) "And mysterious. Don't you think so? But also it is only itself, so we can lose ourselves in it utterly. That's the main thing, I think."

Now it is Sally Hemings's turn to be silent.

"I'm not sure I see what you mean," she says.

"If there is nothing to hope for, or dread, or plan for, or mourn, if nothing we do or say can have any consequences, then there is nothing for us to think about except each individual moment as it happens. In an odd way, we are more alive now than we ever were when we were living."

"But we are not alive. We are nothing. We are not actually even here."

"I am seeing," says Thomas Jefferson. "I am thinking. I am talking to you. So I am here."

"But if you can *do* nothing, if nothing you do has any effect on the world, then from the point of view of the world you *are* nothing. You don't exist."

"Yes. Exactly. That's what I enjoy most."

"How can you say that? You devoted your entire life to changing the world. That was what you lived for. That was who you really *were*. And now you can't be yourself anymore. There is no Thomas Jefferson. You are not him, and you never will be again."

At first Thomas Jefferson seems to have a ready counterargument. He opens his mouth to speak, but no sound comes out. At last he sighs. "Yes," he says. "That's true. I do regret that aspect of it. But even so—"

Sally Hemings cuts him off. "You say you are in the world, but the world has changed several times since we began talking. So which world are you in? Or are you in any world at all? And which world am I in, for that matter? If I am not in the same world as you, then you may be talking, but you are only talking *at* me, not *to* me or *with* me. It is even possible that you are not *with* me at all. I may be somewhere else."

"I am lying in bed with you," says Thomas Jefferson. "We are both entirely undressed, and you are as beautiful as you have ever been. I am leaning on my elbow, looking down into your eyes. My thigh is across your thigh, and my foot rests between your feet. In a moment, perhaps, we will make love. But now we are only talking, and we could hardly be more content."

Sally Hemings smiles, then sighs heavily.

"But what if we never make love?" she says. "Or what if we do make love but in the next instant everything changes and it turns out we have not made love at all? And what if it turns out that we have never said any of the things we are saying now and all of this never happened, even in our memories?"

"But now—in this solitary instant, at least—it *is* happening. Even if we never make love, now we are together in a moment in which we want to make love and in which we know that our lovemaking is imminent. This is a very good moment all by itself. Why should we need anything more?"

"But won't it be a loss if we never do make love? Or if, all at once, we have no memory of having made love? Or even of being together? Or if, in an instant, we mean as little to each other as two people separated by a thousand years and a thousand miles?"

"It will only be a loss," says Thomas Jefferson, "if we know what we have lost. And if we don't, then each moment is only itself. It is absolutely pure."

Account Book

1. While Thomas Jefferson was assiduous about listing all of his expenditures in his Memorandum Books, which he kept from the start of his law practice in 1767 until his death, he was far less assiduous about totaling up those expenditures against his income, and so, until very late in life, and despite having to pay off the occasional pressing loan from a bank, he operated on the assumption that he was a wealthy man, without serious financial worries.

2. At the time of his death, he was $107,000 in debt, which would amount to approximately $2.4 million in today's money. The majority of his debt was inherited from his father-in-law, John Wayles, who, like most southern plantation owners, had borrowed heavily from British banks and whose debt was unaffected by the Revolution.

3. In 1801 Thomas Jefferson's salary as president was $25,000, and he spent $33,636.44—including $3,100 for a new carriage and horses that he felt were suitable for the dignity of his new office, and $2,797.38 for wine.

4. In 1815, partially in an attempt to diminish his debt, he sold his collection of 6,847 books to the Library of Congress to replace the 3,000 books burned by the British during the War of 1812. He received $23,950.

5. In 1798 Tadeusz Kościuszko, a Polish general who served in the Continental Army during the American Revolution, drew up a will leaving Thomas Jefferson $20,000 to purchase the freedom of slaves (his own and others) and buy them land. The will was hotly contested by Kościuszko's Polish family when he died in 1817 (and, indeed, the family ultimately won their suit), but even had the money gone to Thomas Jefferson, it would have been only enough to free roughly thirty slaves, which would have meant a 23 percent cut in Monticello's labor force at a time when Thomas Jefferson already owed in excess of

$80,000—a state of affairs that may well have entered into his decision not to claim the bequest.

6. In 1818 Thomas Jefferson guaranteed a loan of $20,000 to Wilson Cary Nicholas, a former governor of Virginia, who subsequently defaulted on his debt, leaving Thomas Jefferson responsible for that money, too, the interest payments on which amounted to $1,200 per year.

Often they are bored, in the manner of misty rain under pale cloud light, or of after-dinner whist-table restlessness, or of a head cold that makes every possibility seem pointless and squalid. Other times Thomas Jefferson might come upon Sally Hemings, momentarily looking up from her sewing, her face in that lost vacancy that so often comes over it when she is thinking, and he will ache with such tenderness that he will want to sweep her into his arms and cover her neck with kisses, even though the ever-vigilant Martha is eyeing him ruefully from her chair by the fire. Or Sally Hemings will look away from him as a means of controlling her trembling rage as he tells her yet again that the world will not allow him to love her openly and therefore that she should not expect him to show his love, and finally she will turn to him and say, "What makes you think I even want your love, Mr. Jefferson?" Or he will say, "How I wish that we could marry!" and she will put her hand on top of his and say, "Don't," or she will say, "But we *are* married!" and then feel a knot of humiliation in her chest. Or they will be walking beside a lake on an autumn morning and, with a sound like a gigantic sigh, a great blue heron will lift out of the reeds and, gathering masses of air under its huge, wafting wings, it will arc above its own reflection, then soar over the tops of the trees, and she will cry out, "Oh, Tom, look! Isn't that so beautiful! Isn't that the most magnificent bird!" Or they will be naked together in the bed of the lodge, and they will be gasping, tasting each other's sweat, and each will pour through the body of the other like a wild river. Or she will be wound up tightly in the sheets, sulking, and he will be out on the porch with a headache, thinking of the farmer in Amherst who told him that when his slave mistresses get to be too much trouble, he just sells them cheap. Or she will be looking at his brown teeth, his folded neck, the vertical grooves in his cheeks, and she will be think, *This is an old body. This is a body that is wearing down, getting uglier every day.* Or she will be lying with her head on his shoulder, listening to the rumble inside his chest as he tells her about the letter he wrote that morning to Napoleon, and she will be thinking, *How is it possible that this man was just inside my body, this man who will never be forgotten as long as there are men and women walking this earth?*

But mostly this will be their life together:

She will pour him a glass of water and then pour one for herself, and then their throats will make glugging clicks while they both drink deeply, and when at last they take the glasses away from their mouths, they will both make crisp, satisfied sighs. Or they will both be reading on the porch, and she will be aware of the loud flap every time he turns a page, which sometimes will annoy her, other times not at all. Or seated diagonally across the table, he will tell her again, between bites, that he has little taste for lamb, and she will tell him again that lamb is her favorite among meats. Or they will be sitting on the slanted rock on the edge of the Rivanna. She will dive in and a moment later he will follow, and when their heads rise above the surface, they will already be several yards downstream, and they will continue to slide between the wooded riverbanks as they chat, trade splashes, swim.

I was born . . . at Monticello, Jefferson's beautiful Virginia home, on June 6, 1815, just before Waterloo. Jefferson was an ideal master. He was a democrat in practice as well as theory, was opposed to the slave trade, tried to keep it out of the Territories beyond the Ohio river and was in favor of freeing the slaves in Virginia. In 1787 he introduced that famous "Jefferson proviso" in Congress, prohibiting slavery in all the Northwestern Territory, comprising the States of Ohio, Indiana, Illinois and Missouri. He had made all arrangements to free his slaves at his death by making three prizes of his property, &c.

—The Reverend Peter Fossett
"Once the Slave of Thomas Jefferson"
New York Sunday World
January 30, 1898

It is 1809, and the world is white, particulate, hurtling and loud. First Thomas Jefferson cannot feel his fingertips, then his feet fade away, and then the outside of his right leg. His lead horse leaves bloody tracks in the snow.

He has a boiled egg and two glasses of cider at the posthouse while his horses are being changed. The hostler stamps the snow off his boots, scattering white chunks across the gray floorboards. "Everything's ready, Your Excellency."

"No," says Thomas Jefferson. "Don't call me that."

"Sorry," says the hostler, his nose claret red, his cheeks the unsteady red of a not-quite-ripe peach. After half a breath's hesitation, he adds, "President Jefferson," and lowers his head.

Thomas Jefferson is not the president either. Not anymore. He will never return to Washington. One last swallow. The tankard comes down on the hacked tabletop with a satisfying bang. He thanks the hostler and the innkeeper.

The hostler follows Thomas Jefferson outside and watches from the porch as he is taken apart by the hurtling snow. The harness clinks, the muffled thumps of eight hooves grow ever quieter. Thomas Jefferson diminishes. Grays. His body fragments. And between the fragments is a fierce gray-white. The fragments whirl away. Vanish. First one. Then another. Then another and another. Then dozens at once. Finally there is nothing left but that gray snow, which is only white snow in the shadows of the numberless flakes hurtling sideways between the earth and that clean, clear emptiness above the clouds.

Account Book

1. After having refused to pursue Tadeusz Kościuszko's bequest of $20,000 to buy his slaves freedom, Thomas Jefferson, desperate to pay off some of his debt, sold a large number of them to Francis Eppes, his daughter Maria's only surviving child, for $3,500—an arrangement that kept the slaves within his own family and the slave families relatively intact.

2. On February 20, 1826, the Virginia state legislature agreed to allow Thomas Jefferson to pay his debts by disposing of most of his land and buildings—the Monticello great house excluded—through a lottery, which he expected would bring him $112,500. The plan was put aside when a committee of New Yorkers convinced his grandson, Jefferson Randolph, that more money could be raised through contributions from wealthy patriots throughout the country. Unfortunately, this effort returned only $16,500, though Thomas Jefferson never learned of this fact, and went to his grave believing that his grandson's efforts to save the plantation had been successful.

3. After Thomas Jefferson's death, Jeff Randolph attempted to hold the lottery after all, but people were far less interested in helping the Jefferson family than in helping Thomas Jefferson himself, and so the effort failed, leaving the family only one alternative.

4. On November 3, 1826, Jeff Randolph placed the following advertisement in local newspapers:

EXECUTOR'S SALE

Will be sold on the premises, on the first day of January, 1827, that well known and valuable estate called Poplar Forest, lying in the counties of Bedford and Campbell, the property of Thomas Jefferson, dec. within eight miles of Lynchburg and three of New London; also about 70 likely and valuable negroes, with stock, crops, &c. The terms of the sale will be accommodating and made known previous to the day.

On the fifteenth of January, at Monticello, in the county of Albemarle; the whole of the residue of the personal property of Thomas Jefferson, dec., consisting of 130 valuable negroes, stock, crop, &c. household and kitchen furniture. The attention of the public is earnestly invited to this property. The negroes are believed to be the most valuable for their number ever offered at one time in the State of Virginia. . . .

. . . Joey touched my shoulder and said, "Aunt Sally," his voice an urgent whisper. I turned around and saw a man walking toward the stable with two sets of shackles, one in his hand, the other draped over his shoulder. Two other men walked behind him. One of them had an antique musket slung through the crook of his arm; the other carried a coiled cowskin in his hand and had a pistol in his belt.

The sun had barely risen, and we were standing in front of the solitary open stable door. The opposite door had been nailed shut and was fortified by having a wagon backed against it. The wagon was also to serve as the auction platform, and Mr. Broomfield, the auctioneer, was standing on it issuing instructions concerning the arrangement of crates into a sort of staircase to make ascent and descent more expeditious. A rough fence, with a gate only wide enough to allow the passage of one person at a time, had been built inside the open stable door. And behind that fence stood all the good people whom I had known since they or I were born. A couple of babies were crying, but most everyone else was silent or murmuring in the lowest of voices. Even the children were silent, clutching at their mothers' skirts or standing alone, eyes wide in infantile astonishment, hugging themselves against the cold.

An acrid tang, such as I had never smelled outside of a slaughterhouse, hung densely in the dim air inside the stable. Even before I fully apprehended the nature of that odor, I became wild with the desire to flee—not out of any fear for my person but simply because I knew that the world was about to be revealed to me as a miasma of agony and shame. Yet I could not, for I had promised Joey that I would stand by him—dear Joey, whom I had thought of as my own child during the years after his mother, my sister Mary, was sold to her husband, Colonel Thomas Bell. Joey and I were among the handful whom Mr. Jefferson had chosen to free—as were my own two boys, who were in Charlottesville with Joey's mother, looking for a house in which they and I might live. Of my immediate family, only Critta and Peter were to be sold, but Miss Maria's son had solemnly promised that he would buy and free Critta, and Danny Farley (who was Joey's brother and who had already bought his own freedom) agreed to do the same for Peter. Joey had returned from Charlottesville only an hour earlier, having received similar promises regarding his wife and nine children, and he had come to the stable door to give his family the news, as well as a parcel of oatcakes made by Mary.

And so I stood my ground, though it might be better to say I swayed upon it, for my mind was aswirl with such a diversity of passions and worries that I had to clutch at Joey's hard shoulder to keep from falling.

Mr. Jeff was walking toward the man with the shackles. "Good morning, gentlemen," he said. Not two minutes previously, he had been standing beside Joey and me, telling the crowd inside the stable that although he had gotten bids from Georgia farmers, he would not allow "my people" to go to anyone but "good Virginians." And now here he was, walking toward these grim and unwashed men—"good Virginians" presumably, whose virtue was exemplified by the shackles, guns and whip they carried.

"Welcome!" he said. "Welcome!" And in a voice that couldn't have been more amiable were he speaking to dearest friends, he told them that the "viewing" wouldn't begin for another hour but that they should feel free to look around the house, the entire contents of which would be put up for sale in the coming days.

It is happening, I thought as I watched this scene. Nothing can stop it now. And yet, despite these asseverations, I simply could not believe that Mr. Jeff, who had always seemed the quintessence of decency and good cheer, should be a party to this impending monstrosity. As Mr. Jefferson reached the extreme of his old age, he had become far less active in the affairs of his plantation, with the result that his overseers had been exercising more and more control, and many of them had been unable to suppress their intrinsic cruelty. On being installed as steward by his grandfather, Mr. Jeff had dismissed the most abusive overseers and encouraged the remainder to exercise a policy of fairness and restraint. Cruelty was not banished from the plantation. In fact, Mr. Jeff himself had presided over a thrashing, but life definitely became easier for all the slaves. And so when word got around about how deeply Mr. Jefferson was in debt, most people believed that Mr. Jeff would find a way to discharge that debt with minimal pain. I had myself. There was even talk that he had come up with a scheme whereby enough money might be raised through a lottery to enable Mr. Jefferson to free all of his slaves upon his death. But absolutely no one had ever imagined that Monticello would simply cease to exist. So here we all were, staggering in disbelief and terror, and here was our supposed savior in congenial conversation with two men sure to bring misery to any number of us.

After his first glance, Joey had turned his back on Mr. Jeff and the men and was calling out to his wife, who was not visible in the central part of the stable and must have been huddling in one of the stalls to keep warm. Hearing no reply, he called again and again, "Edy! Edy! Edy!," his voice growing ever more worried and shrill.

Joey's anxiety seemed to awaken the fear in the stable. Children began to cry. A woman called out, "Please, Jesus!"—it was Evelina, who had cared for my Beverly and Harriet when they were babies and who now had three young girls of her own. Her cry of despair was answered by others from around the room: "Help me, Lord!" "Precious Savior!" Slowly people began to emerge from the stalls and get up off of the benches, buckets and heaps of hay where they had been sitting, and crowd toward the fenced door.

"All right!" said Mr. Byrd, who, with Mr. Henderson, was standing guard outside the door—each of them holding a stout staff about five feet long. Mr. Jeff had stationed other overseers carrying firearms around the back and sides of the stable, so as not to "unduly disturb" the people inside with the sight of their weapons. "All right!" Mr. Byrd said again, putting his staff between Joey and the fence, as if to pry him away. "You best be going, Fossett."

"I've got to speak to my wife."

"You best be going," said Mr. Byrd. "We ain't got no time for such carrying-on."

"I've got to speak to her," said Joey. "Just let me speak to her!"

By now a crowd had gathered at the fence, and from the back of it Edy called, "I'm here, Joe! I'm here!"

Mr. Henderson banged his staff repeatedly against the stable door, waved with his other hand and shouted, "All right, everybody! Just you calm down! There's no cause for consternation. Just go back to where you was sitting!"

"Edy!" Joey called out.

"I asked you nicely," said Mr. Byrd, now brandishing his staff like a club.

"Please, Mr. Byrd," I said. "He only wants to comfort his wife and children."

"Let him speak!" called a firm male voice from the crowd inside the stable.

Mr. Henderson was now pounding on the door with his staff as if he wanted to break it down. "That's enough, now!"

"You see?" Mr. Byrd said. "Look at the trouble you started!" He jabbed Joey in the ribs. "You best get away now, or you gonna find yourself on the other side of that fence."

Joey didn't utter a sound but looked Mr. Byrd straight in the eyes, trembling with rage.

Mr. Byrd raised his staff high into the air, as if he were going to smash it down on Joey's head.

Without thinking, I grabbed the raised arm and cried, "Please! No!"

Mr. Byrd shoved me aside and shouted, "Out of my way, Miss Sally!" Then he swung the staff down hard on the frozen ground between Joey and me. "I don't care what Mr. Jefferson said! Or Mrs. Randolph! Or anybody! You cause trouble here, you gonna find yourself inside that fence!"

Hearing the commotion, a pair of overseers had come around from the right side of the stable—both carrying muskets—and a man with a blunderbuss was standing in front of Mr. Broomfield's wagon.

I was so filled with fury at that moment that I wanted to grab Mr. Byrd's staff right out of his hand. There were one hundred and twenty-six people inside that stable and only some ten armed men outside—including the men with the shackles. If all of those inside rushed that makeshift fence, they could have burst right through it. Certainly some of them would have been shot, but they had the white men so grossly outnumbered they could easily have overpowered them, taken their guns and headed off to freedom in the north. In my rage, nothing seemed simpler to me.

As I stood glaring at Mr. Byrd, the crowd quieted and Mr. Henderson stopped banging his staff against the wall. A voice called out from behind me, "I'm sorry, everybody."

It was Mr. Jeff, walking back from the men with shackles—who had their weapons at the ready and a grim eagerness in their eyes.

"I know how you feel," said Mr. Jeff, his voice unsteady with emotion. "I, too, wish that this day had never come. Mr. Jefferson and I did everything we could to prevent it, but we were defeated by the banks and by some very bad luck. And now that this terrible day is upon us, all that we can do is try to get through it in the best way possible. I know that nothing I can say will take away your worries and sorrow. And I am sorry about that. I promise you that I will do everything in my power to make sure you go to the very best masters possible. But the only way I'm going to be able to do that is if this auction proceeds in a calm and orderly fashion. If you show yourselves as the good people I know you are, then good people are going to want"—he fell silent a long moment before he finally swallowed and finished his sentence—"to take you home." He swallowed again. "I am sorry. I wish there was another way."

I was standing just behind Mr. Jeff, and I wanted to jab my fingernails into his pink neck. He had ceased being anyone I knew, let alone my own nephew and a man I had liked and respected. He was evil incarnate, and I wanted to drag him to the ground and stamp on his face.

I did nothing, of course.

Inside the stable a couple of women began to weep, but everyone else remained silent and still.

Over Mr. Jeff's shoulder, I saw a man named Moak Mobley standing at the back of the crowd. Just from the set of his shoulders and jaw, I knew that every muscle in his strong body was rigid with fury, and the same rigidity was in his eyes, which were looking directly at me. He was well within the shadows, but there was such ferocity in his gaze that his eyes seemed alight with white fire.

Mr. Mobley had done me a grave disservice many, many years ago, and in all the time since, I had scrupulously avoided being in his presence and had kept my head averted when our paths had happened to cross. But now I looked straight into his eyes and hoped that the intensity of my rage would be a match to his. I wanted him to know that I, too, despised the shameless duplicity of Jeff Randolph and of all his family, whose protestations of sympathy, sorrow and regret were simply their way of hiding their damnable guilt from themselves. I wanted Mr. Mobley to know that with every fiber of my heart I desired nothing more than for all Negro people to rise up as one and rid themselves of white tyranny. But the longer I looked into his eyes, the more I came to feel that he did not see me at all, that his rage was so ferocious it had blinded him and that I was nothing before his eyes but a vapor, a ghost, a last crumbling atom of a world obliterated by hate. . . .

J ust before Thomas Jefferson stepped into the subway car where he spotted Sally Hemings, he was standing on the platform furiously scribbling into his journal. "Our very perceptions are works of art," he wrote, "but also moral acts. This is because we are the ones who create the 'facts' we live by. Nothing we see, or hear, or believe is given to us by God, or is even real in any straightforward way. It is all our construction. All our responsibility. Therefore every perception, even the most fleeting, is a moment of truth, during which our souls are in peril. With every perception we create one particle of the world in which we live. As perception is added to perception, we forge the context in which we act, and therefore our perceptions dictate our acts, our morality, our selves, our souls. It is all our own doing. There is no one else to credit or blame. We wrestle, in every instant of our being, with perdition." The train was coming into the station as he scribbled the last words—so rapidly he wasn't sure he'd be able to read them when he opened his journal again. He slipped his pen into the journal's spiral binding. There was a roar. A wind struck his face. He flung his journal into his backpack. The train had stopped. He stepped into the car and sat down. Then he recognized those high cheekbones, those narrow cloud gray eyes, that stricken expression that was only her face at rest (she was reading) and that long arc along her rib cage to her pelvis, every inch of which he could still feel beneath his fingers. Then the car filled with the screeches of mechanical birds. She put her book under her arm and her fingers in her ears. Darkness.

Thomas Jefferson is out for a morning walk when he sees Beverly sitting on the nailery porch, his elbow on his knee, his head resting on his hand, the other hand poking at the dust with a stick. He is ten years old and seems entirely unaware of his father's approach or of anything other than the mark his stick is making in the dusty road.

Thomas Jefferson walks straight over to him and, planting his cane firmly between his own feet, calls out, "Good day, sir!"

Beverly lifts his head and, for half an instant, seems not to recognize the man he is looking at. "Good day," he says softly, his face the picture of melancholy.

"Is anything the matter?" Thomas Jefferson asks.

The boy shrugs.

"What have you been doing?" asks Thomas Jefferson.

"Nothing." He has made a line in the red dust, and now he crosses it. "Thinking."

"About what?"

"Nothing."

Thomas Jefferson does not know whether to be concerned or to reprimand the boy for his rudeness. In the end he says, "That doesn't sound very interesting."

"I was thinking about a lot of things." Beverly looks up again and squints his eye against the brilliance of the hazy sky. "Mostly I was thinking about why I can't fly."

Thomas Jefferson makes a bemused grunt and, clutching his cane with both hands, hunches over a bit to be closer to the boy. "Did you reach a conclusion?"

Beverly seems to think his father has just asked a very stupid question. "I don't have wings," he said.

"Would you like to have wings?"

"I was thinking about that, too."

"And?"

"Only if I could still have arms. I don't think I'd like it if I only had wings. How would I eat? I'd have to have a beak, and I don't want to have a beak."

Thomas Jefferson laughs. "There are other ways that people can fly than on wings."

The boy's brow knits with both curiosity and skepticism.

"Come along with me," says Thomas Jefferson, "and I will tell you about the time your mother and I saw a man fly."

Beverly flings his stick to the side of the road and gets to his feet. As he walks beside his father on the road leading back to the great house, he hears the story of le Comte de Toytot's ascent in the *ballon*. Thomas Jefferson has nearly finished the story when it becomes apparent to him that the boy does not believe him.

"It is true," Thomas Jefferson says. "The *ballon* rose over the treetops, and the wind carried it for many miles before the count came down in a field."

"Did he die?"

"No. The air in the *ballon* cooled very slowly, so he descended to the earth as gently as a feather. Though once he was on the ground, a big wind blew the *ballon* into a river."

"Did he drown?"

Thomas Jefferson laughs. "No. He was already out of the *ballon*. Nothing bad happened to him at all."

Beverly stops walking. He is looking at the sky, his eyebrows lifted and his brown eyes filled with an unabashed curiosity.

All at once Thomas Jefferson realizes that what he has been interpreting as skepticism is, in fact, so fierce a desire to believe that it makes Beverly think that what he is hearing is too good to be true, and in this conflict Thomas Jefferson recognizes the two most essential qualities of the philosophical mind: a passion for beautiful ideas coupled with an entirely rational understanding that one's own passion does not make even the most sublimely beautiful idea true.

"But why does hot air make a man fly?" asks Beverly.

Thomas Jefferson explains about hot air being lighter than cool air.

"But when I breathe," says Beverly, "my breath is hot, but I don't go up in the air."

Thomas Jefferson explains how the upward force of the hot air has to be greater than the downward force created by weight. "You're too heavy," he says at last.

"But *why* is hot air lighter than cold air?" asks Beverly.

"It has something to do with the motion," says Thomas Jefferson. "You've seen the way the air ripples over the brick kiln or the way smoke billows as it rises." He stops talking, because he realizes that what he is saying does not make sense and that he does not, in fact, know why hot air is lighter.

"The best way to understand how it works," says Thomas Jefferson, "would be for us to make our own *ballon*."

The boy's eyes and mouth both go round.

"Not a big one," says Thomas Jefferson. "It would take much too long to build one that we could actually fly in. But perhaps we could build a small one before dinner."

"Big enough to fly Hurly?" Hurly, a beagle, used to belong to Betty Hemings, and Beverly has been caring for him during the year since his grandmother died.

"No, Hurly's too heavy, I think."

"A mouse?"

"Maybe a beetle," says Thomas Jefferson.

He sends Beverly to his Uncle John for a bit of pine glue, and crosses the lawn to his own chambers to look for a silk scarf and a sheet of vellum. By the time Beverly returns with the glue, Thomas Jefferson has cut the vellum into strips. He glues one strip into a ring and makes a small canoe of the others. Then he uses the glue to attach the four corners of the scarf to the ring and then to attach the edges of the scarf to themselves so that they form a sort of sack. And lastly he dangles the canoe from the bottom of the ring on four threads.

They have finished making the *ballon* by dinner but have to wait until the afternoon to start a twig fire in the brickyard to one side of the kiln. Thomas Jefferson places two pebbles in the canoe to serve as ballast. Beverly does, in fact, manage to trap a beetle, but the only way to keep the insect from immediately crawling out of the canoe would be to kill it, and father and son agree that launching a dead beetle would be entirely beside the point.

When at last the fire is sufficiently hot and low, Thomas Jefferson holds the *ballon* upside down and grips the lowest point of the scarf between his thumb and forefinger. He carefully lifts the scarf so that the ring and the canoe swing to the bottom, and then he gently draws the whole contraption over the fire, instructing Beverly to clip the vellum ring between two Y-shaped sticks. As soon as the scarf begins to inflate, Thomas Jefferson releases his grip on the top, and he and Beverly are equally excited when the scarf defies gravity and remains aloft.

It takes no more than fifteen seconds for the scarf to completely inflate, and then, at the count of three, Beverly pulls aside the Y-shaped sticks and the *ballon* shoots straight into the air. It doesn't get more than ten feet above the ground, however, before a breeze causes it to lurch onto its side and drop like a shot duck, straight to the earth, narrowly missing Beverly as he dodges to one side.

He cries out in disappointment, then hangs his head. "I wanted it to fly over the trees," he says.

"Next time," says Thomas Jefferson.

"No. It will never work."

"Nonsense!" Thomas Jefferson gives Beverly an encouraging pat, but the boy only shrugs his hand away. Tears sparkle in the corners of his eyes.

"We didn't have enough ballast," says Thomas Jefferson. "If we'd put in another pebble, it would have gone up straight. Let's give it another try."

"No," says Beverly. "It will never work. I can tell." He starts to walk away.

Mystified by the sudden change in Beverly's mood, Thomas Jefferson says, "I brought plans for the *ballon* your mother and I saw in Paris back with me. They must be in a trunk somewhere. If I can find them, I'll show them to you."

Beverly looks around at his father but doesn't say anything.

"Perhaps one day," Thomas Jefferson continues, "we can construct a real *ballon* together—a big one! Maybe even bigger than le Comte de Toytot's! I'll bet the winds could carry us all the way to Charlottesville. Perhaps we could even fly as far as Washington. Wouldn't President Madison be surprised if we were to drop out of the sky and visit him!"

Beverly smiles weakly, then says, "I have to go."

As the boy walks in the direction of his mother's cabin, Thomas Jefferson bends and picks up the fallen *ballon*. He wants to put a third pebble into the canoe and make another attempt—but not on his own. He holds the top of the *ballon* between his thumb and forefinger, and as Beverly disappears into his mother's door, Thomas Jefferson turns and carries the *ballon* to his own chambers.

Perhaps the boy will feel differently tomorrow.

In 1815 Francis C. Gray, a lawyer, asked how many generations of intermarriage with whites would it take for the offspring of a mulatto family to be considered white, and Thomas Jefferson replied by letter: "Our canon considers two crosses with pure white, and a third with any degree of mixture, however small, as clearing the issue of negro blood." If we consider the relationship of Betty Hemings's mother, Parthenia, with Captain Hemings as the first "crossing" and Betty's own relationship with John Wayles as the second, then, by this calculus, Thomas Jefferson understood that his children with Sally Hemings more than qualified as "white."

As a master Jefferson was kind and indulgent. Under his management his slaves were seldom punished, except for stealing and fighting. They were tried for any offense as at court and allowed to make their own defense. The slave children were nursed until they were three years old, and left with their parents until thirteen. They were then sent to the overseers' wives to learn trades. Every male child's father received $5 at its birth.

Jefferson was a man of sober habits, although his cellars were stocked with wines. No one ever saw him under the influence of liquor. His servants about the house were tasked. If you did your task well you were rewarded; if not, punished. Mrs. Randolph would not let any of the young ladies go anywhere with gentlemen with the exception of their brothers, unless a colored servant accompanied them.

—The Reverend Peter Fossett
"Once the Slave of Thomas Jefferson"
New York Sunday World
January 30, 1898

. . . Mr. Jeff allowed Joey to go into the stable, but only long enough to embrace Edy, tell her of the success of his plans and give her the oatcakes. Afterward, when Joey and I sat shoulder to shoulder on the mounting block just outside the stable, he told me he wasn't sure of the success of his plans. "I don't trust white people anymore," he said. "Not a one of them thinks a promise to a nigger is a real promise. That Mr. Jones especially. He was just like Mr. Jeff, saying, 'My heart is breaking. I'm so sorry. I'll do anything I can.' But I saw it in his eyes— all he was thinking was he was gonna get some niggers cheap."

Cheap because Mr. Jeff had told us that he would cut off the bidding early on our family members so that whoever had promised us to buy them would pay the lowest possible price. "Virtue never flourishes so well," he told me, "as when it coincides with monetary reward." This had seemed a wise strategy at the time, but now I wondered if the reward wouldn't undermine the virtue.

"No!" Joey cried, as if he had read my thoughts. His voice wavering, on the verge of breaking into a sob, he continued, "I've got to stop thinking like that. Mr. Jeff made me a promise. I've got to trust him. I've got to have faith."

My own anxiety and sorrow having reduced me to something close to paralytic numbness, I could only answer Joey by giving his hand a squeeze. If I spoke a single word, I would burst into tears.

The "viewing" began at eight o'clock; the yard around the stable and the whole of the lawn in front of the great house had filled with wagons and carriages. A crowd of forty or fifty white people—mainly men—had gathered in front of the open stable door, and when Mr. Jeff gave the word, they filed into the stable one by one. I had never seen a slave auction, so I had no clear idea of what actually happened at a viewing.

Despite the cold, Mr. Jeff told the slaves to remove their cloaks, coats and shawls so the "visitors" could get "a better look." And look they did, at all of these dear men, women and children, as if they were merely animals. Arms were squeezed, and thighs; stomachs were poked and grabbed. Fingers were stuck into *open mouths to test the solidity of teeth. At one point a man with bushy black eyebrows and a yellowed periwig approached Joey's second-eldest daughter, Patsy, a fine-featured and stately girl of sixteen, and yanked down the front of her shift, tearing it and exposing one of her breasts. Joey leapt off the mounting block and raced across the yard, shouting at the man in the periwig, "No! You can't do that! Don't you dare touch her!" He was caught and restrained by Mr. Henderson and Mr. Byrd just outside the makeshift fence, but he continued to shout, and the man who had accosted Patsy kept his back turned, as if he didn't hear a word.*

Mr. Jeff, however, had heard Joey, and, seeing Patsy clutching the ripped neck of her shift, he immediately walked up to the man, saying, "There is no cause for you to treat a young woman like that."

"Don't I have the right to see what I'm buying?" the man said.

"If you cannot treat a woman with due respect," Mr. Jeff said, "I must ask you to leave this plantation immediately."

"I thought this was an auction, not a cotillion!" the man replied, but he turned away, leaving Patsy staring fixedly up toward the rafters as if she could not bear to see anything around her.

I had trailed after Joey and was standing speechless beside him as he—motionless now, still gripped by the two overseers—watched fiercely while the man in the periwig went on to inspect another young woman.

White people had streamed in ever-greater numbers toward the stable after the commencement of the viewing. One of them, Mr. McFlynn, a cooper from Charlottesville, gaunt and near seventy, with a face the color of a butcher's hands, had arrived just as Mr. Jeff had issued his ultimatum to the man in the periwig, and he had stopped in his tracks not five feet from where I was standing. He snorted at Mr. Jeff's words, and when he saw that the man in the periwig was not going to put up a fight, he raised his arm in my direction and called out, "How much do you want for old master's whore?" Mr. Jeff either didn't hear him or didn't want to dignify his question with a response, so Mr. McFlynn asked again, "How much for old master's whore?" . . .

I t is June 1816. Thomas Jefferson is seventy-three, and sleeping. Sally Hemings, in her white shift, having just picked up her gown from the chair next to the night table, stands beside the bed looking down. Gold tinges the blue trees outside the lodge windows, and the birds are filling the quiet with their squeaks, trills, burbles and peeps.

What she sees, not for the first time, is that Thomas Jefferson is elderly. His cheeks are like weathered canvas, sagging over the armature of his facial bones. That chin, which once had seemed the embodiment of wit and pride, now juts like a tree stump on a barren hilltop. *This is how he will look when he is dead*, Sally Hemings thinks.

His eyelids flutter and open. At first he doesn't seem to see her, but then his coppery yellow eyes focus and his thin lips lift into a one-sided smile. His voice phlegm-cracked, he asks, "What are you up to, sweet nymph?"

"Shhh," says Sally Hemings, who got out of bed with the intention of making a cup of tea and drinking it alone out on the porch.

Thomas Jefferson slides his hand off his belly and pats her side of the bed. Without a word, she pulls back the covers and slips under. He lifts his arm so that she might nestle against him, her head on his shoulder, and once she has done so, he lowers his arm and lets his fingers rest on the rim of her pelvis. "I've finally figured out what I am going to do with my freedom," he tells her.

He no longer has any official responsibilities. He has been home from Washington for seven years.

"What now?" she says.

"A balloon!"

Sally Hemings sighs and idly circles her fingers amid the white hairs on his chest.

"Beverly is going to help me," he says. "I was talking to him about it yesterday. He had an excellent idea." Beverly is now seventeen.

"Oh?"

"We were talking," says Thomas Jefferson, "about how the weight of a

567

balloon limits the altitude to which it can ascend. And he suggested that the gondola should be fishnet on a wicker frame instead of solid wicker. I think that's admirably practical. The fishnet's far lighter, and there'd be no danger of falling through."

"What about the silk?" says Sally Hemings.

"The silk?" says Thomas Jefferson. "You mean a silk fishnet?"

"No. I mean how are you going to afford all that silk?"

Thomas Jefferson remains silent.

Sally Hemings continues, "Wouldn't your balloon require enough silk to make one hundred gowns? Or *five* hundred? Or a thousand?"

"Not a thousand," he says. "Not five hundred either, I think."

"Still," asserts Sally Hemings.

Thomas Jefferson doesn't speak for a long time; then he says, "You've grown so practical in your old age."

"Someone has to be."

"Not you!" He smiles mischievously. "You should leave practicality to Martha. She's the mistress of Monticello, after all."

Sally Hemings is silent. She knows that the servants have been discussing whether Thomas Jefferson will have to sell them off to make good his debts.

He slides his hand off her pelvis and slaps her buttock. "I'm making it for you, you know!" he says. "Didn't I promise I'd take you up in a balloon? Remember how you wanted to fly when we were in Paris? *Voler comme un oiseau!* Don't you want me to keep my promises?"

"Only the ones you can afford to keep."

"I'm going to call it 'Dusky Sal'!" he says.

Sally Hemings laughs. "I think you should call it 'Howling Atheist'! That's a much better name for a balloon!"

"Dusky Sal and the Howling Atheist," says Thomas Jefferson. "I'm going to inscribe that in letters twenty feet high—big enough to be read from a mile away! Then you and I can ride our balloon across the Potomac and over Washington—then Philadelphia, New York, Boston. And anyone who sees us can write all the slanderous doggerel they want. We won't care. We'll just go up and up until we have reached the very top of the tallest cloud in the sky. I'll fling a rug out across it. We'll unload a basket filled with sausages, figs, bread and champagne, then lie on our rug in the warm sun, feeling gentle breezes blowing about us, and we won't give a thought to anything anyone might be saying or thinking down below. We'll just sip our champagne, talk nonsense, watch the birds fly."

Thomas Jefferson is silent a moment, then kisses Sally Hemings's head. "How does that sound?" he asks.

"We'll fall through," she answers.

"**I** am making arrangements," Thomas Jefferson says.

"You have to trust me," he says.

"I already know," he says.

He is impatient. He is always impatient. "Please, there is no need to worry."

"It is an immensely complicated business, but I have everyone's best interest at heart."

He pounds his hand on the table and speaks in a low, firm voice. "How many times do I have to tell you?"

"Why do you have so little faith in me?"

"Sally, Sally, Sally!"

What is the matter? Something is the matter. "No, nothing."

"That's not what I meant." *Then what? What did you mean?* "This is a tiresome subject. I will be making the final arrangements this week."

He puts his hands against his temples. "I can assure you that not a day goes by when it is not on my mind."

"Why are you worried?"

"It is a simple matter. There is nothing to worry about."

"I have had setbacks, but I will surmount them."

"You have to stop listening to those people."

"It is done."

"Mr. Cartney is trying to make things difficult, as usual, but the legislature is entirely on my side."

"It is impossible to make everyone happy, but no one can fault my arrangements."

He speaks so softly she can hardly hear. "Oh, Sally, I wonder if you shall ever forgive me."

He shouts, "I've told you a thousand times!"

"It's not a question of *if*, it's a question of when. And, in fact, I've already acquired all the resources I need."

He takes her hand in both of his and speaks tenderly. "Dear, dear Sally. You are a very good woman, but you worry too much."

"The House of Delegates is having one of its monarchist moments, but they will come round in the end." *Are you sure?*

"It is done," he says. "I have arranged it. It is done, it is done, it is done."

A nd since Sally Hemings is doing an entirely adequate job of steering, Thomas Jefferson lays his oar across the canoe's gunwales and looks around. It seems that they have traveled very far from Virginia—west, for hundreds and hundreds of miles. The quality of the forest has changed. The trees have grown massive, their boughs are like roads going off into a wilderness of foliage, air and sun, and above the trees are mountains that ascend jaggedly to such a height that their peaks shred the clouds. There is a low trumpeting along the banks, a splintering of wood and a sound that makes Thomas Jefferson think of stones being uprooted and slammed back into the earth, over and over. It takes him a while to see through the tangle of shadows and sun-shot foliage, but then everything comes clear: Walking along both banks are hirsute creatures so enormous that they are like moving hillsides, and they have long, arcing tusks and proboscises that slither and curl in the manner of snakes. These creatures are mammoths, and Thomas Jefferson is so excited that he cannot help but turn to Sally Hemings and tell her he had always known that mammoths still traversed the American continent. "I specifically directed Meriwether Lewis to bring me back one of these creatures," he tells her, "but he disappointed me." Sally Hemings says not a word. She has been silent throughout the entire trip, and now her silence has become a towering absence that he hardly dares to contemplate. Time passes. The mountains grow more distant, and the forest gives way to plains of such robust fertility that in the time it takes the canoe to pass, apples burst from branch tips in a shower of petals and go from green to purple-red; vines rise out of the earth, writhe along the ground and sprout pea pods, pumpkins and tomatoes; and acre after acre bristles with green blades that burgeon and elaborate until they make an ocean of shoulder-high wheat, glinting, hissing and swaying under restless breezes. And in the midst of these fields are villages of fountains and tree-shaded plazas, where each house is so perfectly proportioned it seems as light as an idea, and the citizens are all tall and broad-shouldered, strolling at their ease, strangers to poverty, illness and vice. "Such incredible beauty!" says Thomas Jefferson. "Are we not blessed to inhabit a continent so abundantly and spectacularly beautiful? Is there any doubt that here is where humanity shall finally be fashioned in God's image?" Sally Hemings has lifted her oar out of the water, and the canoe begins to drift in slow circles. "I have no use for beauty," she says. "It is only the mask by which we hide from ourselves the barbarity of life on this earth and the coldness of our own hearts. You think it enough to speak beautiful words, but that beauty is nothing unless those words are lived." And now it is Thomas Jefferson whose silence becomes monumental. The canoe rotates slowly on the water as the sky darkens. It is night, then more than night, and soon nothing can be perceived but the sound of water over rocks.

June 20, 1826. He grows birdlike with time. The flesh melts away, and his bones grow light, his gestures tentative, even when he intends to be forceful. He covers his good ear with his right hand and points to the door with his left, telling Martha, "Go! Go! Why are you bothering me with such trivialities!" Where once there would have been rage and hurt in his daughter, who is now fifty-four, there is only a flicker of irritation. And she leaves, not out of respect, or even a desire to save herself from further pain, but out of pity.

He is eighty-three. His eyes have grown larger in his shrinking skull and are often filled with the bewilderment of someone who has found himself in a place and among people he neither recognizes nor comprehends. When Martha has pulled the door shut behind her with an impatient bang, he brings the pursed fingertips of his hands together in that habit he has developed recently, the fingertips of the right nibbling at the fingers of the left, in the way that birds kiss.

"Now, what were we doing, Sally?" he says after a moment of looking off into the dimness of his shuttered study.

"Boots or shoes?" says Sally Hemings, holding a pair of each in either hand. "It's muddy outside. I think the boots would be better."

A wrinkle of consternation interrupts the pink space between his white eyebrows. Without looking, he reaches behind and touches the counterpane of the bed. "Neither," he says, sitting down and sighing heavily. "I've changed my mind. The boys can get on without me. There's reading I have to do."

He adjusts the pillows at the head of the bed, and, fully dressed, with even his coat on, he leans against the pillows and lifts his bare feet onto the counterpane. The nails on his big toes are exactly the color and texture of corn husks in October.

Sally Hemings puts the boots and the shoes back into the closet from which she has just taken them. Then she takes a woolen blanket from the chair by the fire and covers his feet.

"Thank you, Sally," he says contentedly, looking up at her as a boy might look up at his mother just before taking her hand. "Could you get me my Vergil?" He gestures in the direction of his desk. "And my spectacles."

Sally Hemings walks around to his study and then pauses, looking down at the several volumes on his desk.

"It's the red one," he said.

She knows. How could she not know? He has read to her from it so many times, in Latin and in English, especially that beautiful passage about the stars and spring planting, and she has even browsed the translation herself, more than once, and she has talked to him about it. But now she only picks up the book and the silver spectacles.

"Thank you," he says when she hands them to him. He places them on his belly and then takes hold of her hand. "You are very patient with me. I'm sorry." He gives her hand a squeeze, then lets it go.

As he pushes his spectacles onto the bridge of his nose, he says, "Could you ask Burwell to record the exact weight of each boy's rod and bring it to me before lunch."

"Certainly, Mr. Jefferson."

Again he says, "Thank you, Sally."

His face brightens, and he looks almost his old self.

"I'm thinking of having Eagle and Tecumseh saddled first thing in the morning," he says. "The weather's going to be wonderful, I believe. We could go out before anyone is up and watch the sun rise over the lake, then ride down the valley and along the river as far as Castle Rock? How would you like that?"

She tells him she would like it fine. He is still smiling.

After that, her throat becomes so constricted that she cannot speak.

And if he notices, he never says a word.

. . . Mr. Henderson nailed a list on the stable wall of all the slaves' names in the order in which they would be sold. As Mr. Jeff had promised me, Critta and Peter went first. I wasn't worried about Peter. He had been thrown by a horse two years previously, and ever since then his right leg had been so lame he could hardly put weight on it. Indeed, he couldn't climb up onto Mr. Broomfield's cart without the aid of both Mr. Henderson and Mr. Evans. The only bid was from Daniel Farley, and so my brother gained his freedom for a mere dollar.

Three people in addition to Mr. Eppes seemed determined to purchase Critta, and Mr. Broomfield let the bidding go for several rounds—long enough for me to become very worried—but then Mr. Eppes made another bid, and Mr. Broomfield cried "Sold!" without allowing the other interested parties time to raise their bids—with the result that those parties shouted outraged objections and the whole crowd murmured its disapproval. Looking alarmed at the crowd's reaction to his stratagem, Mr. Broomfield silenced further protest by beginning the bidding on George's Ginny before she had even climbed up onto the cart.

And thus the last member of my immediate family had found a hospitable situation in which she might live out the rest of her days as if free. No other of the dozens of families who had abided at Monticello for five decades and more had been so lucky. I was well aware of the injustice of our good fortune, even as I was exceedingly grateful for it.

Despite the cold, Joey's broad forehead was glossy with the sweat of his anxiety for Edy and the children. When I touched his forearm, he grabbed my hand, drew his face so close to mine that I thought at first he would kiss me, and in a breathy, emphatic voice he declared, "Danny and Mr. Eppes kept their word. Mr. Jeff, too. That's a blessing. Lord be praised! I don't even care about Mr. Jones anymore. As long as my family stays right here in Albemarle where I can see them, that's all I care about."

I squeezed his hand with my own. But when I tried to speak, my words came out in a strangled croak. "Yes, that is good. But let us hope for more."

His hand closed so hard upon my fingers I thought he might snap them off. "I feel like I'm going mad. I'm trying to get a hold on myself, but I don't know how much of this I can stand."

"Oh, Joey." I kissed his forehead and tasted salt on my lips. "Oh, Joey. Oh, Joey." I was so possessed by foreboding that I couldn't say anything else.

The reason I had touched his forearm was to see if I might excuse myself for a minute. My hands were trembling. I was nauseated. I thought a quick walk might fortify me and restore some of my composure. There were twelve people on the list before Edy and the children, and of those twelve, only the last four, Evelina and her children, were people to whom I had been close. It seemed to me that I had easily enough time to make it out to Carter's Bluff and back. I felt it was wrong of me to abandon Joey, though I didn't see how I could possibly stay. I, too, felt as if I were on the verge of losing my mind. So when I asked if I might walk for ten minutes, I added that he should come with me if he wanted.

"Oh, no!" he said. "I can't do that. I've got to stay right here so I can see what's happening." He released my hand with a gentle pat. "You go, though. I'll keep your spot warm."

I don't know whether the walk did me any good at all. I strode along Mulberry Row away from the crowd, my head down, my arms gripping my cloak tight against my body. I was shivering, though not, I think, from the cold. I had hoped that my head might clear when I had some space around me and could feel the enlivening stirring of the open air, but my mind was roiling with sentiments and ideas, not one of which I could bear to consider—a state not unlike, I imagine, that of someone plummeting off a precipice toward a heap of jagged rocks. I strode to Carter's Bluff and back in almost complete unconsciousness of my surroundings. Just as I was approaching the fringe of the crowd once again, I heard a voice call out my name. I looked up to see broadfaced and heavy-shouldered Burwell Colbert, who, as Mr. Jefferson's body servant, had been at my side most days and many of the nights during our master's last weeks. He had been a great relief to me then, for he seemed possessed of nothing but congenial spirits and could always find something to appreciate, even in the bleakest circumstances. He was also a calming presence for Mrs. Martha, who couldn't deny me my place at her father's bedside, although she never wanted me there.

I remember late one night, three or four days before Mr. Jefferson died, Martha had gone to bed and Burwell and I were alone. Something had gone wrong with Mr. Jefferson's breathing, and instead of snoring his every breath came as a long, trumpeting groan, over and over and over, relentlessly, the whole night through. The sound was a torture to listen to, not merely because it put one in mind of how unsatisfying those breaths must have been (the sound could only be caused by a constriction of the throat) but because it was almost impossible to resist breathing at the same unnatural rhythm.

There was a full moon out that night, and as Burwell and I sat side by side in the darkness, in a room lit by a solitary taper resting on the mantelpiece at our backs, Burwell made a soft, happy laugh. "I sure do hope, Mr. Jefferson's listening to that! Ain't nothing he like better in the world than a mockingbird song, and I ain't never heard a mockingbird sing as fine as this one here tonight!" I didn't know what he was talking about at first, but as soon as he mentioned the mockingbird, my mind left Mr. Jefferson's agony, and it was as if I were out in the moonlight myself, hearing nothing but the free and happy inventions of that perky gray bird.

I was profoundly grateful to Burwell that night and on many others, during which he alone seemed to remember that the world contained joys, even as it surrounded us with sorrow and pain. And, indeed, he was smiling as he called out to me and as he lumbered the five steps from the great house lawn onto Mulberry Row. "Hey there, Miss Sally!" he said as he drew up beside me. "Look what I got here!" He held out two framed etchings, attached by a hinge, of Mr. Jefferson and the Marquis de Lafayette that had been standing on a marble-topped table in a corner of the parlor for as long as I could remember. "Ain't they wonderful! Don't they just bring you back to your Paris days? Mrs. Martha let me have them for cheap. She saw me looking at them, and she came over. 'How much you asking for these?' I said, and she said, 'How much you got in your pocket?' 'Not but four cents,' I told her, and she said, 'That's just what I'm asking!' Ain't that so nice of her? Ain't these just the perfect likeness?"

This was one time when Burwell's smiles brought me no cheer at all. He, too, had been freed by Mr. Jefferson. His wife was dead, but his eight children were to be sold that very afternoon. I was so aghast that I did nothing to censor my thoughts. "How can you waste your money on things like that," I said, "when you could be buying your family out of slavery?"

He smiled and shook his head slowly, as if amused by my stupidity. "Oh, Miss Sally, I don't have near enough to do that now. Mrs. Martha says she can't pay me my $300 from Mr. Jefferson until after everything's been sold."

I heard a woman screaming frantically from the area of the stable. I hurried away from Burwell, loathing him for his inability to grasp the injustice that was being done to him, vowing that I would cut him out of my life, that I would never again address a single word to him.

I had to push my way through the huge crowd that had now gathered around the stable, and when at last I reached Joey's side, I found him clutching the top rail of the paddock fence and leaning forward so far he would have fallen if he had let go. His entire attention was directed at the stable, in the depths of which the woman was still screaming and being cursed by white male voices. Only when he felt me draw up beside him did he turn and look at me with the open, slot-shaped mouth and the wide, wavery eyes of someone on the verge of vomiting.

"What's happening?" I said.

"Evelina," was all he answered.

"What? What are they doing to her?"

"Her children have gone to farmers in Amherst and Petersburg, and she's just been sold to McFlynn."

Only now could I understand what she was screaming: "I won't go! You can't take a mother from her children! You can't take my babies away!"

As I listened to her, I remembered a time when she was taking care of my Harriet and I had run off into the woods in such a state of confusion and despair that I wasn't sure if I was going for a walk or to end my life. When at last, hours later, I was driven back to the house by a rainstorm, Harriet ran to greet me as she did every time we were separated, but I saw real fear in Evelina's eyes. She was hardly more than a baby herself, but old enough to know what had driven me from the house and to worry that she had been abandoned in a world of cruel strangers.

"What are we going to do?" I asked.

Joey only met my gaze with that same slot-mouthed, wide-eyed expression, then turned to look at Mr. Broomfield's cart, onto which Edy and their two youngest children had just climbed. Evelina was still screaming.

"All right, everybody," said Mr. Broomfield, "while Mr. McFlynn's talking sense to that girl, we'll just go on with our business."

There was scattered, subdued laughter, and the bidding began. At first everything went as Joey had arranged. Edy and their two youngest children were bought and would be freed by Jesse Scott, a half-white, half-Indian man who had married Joey's youngest sister. Maria and Isabella were bought by a friend of Mr. Scott, who lived not far from Shadwell. Mr. Jones bought Peter. And then, at last, it was Patsy's turn on the block.

The first person to bid was the man in the yellowed periwig who had ripped her shift. Mr. Scott's friend, who had agreed to take all the older girls, bid next and was instantly topped by the man in the periwig. Other people bid, but the contest was clearly between Mr. Scott's friend and that yellow-wigged man. And so, one after another, the other bidders dropped away. All this time Joey clutched my hands tightly in his own, crushing them every time the man in the periwig made another bid. I kept assuring Joey that Mr. Scott's friend would not let him down, but I am not sure he heard a word I uttered.

When at last only Mr. Scott's friend and the man in the periwig were bidding, a terrible pattern ensued. With growing hesitancy Mr. Scott's friend would raise his bid in increments of ten dollars, which the man in the periwig would instantly top by twenty-five. At first I thought that the man in the periwig was bidding so rapidly in order to stop Mr. Broomfield from calling out "Sold!" after Mr. Scott's friend's bid, but then I realized that Mr. Broomfield had not done so with any of the other Fossett children and that he must have been dissuaded from that strategy by the outcry that had followed his cutting off Critta's bidder. After that I uttered no further encouragement.

When the bidding reached $645, Mr. Scott's friend took so long upping the bid that Mr. Broomfield called out, "Going once! Going twice!" before the friend finally bid $655, his face contorted and pale. He had pulled his hat off his head and was twisting the brim in his fists. When the man in the periwig bid $700, Mr. Scott's friend flung his hat to the ground. He was done. But then Mr. Scott called out, "Eight hundred!" and with gestures indicated to the friend that they would split the price.

"Thank the Lord!" Joey cried, but in the next instant the man in the periwig raised his bid to $1,000.

The scant seconds while we waited for Mr. Scott or his friend to raise the bid seemed an eternity in hell. During the whole time, I heard a woman screaming and was in such a state of distraction that I thought it was Patsy, even though she was standing motionless, her eyes uplifted, as she had been in the barn. When at last Mr. Broomfield lowered his hammer, confirming the sale to the man in the periwig, Joey cried out to God, fell to his knees and began to bang his head against the frozen earth. "Stop! Stop!" I cried. "Don't, Joey! Don't!" I grabbed at his shoulders and tried to pull him up from the ground but could think of nothing that might give him hope—especially because it seemed to me that the outcry following the hasty conclusions of Critta's sale had deprived Mr. Broomfield of the only means by which Patsy might have been saved from the clutches of that repulsive man.

This thought entirely deprived me of strength. I looked around the yard in front of the stable, where hundreds of white people were taking absolutely no notice of Joey's suffering or of Patsy's plight.

It was then I heard the screaming again, and for the first time since I had returned from my walk, I actually caught sight of Evelina. McFlynn and another white man were shoving her from around the far side of the stable toward the lawn where all the carts and carriages were waiting, their horses attended by servants or merely tied to a fence or tree. Evelina had her head and shoulders hunched, and she was taking very small steps. At first I thought that this was merely her way of protecting herself from the blows of her captors, but then I saw the swinging chains and realized that not merely was she shackled wrist to wrist, ankle to ankle but that an iron collar had been put around her neck, and it was fastened to the chain between her ankles by another chain too short to allow her to fully stand.

I felt a sort of crack inside my head, as if something had broken, and in an instant I was shoving through the crowd of white people, desperate to get to Evelina, having no clear intention of what I would do when I had reached her, only feeling that if I could speak to her or touch her hand, I could somehow undo everything, not just what had happened to her but the grim and unjust fates meted out to virtually every one of the men, women and children who had been confined like animals in that stable.

The white people amid whom I was attempting to pass soon made it abundantly clear, through their own shoves and curses, that I would never make it to Evelina if I did not master my rage, that my only hope was to take advantage of my own white skin and flowing hair, and so, instead of cursing, pushing and pummeling, I kept my arms at my sides and said, over and over, "I'm sorry. Excuse me. I have to get through. Please. I'm terribly sorry." Despite all my efforts, I must still have been a bizarre spectacle, because it is impossible for me to imagine that I could have concealed the utter contempt that propelled each one of these niceties from my lips. Nevertheless, my strategy worked; the curses ceased, shoulders parted to allow my passage, and there were places in the crowd where I had plainly been recognized, and scores of people stood aside to let me pass as if I were royalty.

I was not tall enough to see over the heads surrounding me, and so I did not once glimpse Evelina during the whole of my progress to the crowd's far edge. And then all I saw was a chaotic assemblage of horses, wheels and Negro men, some dressed in full livery, others in straw hats and sackcloth coats. I began running from one of these servants to the other, asking—shouting, really—if anyone knew where I might be able to find McFlynn's carriage, and most of them—no doubt thinking me an insane white woman—merely looked over my head, down at their feet or otherwise pretended not to hear me.

In the end it was only one servant's involuntary glance across the road that enabled me to spot Evelina, hunched and silent, seated in a fenced enclosure on the back of a hay wagon that was already rocking and rumbling off a brown field and onto the road. McFlynn and his driver were seated at the front with their backs to me.

And here, at last, I became the insane woman whom everyone had imagined me to be, as I ran after the retreating wagon, shouting out, "Evelina! I'm sorry! I'm sorry! I love you! I love you! Evelina! I love you!" Now it seems odd to me that I should have professed my love to this woman, because during most of my association with her, especially when she was my own servant, she had often irritated me, and I had never found her sufficiently industrious or remotely intelligent. But as I ran after that wagon, my love for her was passionate and true, and if it had been possible to gain her freedom by throwing myself under the wheels of the wagon, I would have done so without a thought.

But the wagon only gathered speed as I raced toward it over the frozen, rutted, red earth of the East Road, and it was clear that even if my heart had not already been pounding and my breaths had not been burning in my throat, I had no chance of catching up with it.

But then a horse by the side of the road started—perhaps at McFlynn's driver's cries—and lurched in front of the wagon, pulling its gig along with it. McFlynn's horses veered left, and the driver yanked on the reins, avoiding a collision and bringing the wagon to a halt. And so, still shouting my love and my sorrow and not caring who heard me, I redoubled my pace, and in instants I was gripping the posts at the rear of the wagon.

I had not been able to tell as I ran if Evelina had been even aware of my pursuit, but now she was looking straight at me under her lowered brow. As I, unable to gather air sufficient for speech, only sobbed and gasped wordlessly, she placed her hands on the bed of the wagon and dragged herself as close to me as her chains—fastened to the base of the driver's seat—would allow. Over her shoulder I saw that McFlynn had turned to look at me. He yanked the whip out of the hand of his driver—who was exchanging curses with the driver of the gig—and lifted his leg so that he might step over the seat and into the back of the wagon.

I didn't care what he did with that whip. I almost longed to feel its sting on my shoulders and cheek. Evelina's face was now only inches from mine. I looked into her eyes, which seemed filled with animal fury. She was milling her mouth in a peculiar fashion, as if she were engaged in some terrific struggle to regain the power of speech, and then, exactly as the driver cried out and the wagon jerked forward, yanking the posts from my grip, something white shot across the space between us.

As I watched Evelina draw away from me, her new master behind her, one hand gripping the back of his bench, the other holding his whip high in the air—though only to steady himself as the wagon tilted into and then out of a rut—I felt her warm saliva, still fragrant of the inside of her mouth, oozing down my nose and onto my lips. . . .

The story of my own life is like a fairy tale, and you would not believe me if I told to you the scenes enacted during my life of slavery. It passes through my mind like a dream. Born and reared as free, not knowing that I was a slave, then suddenly, at the death of Jefferson, put upon an auction block and sold to strangers. I then commenced an eventful life.

I was sold to Col. John R. Jones. My father was freed by the Legislature of Virginia. At the request of Mr. Jefferson, my father made an agreement with Mr. Jones that when he was able to raise the amount that Col. Jones paid for me he would give me back to my father, and he also promised to let me learn the blacksmith trade with my father as soon as I was old enough. My father then made a bargain with two sons of Col. Jones—William Jones and James Lawrence Jones—to teach me. They attended the University of Virginia.

Mr. Jefferson allowed his grandson to teach any of his slaves who desired to learn, and Lewis Randolph first taught me how to read. When I was sold to Col. Jones I took my books along with me. One day I was kneeling before the fireplace spelling the word "baker," when Col. Jones opened the door, and I shall never forget the scene as long as I live.

"What have you got there, sir?" were his words.

I told him.

"If I ever catch you with a book in your hands, thirty-and-nine lashes on your bare back." He took the book and threw it into the fire, then called up his sons and told them that if they ever taught me they would receive the same punishment. But they helped me all they could, as did his daughter Ariadne.

Among my things was a copy-book that my father gave me, and which I kept hid in the bottom of my trunk. I used to get permission to take a bath, and by the dying embers I learned to write. The first copy was this sentence, "Art improves nature."

—The Reverend Peter Fossett
"Once the Slave of Thomas Jefferson"
New York Sunday World
January 30, 1898

Account Book

1. Sally Hemings was not freed in Thomas Jefferson's will but "given her time" by Martha Randolph, an arrangement that simultaneously avoided the scandal that might have arisen had Thomas Jefferson freed her himself and, since she was not technically free but only allowed to live as free, enabled her to evade the Virginia law that required freed slaves to leave the state. Her sons, Madison and Eston, were exempted from the law through a dispensation granted, at the request of their father, by the state legislature.

2. Joseph Fossett worked many years to earn enough money to buy back his wife, five of his children and five grandchildren. In 1840, once it became clear that Colonel John R. Jones would never allow Fossett to buy back his son Peter, the family moved to Cincinnati, Ohio. Although he was also unable to buy back his daughter, Patsy, she ran away from her new master within the year and was living in Cincinnati at the time of the 1850 census.

3. Burwell Colbert never rescued any of his children from slavery. His elderly mother lived at Monticello until the great house was finally sold in 1831. He would visit her from time to time, clean up the house and tend the garden, but mostly he worked as a painter and glazier at the University of Virginia. When he was fifty-one, he married a twenty-year-old freewoman and started a new family.

4. Wormley Hughes, a favorite servant, who dug Thomas Jefferson's grave, was also given his time by Martha Randolph, but his wife and their eight children were sold to separate buyers in Charlottesville. Jeff Randolph bought them all back immediately after the auction, and over the next four years, he bought eighteen more members of Hughes's extended family, all of whom were reunited at Randolph's Edgehill Plantation.

5. Forty-two of the approximately two hundred human beings auctioned at Poplar Forest and Monticello ultimately found freedom or lived out their lives in comparatively beneficent servitude with members of Thomas Jefferson's extended family. The rest were dispersed among households and plantations across Virginia and perhaps in neighboring states. Their fates are entirely unknown.

. . . *It is late. The fire is out. So maybe it is five or six in the morning. The room is frigid and still dark. I can see my breath by candlelight. I don't know why I have been writing all of this.*

No. I do. I do.

I said that I wanted to understand, but that is not true. What I wanted was absolution. I thought that by admitting my sins I would somehow be freed of them. That is all I really cared about. Instead I am only more despicable to myself. When I finished my narrative, I needed company. In truth, I wanted my mother—which shows how friendless I have made myself. Mrs. Martha is here. And Mr. Jeff. And their servants. But I can no longer stomach white people, and the servants won't talk to me. In my presence they behave as if they can neither see nor hear me. I am invisible to them. I am nothing. And it is true: I am not white. I am not black. So I am nothing.

I wrote earlier that I could have said no to Mr. Jefferson, but that is not true either, because were I to have said no to him, I would have been saying no to myself, and because whatever else I may have gotten from him, I also got the world. I don't mean only that I went to France, though had I not, perhaps nothing that happened afterward would have been possible. I mean that he opened up the world to me through his conversation, his great, endlessly restless mind, through his brilliant and powerful friends and, perhaps most of all, through his books. To reject all of that would be to reject the person that at so many moments along the way I was so thrilled to be becoming. And even now, the notion of emptying my mind of everything that I have gained through my association with Mr. Jefferson fills me with a sort of panic, as if I am pulling a coffin lid down upon myself.

There should be nothing wrong with what I have done. The right to know, to learn, to be able to investigate, savor and inhabit the world through one's mind as well as one's person, ought to be as "unalienable" as any of the other rights Mr. Jefferson enshrined in his Declaration. Yet for me the exercise of this right has come at too high a moral cost. By becoming the woman I am now, I lost my self—if by "self" we mean a way of being in the world that one can recognize as one's own.

Earlier tonight, after finishing my narrative, I went down to the kitchen and stole a bottle of Mr. Jefferson's wine—a very good Ledanon. I say "stole" because it had already been packed for auction, as tomorrow everything in this room will be similarly packed. This is the last time I shall ever stay here. After tomorrow this room will be an empty space, containing nothing but echoes and dust. I wanted the wine because I thought it would give me comfort. And when I had finished the bottle without feeling comforted in the least, I "stole" another, hoping it might give me sleep—and that it did, but only the sort of sleep which is a senseless whirling in a dark that is itself whirling with lurid fancies and fears.

And then, only minutes ago, I was awakened by a vivid memory that had come suddenly into my head. I remembered Mr. Jefferson laughing. It was in Paris, not long after our love had truly commenced. We were lying side by side in bed, looking into each other's face, exchanging small kisses. Then, all at once, he shook his head and said, "Oh, Sally, what are we doing?" And then he began to laugh, out of sheer happiness at what had come to pass between us, and I laughed, too. I laughed for joy.

As soon as that memory took possession of me, I began to sob. I sobbed and sobbed and couldn't stop, thinking what a hell life is that such moments of goodness and beauty should end up being so damnable and depraved. I sobbed until, exhausted, I turned on my side, hoping for a little more sleep. And as my face pressed into the pillow, I realized that I could still smell Mr. Jefferson. He was still there. Thomas. Tom. My Tom. And I breathed deeply, thinking that this would be the last time I would ever have any part of him inside me.

EPILOGUE

B everly left Monticello and went to Washington as a white man. He married a white woman in Maryland, and their only child, a daughter, was not known by the white folks to have any colored blood coursing in her veins. Beverly's wife's family were people in good circumstances.

Harriet married a white man in good standing in Washington City, whose name I could give, but will not, for prudential reasons. She raised a family of children, and so far as I know they were never suspected of being tainted with African blood in the community where she lived or lives. I have not heard from her for ten years, and do not know whether she is dead or alive. She thought it to her interest, on going to Washington, to assume the role of a white woman, and by her dress and conduct as such I am not aware that her identity as Harriet Hemings of Monticello has ever been discovered.

Eston married a colored woman in Virginia, and moved from there to Ohio, and lived in Chillicothe several years. In the fall of 1852, he removed to Wisconsin, where he died a year or two afterwards. He left three children.

—Madison Hemings
"Life Among the Lowly, No. 1"
Pike County (Ohio) *Republican*
March 13, 1873

A drizzle grays the air when Thomas Jefferson and Sally Hemings visit the Museum of Miscegenation. They approach the columned and domed marble edifice (which Thomas Jefferson cannot help but notice is in the Palladian style) along an avenue of plane trees, all-but-invisible droplets drifting between bare branches tipped with the tiny lettuces of just-bursting buds. The drizzle coats the square cobbles like breath upon a mirror, and Sally Hemings, wearing leather-soled shoes, finds the footing so slippery she has to cling to Thomas Jefferson's arm until they are inside the museum.

They have come unannounced, but as soon as they step through the glass doors into the cavernous lobby, a security guard nudges a young man in a trim black suit standing next to him and nods in Thomas Jefferson's direction (no one, of course, knows what Sally Hemings actually looks like). The young man immediately goes over to the information desk, picks up a telephone and dials.

Swimming-pool-size banners hanging from the ceiling advertise two new shows: THE MYTH OF PURITY and EUGENICS: PAST, PRESENT AND FUTURE, but Thomas Jefferson and Sally Hemings are interested in neither. They have come, after many second thoughts and much procrastination, to view the entire wing of the museum devoted to their thirty-seven-year relationship.

The young man has put down his telephone and seems on the verge of approaching them, so they turn their backs and hurry across the lobby toward a considerably smaller banner:

THOMAS JEFFERSON & SALLY HEMINGS
AN IMPOSSIBLE LOVE

Just as they pass through the doorway beneath the banner, Sally Hemings looks over her shoulder and sees that the young man has been joined by a stocky gray-haired woman in a magenta suit with a knee-length skirt. She has one hand on the young man's forearm, as if holding him back. They are both staring at Sally Hemings, but neither budges nor makes any show of greeting.

The interior of the gallery is so dim that the spaces between the spot-lit exhibits seem fogged with granulated pencil lead. Thomas Jefferson is already standing beside a vitrine. Sally Hemings rushes over and takes his arm again, feeling less exposed pressed against his side.

It seems that in their hurry to escape notice, they have entered the show through its exit. The vitrine into which Thomas Jefferson is looking contains his silver spectacles, star-shaped inkwell and shoe buckle. Sally Hemings carried these in her bag when she left Monticello, and she gave them to their son Madison shortly before her own death. These items look far too paltry to be arrayed on velvet under a golden spotlight. But seeing them after such a long time, Sally Hemings is so weakened by sorrow that her fingertips and legs go trembly. Thomas Jefferson glances at her with a sad smile.

"I'm glad you kept these," he says. "The inkwell especially."

She smiles hesitantly and nods. She cannot answer. She lets go of his arm.

"I don't recognize the buckle, though," he says. "Are you sure it's mine?"

"It was in the lodge. I went there not long before I left Monticello. It was under the night table."

Thomas Jefferson's smile has vanished. He gives her hand a long, firm squeeze. "Oh, God, Sally."

"Do you want to go?"

"No. That would be a waste. We've come all this way."

Some of the displays are amusing—particularly the dioramas. One shows Thomas Jefferson standing in front of a fireplace playing a violin while mannequins representing his granddaughters, Ellen and Cornelia, both looking about eleven years old, whirl, elbows linked, in a merry jig. Almost everything is wrong with this exhibit. First of all, Cornelia absolutely hated dancing, in part because her actual proportions—unlike the mannequin's—verged on the elephantine. Second of all, no one's clothes make sense. Thomas Jefferson is wearing a braided, gold-buttoned, royal blue frock coat, which is far too formal for so humble and domestic an occasion. And his waistcoat is an absurd geranium red, such as a tavern keeper might wear. The girls, by contrast, are in mauves and pigeon gray, which they would have considered too dour and old-fashioned even for their grandmothers.

Most ludicrous of all are the faces of the mannequins, ostensibly based on portraits painted "from life." Thomas Jefferson, at least, looks as if he belongs to his own family—though not any closer to himself than a second or third cousin, and the grin on his face is the sort that only accompanies intense discomfort of the lower intestine. The mannequins representing the girls both look like demented elves, neither bearing the faintest resemblance to the actual Ellen and Cornelia.

Sally Hemings is also in the scene, though her face is not visible, since she is shown watching the family merriment from a dark hallway.

In every single one of the dioramas and modern illustrations, Sally Hemings's face is either in shadow or turned away from the viewer. This is because, as the captions to the displays repeat time and again, if any portraits of her were ever made, none has survived. She understands that the absence of her face represents the museum curator's desire both for historical accuracy and to make a statement about her "invisibility" in Thomas Jefferson's world, yet she can't help but feel affronted that she alone, of all the people represented, is deprived of the most significant physical manifestation of identity, especially since the faces of every other member of the Jefferson family and social circle could hardly be less historically accurate.

She is also disturbed to see the knives, forks and spoons she remembers as shiny copper and silver looking black and withered, and the blue china plates off which she ate thousands of meals now only partially reconstructed assemblages of variously discolored fragments. Particularly disturbing is a display of miscellaneous bits of pottery unearthed at Monticello, in which she notices two arced pieces of the jam jar in which she buried La Petite. Thomas Jefferson passes right over this display without even noticing what it contains, and she doesn't bother to inform him. She lingers behind as he moves on to other exhibits, however, and it is a long while before she can bring herself to stand near or talk to him again.

In the end she is moved to return to his side and, finally, to take hold of his hand by the responses of the other people in the gallery—about half of whom obviously have African ancestry. The overwhelming message of the show, rendered anew in exhibit after exhibit, is that when it came to the Africans with whom he spent almost every day of his life, Thomas Jefferson was a selfish and spitefully prejudiced hypocrite—which, indeed, he was, Sally Hemings realizes far more clearly now than she ever did at the time, though that is not all that he was. As he and she move between pools of illumination in the twilit rooms, people are constantly murmuring sourly to one another and making comments like, "What a bastard!" Or, "I used to admire this guy!"

Thomas Jefferson gets few second glances, however, and maybe one or two stares, but no one comes up to him, no one cups a hand over his or her mouth and whispers into a neighbor's ear while glaring at him fiercely. But as he and Sally Hemings are watching a video in which some of his writings on slavery are read aloud by an actor, a man of African descent does look directly at Thomas Jefferson, and says in a loud voice, "This country would have been a hell of a lot better if all the *white* people had been sent to Ohio or Canada!"

Thomas Jefferson responds to this man's words and, indeed, to every other overt or implicit disparagement he receives that day, as he always responds to criticism: by pretending not to notice it.

As he and Sally Hemings are leaving the video, she takes his hand in both of hers, moves her lips next to his ear. "I hope this is not more than you can bear," she says.

At first he only sighs heavily without speaking. But after a long moment, he says, "It seems that I never . . ." He is silent another long moment, then shrugs and pats her hand. He doesn't look her in the eye.

As they draw near the end—which is to say the beginning—of the show, they come to a vitrine displaying the very gown that Sally Hemings was wearing the day they went to see le Comte de Toytot fly in a hot-air balloon and that she was also wearing later that night, when Thomas Jefferson forced himself into her room.

They stand side by side in front of the vitrine, as if before an apparition, their faces tremulous with the repeated impacts of possibility and doubt. The gown, suspended in midair by nearly invisible fishing line, is the only item in the whole exhibit that seems untarnished by time, its yellow silk radiant in the spotlight and its white underskirts as brilliant and luxurious as clouds.

After a moment they notice a guard standing next to them. He is dark-skinned and heavyset, and he is smiling at Sally Hemings. "Would you like to try it on?" he says.

"Is that allowed?" she asks.

The guard nods beneficently. "For you, of course."

He pulls out a set of keys, attached to his belt by a chain, unlocks the back of the vitrine and detaches the gown and its underskirts from the fishing line. As he hands them to Sally Hemings, he nods wordlessly toward the door of a women's room.

She takes the gown and skirts into her arms as if they are the wasted body of a child. When she emerges from the women's room, her expression is solemn and intent. She is barefoot, clutching her raincoat against her chest.

The guard has left the room, and for the first time since they entered the museum, Sally Hemings and Thomas Jefferson are entirely alone. "You have to do me up," she tells him, and turns her back. "The stays are missing, and there is no hoop. I'm sure I'll look terrible."

"It will be fine," says Thomas Jefferson as he fastens the many little buttons from just below her waist to the nape of her neck.

And, indeed, when she hands him her raincoat and turns to face him, she seems hardly to have changed since she last wore the gown so many years ago.

She is looking into his eyes, waiting, still solemn and intent. He is afraid to speak. He is feeling so many different kinds of sorrow, but also a lightening of spirit—something very like hope.

She swallows and parts her lips, as if to form a word. But then she clamps her mouth into a thin seam, and the skin around it goes yellow. She is still looking into his eyes, and he is looking into hers.

The guard has returned, stepping sideways through the door, glancing over his shoulder toward the room he has just left. Then he looks directly at Sally Hemings, tilting his head to one side, his brow furrowing and his lips going into the lumps and twists of someone who wants to smile. Finally he shrugs and parts his open hands in the gesture that signifies helplessness. There are murmurs in the next room, and the whisper of shoe soles on polished wood.

C ol. Jones had by this time become very fond of me, and would not arrange any terms by which I could gain my freedom. He respected me, and would not let me see him take his "bitters." He was surprised and pleased to find that I did not touch liquor. Being with and coming from such a family as Mr. Jefferson's, I knew more than they did about many things. This also raised me in their esteem. My sister Isabel was also left a slave in Virginia. I wrote her a free pass, sent her to Boston, and made [an?] attempt to gain my own freedom. The first time [I fai?]led and had to return. My parents were here in Ohio and I wanted to be with them and be free, so I resolved to get free or die in the attempt. I started the second time, was caught, handcuffed, and taken back and carried to Richmond and put in jail. For the second time I was put up on the auction block and sold like a horse. But friends from among my master's best friends bought me in and sent me to my father in Cincinnati, and I am here to-day.

—The Reverend Peter Fossett
"Once the Slave of Thomas Jefferson"
New York Sunday World
January 30, 1898

The movie once seemed it would never end, but now the actor who wore the copper-colored wig is wearing a skinlike skullcap: pink, freckled and crossed by cobwebs of white. A pinkish putty has been attached to his face, and it does look remarkably like aged flesh, though unnaturally inflexible. The putty and skullcap are good enough, though, that the actor is clearly portraying a man in his mid-eighties, possibly even his nineties—which strikes Thomas Jefferson as a respectable life span; to want to live longer would be to ask for more than one's fair allotment, unseemly in a democracy where all are meant to be equal.

Thomas Jefferson finds himself strangely content as he watches the actor compose his character's end. There is something geological in the swirl of white sheets on the bed, and there is a dawnlike luminescence in the death chamber, as if the actor were a mountain range catching the first silver beams of a sun returning after a long season of darkness, so that his death seems a new beginning.

There is, indeed, much beauty in this death. The aesthetic dimensions of every detail have been maximized: The hands on the sheets, for example, approach each other upon the axes of a tilted 125-degree angle—they approach but never touch. Within these hands is the potential for a clasp, but that potential will be eternally unrealized. Likewise, strength is latent in their musculature, but they are the quintessence of frailty. The actor's half-closed eyes, granted a bluebird brilliance by the silver light, appear the most flawless visual organs imaginable, and yet the images projected onto their internal concavity can only be mere shadows, unaccompanied by answering projections within the mind. And those putty-covered lips are so clearly poised to pronounce a word— What is it? *Freedom? Sorrow? Equality? I?*

No one will ever know.

Yet the true beauty of this scene is not in its splendidly articulated and suggestive composition but in its relationship to everything that has preceded it—a realization that throws Thomas Jefferson into perplexity. For what has this movie been to him besides an unending ordeal of humiliation, betrayal, idiocy and insult? And yet with all of its drawbacks, the life portrayed by the actor in the copper-colored wig and now the pink skullcap has a significance and sweep that Thomas Jefferson's own life has never had and that he can only envy.

At first the tableau of the actor, the silver luminescence and the geological sheets seem to be disintegrating, but then Thomas Jefferson realizes that phrases composed of bronze letters affixed to stone are drifting in front of the tableau, or perhaps right through it, like ghosts. He recognizes the phrases as his own: "I tremble for my country when I reflect that God is just" . . . "All men are created equal" . . . "Commerce between master and slave is despotism" . . . "No man shall be compelled to frequent or support any religious worship" . . . "Nothing is more certainly written in the book of fate than that these people are to be free."

What Thomas Jefferson envies is the unity of these words and the man portrayed by the actor. They are one with the sweep and sentiment of his life, and he will live within them, in every way that matters, for at least as long as the words are remembered. The man within the movie is both the musician and the music, while Thomas Jefferson is only noise and a maker of noises. Yes, these words may have trailed behind his pen, but they are no closer to his essence than his ripping flatulence, his fearful shouts in the night, his groans, his burps, his donkey laughs, his exhausted panting, his moronic limericks and puns, his sobs, his lustful moans, his shouts of fury, his envious muttering, his lies, his dissimulations, his unrelenting inability to unite his words and his life.

Perhaps this death is exactly what Dolley Madison had thought so uplifting, but the longer its manifold beauty works upon Thomas Jefferson, the more profoundly he feels himself undone. There is a lie between himself and the man who is passing on with such quiet grandeur, but he doesn't know whose lie it is, and he doesn't know what the existence of the lie means—although he worries that it means that nothing good is true, that nothing he believes is real, that his very love is a betrayal of everyone and everything he wants so much to be happy or the occasion of happiness.

He looks for Dolley Madison so that he might tell her what the movie has done to him, but her seat is empty. And so is the seat where James Madison once sat stupefied and wonder-filled. And so, Thomas Jefferson soon discovers, is every other seat in the theater, from those in the very front row to those all but lost in obscurity beneath the single flickering blue beam. He is alone in the dark and the brilliance and the noise, the only one left to witness the actor achieve his ultimate significance.

Beverly Hemings is a white man and has been since 1822, when their father gave Harriet and him coach tickets and fifty dollars each so they could "run off" to Washington City. It is July 4, 1834, exactly eight years since his father's death. When Beverly agreed to return to Virginia for the first time in more than a decade, he saw himself as fulfilling a promise. He wrote to his brothers, Madison and Eston, hoping they would bring their mother when they came, but only Madison stands among the crowd of upturned faces on Poplar Lawn. At the last minute, their mother said she didn't have the strength. She told her boys to go without her, but Eston stayed behind.

As the earth falls away and Beverly's wicker gondola swings gently beneath a huge sack of hydrogen gas, he looks toward the hazy silhouette of the mountains where he was born, and when he looks back, he can no longer distinguish his brother amid the crowd, which has begun to run. A smooth breeze has caught him and is sending him across Jefferson Street and out over the open countryside east of the city. The foremost members of the crowd have leapt a rail fence and are charging down through a meadow toward Great Run, but they will never keep up. Beverly Hemings is some two hundred feet above their heads and moving ever faster. He has already passed the meadow and is over a wooded valley. In seconds he will be looking down again on fields and streams and houses and barns. Farmers on their hay wagons, farmwives flinging potatoes to pigs, barefoot boys and old men trailing fishhooks in glinting creeks will look up and shield their eyes to be sure of what they see. Beverly will lean out over the rim of his gondola and give them each a wave, as if there were nothing more natural than to be drifting in the sunshine between treetop and cloud.

Thomas Jefferson sways in the middle of the hammering subway car. The lights flicker out again, and when they come back, he knows that Sally Hemings has seen him. How could she not? He is standing so close. The screech abates for a moment, then starts all over, drilling his ears. He is looking down at the tip of Sally Hemings's boot. He doesn't know what to do or say. He has no idea what will happen when, at last, his eyes meet hers.

. . .

AUTHOR'S NOTE

There is no greater gap in the record of Thomas Jefferson's life than his relationship with Sally Hemings. The direct references to Hemings in the writings of people who actually knew her don't add up to more than several hundred words, most of these being in Madison Hemings's two-thousand-word memoir, and none of the references provide anything like a full portrait of her character, her appearance or her relationship with Jefferson; indeed the majority consist only of a sentence or two.

Beyond these references, her name, birth year and an account of the food, clothing and bedding she was given at Monticello are noted in Jefferson's record books, as is the same information about her mother, siblings and children, but not in a way that significantly distinguishes Hemings or her family from any of the other enslaved people who also appear in the record books. We know how much Jefferson paid for her clothing while she was in France and that he boarded her for five weeks with his laundress in the spring of 1789, but we know nothing about the motives or consequences of either of these expenditures. She comes up in two Charlottesville censuses after she left Monticello following Jefferson's death. In 1830 she and her sons Madison and Eston are classified as white, and in a special 1833 census of black residents of the parish, the family is listed among the "free Negroes & Mulattoes." And lastly, a 1998 genetic test established that Eston Hemings was the child of a man bearing a Jefferson Y chromosome. The Jefferson family had long maintained that Sally Hemings's children had been fathered by Thomas Jefferson's brother, who would indeed have had the crucial chromosome, but there is no evidence that he was ever at Monticello when Hemings's children were conceived, whereas Jefferson always was—a detail supported by numerous documents.

And that is just about all we have in the way of facts specifically concerning Sally Hemings. While it is hard to imagine that Jefferson would never have mentioned her in a letter during the thirty-seven years of their relationship, the twenty thousand pages of correspondence that he or his white family saw fit to preserve contain not even one clear reference to Hemings—although it is true that the letters he exchanged with his wife, Martha, are also absent from the trove. If Sally Hemings herself ever put a word to paper, it, too, has not survived, though we do have writing by two of her brothers—none of it mentioning her. And although there are dozens of paintings, drawings, etchings and statues of Thomas Jefferson, no image of Sally Hemings taken from life has ever been identified.

While biographers and historians are expected to be rigorously factual, in novels the primary function of fact is to facilitate readers' suspension of disbelief. Factual accuracy is somewhat more important in realistic novels that purport to represent significant historic or political events, but even so, fiction writers are generally given license to do whatever they want in the gaps between facts. Under such circumstances, the dearth of verifiable information concerning Jefferson and Hemings's relationship ought to have given me a field day, but, as it happens, Thomas Jefferson presents rather specific challenges to any writer.

With the possible exception of Abraham Lincoln, he is the most written-about and well-documented figure in American history, and his relationship with Sally Hemings has also made him one of the most controversial. I was terribly worried when I first began working on this novel that the sheer volume of information concerning Jefferson would so dominate my thinking that the book would end up as hackneyed and plodding as a dutiful docudrama. And I was even more afraid that the intense political debate regarding his relationship with Hemings (of which I was reminded every single time I told anyone what I was writing) would make it impossible for me to give my characters enough psychological and moral complexity to feel like living, breathing, passionate and perplexed human beings.

The first thing I did when I began to work on this novel was read three biographies: Annette Gordon-Reed's *Hemingses of Monticello*, Fawn M. Brodie's *Thomas Jefferson: An Intimate History* and Joseph J. Ellis's *American Sphinx*. But as soon as I felt I had grasped the basic facts of my protagonists' lives, I stopped research and leapt straight into writing, composing scenes entirely out of chronological order and switching randomly between realism, fabulism, essay, prose poetry and quotation. My hope was that by never knowing what I was going to write next or how these pieces might link up in the finished work, my mind would be freer to imagine Jefferson and Hemings in fresh and surprising ways and with minimal influence from other people's narratives or opinions. And, indeed, it was during this phase that Jefferson became an ape, a blimp and an art student in New York and that Sally Hemings created an invention that eventually became the world that Jefferson would have to inhabit. It was also during this phase that I "discovered" my protagonists' lonely childhoods and the extremity of their passions, be they love, loathing, fury or fear.

Once I had staked out what seemed sufficiently fertile and fresh imaginative territory to guarantee my novel a margin of originality (or so I hoped), I felt free to return to my research. I found two biographies especially useful: *Thomas Jefferson: The Art of Power*, by Jon Meacham, and *Master of the Mountain*, by Henry Wiencek—a pair of books that could hardly have diverged more radically in their portrayal of their subject, with Meacham's Jefferson corresponding fairly closely to the familiar figure of the brilliant if excessively idealistic Founding Father, while the most direct precursor to Wiencek's Jefferson is Simon Legree—the cruel slaveholder in *Uncle Tom's Cabin*. The stark contradiction of these portraits was instructive all on its own, because it helped solidify my sense that Jefferson was an amalgam of opposites—which is not to say that he occupied any sort of bland midpoint between the extremes of virtue and monstrosity but that he was brilliant, idealistic, ignorant and evil all at once. And while I had many problems with Wiencek's often absurd interpretations of decidedly cherry-picked facts, his book nevertheless forced me to confront Jefferson's dark side over and over—a process that turned out to be immensely productive.

In addition to these and other biographies, I also read Jefferson's *Autobiography*, his most significant political writings (including *Notes on the State of Virginia*) and two especially revealing collections of his letters: *The Domestic Life of Thomas Jefferson*, edited by his great-granddaughter, Sarah N. Randolph, and *Jefferson in Love: The Love Letters Between Thomas Jefferson and Maria Cosway*, edited by John P. Kaminski. Apart from Annette Gordon-Reed's masterful account of the whole Hemings family, the book that best helped me envision Sally Hemings's experience was *Incidents in the Life of a Slave Girl*, a memoir by Harriet Jacobs, first published in 1861, although I also gathered extremely useful insights and background details from *Narrative of the Life of Frederick Douglass* (both books are included in *The Classic Slave Narratives*, edited by Henry Louis Gates Jr.). The brief memoirs by Madison Hemings, Peter Fossett and Isaac Jefferson also deepened my understanding of Hemings, of course, but, more important, they gave me a rich sense of life at Monticello, even if all three of these men clearly allowed their narratives to reflect many of the interests and prejudices of their white interlocutors or readers. And lastly, I visited the places where Jefferson and/or Hemings had lived— Monticello, Poplar Forest, Williamsburg, Philadelphia, London and Paris—and I wrote substantial portions of my novel at the Virginia Center for the Creative Arts, not far from Charlottesville, where I came to have an intimate sense of the smells, sounds, weather and beauties of the Blue Ridge Mountains.

One of the reasons I was so anxious about the effects of the intense political passions regarding Hemings and Jefferson was that I shared those passions to a very considerable extent, especially concerning race and gender. During the early improvisatory phase of my writing, however, I did my best to put such issues out of my mind and just write what seemed most natural and necessary for each individual scene or meditation as it came along. But once I had that first draft, and ever more so as I wrote my final ones, I constantly interrogated myself to be sure that my vision had not been clouded by unconscious prejudice or simple ignorance. I also gave successive drafts to trusted friends—black and white, male and female—and listened carefully to what they said, making corrections where I felt I had misunderstood the reality of the experiences I was trying to render. My goal always was to add depth and specificity to my portrayal of my protagonists, without ever confining them to any preexisting ideas of who they were or what their lives might mean—and I can only hope that I succeeded in this regard.

My understanding of my characters and their story evolved considerably over the course of my research and writing. At the beginning I assumed that Jefferson and Hemings's relationship had commenced with rape and amounted to, at best, a grudging submission on her part to demands she was powerless to resist. But the more I read, the more I encountered evidence suggesting that the relationship might have been much more complicated. I was struck, in particular, by the fact that when Sally Hemings finally left Monticello, she took three items that had belonged to Thomas Jefferson: his inkwell, a pair of his spectacles and a shoe buckle. It just didn't seem possible that if her life with him had been nothing but sexual torture, she would have wanted to possess such intimate belongings, nor that she would have passed them on to her son Madison, who gave them, in turn, to his daughter.

Eventually I came to believe that Hemings's feelings for Jefferson might well have fallen somewhere along the spectrum between love and Stockholm syndrome—the latter being that tendency of kidnap victims to identify with their captors and even to develop extremely positive feelings for them. There is no way I can know whether this supposition is correct, but I did think it made for a much more interesting story than had my original understanding. A narrative in which Sally Hemings was simply tortured and abused by her master would be only a recapitulation of very familiar ideas about the nature of slavery (which is not to say that such ideas should ever be forgotten), whereas a novel in which she felt—or even only believed she felt—something closer to love for her master would amount to an exploration of the mysterious and disturbing underside of an emotion that many of us consider the chief source of human happiness.

While I did my best to make the relationships and events of the realistic segments of my narrative consistent with the historical record (to the point that I hope my book might give readers some insight into what Hemings and Jefferson might actually have been like), there are several elements of the story that have almost no basis in fact. I think it highly unlikely, for example, that Sally Hemings was literate (if that were the case, then *she* would have been the one to teach Madison Hemings to read, rather than Jefferson's grandchildren), yet I felt that if I made her not just literate but well read, I would be intensifying the fundamental equality between her and Jefferson and thereby adding illuminating moral complexities to both sides of their relationship. I also felt that by having her write her own confession, I would be giving her a much more powerful voice—one that might help counterbalance the imposing gravity that Jefferson possesses merely by virtue of his historical significance.

The scene in which Hemings and Jefferson watch a hot-air balloon take off from a farmer's field outside of Paris is complete invention. While Jefferson did witness a balloon flight in Philadelphia, there is no evidence that he or Hemings ever attended such a spectacle in France. I wrote the scene partly because the idea simply delighted me, but also because I knew early on that toward the end of the novel I would describe Beverly

Hemings's balloon flight (for which there is some historical evidence), and I thought this earlier flight might give his experience greater emotional and thematic power. The lodge to which Hemings and Jefferson retreated to be alone is also an invention. There is, in fact, no evidence whatsoever as to where they conducted their sexual relationship.

Moak Mobley and Sam Holywell are likewise products of my imagination, as are all the street vendors and white servants in Paris (apart from Adrien Petit) and the white servants and shopkeepers in Virginia. Some of the stewards and overseers at Monticello bear the names of real people, but when I was unable to discover the names of the people who actually held these jobs during a particular period of my story, I simply made up a name. Otherwise all the characters with "speaking parts" are based to some extent on real people in Hemings's and Jefferson's lives.

And lastly, all of the statistics relating to fertility and life expectancy cited on page 37 are not from the late eighteenth century but from the 1850s, the earliest era at which such data was compiled. I chose not to indicate the provenance of these figures when I cited them, because I felt there was only so much scholarly awkwardness a novel could stand. And I had similar reasons for not revealing that estimates of maternal mortality rates during the mid-nineteenth century range from 1 to 16 percent, depending on the structure of the study and the source of the underlying data. I settled on 4 percent, a figure cited by more than one source, primarily because I wanted to err on the side of caution.

ACKNOWLEDGMENTS

None of my books has ever been the result of my efforts alone, but never have I so benefited from the insight, generosity and, in some cases, hard labor of my friends and colleagues as I have this time around.

I want to thank, first of all, my wife, Helen Benedict, who has read many iterations of this book over the last five and a half years and given me much extremely beneficial advice about countless aspects of its content, style and political ramifications, and who has demonstrated admirable patience with my endless midnight panics and my tendency to infuse dinner-party conversations with gossip about the Founding Fathers.

I also want to thank those dear, wise and exceedingly kind friends who read my ten-pound manuscript and had the courage to tell me exactly what they thought, thereby giving me the chance to save myself and my readers from my ignorance and manifold weaknesses of character. Thank you, Idra Novy, Robert Marshall, Kathryn Kuitenbrouwer, Ellery Washington, Cassandra Medley and Anja Konig.

Several good friends read excerpts from the manuscript and likewise helped shield the world from my deficiencies: Christine Hiebert, Mary Mc-Donnell, Ellen Kozak, Amy Bonnaffons, Pascal Aubier, André Pozner, Erwan Benezet, Olivier Renouf, Abby Rasminsky, David Goldstein and Julia Deck. I'd also like to thank Christa Dierksheide and Anna Berkes at Monticello for providing me with crucial details about the way Jefferson's slaves actually lived.

I owe a huge debt of thanks to my wonderful agent, Jennifer Lyons, for her hard work on my behalf, her unflagging belief in me and in my books and for her excellent editorial advice. I also want to thank her assistant, Kit Haggard, for her consummate efficiency and all-around good nature.

This book never would have come into being if James Yeh, coeditor of *Gigantic*, hadn't invited me back in 2009 to write a three-hundred-word piece on a historical character for his journal. I sat down at my desk and, without thinking, wrote, "Sally Hemings is sleeping," and thereby commenced a surprisingly long journey. Thanks, James.

Since that first piece I have benefited from the intelligence and excellent advice of a number of editors—the first and foremost being Paul Slovak, my editor at Viking Penguin, whose careful reading, spot-on marginal remarks, literary savvy and unfailing enthusiasm and generosity have done so much to help me transform this book into its best self. I consider myself hugely lucky that he wanted to work with my book and with me. Thanks, too, to Carolyn Coleburn, Rebecca Lang and to the many other extremely helpful people at Viking.

I am also indebted to Andy Hunter, a founding editor of *Electric Literature*, for his interest in and smart edits of this novel's earliest incarnation as a short story; to Halimah Marcus for remembering that story and wanting to publish an updated version of it in *Electric Literature's Recommended Reading*; to Ben Samuel for his own astute editing; and to Martha Colburn for her surprising, suggestive and beautiful video and for the art book that came along with it.

I did an enormous amount of work on this novel during three summers at the Virginia Center for the Creative Arts and will be forever grateful to the entire staff, but especially to Sheila and Craig Pleasants for their hospitality and support and for insisting that I visit Poplar Forest. Substantial portions of this book were also written during residencies at the Ucross Foundation, Yaddo, the MacDowell Colony and the Palazzo Rinaldi in Noepoli, Italy.

And, lastly, for giving me advice, listening to my gripes, bolstering my spirits, making me welcome and for assorted other kindnesses, I want to thank Bruce Baumann, Patti Capaldi, Courtney O'Connor, Marcus Grant, Marika and Kasya O'Connor Grant, Elizabeth Harris, Nell Boeschenstein and an extremely helpful young woman at the Millinery Shop in Colonial Williamsburg.

Throughout the research and composition of this book, I tried to jot down the names of everyone who helped me in any significant way. Nevertheless, I am sure that there is at least one person whose name has been left off the foregoing list. Should that be you, please forgive me and know that I am deeply grateful for your wisdom, your encouragement, your inspiration. Thank you.

9/6/09–8/20/15